PRAISE FOR THE NOVELS
OF ALEXIS MORGAN

Her Knight's Quest

"Morgan has the gift of bringing her characters to life—
both good and bad—and keeping you invested in them
and their lives." — *Fresh Fiction*

"Readers will enjoy passages about the warriors' tender-
ness toward their animal avatars and the strong, equal
partnerships between the warriors and their lovers."
— *Publishers Weekly*

"Morgan provides a richly woven story that places her
damned heroes on a quest for redemption that may or
may not culminate in their salvation."
— *RT Book Reviews*

My Lady Mage

"The first book in her Warriors of the Mist series shows
Morgan at her storytelling best.... Morgan provides
plenty of mystery, action, and passion to keep you flipping pages well into the night. I didn't want *My Lady
Mage* to end." — *Fresh Fiction*

continued ...

Honor's Price

A Warriors of the Mist Novel

Alexis Morgan

A SIGNET ECLIPSE BOOK

SIGNET ECLIPSE
Published by the Penguin Group
Penguin Group (USA) LLC, 375 Hudson Street,
New York, New York 10014

USA | Canada | UK | Ireland | Australia | New Zealand | India | South Africa | China
penguin.com
A Penguin Random House Company

First published by Signet Eclipse, an imprint of New American Library,
a division of Penguin Group (USA) LLC

First Printing, September 2014

Copyright © Patricia L. Pritchard, 2014
Agathia map © Delilah Stephans Designs, 2013
Excerpt from *A Time for Home* © Patricia L. Pritchard, 2013

SIGNET ECLIPSE and logo are trademarks of Penguin Group (USA) LLC.

ISBN 978-0-451-23997-6

Printed in the United States of America
10 9 8 7 6 5 4 3 2 1

I want to dedicate this book to the usual suspects: to my husband for his constant support and for still making me laugh after all these years; to my agent, Michelle Grajkowski, for always being there for me; and to Kerry Donovan for understanding why Kane was my favorite and for helping make his book shine!

Acknowledgments

I want to thank my friend Janice Kay Johnson for all the brainstorming sessions over lunch. I love thinking back over how many books have we plotted over burgers and fries.

River of the Damned

*T*he Warriors of the Mist are a legend, their origins lost in the shadows of the past. In dark times, it is whispered that the warriors can be summoned from beneath the roiling currents when a champion is needed and if the cause is just.

However, the cost will be high and the risks are great. For if the battle is won, the champion faces judgment by the same gods who had once condemned him to the cold chill of the mountain river. If his performance is found worthy and valiant, at long last the warrior will make the final journey to the great hall where the noble knights of the past dwell for all eternity. However, if the champion is found lacking still, he returns with his brothers to the river.

If the battle is lost, regardless of fault, both the champion and the supplicant will be condemned to the netherworld. Together they will wander without hope and without light, lost in cold darkness until the ages have passed and all that exists ceases to be. Only the powerless and the desperate dare approach the Warriors of the Mist to plead for their cause.

Many years have passed since last a worthy supplicant journeyed to the river's edge, but times are dark and desperation has once again come to the people of Agathia. There is a disturbance in the mists, and the waters grow restless. Someone comes, bringing either disaster or redemption.

The Warriors of the Mist ready their weapons and prepare to meet the enemy.

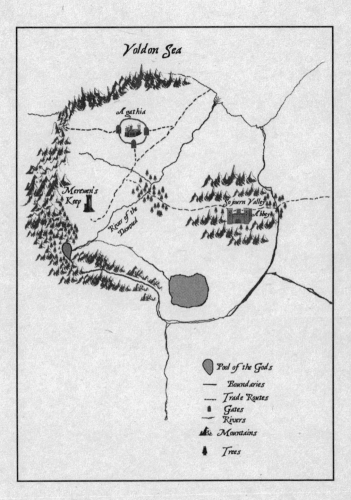

Chapter 1

*I*t had been three days since Kane first rode through the arched gates of Agathia, capital of the kingdom with the same name. He already hated everything about the place: the throngs of people, the constant noise, and especially the spicy miasma of dark magic that permeated every corner of the city.

During the daylight hours, he slept. Afternoons he prowled the streets, memorizing the layout of the city. Knowing which walls could be scaled and where the guards dozed while on duty could make the difference between life and death if his mission were to go badly.

His nights were spent visiting taverns to gauge the mood of the patrons. They definitely weren't happy, not with the heavy dose of sour fear mixed with the usual smells of greasy food and cheap wine.

He'd hoped to cross paths with Duke Keirthan's personal guard while they were off duty. Yet he hadn't seen any in the places he'd been so far, and it wouldn't be prudent to ask strangers to direct his footsteps. In this city, anyone who showed too much interest in the duke's men was likely to end up dead.

The Broken Sword was the fourth such place he'd been in tonight, but this time he planned to stay awhile. Long enough to finish a second tankard of ale, maybe even a third.

He looked around the crowded room. Had all of these fine citizens of Agathia taken to drinking in reaction to the growing evil trapped within the city walls? Kane felt sure it wasn't the quality of the food that drew them to this piss pot. He choked down another bite of the greasy stew and shoved the bowl aside.

At least he had a table to himself. Several people had started to sit down with him but had quickly changed their minds. Evidently, Agathians were reluctant to share space with a man who bore a mage mark on his cheek and had eyes the color of death.

Fine with him. The company of strangers always made his skin crawl.

The evening's entertainment was about to start, the real reason Kane was there. Averel, the newly hired troubadour, sat in the far corner, tuning his lute and warming up his voice for his debut performance in the city. Two oversized dogs lay sprawled at his feet, their relaxed air deceptive. One hostile move toward their master and these people would learn all too quickly how much damage a pair of war dogs could do.

Kane leaned back in his chair with his arms crossed over his chest, watching the crowd while keeping a wary eye on the young musician. There was a definite air of innocence about the youth. Most of these fools probably thought the calluses on Averel's hands came from hours of plucking the strings on his lute. In truth, they'd come from years of gripping the pommel of a sword.

If Kane hadn't spent centuries of fighting side by side with the young knight, he might well have bought the innocent act himself. However, despite their long friendship, tonight they were strangers to each other. He'd keep his distance to minimize the chance of someone noticing the two of them shared the same unusual eye color. Those who clung to the old superstitions would say they'd been marked by the gods.

They would be right.

Both Kane and Averel served the Lord and Lady of the River. Along with their captain and two other warriors, they were the Warriors of the Mist or, as Kane actually preferred, they were simply called the Damned.

The gods had sent them to make this land safe for Lady Merewen, the woman who'd risked everything to call the warriors from their sleep beneath the river back on the spring equinox.

Averel headed toward the small platform in the front of the room. Silence followed in his footsteps as he made his way through the jumble of tables and benches. By the time he took a seat on a tall stool, every eye in the room was on him. Kane would have hated that, but Averel took all the attention in stride.

It seemed as if everyone was leaning forward a bit, anxious for the performance to begin. No doubt in these dark days, the promise of any entertainment was a welcome diversion. Even a poor musician would serve the purpose; tonight they were in for a surprise.

Averel had a true gift for music and a voice that lent itself to both the beautiful and the bawdy, depending on the crowd and his mood. Kane waited to see which direction his friend would choose tonight.

"Good evening," the young minstrel began, pitching his voice just loud enough to be heard over the quiet murmurings of the crowd. "As your humble servant, I will begin with a few personal favorites. Later I will take suggestions, but I make no promises. My master specialized in the old songs, so I have not yet learned the newer melodies."

Kane was impressed. Averel had come up with the perfect excuse for not performing all the popular ballads. Considering how long they'd been absent from the world, it was unlikely he knew anything that had been composed in several hundred years.

It wasn't long before Averel had the crowd singing along with him. Kane looked around for the tavern owner. The grinning fool was behind the bar, serving up pitchers of ale as fast as he could fill them. Obviously, singing was thirsty work, which boded well for Averel's chances of being hired on for an extended stay.

Kane's situation was trickier. His assignment was to

get close to Duke Keirthan himself. His best option would be as a member of the duke's personal guard, but the man had a reputation of being careful about letting strangers get too close. Considering the man harvested his own people like a crop to feed his blood magic, the caution was understandable.

A movement off to his side had Kane reaching for his knife. Realizing it was one of Averel's idiot dogs, he forced himself to relax. Both of the mutts were working their way through the crowd, mooching for bits of bread and meat. The white one stopped only inches from Kane's table.

Everyone in his immediate vicinity watched the interchange with understandable caution. After all, the dog was tall enough to look a seated man in the eye.

Kane glared at the offending beast. "What do you want?"

The dog responded by wagging his tail and then laying his head in Kane's lap. It would be more in Kane's character to shove the dog away, but then he glanced up at Averel, who gave him a slight nod before looking away.

All right, then. The animal was there for a purpose. Kane relented and gave him a thorough scratching, in the process palming the message Averel had stuck inside the dog's collar. After a few seconds, Kane gave the dog a gruff push.

"That's enough. Be off with you."

The dog stopped at a few more tables before rejoining the other beast in the back corner. Well done. The message had been delivered without Averel having to approach Kane directly or his dogs singling Kane out for attention.

Averel started a new song, one that had everyone clapping their hands and stamping their feet in time to the music. Kane sipped more of his ale and waited until the song ended before making his escape. Aiming for the back door where the privies were located, he staggered as if he were feeling the effects of all the ale he'd consumed.

When he was sure he wasn't being followed, he dropped the act and continued on down the alley for several blocks before cutting back over to the main road through town. Thanks to the late hour, the streets were dark except for the occasional pool of light from a window along the way. Kane kept to the shadows, where he felt most at home. The few people he passed gave him a furtive look and hurried on their way. He didn't blame them. There were many scary things that prowled in the darkness; Kane was one of them.

His own destination was close by now. He'd taken a room at an inexpensive inn on the edge of town, the kind of place where a few coins ensured privacy. Add another piece of silver to the price, and the staff would turn a blind eye to anything short of murder in the dining hall. While Kane had no immediate intentions of killing anyone, he did have an unusual companion sharing his quarters. Hob wouldn't attack unless provoked, but just the sight of him would likely throw the whole inn into chaos and draw unwanted attention to Kane himself.

Gargoyles had that effect on most people.

Kane entered the building through a side door. At this time of night, few guests would still be up, but he preferred to keep his movements as private as possible. For the same reason, he automatically avoided the fourth step, the one that creaked.

His room was at the far end of the hall with a window that overlooked the courtyard below. If he needed to make a quick escape, Kane could easily jump to the roof of the stable and then to the street below. A smart man slept better knowing he wasn't trapped in a room with only one way out.

All was quiet as he slipped inside his room and locked the door. Making his way to the small table by the bed, he lit a candle. Averel's note could wait until Kane released Hob and got comfortable.

He kept the shutters closed even though the air in the room reeked of boiled cabbage and stale beer from the dining room below. Murmuring the words to release Hob from his magical resting place on Kane's shield, he averted his eyes from the sudden burst of light that accompanied the gargoyle's appearance.

Hob looked around and shook from the tip of his nose to the tip of his tail before leaning back on his haunches in a long stretch. Then he circled around Kane's legs, bumping him in a show of affection.

Kane patted the beast on his scaly head. "Sorry to be so late in returning, boy."

When Kane opened the shutters, Hob laid his head on the sill to taste the night air with a few flicks of his tongue and then gave the rest of their quarters a thorough sniff. Satisfied all was well, he turned a few circles before curling up on the floor at Kane's feet.

Unfolding Averel's note, Kane spread it out on the table near the candle for light. All it said was *The Empty Keg* and *The Rooster's Crow*. No other explanation was needed. Averel knew Kane was hunting for the tavern where the guards spent their off hours. He must have heard something about these two places.

Kane would visit them as soon as the sun went down tomorrow night. He needed to evaluate the caliber of man the duke was hiring but also hoped to bring himself to their attention. The best way to get a job as a hired sword was through a recommendation from someone already on the payroll.

It wasn't much of a plan, but before meeting Captain Gideon all those centuries ago, Kane had made his living as a mercenary. Some things never changed, especially the demand for men who could wield a sword and weren't too picky about who they worked for.

He stripped out of his clothes and stretched out on the thin mattress. When Kane was situated and had the threadbare blanket pulled up to his chest, Hob crawled onto the bed and curled up at his feet. The damned animal took up too much room, but he and Hob had been partners since Kane's grandfather had presented him with the freshly hatched gargoyle. He'd intended it as a bribe to purchase his grandson's willing assistance in his magery. The ploy hadn't worked, but Kane and Hob had formed a bond that had proven unbreakable.

That wasn't the only reason he tolerated Hob sprawling across his ankles. The Damned had fought as a unit even before the goddess had taken them into her service. Not that he'd admit it to his friends, but Kane missed them on this solo mission. Hob's solid presence close by helped fill the gap.

Before dozing off, Kane offered up a prayer that his time here in the city would be short. He'd volunteered for this duty, but war was coming; he sensed it in his bones. When it came time to fight, the Damned would face their enemy together.

An hour after sundown, Kane left the Empty Keg to move on to the next tavern. Outside, he overheard an argument in the nearby alley. He crept closer, his pulse quickening at the possibility that he may have just stumbled across exactly the kind of situation he'd been looking for. He peeked around the corner to see one of the guards facing off against a middle-aged man dressed in clothing suited for a well-to-do merchant.

The guardsman shoved the older man back a few steps. "Hold your tongue, you twice-cursed fool! Quit spreading false lies about your ruler! I'm off duty or else you'd already be on your way to prison for such traitorous remarks."

Rather than listen to the sound advice, the man pushed back. "The truth cannot be silenced no matter how many of you brutes the duke hires, Captain Bayar. Does he think we don't know what he's done? How many of his own people have died at his hands?"

The guard was both drunk and belligerent, a volatile combination, but it was his opponent who had Kane worried. The merchant's words echoed with grief and righteous anger. The man might have good cause, but he was asking to get skewered.

The argument turned lethal as both men drew their swords. Kane charged forward, hoping to distract the two long enough for them to back away from the precipice.

The guard reeled forward, but even drunk, he disarmed his opponent easily. He could have stopped there, the fight done before it had really started. Instead, he sneered and held the tip of his blade at the merchant's throat.

"Do you really think you can insult both me and the duke and live?"

Kane drew his own sword as he closed the distance between himself and the two men. Hoping the guard would respond to the bark of an order, he shouted, "Drop your weapon!"

He was too late. The merchant dropped to the ground, his throat slit. Kane took up his cause. Drunk or not, the captain was paid to protect the citizens of Agathia, not to execute them over a few ill-advised words. Yes, the merchant had been foolish to cross swords with the guard, but he didn't deserve to die for it.

But maybe the captain did.

Bayar blinked at Kane. "What do you want?"

Kane smiled. "To ensure you face the judgment of the gods tonight for crimes against Agathia, including murder."

The fool bellowed in fury and went on the attack. Kane sidestepped him easily. Despite the alcohol he'd consumed, the captain still put up a credible showing. It was tempting to play with him for a while, but the other guards might be looking for him.

Kane ended the battle with one stroke. It was a quick kill, although Kane doubted the man would be grateful for the small mercy. After all, dead was dead.

Kane murmured a prayer for the merchant and grudgingly added a shorter one for the dead guard. As soon as he quit speaking, he caught the sound of voices in the distance. They were moving in this direction. Kane froze when he made sense of what they were saying.

"Captain, where did you go?"

A second voice asked, "Where did he disappear to this time?"

"Most likely into an alley to take a piss." The speaker sounded disgusted.

Kane ducked farther back into the shadows, debating his limited choices. Just as he'd feared, the captain hadn't been alone. If his friends found Kane standing over their dead leader, more would die in that alley.

It would be but a minute, maybe two, before the guardsmen reached the alley. He couldn't count on them simply passing by, and it was his misfortune that the alleyway came to an abrupt end at a high wall. After studying the two bodies, Kane made his decision. Apologizing to the merchant's spirit, Kane quickly rearranged the bodies and the weapons. He retrieved the merchant's weapon and closed the dead man's fingers around the grip.

Then he wiped the captain's blade clean and sheathed it, making it look as if the merchant had assassinated the guard with no provocation. Then Kane rushed to the street and waved his hands to attract the attention of the three guardsmen searching for their leader.

"Help! I tried to stop him, but it was too late! Captain Bayar has been murdered!"

Unlike their leader, these three were sober and smart enough to approach Kane with swords drawn and a great deal of suspicion.

Two of them pinned Kane against the wall and stripped him of his sword while the third investigated. It didn't take him long to assess the situation. When he rejoined his friends at the mouth of the alley, he grabbed Kane by the throat, choking off his air.

One of the others glanced toward the alley. "Sergeant, is it true? Is the captain dead?"

The man jerked his head in a quick nod and then leaned in close to Kane's face. "When I let you breathe, start talking. Tell me everything that happened. If I believe your story, you get to live. For now. If I don't, you might want to end your explanation with a prayer for an easy death."

He tightened his grip. "Nod if you understand me and what's at stake."

As one of the goddess's avatars, it went against Kane's nature to surrender without a fight, but he was playing the role of a mercenary down on his luck. Pretending a fear he didn't feel, he bobbed his head and managed to whisper, "I understand."

"Good. Mayhap you're smarter than you look."

The guard dropped his hand and retreated a step. Kane jerked his hands free of the other two fools and rubbed his neck as if he were in pain. The action bought him a few seconds to organize his thoughts.

He decided to throw the dice and see where it got him. "I had a drink with Captain Bayar, and he mentioned the possibility of a job. I stopped to use the privy and was supposed to catch up with him.

"By the time I got here, he was dead. I never heard the other man's name, but Bayar was already down and wounded. He obviously hadn't even had a chance to draw his own weapon. The merchant was standing over him with a bloody sword and stabbed Bayar a second time."

Kane drew another breath and finished his hastily assembled tale. "I rushed forward, hoping to block the blow, but I was too late. When the crazy bastard came at me next, I killed him."

There. His explanation covered all the observable facts. He waited to see if these three believed him or not. If they didn't, there'd be another fight, although he really hoped it wouldn't come to that. There was no telling how the duke's guards would react to finding four of their own dead in one night.

Kane had no doubt of the outcome of the possible fight. These fools might be well trained by their standards, but they'd never faced one of the Damned in armed combat before. Finally, the sergeant glared at Kane and then at his two companions. He pointed at the one on the right.

"Corporal, fetch the rest of the men and bring them here along with something to carry the bodies on."

As the corporal took off running, the sergeant told the third guard, "Bring a pair of lanterns so I can see better what happened back there."

Then he turned his attention back to Kane. "You stay right where you are. Try to leave and I'll gut you like a pig. If your story holds water, we'll give your sword back. I'm Sergeant Markus."

"I'm called Kane." He leaned back against the wall, crossing his feet at the ankles. "I've got no place to be. Let me know when you've made up your mind."

Even knowing Kane didn't have his sword, the guard didn't turn his back until he was halfway down the alley. Kane smiled. Maybe the man was smarter than *he* looked.

For now he would wait to see if he'd taken his first step toward infiltrating the duke's inner circle.

Chapter 2

"*W*e need her."

"Are you certain?" Murdoch glared across the table at Gideon as he waited for him to defend his decision.

Normally he would accept his captain's opinion without question. Gideon had led their small band of warriors wisely and well. The sole exception had led them right to this point in time, with all five of them damned to an endless cycle of bloody battles alternating with long periods of time sleeping under the river.

Gideon rubbed his temples and briefly closed his eyes. When he opened them again, his words conveyed his own reluctance, as if he needed to convince himself as much as Murdoch. They'd all been in the pasture trying to calm the horses when Duncan and his lady had come charging into the keep just as the enemy had attacked. Lavinia had wielded her own powerful magic to block the blasts of destructive power Duke Keirthan had sent their way. At the same time, Duncan had shielded everyone else from harm, using a spell Lavinia had taught him.

Gideon was struggling to come to terms with all that had happened. They all were. "You saw what happened out there, same as I did. If Lady Lavinia hadn't been there to intervene, we would have all died. She almost did."

Murdoch frowned as he nodded. "True, but she's Keirthan's blood kin. Could that connection have led his attack right to our doorstep?"

Duncan had remained quiet until that point. He surged to his feet and slammed his hands down on the table. "Murdoch, I share your mistrust of magic, but do not accuse Lavinia of being in league with her brother. Her honor is above question. I stake my own upon that being true. She saved every one of us from the duke's attack."

Murdoch wasn't ready to concede the point. He aimed for speaking reasonably but wasn't sure if he succeeded. "But the goddess forbids the use of dark magic. How are we to know if the source of her power is any different from his?"

Duncan's expression went flat. To a stranger he might have looked bored, as if the conversation no longer interested him. Murdoch knew better. So did Gideon. The captain was already up and moving, hoping to provide a buffer between the two men.

Lady Alina put her fine-boned hand gently on Murdoch's thick wrist. Her soft touch was enough to render him helpless to move. Meanwhile, Gideon convinced Duncan to sit back down even though the man would clearly prefer to continue the discussion with his fists.

Once they were all seated again, Gideon took charge of the conversation. "Duncan, tell us what you learned while you were at the abbey. Start from when you left here. Leave out nothing, even if the details seem inconsequential. Once we've heard the entire story, we will better understand what happened out there as well as the source of Lady Lavinia's power."

Then he shot Murdoch a hard look. "Agreed?"

"Agreed."

He'd listen, but that didn't mean he had to like it. The goddess's disapproval of all kinds of dark magic had been one of the axioms they'd lived by since entering her service. But this time, they'd already accepted Lady Merewen's special gift with horses. Now Duncan was wanting them to accept Lady Lavinia's gift for combat magic. She claimed she'd merely shielded them from Keirthan's attack, but they'd all seen what she'd done. What was worse, she'd taught Duncan how to build a magical construct he called a ward.

Magic was magic, and Murdoch hated it all.

However, Duncan had been a good friend for centuries, and he owed it to the man to at least listen. He met Duncan's gaze and slowly nodded, hoping he understood that Murdoch's anger was aimed at the situation, not at Duncan himself.

Duncan nodded in return and began speaking. He began with the moment he'd first felt Lavinia's presence, long before he'd actually reached the abbey. From there, he explained Keirthan's attacks on Lady Lavinia and the abbey where she was acting as the abbess.

A ripple of shock circled the table when he revealed the Lady of the River had spoken directly to Lavinia. A second wave swept through when Duncan admitted that he'd almost succumbed to the hunger for the power magic could give him, but that he'd stepped back from the precipice at the last moment.

He brought them full circle back to the attack they'd all survived out in the pasture. An uneasy silence settled over the room as they absorbed all the information they'd just been given.

Gideon broke the silence. "Are you all right?"

Leave it to the captain to be more worried about his men than he was the situation, Murdoch thought to himself.

Duncan offered him a weary smile. "I'll be fine after some food and rest. It's a relief to be here because I'm worried about what Ifre Keirthan will do now; he won't take defeat well. This is the third time Lady Lavinia has thwarted him, the fourth if we count destroying the talisman one of our pursuers was carrying."

He glanced toward the door. "And I'm worried about the effect projecting all that power will have on Lavinia. It almost killed her."

Duncan paused as his face went pale. "No, it did kill her. She awoke saying the Lady led her back to me."

He took a long drink of wine and looked first at Gideon and then at Murdoch. "I don't ever want to see her like that again. But how do I protect her from something that comes flying across the sky with no warning? What good is my sword against an enemy I can't see?"

There was no easy answer to that question, and they all knew it. Once again, Gideon took charge.

"You've given us all a lot to think about, and we'll all do a better job of that after a good night's sleep. Tomorrow morning will be soon enough to start making more plans."

"Murdoch, check in with the guards and let them know to send for me if they notice anything at all unusual during their watch. After that, turn in for the night. I want all of us rested in the morning. I plan to ask Lady Lavinia to join us. We need to better understand what she can and cannot do with her gift. Perhaps she has suggestions about reinforcing our defenses, as well."

For the first time since the meeting started, Duncan looked happier. "I will tell her."

He walked out of the room without another word. Murdoch stared at the closed door.

"He's fine."

It was the first thing Alina had said since they all filed into the library to talk about the day's events. She gave Murdoch's arm a soft squeeze.

"None of you are accustomed to letting your hearts direct your actions, but obviously your goddess approves of Duncan's involvement with Lady Lavinia. And clearly we're going to need her as an ally when we make a stand against the duke."

Then she rose to her feet. "Now, if you'll excuse me, I'll check with Ellie to review the menus for tomorrow."

When she reached the door, she smiled directly at Murdoch. "Just so you know, Shadow is in my room. You might want to stop by to check on her."

There was a hint of heat in those soft gray eyes as she spoke. Several days ago, she'd invited Murdoch to share her bed, but he'd been called away. Was this her way of letting him know that invitation still stood?

Please, gods above, he hoped so. "I will come as soon as I speak to the guards."

"I look forward to it."

Then she swept from the room, taking his last coherent thought with her. When Gideon laughed, Murdoch glared at his friend.

"You find something amusing? Because as tired as I am, I think I can still find the strength to teach you some manners."

All right, maybe he couldn't, but he'd give it his best effort. Besides, what energy he did have he hoped to put to better use with Lady Alina.

Fortunately, Lady Merewen intervened. "Gideon, be nice. The man is clearly exhausted. So is Duncan, not to mention Sigil. Save your teasing for a time that's more appropriate."

Then she gave the captain a look that was all too similar to the one Alina had given Murdoch. "We've all had a trying day and should retire early. Right now I need to see how the horses are faring after the attack."

When she left the room, Gideon sighed and shook his head. "Did you think we'd ever meet women who could wield such power over us? Besides the goddess herself, of course."

The last of Murdoch's bad mood faded away. "No, I didn't. We'll know that the world has truly turned upside down if the same thing were to happen to Kane."

They both laughed over that thought. "Any word from him or Averel as yet?"

Gideon shook his head again. "No, and I don't expect to receive word for a while. They won't send the dogs until they have something to report."

He settled back in his chair. "Now that I've heard Duncan's story, tell me what you saw. How did Sigil do? Any worries about him?"

Murdoch reached for his wine. "None. In truth, the only reason we reached Duncan in time was that Sigil sensed something was wrong. We abandoned our camp in our rush to find him, Lady Lavinia, and the little girl Sarra."

He ran through the events in his mind. "Sarra also carries the taint of magic, although you'd have to ask Duncan more about the nature of it. She's the one who cried out that we needed to get to the horses before they were killed."

Gideon put his hand on Murdoch's shoulder. "I'll add that to the list of things to talk about tomorrow. For now let's see to the guards and call it a day."

Time dragged. What was taking Murdoch so long?

Surely he didn't doubt his welcome at her door. But then, Alina had her own reasons for being nervous about what they had planned. After all, until her husband's death, he was the only man she'd been with, and Fagan's brutality had left her terrorized every time he'd demanded she share his bed.

While waiting for Murdoch, her elderly maid helped her change into a nightgown and let her hair down. After Magda left, Alina added wood to the fire and turned down the bed.

It was another hour before the knock at the door finally came.

"Alina, I'm here."

She swung the door open, relieved that the moment had finally arrived. "Come in."

"I'm sorry if I kept you waiting, but I wanted to wash the trail dust off before I came to you."

She should have thought of that. "I wish I'd known. I would have had the servants bring the tub in here."

But then the image of helping Murdoch bathe had her blushing. It wasn't as if she hadn't seen a naked man before. In fact, she'd seen all of Murdoch when she'd nursed him back to health after he was wounded. Though that wasn't at all the same as the intimacy of a wife assisting her husband with his bath.

Not that Murdoch was her husband, but he would be her lover. *Oh, but how to begin?* In her marriage, her husband had always dictated the details of how and when.

"Murdoch?"

His stern mouth spread in a slow smile as he reached out to trace her cheek with a single fingertip. "I can only imagine the thoughts racing through your mind right now. Upon my honor, Alina, I will go as slowly as you need me to and only as far as you are willing to go."

The sweetness of his touch combined with the raw hunger in his eyes gave her the courage she needed. Taking his hand in hers, Alina tugged him toward the bed.

"Murdoch, I want it all."

From the angle of the light streaming in through the window, the sun had already been up for several hours. No doubt everyone else was awake and about, but Murdoch refused to feel guilty about stealing a few precious hours in Alina's bed, in her arms.

Last night had been . . . Truly, he had no words to describe it. All he knew for certain was that he'd never experienced anything like it before. Right now his lady lay cuddled at his side, her hand over his heart, her leg over his.

Her pale blond hair spilled across his arm and shoulder in a tangle of silk. He loved the feel of it against his skin. Loved the feel of her against his skin.

Loved her.

His desire stirred to life again, along with the impulse to pick up where they'd left off just before dawn. He'd taken her three times during the night, and she would probably appreciate some time to recuperate. He shifted slightly away from her, hoping that little bit of space would help.

It didn't.

His movement woke his lover. She blinked up at him. Her eyes widened and her mouth opened in a circle of surprise. Had she thought it was all a dream? Or mayhap hoped that he would have slipped out of her bed to go skulking back to his own? He hadn't thought to ask her.

"Should I go?"

She scooted toward him, closing the small gap he'd just created. "Only if that's what you want. I mean, I'd understand."

Damn her late husband all over again! Murdoch had spent the night worshipping this woman with everything he had, and yet she still worried she might not have pleased him.

"If I could figure out a way to manage it, we wouldn't leave this bed for at least a week, Alina."

He took her hand and led her down to the rock-solid proof of how much he still wanted her. To his delight, she gripped his cock and gave it a promising squeeze. He had to stop her before he lost all control.

"Alina, you might not want to stoke that fire again."

"Why not? Don't you like it when I do this?" She repeated a slow stroke. "Or this?" she asked as she cupped his sac with a firm squeeze.

His head kicked back at the jolt of pleasure. "I like it a little too much. Keep that up, and I won't be able to stop."

Instead of retreating, she slid up on top of his body, settling her core right over his cock and pressing her sweet breasts against his chest. Then she wiggled up to kiss him.

He rolled to the side and trapped her arms and legs with his, immobilizing her for the moment. "Sweetling, I want you so badly that I ache. But given what all we did last night, I'm afraid you'll be uncomfortable and won't say anything."

His lover finally showed a spark of temper. "I'll decide what's too much for me to handle. Eventually, someone will come looking for you or for me. Do you really want to miss this chance before the rest of the world intrudes?"

She had a point.

"I surrender, my lady. Use me as you will."

He sprawled onto his back and then lifted his lady to settle her over his hips. Her eyes widened as she realized that he wanted her to take control. He doubted she'd ever been allowed to do so before, but she was a quick study. As she took him deep inside her slick heat, he forgot how to breathe.

When she found her rhythm, she was so beautiful, with her hair flowing down her shoulders, her head tipped back, and her eyes closed. The sight took him right to the edge. He grabbed her hips and thrust upward, shuddering in release deep within the welcoming heat of her body. She followed him in the dance, calling his name over and over as she shivered in his arms.

He grinned as she collapsed on his chest, boneless and content. He stroked the elegant length of her back, calming them both.

Then, just as she'd predicted, the world intruded. After knocking on the door, Sigil called softly, "Lady Alina, I apologize for disturbing you, but it would seem that Murdoch has gone missing. Gideon is hunting all over for him. If you've, ah, seen him recently, would you let him know?"

"I'll tell him. Thank you, Sigil."

Alina sat up and pushed her hair back from her face. It was impossible to know if the rosy tint to her complexion was a result of their lovemaking or that Sigil had known exactly where to find Murdoch. Either way, their time together was at an end. For now.

Evidently, she was thinking along the same lines. "I will be counting the minutes until nightfall."

He kissed her one last time. "As will I, my lady."

Time to go to work. The Damned had plans to make and people to protect, including Alina herself. Murdoch knew his duty and would see it done. Even so, it took all of his considerable strength to make him leave the bed and start looking for his scattered clothing.

Chapter 3

*K*ane stood in a ragged line of mercenaries and farmers' sons and tried to blend in. Sergeant Markus had finally accepted his explanation of how their captain came to be lying dead in an alley. As a result, he'd promised Kane a chance at being hired as one of the duke's guard. As he'd explained, there were two different divisions of military in Agathia.

The largest group was the troops who served the country as a whole. They dealt with bandits and other threats. The second set was comprised of the elite fighters, the ones assigned to protect Ifre Keirthan himself. They patrolled the city, but especially his residence.

It was interesting that the duke personally viewed all of the potential applicants, deciding who would be offered a position and where each recruit should be assigned. From the rumors that flowed like water up and down the line, the majority of the hires were being assigned to the regular troops. Recently, several patrols had come under attack, greatly reducing their numbers.

Kane knew firsthand about one such attack. He and Hob had themselves accounted for a number of those deaths. There'd been at least two more skirmishes since then. Had his friends been involved? He prayed to the goddess that she keep the Damned safe until he was able once again to stand beside them in battle.

The line shuffled forward again. It should be only a few more minutes before he came face-to-face with the man the Damned were determined to topple from his throne. It was tempting to take advantage of this unexpected audience to execute the bastard immediately.

He rejected that idea as soon as he crossed the threshold into the dim interior of the building. Keirthan's personal guard kept him surrounded, and Kane would have to fight his way through at least two layers of defense to get close to the duke.

It wasn't difficult to pick Keirthan out in the crowd. He was the one with an oily cloud of evil clinging to him like a second skin, following his every move. It was not an accident that no one stood within arm's reach of the man. Even those with little or no sensitivity to magic would be repulsed by the chilly blackness that writhed and swirled around their ruler.

How many of their countrymen had died to create that abomination? Kane kept his hands away from his weapons, but in his head he imagined the sweet slide of his sword through Keirthan's flesh, plunging it deep and twisting it hard to make sure the man suffered for his crimes.

Better yet, Kane wanted to wrest control of that darkness for himself, turn it back on its master, and let it eat its fill of Keirthan's soul. The image set the mage mark on Kane's cheek afire, as for the first time in centuries he hungered to wield the kind of magic that was his family heritage.

Dear Lady, what was he thinking? The last thing he wanted was to touch the blackness that Keirthan had flowing in his veins like poison. He'd seen how that kind of craving for power had warped his own grandfather, turning the man into a coldhearted bastard who sacrificed even his own kin to feed his hunger. If it hadn't been for the gentle influence of Kane's mother, he might have very well followed in his grandfather's path. It had been a hard-fought battle, but he'd walked away from his heritage. Despite his best efforts, the magic still left its mark on him, the one on his face only the most obvious.

He forced his attention back to the moment at hand,

watching closely as Sergeant Markus assessed the group of men just ahead of Kane. Each applicant drew his sword and held it out pommel first. What was Markus looking for?

The sergeant made his way down the line of eight men. When he'd hefted the last sword in the bunch, he stepped back and gave the men their orders. From the dejected posture of the first two, they'd been turned down. The next five were directed toward a side door, presumably to join the regular troops.

After they filed out, the duke approached the one remaining applicant. The mercenary started to step back, but then stopped midstep, frozen in an awkward position and clearly not in command of his own movements. Sweat broke out on his forehead and his jaw worked hard, as if trying to force words through his clenched teeth.

The duke smiled and nodded to Markus as he released his hold on the man's body and mind. Markus waited until the duke stepped back behind the safety of his guards before directing the merc toward a door in the back corner. Obviously, he possessed whatever quality the duke had been hunting for.

Markus returned to his position. "The next eight line up here."

Kane and seven others slowly shuffled forward to stand in front of the sergeant.

"Weapons out."

Markus made quick work of the first seven swords, but frowned when he examined Kane's. What could he possibly be checking for? Kane's blade was high quality with a curved cutting edge, but carried no taint of magic. The sergeant returned Kane's weapon and stepped back.

"All but Kane go through the second door. Someone will be waiting to show you to your new quarters."

After they filed out, the duke stepped down off the dais again. "Is this the man you spoke of, Sergeant?"

"Yes, Sire. This is Kane. He personally executed the

man who killed Captain Bayar. Since he was looking for a position with the guard, I thought it was appropriate to invite him here today."

Keirthan studied Kane with greedy interest. "Thank you for defending the honor of my guard, Kane. Captain Bayar will be missed. It will be difficult to replace him."

As Keirthan stepped closer, the shadow of darkness slithered forward to wrap around Kane's body. It sent a burning chill straight through to his bones, requiring considerable effort to hide his reaction and hold his ground. The inside of his skull itched as Keirthan's mind pushed at the boundaries of Kane's own. It had been centuries since Kane had last been subjected to such treatment, but his grandfather had taught him well how to defend himself against such an intimate invasion.

The duke's eyes narrowed as his efforts intensified. Kane held strong, but he wasn't sure if that was a good thing. It might cost him this opportunity to join the guard, but it would cost him his life if the duke managed to breach his defenses. All he could do was wait Keirthan out.

After a few seconds, the pressure lessened and then disappeared altogether. Keirthan remained close, though.

"Turn your face to the side."

Kane didn't bother to ask which way. Keirthan wanted to see his mage mark. He could look all he wanted. If he tried to touch him, mayhap it would be the duke's day to die. Kane's, as well, but it might be worth the price.

Keirthan held his hand palm out but didn't actually touch the mark. "I've read of such sigils, but I've never actually seen one before. How did you come by it?"

"It was a gift from my grandfather." One Kane would have gladly gutted the old bastard for, but he made sure none of his anger leaked into his voice.

"Have you much practice wielding the magic behind it?"

Keirthan sounded more curious than cautious. If he

truly knew much about the marking, he would have been more prudent. This time Kane could answer without hesitation.

"He was killed before he could infuse the mark with its full potential." True enough, although Kane had taken care of that himself before he'd finally renounced his magical heritage.

The duke looked like a child whose new toy didn't perform as expected. "And your father couldn't finish it for you?"

"I never knew him. It was my maternal grandfather who was the mage."

Also true. Kane's father had been sacrificed to Grandfather's ever-growing need for blood to fuel his magic. He'd even used his own daughter for the same foul purpose, while she carried Kane in her womb. Unlike most of the mage marked, Kane had been born with his.

"Your eye color is also odd."

Kane shrugged. "Another gift."

One from the goddess herself, but that truth would get him killed right where he stood. Keirthan continued to stare at Kane for several long seconds, clearly waging an internal battle as to what Kane's fate should be. Finally, he gave a decisive nod.

"I will offer you a position in my personal guard. For now Markus here will get you settled in. In three days' time, there will be a trial by combat so we can evaluate the new recruits. I expect you to participate."

Without waiting for Kane to respond, Keirthan stalked away, his guards scurrying to catch up with him. For a man with an ever-growing number of enemies, he was careless with his own safety. No doubt he thought his cloak of magic would keep him safe. An ordinary man would stand little chance against the lethal combination of Keirthan's personal guard and blood magic.

But there was one thing Keirthan hadn't taken into consideration: Kane was not an ordinary man.

*   *   *

"Lady Theda, the duke would like to speak with you."

She paused, wishing she had the courage to simply ignore her brother-in-law's summons. She knew full well that any show of rebellion would only make her already tenuous situation at court far worse. If Ifre ever decided she was more trouble than she was worth, she would die.

She hated the fact that there were days the idea held some appeal. However, the other people under her care would face the same fate, and she would not risk their lives needlessly.

Theda turned to Lady Margaret and her other lady-in-waiting. "Return to the solar. I will join you shortly."

Her young friend knew better than to let her worry show in such a public venue. Keeping her voice to a low whisper, she asked, "Would you prefer that I came with you?"

Theda smiled, as always maintaining a calm facade. Sometimes her face ached from the strain of the mask of pleasantry she was forced to wear when what she really wanted was to scream. "I'll be fine. I'm sure it's nothing."

She waited until her two friends safely made their way through the crowded room toward the stairs. They'd all put in their token appearance in front of Keirthan's associates. The man didn't have friends, only those who curried his favor. Anyone who felt differently about the man either stayed tucked away on their family estates or mysteriously disappeared.

On her way to where Keirthan waited, Theda made the effort to greet several acquaintances. There were so few left who were overtly friendly to her anymore, a depressing change from when her late husband was the duke. With Ifre's ascension to power, her own position at court had fallen into disfavor.

Finally, she reached the throne where Ifre liked to sit and watch the ebb and flow of those who sought his favor. Her husband had understood the politics of ruling, but Armel hadn't basked in the power he had over his people. Instead, he'd worked hard to ensure that they were cared for and protected. In contrast, Ifre was a selfish bastard who never saw beyond his own best interests.

Right now he was busy ignoring her as one of the nobles from a nearby estate described the mare he'd just purchased for his wife. She waited until he paused to take a breath to make her presence known. Ifre was well aware of her standing there, but he enjoyed treating her like a servant whenever possible.

She dropped into a short curtsy. "You wanted to see me?"

"You will attend the trials this afternoon as my hostess. I have guests who will need to be served refreshments. Bring those two women who flutter around you as well. They're not good for much, but at least they look pretty and can serve the wine."

Theda dug her fingernails into the palms of her hands to avoid lashing out in response to the insult. Ifre made remarks like that for the sole purpose of goading her. She never let him win.

"We will be there."

Not that she had any interest in watching men beat one another bloody with swords for the entertainment of Ifre and his cronies. She'd heard trials were being held in part to replace the late Captain Bayar, who'd died unmourned in an alley. As far as Theda was concerned, he'd met a fitting end.

"If you'll excuse me, I will check with the kitchen to make sure that the refreshments and drinks will be ready."

Ifre smiled as she backed away. "They'd better be, Theda. It wouldn't do for my guests to be disappointed in any way."

"I understand." All too well. With another curtsy, she made her escape.

Although his tone was intended to convey concern for his friends, the implied threat was real. If anything went wrong with his plans, someone would suffer. Someone she cared about. As yet, Ifre had never raised a hand to her, but he barely kept a leash on those animals who served as his personal guard.

She lived in constant fear that he'd tell them her ladies-in-waiting were fair game. If that ever happened, he would die. She spent long hours imagining all the ways that could happen.

If it were up to her, Ifre wouldn't have lived this long. However, he had one other weapon in his arsenal that served to keep her in line. He held her stepson in his thrall. She hadn't seen him in weeks now, but Keirthan had made it clear that Theda had to do exactly as he ordered or her stepson would die.

As she headed for the kitchen, she sent a prayer skyward that the gods would have mercy on her people and end Ifre's tyranny once and for all.

The tent offered shade against the afternoon sun but also blocked what little breeze there was. Theda sipped her drink and pretended an interest in her companion's endless prattle about his prowess with a sword.

"If you will excuse me, I have to see to my duties as hostess."

She smiled and made a pretense of studying the crowd to make sure everyone had a drink and looked reasonably content. Her ladies were mingling in the crowd yet being careful to not single out any one man for very long. To do so ran the risk of encouraging unwanted attention.

Everything was flowing along smoothly, which meant Ifre had nothing to complain about. Even knowing the potential risk that she'd miss something, Theda desperately needed to slip away for a few minutes' respite from the crowd and heat. She wouldn't go far.

There was a small space between two of the tents that was currently unoccupied. What a relief to be alone even if all that separated her from the rest of the world was the thick fabric of the tent walls. A few minutes of stolen time away from her odious brother-in-law and his friends was truly a gift from the gods.

The crowd's constant cheering of the fighters taking part in the tournament had given her a headache. The noise formed a constant drone, punctuated occasionally with applause or catcalls when a fighter failed to live up to everyone's expectations. Despite Ifre's orders that no one was to die in the practice battles, that didn't mean blood wasn't shed when either a sword or a temper slipped out of control.

She had dampened a handkerchief in water before escaping the tent. It served to cool her face and the back of her neck. Feeling slightly better, she wandered closer to the railing that separated the fighters from the spectators. The field was empty, but there was a sense of growing excitement in the crowd.

A single fighter appeared at the closest end of the field. He had the build and coloring of the raiders from the far northern lands, with hair the color of fire and fair skin that would burn red in the sun. His weapon was an enormous broadsword, one that most men would have trouble drawing, much less wielding for the length of a battle.

A movement at the other end of the field caught Theda's attention. The second combatant had arrived. She watched as the two men met in the middle and then turned to approach the fence in front of Keirthan's tent. Where the redhead was mammoth, all muscle and power, this warrior moved with a lethal grace. He was nearly as tall, but built along much leaner lines. If the other man's hair sparked hot in the sun, this one's was an unrelenting black, a shadow too powerful for mere sunlight to overcome.

In contrast, his eyes were surprisingly pale, an odd shade of gray or perhaps light blue. His face wasn't handsome, not in the superficial way that Ifre's was, but it was compelling. There wasn't even a hint of softness about the warrior, as if life had carved it all away, leaving nothing but the bedrock of grim strength. He would never go unnoticed in a crowd. Men would step aside while women would be tempted to get all too close.

Theda couldn't tear her eyes away from him.

If he was taken aback by the size of his opponent, he gave no sign of it as both men had stripped off their tunics. Then they held their swords aloft in salute to the duke, bowing first to him and then to each other before moving farther away to face each other with their weapons ready. Normally, Theda had little interest in the dangerous games men played, but for some inexplicable reason, she was riveted.

She watched in utter fascination as Sergeant Markus barked the order to begin. This time the crowd remained strangely silent as the two men put on a display unlike anything she'd ever seen before. It was brute force facing off against speed and grace, with neither man willing to give an inch.

If their fighting styles were at all hampered by the duke's order to avoid serious injuries, it didn't show. In fact, the dark warrior was grinning now, clearly enjoying facing off against another talented fighter. If she had to predict the victor, her first instinct would be that size and overwhelming power would win the day.

And she would've been wrong. After a sudden flurry of blows, the pale-eyed fighter had his huge opponent in full retreat. Realizing that defeat was upon him, the redhead bellowed in challenge and charged forward. The two men came together in a clash of weapons that echoed across the silent field.

How was Ifre reacting to the display? It wasn't hard to spot him leaning forward over the fence, his hands holding on to the top railing with a white-knuckled grip. The expression on his face was greed, pure and simple. But which of the two warriors was he so interested in?

Sergeant Markus had made his way to the fence, as always, trailing after Ifre, watching his back and keeping an eye on the crowd. She approached slowly, careful not to startle him. He glanced down at her, the expression in his dark eyes flat and suspicious. She didn't take it personally. He didn't trust anyone who got too close to Ifre.

"Lady Theda."

"Sergeant, who are those two men?"

"The redhead is Johan. He normally rides guard for one of the caravans but lost his position when he got caught with one of the trader's daughters. He's hoping to get a job with the troops who ride patrol, but the duke is considering him for his personal guard."

"And the other?"

Markus glanced at her out of the corner of his eye. She was known for actively avoiding the guardsmen as much as possible. Her curiosity must seem out of place to him.

A little bit of honesty might go a long way toward assuaging his concern. "I often watched the weapons practice when my late husband was the duke, but I've never seen anything like his style of fighting."

Markus grunted. "Neither have I. Johan is a talented swordsman, but Kane is just playing with him. If this were a real fight, Johan would have been dead seconds after they drew steel."

As if his words were prophetic, a shout went up. They both looked to see what had caused the uproar. Just as Markus had predicted, the one called Kane stood over Johan, the tip of his sword at Johan's throat. A single thrust would have ended the big man's life right there in the dust.

Her brother-in-law had joined them. "Markus, send Johan to the troops."

"And Kane?"

Ifre smiled with obvious glee. "I shall be keeping a close eye on him. Keep me apprised of how he does."

"As you wish, Sire."

Markus bowed and backed away. Neither man paid any attention to Theda, but that was fine with her. She was too busy staring at the dark-haired warrior as he helped Johan back to his feet. What about him drew her attention? She normally had little use for the men who served Ifre.

As if sensing her interest, the dark warrior turned to stare right at her. The power of his cold gaze swept over her, leaving her chilled in the hot summer sun. When he abruptly looked away, she stumbled away from the fence. Deciding she should resume her hostess duties, she lifted her skirts and all but ran toward the questionable safety of Ifre's tent.

Chapter 4

*K*ane tugged at the collar of his uniform. The cursed thing wasn't tight, but still it choked him. Both the fit and fabric of the tunic were fine; it was what the uniform represented that chaffed. He was a Warrior of the Mist and sworn to serve the Lord and Lady of the River, not a corrupt blood mage like Ifre Keirthan.

He left the barracks to head for the stone building that served as Keirthan's home as well as the center of government for Agathia and its people. According to Markus, servants and tradesmen used the side doors, which were never left unattended. The guard on duty nodded to Kane. "Saw you fight Johan yesterday. That was something."

"I got lucky. It's been a while since I've faced off against someone that good."

Another lie, but he had to play the part. "Sergeant Markus told me to find him so he can show me the layout of the duke's keep. Have you seen him?"

"Not recently, but the men on duty at the front entrance will likely know where he is. You can either go through the building or walk along the edge of the garden to the front."

A little more time spent outside and away from the stench of Keirthan's magic held a great deal of appeal. It was also gave Kane an excuse to explore the area on his own. "I'll go around."

He walked away without thanking the man. Knowing he would face the guards in battle, he had no desire to make friends with them. He strolled along the side of the building and studied his surroundings. The garden on his right was quite elaborate. The morning breeze carried the scent of flowers as well as the sound of women's laughter in the distance.

Instantly, the memory of that dark-haired woman who'd watched his bout yesterday flashed through his mind. He hadn't noticed her until after the fight was over; he'd been too busy trying to keep from being knocked senseless by the flat of Johan's sword. But the moment their eyes had connected, everything else faded away completely, as if the entire world had narrowed down to just the two of them.

The whole encounter had lasted but a heartbeat, but she'd felt the impact, too. It was there in the way she drew a sharp breath and froze like a deer trying not to draw the attention of a wolf. Her reaction had made him mad then, and the memory stirred his temper even now. He was no threat to her.

Yet she'd fled into the duke's private tent, which also meant she was part of Keirthan's household. She lived with that monster and yet feared Kane at first sight? He should be used to it by now, but he grew weary of being feared by the very people he was sworn to protect.

Some things never changed. For now he would hunt down Markus and get to work. He rounded the front of the building, where two guards flanked each side of the huge wooden door. He approached slowly, making sure they saw him coming. Even then, they looked suspicious. After all, if an assassin were planning to kill the duke, wearing the uniform of his personal guard would be a logical way to slip inside the hall.

Sergeant Markus's honor might be called into question because of his choice of employers, but Kane couldn't fault him on how he did the job. At least these men were alert and constantly scanning the area for anyone who looked out of place. When they spotted Kane, the closest pair stared at him in suspicion until one of the guards on the other side said something.

They all relaxed but only a little. "You're not on the duty roster. What's your business here?"

Kane kept his hands away from his weapons. "Sergeant Markus asked me to meet him this morning."

The closest guard jerked his head toward the door. "The sergeant usually stands near the staircase so the duke can find him easily if he wants him. If he's not there, try the practice field."

"If you see him, tell him that I'm looking for him." Kane injected enough authority in his voice to have all four guards standing at attention.

"Yes, sir."

Kane crossed the threshold of the duke's stronghold for the first time. Once inside, his eyes, always sensitive to the light, took longer than usual to adapt from the bright sunshine outside to the dark interior of the building. He blinked several times only to realize that the enormous room wasn't actually poorly lit.

No, what he was sensing was the shadow cast by Keirthan's blood magic. Everyone else in the room was going about business as if nothing were wrong. Either they were completely blind to magic or else they'd grown accustomed to its taint.

The air was thick with it, and Kane could feel the pulsing of Keirthan's blood magic coming from beneath his feet. Logically, that meant the mage's private workroom was located immediately below the great hall, not that he had any desire to find out for certain. If he ever ended up down there, it would mean Keirthan had discovered the real reason Kane had sought a position with his personal guard.

Right now he needed to do something besides standing there and blocking the doorway. He aimed toward the side of the room, taking time to study the ebb and flow of the people around him. Interesting that only the servants had a furtive air about their movements, clearly trying to avoid drawing attention to themselves.

In sharp contrast were the courtiers, mostly nobles

and wealthy merchants, judging by the style and quality of their clothing. The lot of them strutted through the room as if they owned the very air they breathed. How did Keirthan hide his true nature from these people? Did they suspect but believe they were immune from his predations?

If so, they were fools.

Right now, while Keirthan was still building his power, he would limit his victims to those who wouldn't be missed by anyone other than their families. But once he unleashed his full fury upon Agathia, no one would be safe. If these people didn't wake up soon, it would be too late to make an organized stand against the mage. They'd be dead before they could lift a sword.

He spotted Markus standing in the shadow of the staircase exactly where the guards said he would be. The sergeant would find it odd if Kane continued to meander through the room, so he cut straight through the crowd to where Markus stood waiting.

"I wondered if you'd gotten lost. The duke doesn't tolerate tardiness." Then he raked Kane with a cold-eyed look. "Neither do I. Understand?"

Kane shrugged. "I wasn't aware we'd agreed upon a specific time."

"If it were just me waiting to talk to you, that wouldn't be a problem. However, Duke Keirthan wants to see you after he finishes hearing petitions. Luckily, the line is long today. Otherwise you'd be explaining to him why you dawdled along the way. And if I had been the one having to make excuses for your absence, well, let's just say that I have ways of making my displeasure known."

Right now Kane cared less about incurring Markus's wrath than he did about why Keirthan was singling him out for attention. From the way Markus was staring at him, he was wondering the same thing.

There was no use in worrying about it overmuch. They'd both find out soon enough. Meanwhile, Kane continued to study the people in the hall. As he watched, two men got in a heated discussion, but they seemed to be a threat only to each other. As they argued, the doors opened again and a trio of women filed in, including the one who had watched Kane's fight with such interest.

From her demeanor, he had to think that she was a noblewoman surrounded by her ladies-in-waiting. He cast about for a way to learn her identity without singling her out of the group.

Did she remember him, and would she admit it if she did? He noticed Markus also had his attention on the women as they cut across the room, heading directly for the staircase at Kane's back. Finally, he nodded in the direction of the approaching women.

"I hadn't heard the duke was married."

Markus looked disgusted. "He's not. The woman in blue is Lady Theda, the widow of the duke's older brother. She does serve as Keirthan's hostess when he needs one, which is why she and her ladies-in-waiting attended the trials yesterday. Ordinarily, she acts as the chatelaine and oversees the servants and the kitchen."

Interesting. By all reports, Keirthan had been jealous of his late brother. Maybe he was just petty enough to take it out on the man's widow.

The women were now but a few feet away. At the last second, Markus moved to stand in front of the staircase, partially blocking their way and forcing them to squeeze past him. Obviously, part of Keirthan's lack of regard for his sister-in-law included letting his men treat her shabbily.

Kane wanted to shove Markus out of the way and teach him some manners. But that would be out of character, especially for a new hire who was looking to fit in. Lady Theda waited until the other women made it safely past the sergeant before following after them. When she reached the third step, she paused to shoot Kane a sideways look before continuing on up the stairs.

"Lady Theda thinks she and those others are too good for the likes of us, but her day is coming."

Markus's sly smile revealed much about what he thought would happen then. Kane sincerely hoped that the women slept behind locked doors. It reminded him of the terror Lady Merewen had lived with while her uncle had been alive. If Fagan hadn't promised her to Duke Keirthan for his blood magic, she would have suffered greatly at the hands of the captain of Fagan's guard.

There were obvious reasons why Fagan had been a favorite of the duke's. The two men had much in common, all traits that had led to Fagan's death and, with the goddess's blessing, would lead to Keirthan's downfall as well.

While they watched the women disappear upstairs, a servant had joined them. Markus glared at him. "What do you want?"

"Sergeant, Duke Keirthan would like to speak with the new recruit now. He said to tell you that he'll send him back to you shortly."

Kane started to follow, but Markus blocked his way. At the same time, he grabbed the servant by the arm and spun him back around. "You haven't been dismissed."

The man kept his eyes firmly chest high on the guard, his free hand clenched down at his side. "Sorry, sir. I meant no disrespect."

"Repeat what the duke said exactly."

Fear had sweat beading up on the servant's face, and his voice cracked as he spoke. "He said, 'Bring the new recruit named Kane to see me. Tell any of the rest of the guards to stay away. I don't need them muddling things up.' Those were his exact words, sir."

"You insolent idiot," Markus snarled and raised his hand as if to smack the servant. Kane caught his arm before he could strike.

The sergeant stared at Kane's hand. "You dare interfere? You have no right to question my actions."

Kane got right in his face, forcing Markus to listen. "Do you want to explain to the duke why you sent his servant back to him bruised and bleeding? Especially when the man's only crimes were doing exactly what the duke ordered and then answering your question. It is hardly this man's fault you didn't like what the duke had to say."

He held on to Markus's arm until he was sure the man had heard what he'd said and understood. Finally, the sergeant relaxed.

Ignoring the servant now, Markus stared at Kane. "Go, but report back to me when he's done with you. Then I'll let you know what your duties will be for the next few days."

Kane bowed slightly and followed the servant to a door on the far side of the room. There were a few people standing in a row along the wall, but the two of them walked past them to the head of the line. Kane's guide started to open the door but then hesitated.

After a quick look around, he whispered, "Thank you, sir, for what you did back there."

Without giving Kane a chance to respond, he opened the door and led Kane inside.

"Sire, Kane is here. I'll be outside if you have further need of me." He left Kane standing in the middle of the room as Keirthan finished writing something down.

Keirthan made a show of closing the ledger and setting his pen aside before he acknowledged Kane's presence.

Steepling his fingers, Keirthan leaned back in his chair and stared at Kane for an uncomfortable amount of time. Kane stood with feet apart, his hands clasped behind his back, not quite at full attention. Now wasn't the time for insolence, but neither would he act cowed by the duke's presence.

"Tell me, Kane, have you ever held a position of authority?"

"I've led my share of men, Sire."

Keirthan nodded as if Kane had confirmed his own suspicions. "As you know, I recently lost the captain of my guard. Normally, I would prefer to replace him with someone I know and trust. Would you agree with that policy?"

Where was he going with this discussion? "A man in your position should be careful about those he allows to get close."

Would the man recognize that as the warning it was? Probably not. Keirthan was the sort of fool who thought he was smarter than anyone else. Considering he'd murdered his own brother, he should know that attacks could come from the most unexpected sources.

"The men in my personal guard were all chosen because of their ability to fight. That's all most of them are good for, although Sergeant Markus is a cut above the rest. What is your impression of him?"

Kane went with the truth. "I've known him only a short time, Sire, but so far he has treated me fairly. Certainly, he didn't have to help me find a job. I am grateful for his assistance."

Keirthan dismissed his comments with a wave of his hand. "All that is fine, but do you think he has the ability to command?"

The ice beneath Kane's feet grew thin. "The men follow his orders promptly."

The duke's laugh was nasty. "That's because he's a vicious bastard and would gut them if they didn't. That doesn't mean he understands battle tactics or how to command in time of war."

"I don't know him well enough to judge. I've known sergeants who had a better feel for command than most generals. Others can train men to fight but little more than that."

Evidently that answer pleased the duke. He picked up what looked like a pin off his desk and studied it.

"I prefer my captains to have an understanding of magic, which Sergeant Markus lacks. You, on the other hand, have great potential in that area."

He tossed Kane the pin. "Put that on, Acting Captain Kane. The appointment isn't final. We'll revisit my decision after you've had time to familiarize yourself with your duties. Any questions?"

"No, Sire. I thank you for the honor. I will endeavor to not disappoint."

"See that you don't."

Kane recognized a dismissal when he heard one. He affixed the pin to his tunic. He bowed and let himself out.

Back out in the great hall, Kane schooled his features, making sure that none of his inner turmoil showed. His mission had been to get close enough to keep an eye on the duke, but being named captain of the guard was an unexpected development. What was behind the man's decision? Kane had done nothing to earn such trust, so his reasons must be linked to the man's hunger for Kane's potential as a mage.

He hated that he'd missed another opportunity to kill Keirthan. But considering how Keirthan's servant hovered right outside the door, there was only a small chance Kane would've made it out of the building before anyone noticed the duke was dead. However, caution wasn't what had stayed Kane's hand.

Until Captain Gideon and their allies solved the mystery of how to counter Keirthan's magic, killing Keirthan by mundane means was too chancy. From what Kane could recall of his grandfather's never-ending lectures, killing a blood mage could be tricky if not done properly. They could run the risk of unleashing all of Keirthan's accrued power in a destructive maelstrom, killing the people the Damned were sworn to protect.

Biding his time, though, wasn't going to be easy. For now he needed to report back to Sergeant Markus. Kane allowed himself a small smile. The man wouldn't be pleased to find out that Kane would now be making all the decisions concerning the duty roster. He'd known he and Markus weren't likely destined to be friends, but he'd hoped to avoid becoming enemies until absolutely necessary.

Kane started back toward the staircase, but Markus was no longer where he'd left him. It didn't take long to spot him standing on the balcony at the top of the steps. Kane headed up to join him, still careful to maintain his calm facade. How the next few minutes unfolded would determine the tenor of his relationship with Markus, not to mention the other men who served under him.

Markus leaned on the railing and stared down at the swirling mass of people on the floor below. "I see you survived your audience with the duke."

When he finally glanced in Kane's direction, his eyes flared wide as he spotted the duke's sigil pinned to Kane's tunic. Markus immediately stood straighter, his shoulders back and his arms rigid at his sides.

"I see congratulations are in order, Captain Kane."

There might have even been a spark of anger in his eyes, but if so, it quickly faded. That was all right. Why wouldn't he be shocked by the turn of events? Kane certainly was.

"Thank you, Sergeant. The promotion is an honor, one I owe entirely to you."

That much was true. If Markus hadn't interceded on Kane's behalf, he might still be wandering the streets of the city looking for a way to insinuate himself into the duke's household. He truly wished Keirthan hadn't done this. Being an officer had immediately opened up a gulf between him and the other man, one that wouldn't be easily crossed.

Markus remained at attention. "What are your orders, sir?"

Kane's immediate options were limited when he still needed to learn the lay of the land. "You were going to show me around the keep. Let's start with that, so I can familiarize myself with its layout. After that, we can review the duty rosters and discuss any concerns you have that have arisen since the death of the prior captain."

For the first time, the sergeant showed a spark of emotion along with a slight smirk. "That would be captains, sir, not just one. We've lost at least three over the past few weeks."

Kane arched his eyebrows as if surprised by that news. "Really? Interesting that the duke didn't mention that. Rest assured, Markus, that I am far harder to kill than most men."

Without waiting to see if the sergeant had anything more to say on the subject, Kane continued. "Shall we start the tour up here and go from there?"

Markus jerked his head in a short nod and walked away, leaving Kane to follow as he would.

●

Chapter 5

*I*fre stared at the closed door for several seconds. It was a shame he couldn't slip out into the hall unnoticed to watch the stir caused by his choice of a new captain for his personal guard. For now he'd remain in his office, considering Kane's reaction to his unexpected promotion.

The mercenary had barely blinked.

An interesting man, to be sure. He probably wondered at the wisdom of Ifre allowing a total stranger to serve in such an important post. He wouldn't be wrong. Ifre knew full well how vulnerable a ruler was if those around him wished him ill.

But few things interested Ifre more than power and magic. He'd lived his entire life surrounded by mages with differing gifts and strengths. But Captain Kane was the first he'd ever met who bore the mark of a true blood mage. Given the man's powerful potential for magic, Ifre would've hired Kane anyway. But it was what Ifre had discovered when he tried to read his mind a few days ago that made it important to keep Kane close enough to keep a wary eye on him.

It took a powerful intellect coupled with a high degree of training to maintain such powerful mental shields. Ifre had run into only a handful of people who'd been able to block his attempts to invade their minds if he was determined to get in. His late brother, Armel, was one of them. Their father had been another, as was Ifre's half sister, Lady Lavinia. Even the mage Ifre's father had hired to mentor his children had had a difficult time shielding his mind.

Kane had not only blocked him; he'd actually pushed back a little before he caught himself. Ifre had spent quite a few of the intervening hours poring through his collection of grimoires to see what he could learn about breaking through Kane's defenses. So far, his search had met with only limited success.

Eventually, he'd find a way to destroy his new captain's defenses. Once that happened, Ifre would have free access to a delicious pool of dark magic. Even now, the badge of office Kane wore was designed to link him to Ifre. The connection would build slowly until it was as powerful as the ones Ifre had used on the late and unlamented Captain Terrick and his men. Eventually, it would insinuate itself deep within Kane's mind, gradually eroding all of Kane's protections. When that happened, Ifre would own him.

He still missed the spicy taste of Terrick's power. Regrets only weakened a man, but he wished he hadn't wasted him on the failed attempt to regain control of that fool Fagan's family estate. If the venture had succeeded, Ifre would have gained another magical asset in Fagan's niece, Lady Merewen. Instead, he'd lost both her and Terrick.

Despite his frustration, Ifre smiled. He'd been afraid he'd never find a new source for the magic he'd drained from Terrick, but Kane had definite possibilities. Meanwhile, he'd also keep looking for other likely candidates. He'd tried without success to drag Lady Lavinia back to the capital for just that purpose.

The blackness in his mind stirred; the pain had him holding the edge of the desk as he waited for it to pass. His magic grew ever more demanding, more hungry. If he didn't find ways to feed the beast, he was very much afraid that—

No, he couldn't think that way. It was weak of him, and the blackness would leap to overwhelm him completely at the first hint of vulnerability on his part. Later tonight, he would feed its needs. Until then, he'd reread the latest report from the men he'd sent after Lady Lavinia, looking for clues to her whereabouts.

Who were these mysterious allies she'd found who had held his men at bay while she escaped? She was clearly behind the vicious counterattack against the latest launch of his weapon. The only reason he hadn't been rendered totally helpless was that he'd been in his secret chambers when the backlash hit.

He'd never cared for Lavinia, although he'd pretended to as a child because his father wouldn't have stood for anything else. Now Ifre was free to hate her. So far she'd withstood his attacks, but eventually he would succeed. When he did, she would suffer tenfold for every bit of pain and frustration she'd caused him. He couldn't wait.

Theda sipped her tea and resumed reading while her ladies gossiped among themselves. Sometimes she yearned to enjoy the warmth and light here in her solar in solitude. If she asked her friends to leave, they would withdraw without question.

However, whenever they were away from her immediate presence, they were vulnerable. So far, none of Ifre's men had dared to lay their filthy hands on either one of her ladies-in-waiting, but it was only a matter of time. Sergeant Markus was growing more bold in showing his total disdain for her and her authority.

And why shouldn't he when the duke publicly treated her with such contempt? She'd taken to carrying a knife tucked in a secret pocket of her dress, but that would do her ladies no good if one of them was caught out alone by Markus or one of his cronies.

She closed her book and set it aside, its words not holding her attention. Perhaps later she would be able to find time to read in peace. For now she reached for one of the sweet cakes Margaret had brought to share with the group.

"Lady Theda, did you watch that final match yesterday?" Margaret babbled on without waiting for her answer. "It was the most terrifying thing I've ever seen."

Theda's own reaction to the fight was powerful as well, but terror wasn't exactly how she would have described her feelings on the subject. The memory of the dark warrior with his pale eyes had haunted her thoughts long after she'd returned to the keep once her duties as Ifre's hostess had ended.

It had come as a shock to see him standing with Sergeant Markus in the great hall when she and her ladies had returned from their stroll through the gardens. The sergeant had been his usual sneering self, but somehow she'd gotten the impression his companion had disapproved of Markus's behavior.

That was no doubt wishful thinking on her part. It had been far too long since anyone had taken up her cause in anything. Her marriage to Armel had been a political alliance, but they'd come to care for each other well enough. She missed him for a lot of reasons, but mostly because if he were still alive, his brother wouldn't have control of her life.

Margaret was still going on and on about the dark warrior's match. Theda was very fond of her young friend, but Margaret was given to exaggerations. It was time to slow her down.

"Margaret, I agree the redhead was a big man, but he hardly qualifies as a true giant." She smiled at the other woman, to keep the moment light. "As for the other man, he was a well-trained warrior, nothing more. His prowess with a sword was due to practice, not magic."

"But what about that mark on his face? And those eyes? I heard whispers that they mean he's a—"

"Enough, Margaret. He's a man, nothing more."

Margaret looked as if she wanted to argue the point, but at the moment the door to the solar was opened with enough force to send it banging against the wall. Theda's two friends squeaked in surprise while she leapt to her feet, gripping the knife in her pocket.

She glared at the guard standing in her doorway. Markus was the only man who would dare intrude on her privacy in such a manner. Theda stepped forward, putting herself firmly between him and the others. Before she could rail at him for his outrageous behavior, she realized he was not alone. She bit back her fury but still made her displeasure known.

"Sergeant, in the future, knock before entering my solar."

"Duke Keirthan has just appointed a new captain of the guard. He asked to be shown around." Markus didn't act in the least bit apologetic as he moved aside to reveal his silent companion. "Captain Kane, this is Lady Theda and her ladies-in-waiting. She's in charge of making sure the duke's household runs smoothly. Come to her if you have problems with the servants or need clean linens."

She wanted to slap Markus for his impudence. It was true that Ifre treated her as if she were little better than a common servant, but few were daring enough to echo his behavior to her face. She was helpless to change her circumstances; she could only pretend the slights didn't hurt.

Kane remained outside the door, his face impassive. Even so, there was something about the set of his mouth that hinted Captain Kane did not approve of his companion's behavior any more than she did.

He met her gaze only briefly, but once again she felt the same jolt of awareness she'd sensed the day before. "Lady Theda, it is my honor to meet you. I hope you will forgive our unexpected intrusion."

She managed to nod. "Congratulations on your new position."

What she really felt was disappointment. Ifre didn't appoint men to positions of authority who weren't willing to carry out his orders without question. She would warn her ladies to be wary of the man until she had sufficient opportunity to evaluate his character.

Markus was too busy staring at Lady Margaret to make any move toward leaving. She was about to suggest they leave when Kane took charge.

"If you'll excuse us, ladies, we should continue on our tour."

When Markus didn't immediately respond, he snapped, "Now, Sergeant."

Sergeant Markus flushed red. He shot Theda a look that warned there would be retribution for the rebuke. They both knew he wouldn't dare take his temper out on Kane, not after having seen the man fight. No, this was just further reason for him to make her life more miserable.

When the two men left, she locked and barred the door. "Ladies, from now on, it would be best if we kept the door locked at all times. Also, when you want in, knock twice, pause, and then knock one more time. I think we'll all feel safer if we know whether or not it's one of us wanting in."

They all exchanged looks and then nodded. Not one of them hadn't experienced a moment or two of fear around the guardsmen. It didn't used to be that way, but things were definitely getting worse. She didn't know if Ifre openly encouraged such behavior in his men or if they simply knew they could get away with almost anything and he wouldn't care.

"You both may remain here for now, but it is time for me to go check to make sure everything is ready for the midday meal. Don't forget to lock the door after I leave."

Theda peeked out into the hallway, checking both ways before pulling the door closed behind her. She was in no mood to confront Markus and the captain again so soon. Before moving on, she listened to be sure her friends took her seriously about locking the door. Satisfied they were as safe as she could make them, she drew a calming breath and made her way to the kitchen.

*   *   *

The cook had things well in hand. Ordinarily, Theda would have simply checked to make sure there were no problems she should be aware of and then leave. This time the cook was lying in wait for her.

"Lady Theda, I had to purchase more supplies today because of the number of them nobles staying on. I thought you'd want to know the miller and the butcher would be looking to get paid extra this week."

"Thank you for letting me know. I'll see to it that payment is made."

She walked away, her already tumultuous emotions surging to new levels. Theda didn't question the necessity of the additional purchases, but she didn't look forward to justifying the unexpected expenditures from the household budget. Ifre had never once refused any extra money she requested, but he also never missed an opportunity to make her practically beg for the funds.

She would've paid the bills out of her own money, but he controlled that as well. He'd taken charge of her wealth after Armel's death and would control it until such time as she remarried. He would also choose her next husband for her.

No doubt he would auction her lands off to the highest bidder. He had hinted at a few men he was considering, each of them with a reputation for cruelty and brutish behavior. She could still remember the chills his words had given her.

If she hadn't already hated Ifre before that moment, she did then. She had no claim on any of his family's property, but she'd inherited several estates and titles that had been handed down from both sides of her own family.

Her personal wealth had equaled or even exceeded her husband's on the date of their marriage. Armel had seen her as a full partner in their marriage, often seeking her counsel when it came to ruling his land. Ifre saw her simply as chattel, something that could be bought and sold like any other possession he owned.

And they both knew her time of mourning was quickly drawing to a close. Even Ifre wouldn't flaunt his power by forcing her into marriage before the traditional time had passed. But all too soon, it would be over and she'd be even more at risk than ever.

Just as she returned to the great hall, Ifre loomed up behind her as if she conjured him out of the dark turn her thoughts had taken. "Ah, Theda, there you are. I've been looking for you."

She swallowed her fear. "I was visiting the kitchen to make sure that the midday meal would be served on time."

He dismissed her comment with a wave of his hand. "I would like you to join me at my table for today. I have a couple of guests who would like to meet you."

"I will be there."

Then in another abrupt change of topics, he went on. "Have you met the new captain of my guard? I think my brother would have found Kane interesting or, on second thought, perhaps not. Kane bears the mark of a blood mage, a gift from his maternal grandsire. Armel's interest in magery always had a rather narrow focus."

Meaning he'd never allowed his interest in his gift to stray into the dark and twisted paths that Ifre currently explored. She saw it as a strength, but her brother-in-law would have scoffed at that idea.

"I should return to my quarters and freshen my attire if I am to join your guests."

"Do that. I want you to look your best for them." He reached out to brush his fingers across her cheek, smiling when she flinched. "A lady should always make a good first impression."

"I know my duty, Ifre, and I'll see it done."

She walked away without a word, her nails biting into the palms of her hands. Before she'd gone five steps, he called after her. "Tomorrow see what you can do about hiring more servants. We seem to be shorthanded again."

She barely paused before continuing on as her stomach roiled with fear. If she didn't do as he asked, he would simply seek his prey elsewhere, perhaps among her ladies. If she did hire the servants, it was with the full knowledge that some of them wouldn't live long enough to collect their first wages.

His laughter trailed after as she all but ran from the dark stench of his evil nature.

Chapter 6

*T*he library was crowded, but its thick walls offered the best chance of privacy for the discussion they were about to have. Gideon looked around the room, counting heads to make sure everyone was there.

Murdoch had been the most recent one through the door, arriving shortly after Lady Alina. Gideon had his suspicions about where his friend had spent the night, but it was not truly any of his business. If Lady Alina chose to offer Murdoch comfort for the remaining days—and nights—of their sworn service to her niece, so be it.

That thought had Gideon automatically reaching out to take Merewen's hand in his. She smiled and gave it a quick squeeze, momentarily distracting him from the task at hand. When the door opened again, Duncan entered with Lady Lavinia holding on to his arm. Murdoch frowned slightly, clearly still not won over to the woman's cause. Gideon had his own misgivings, but he trusted Duncan implicitly and would therefore give her the benefit of the doubt. After all, she'd saved their lives with her heroics.

Duncan led Lavinia down to the far end of the table where they could sit together and present a united front to everyone else in the room. Gideon understood his reasons but wished he hadn't felt that the gesture was necessary.

Maybe he could do something about that. He rose to his feet, always more comfortable speaking while moving around.

"Lady Lavinia, thank you again for rushing to our defense yesterday. Lives would have been lost if you hadn't intervened."

Some of the tension in her face eased. "I'm only glad that we arrived in time."

Her smile seemed genuine as she looked around the table and met each person's gaze. It faltered only when she got to Murdoch. Eventually, the two would have to come to terms, but Gideon liked that she didn't cower. He sensed the same strength in her that he'd found in Merewen—and even Lady Alina was starting to show signs of such a strength. That was good; they would need it if they were all to get through the days ahead.

"Yesterday, Duncan had the opportunity to describe his journey to the abbey and back. Lady Lavinia, I know he explained our circumstances to you and why magic is anathema to us. Our gods have commanded us to forswear the use of all dark powers."

Duncan immediately started to speak, but Lavinia stayed his protest with a wave of her hand. "I understand your concern, Captain. Perhaps I can clarify a few things for you and your men."

She glanced in Murdoch's direction and waited until he nodded before continuing. Duncan immediately leaned back in his chair, further reducing the tension.

"Make no mistake; the kind of magic my half brother practices is evil, both at its source and in its intent. He draws his power from the living to feed the blackness that devours his soul. Eventually, it will grow in strength until he will no longer be able to contain it. When that happens, it will destroy Ifre, leaving it free to ravage all that it touches."

Her blunt words froze Gideon where he stood. "But—"

She cut him off just as she had Duncan. "I would prefer to lay it all before you at once. Then I'll answer what questions I can."

He nodded as he dropped back down in the seat next to Merewen, needing her calming presence. When he was settled, Lavinia resumed her lecture.

"For most mages, the source of their power is the natural energy that surrounds us all. Their talent as a mage comes from their inborn ability to draw on that power and the skill with which they learn to manipulate it. In short, one is born a mage, but most have only a small gift, which limits what they can do with it. Only rarely is someone born with the ability to wield a great deal of power."

Once again she looked at each person in turn. "Magery runs in both sides of my family. My father, the late duke, was a powerful mage, and Armel, his eldest son, was his equal. Both were honorable men, who used their powers only sparingly, preferring to rule their people through justice and wisdom rather than fear."

Her expression turned bleak. "My mother also had a gift for magic, and there were those who accused her of using it to capture the attention and the heart of the duke. I was but a child when they both died, but my memories are of two people who clearly loved each other. Both of my parents made sure that I was taught both the ethics of magic along with the techniques."

Merewen frowned. "And your half brother? What of him?"

"I think it likely that Ifre resented me because of my mother's influence over his father. I am also convinced he was responsible for our brother's death. Ifre will not tolerate interference in his quest for power, and his greed knows no boundaries."

She shivered. When Duncan moved closer to put his arm around her shoulders, she leaned against him, clearly drawing comfort from his touch. Gideon hated to keep pressing her, but time was speeding by them.

"If you have to be born a mage, how were you able to teach Duncan the spell he cast yesterday?"

For the first time, she averted her gaze, focusing on the flickering flame of the candle in the center of the table. He braced himself for an answer he wouldn't like.

"I honestly cannot say if Duncan was born with a gift

for magic or if his connection with the Lady of the River gave rise to the ability."

Gideon had been right. He didn't like the answer, but at least he was willing to listen. Murdoch had a thunderous expression on his face, his huge fists clenched as if readying himself for battle. Lady Alina tried to distract him, but her success was limited.

Gideon couched his response as the order it was. "Explain your reasoning."

Lavinia held up her hand and ticked off her points. "He sensed my scrying before he arrived at the abbey. He was able to detect the magic in the duke's ensorcelled coins but was not affected by it. And in the abbey's library, he not only felt the power in the wards I'd set to protect our collection of forbidden books, but he could see it. No one without at least a smattering of magical talent could have done any of those things."

Murdoch gave voice to his anger. "No insult intended, but until Duncan met you, he has never before carried the taint of magic. He has also admitted to being tempted by its power when using the spell you taught him. Had he not pulled back from that precipice, all of us could've been condemned to a soulless existence for eternity."

Duncan was on his feet, for the second time in two days ready to draw a weapon against one of their own. "Perhaps no insult was intended, Murdoch, but insult was taken. Apologize to the lady now or I'll teach you some manners myself."

At that point, everyone was on their feet. Alina was trying to make herself heard over the deep rumble of Murdoch's voice. Sigil stood beside the big man, making his own loyalties clear. Lavinia had planted herself right in front of Duncan, her face flushed bright with either embarrassment or temper.

Something had to be done and quickly, if for no other reason than their gods would not tolerate one of the Damned turning against another. They'd all come too far, been friends too long, for Gideon to let this happen.

"ENOUGH!" he shouted.

During the brief silence, he repeated himself. "Enough! Everyone, sit down. Now, or it will be me you face."

The women were the first to comply, followed more slowly by Sigil, Murdoch, and finally, Duncan.

Gideon glared at his two friends equally. "The goddess expects better from both of you, as do I. I will remind both of you right now that your primary duty is to Lady Merewen. We have all sworn to protect her at any cost. Have you forgotten that?"

Duncan broke off glaring at Murdoch long enough to shake his head. "I am well aware of my duty to both the goddess and Lady Merewen."

Murdoch growled through clenched teeth, "I have not forgotten."

"Good." Gideon still had more to say. "Murdoch, none of us are comfortable around magic, but do not let your fear blind you to the fact that we can't fight what we refuse to understand."

The big warrior flinched as Gideon's words lashed at him. "I am no coward."

To Gideon's surprise, it was Duncan who responded. "No, you're not, Murdoch. And you weren't wrong about me almost giving in to the magic, but the goddess herself forgave my weakness. It is not your job to judge me, but I would ask you as my friend to help make sure I don't falter again."

Alina smiled at Murdoch in encouragement. He took her hand in his as he stared first at Lavinia and then Duncan. "I would ask for forgiveness from both of you for letting my fear rule me. Duncan, you have never failed the goddess, and you will not this time."

Lavinia managed a small smile. "You are right to fear magic, Sir Murdoch. You've seen firsthand what can happen when it is misused, as have I. I also worry that my own abilities pale in comparison to what Ifre will unleash if we cannot soon put a stop to his predation."

Duncan rejoined the conversation. "These are tense

times, and the situation is grave. It is no surprise that our tempers are easily frayed."

Finally, the atmosphere in the room felt lighter. Perhaps now they could get on with their plans. Gideon cleared his throat, prepared to launch into his thoughts on how best to put their recently acquired allies to good use.

Before he could get a word out, the door opened and Sarra, the little girl who'd arrived with Duncan and Lavinia, walked in. She scurried around the table to whisper in Lavinia's ear. The abbess studied her young friend for several seconds and then turned a worried look in Duncan's direction.

He lifted Sarra onto his lap and murmured something to her in a low voice. Gideon found himself leaning forward, trying to catch what Duncan was saying. Murdoch mirrored his actions while everyone else simply sat and stared. Sarra's small face scrunched up in an angry frown.

Gideon gave voice to the obvious question. "What's wrong now?"

Duncan glanced toward Gideon. "Sarra has a message she needs to deliver."

They'd all learned firsthand yesterday to respect the small girl's pronouncements. If she hadn't warned Lavinia and Duncan of the duke's threat, they would have never reached the keep in time to save the horses or the people who were with them. But that didn't mean that any of them were comfortable with gods speaking through a child.

Gideon had little experience in dealing with children, but he was willing to try. "We're listening, Sarra."

"My message isn't for the Damned, Captain Gideon. I need to speak to the one who has lost his way."

She wiggled down off Duncan's lap and made her way around the table to where Sigil sat watching her as if she were a serpent poised to strike.

In a voice far deeper than a child's, she stared up at him, her expression intense. "Would you hear what we have to say, wanderer?"

Sigil jerked his head in a sharp nod. "I would."

"Come with us, then. Our words are for your ears alone. After you have listened, you can do as you will with what you have learned. I will wait for you in the pasture."

She walked away, leaving the room in stunned silence. Sigil looked first to Murdoch and then toward Lady Lavinia. "What should I do, my lady?"

Lavinia still stared at the door. "I do not understand the source of Sarra's gift, but I have never known her to be wrong. She came to the abbey only a short time ago, after the duke's men killed her father and took her mother. At first Sarra did small things, such as helping people find lost objects and the like. Only recently has her gift grown in power. I have repeatedly cautioned her to come to me in private before she shares her message. Most of the time, she complies, but as you can see, not always."

She finally looked in Sigil's direction. "You may choose not to listen to her, but I fear you would do so at your own peril."

The warrior immediately rose to his feet. "Captain Gideon, if you will give me leave to depart, I think it best that I hear what Sarra has to tell me."

"Of course. Feel free to rejoin us when you are done."

"Yes, sir." He paused in the doorway. "Know that you may count on my sword in any plans that you make."

And with that pronouncement, he was gone.

Outside the library, Sigil put his hand against the wall for support as he struggled to control the hot rush of emotions burning through his veins. What could that child know of him or his past? Did she know his name? Had their paths crossed at some point? If so, why hadn't she said something while they were riding back to the keep?

His instincts were saying no, that they'd never met before the night he and Murdoch had ridden through the darkness to meet up with Duncan and Lavinia. Yet he couldn't deny that when Sarra had spoken to him in the library, her voice had carried a heavy portent of approaching danger. The true question was whether he was its target or its source.

With the same sense of dread he would feel marching into battle, Sigil walked down the stairs, taking care to move normally to avoid drawing attention to either himself or the girl. Lady Merewen's people were already uneasy with everything that had happened recently. The more superstitious ones would do far more than simply shun Sarra if they thought she was possessed by spirits. It was hardly her fault if her gods chose to speak through her, but they certainly put her at risk by doing so.

He stepped out into bright sunshine and turned in the direction of the pasture. It wasn't hard to spot one small girl surrounded by a circle of horses. Her face was bright with happiness as a mare accepted one of the apples Sarra carried in her apron. She giggled when the horse's lips tickled her hand.

Rather than ruin the moment for her, Sigil stood back and waited for her to finish distributing her gifts to her four-legged companions. When she'd delivered the last apple, he started forward. She calmly watched his approach.

She cocked her head to one side when he joined her inside the pasture. "You came. I wasn't sure you would."

"Neither was I."

His honesty surprised them both. He liked that she laughed rather than took offense. "Shall we walk as you tell me what you want me to know?"

Sarra patted the neck of the closest mare. "I'd rather ride."

Sigil recognized a hint when he heard one and lifted her onto the mare's back. Sarra gripped the horse's mane while Sigil led the mare by her halter. The little girl didn't speak until they'd reached the distant end of the pasture.

"This is far enough," Sarra announced as she slid back down to the ground.

The mare moved off a short distance to graze as Sarra

clambered up the fence to perch on the top railing. The maneuver put her closer to Sigil's eye level, which he suspected was a deliberate choice on her point.

"Are you ready, Captain?"

She sounded remarkably calm; he wished he could say the same about himself as he nodded.

Her face immediately changed. The alterations were minor, but the effect was disturbing. Once again, it was as if the girl was gone, and someone else peered out through her eyes. Certainly, when she spoke, the voice was no longer that of a young girl.

"Lost one, how fare you?"

At first Sigil was too stunned to answer, but he finally mumbled, "My wounds have all healed."

Sarra's mouth frowned in disgust. "We can see that much for ourselves. We were asking about your memories. Do you yet fear their return?"

He started to protest but then held back. "In truth, I do. If that were to happen, it will force Captain Gideon and Murdoch to decide what to do about me. We all know that I served a monster. I worry about what that says about me."

Her eyebrows shot up. "But we would ask you this, Captain: If you were the monster Duke Keirthan is, would you even worry about such things?"

Once again she'd surprised him with her wisdom. "Perhaps not. What more can you tell me about myself?"

"Only that by choosing to pledge your sword to the Damned, you will redeem yourself and your honor. Your memories are a burden you do not yet need to bear. You will find your way back to yourself and those who love you, but let the knowledge that you follow the right path suffice for now. We hope that our words have eased your mind."

With no warning, Sarra scrambled down off the fence. When she spoke, her normal voice had returned. "Can I ride the horse again?"

"Of course."

As he followed her toward the mare, the rapid changes in her demeanor had his mind spinning in circles. Yet he realized he also felt better than he had in a long while. Lighter, as if a burden had been lifted from his shoulders.

Instead of setting Sarra on the horse, he boosted himself up on the mare's back first and then held out a hand to tug Sarra up in front of him. When she was settled, he told her, "Hold on tight, little one, and we'll see how fast she can run."

As they circled the pasture, the sound of Sarra's joyous laughter soothed Sigil's soul.

Chapter 7

Kane strolled into the tavern and took his usual table in the back corner away from the few other patrons in the room. Averel had yet to make an appearance for the evening, but Kane was not concerned. He could use a short respite that entailed drinking at least a flagon of ale before resuming his duties. It had been a long day. After the tour Markus had given him, they'd parted ways so Kane could move the rest of his things from the inn to his new quarters in the barracks.

His new room's stark simplicity suited him. As long as he could lock the door and allow Hob time out of the shield without fear of discovery, he was happy. It wasn't as if he intended to take up permanent residence in the city.

He was about halfway into his first drink when Averel entered the tavern. The young warrior was faring well enough in his position as troubadour. His dogs wandered in behind him, stopping to sniff the air before ranging out in front of him to check out the customers.

Both gradually made their way toward Kane, stopping along the way to get petted. Averel followed them, making time to greet several customers before finally arriving at Kane's table.

"I see my dogs have taken a liking to you," he said with a smile. "I noticed you the other night, but we didn't get a chance to talk. My name is Averel."

Kane pushed an empty chair out with his foot in invitation. "I'm Kane, the new captain of the duke's guard. I enjoyed your performance."

His friend managed to disguise his shock at Kane's pronouncement—barely. Then he grinned. "Congratulations are in order then, Captain Kane."

Averel signaled one of the barmaids. "Another flagon for my new friend and one for me as well."

They waited until their drinks arrived before speaking. Averel leaned back in his chair and crossed his feet at the ankles, his relaxed demeanor belying the intensity of his gaze. He glanced around the room before he spoke again.

Pitching his voice low to keep their conversation private, he asked, "I thought you were going to try to get a position with guard, but captain? How did that happen?"

Kane shrugged. "The duke thinks I executed a local merchant in retaliation for him killing my predecessor, Captain Bayar. In truth, it was the other way around. A sergeant and a couple of other guards arrived shortly after it happened, looking for Bayar. Once I convinced them my story was true, Sergeant Markus invited me to join their ranks if I passed the duke's inspection."

Averel blinked. "You've actually met Duke Keirthan?"

Kane couldn't quite hide his revulsion. "Twice now. The bastard reeks of old blood and death, although I seem to be one of the few who notices it."

While Kane swigged down some ale to wash away the foul taste the memory carried with it, Averel asked, "Why did he make you captain?"

"Good question. I easily defeated the favorite in the tournament a couple of days ago, but I'm not convinced that's why." His hand strayed to the mark on his cheek. "Keirthan was far more interested in how I came by this than how I fared against another fighter. Keirthan hungers for more power at any price."

"I'll send one of the dogs to Gideon with the news. Is there anything else he should know?"

"If Keirthan hasn't already started losing control of the magic, he will soon. The path the fool follows will be his undoing. Only a highly trained blood mage like my grandfather would have stood a chance against that much darkness upon his soul."

Kane finished his drink and smiled. "I need to get back and go through the motions of my new position. Seems I am at least the third man to be appointed captain recently. Let's hope that I last longer than Bayar did."

His friend didn't find the jest amusing. "Watch your back, Kane. Send Hob to fetch me if you run into trouble."

Kane's own amusement faded. "I will, my friend. Take care of yourself and the mutts as well. As time allows, I will stop by."

Then he walked away, hoping that it wouldn't be the last time.

Two days had passed since Kane had visited Averel. The brief meeting had helped, but he missed being one of five warriors united in a common cause. He still believed that they were best served by having someone inside the duke's retinue, but at the same time he hated being isolated from the others.

The hour grew late, but he was too restless to sleep. Although not normally given to premonitions, his instincts were telling him that something was wrong or someone was in peril. He wanted to shrug it off, but couldn't. If he was mistaken, fine.

At the worst, the exercise he got from pacing the hallways of the castle would make it that much easier for him to sleep when he finally sought out his bed. But if he were right and failed to investigate, someone would suffer. He wouldn't take that chance.

He wore his black leathers since he wasn't officially on duty. The duke's formal livery with its tan jerkin and dark trousers was too noticeable, while black allowed him to fade into the shadows outside the barracks.

The guard on duty had left his post at the side door, no doubt to relieve himself behind some bushes. Kane took advantage of his absence to slip inside the keep. It was a breach in the duke's defenses that a real captain would have immediately pointed out to Markus. Kane wouldn't bother, not when he might need to exploit the weakness again sometime.

Inside, he followed the hallway to the first passage that opened off to his right, which led toward the great hall. There he paused to listen, to take in all the night sounds that echoed softly along the thick walls of the castle. One by one, he eliminated those that were of no concern. The rattle of a servant carrying a tray of dishes back to the kitchen. The scrape of tables being dragged to the side of the room to clear space for the servants who slept on the floor at night. A few dogs sniffing among the reeds on the floor for any food scraps that had been missed.

All harmless. All normal.

But still he sensed a faint taste of fear in the air. A few seconds later, he located its source. A short distance away, the sound of a deep male voice rumbled in counterpoint to a higher-pitched feminine one. Kane didn't recognize either one, but he knew scared when he heard it. He started forward, his soft-soled boots making but the slightest sound as he stalked his prey.

The voices were nearer now. The woman was insisting that she was expected elsewhere and her mistress wouldn't be happy if she were delayed any longer.

Her unwanted companion only laughed. "Your mistress will have to wait. I have need of you myself."

At the sound of cloth tearing and a muffled whimper, Kane abandoned all attempts at caution. Even if the female was a servant, she shouldn't have to suffer unwanted advances.

He turned the last corner; his already bad mood immediately flared hot. The bastard wore a guard's uniform. While Kane knew Markus turned a blind eye to some of his men's unsavory behavior, rape was beyond the pale. Kane couldn't risk killing one of his own men, but he could make him bleed.

From the guard's slurred speech, he'd been drinking. Good. His memories of tonight's activities would be blurred when he sobered up. Kane ran the last distance, pulling his cudgel from his belt. He shook his head when the woman spotted him, hoping she wouldn't warn her attacker that Kane was there.

When he was within striking distance, he swung hard, bringing the heavy head of the small club cracking down on the back of the guard's skull. The man sank to the ground in a boneless heap. Kane resisted the urge to kick him in the ribs. A lump on the back of his head might be attributed to a drunk's clumsiness, but it would be harder to explain more than that.

The woman looked at the crumpled guard and then at Kane, the fear on her face unchanged. She backed up a step, obviously about to bolt. He should have been used to that reaction by now; that didn't mean it didn't rankle. He'd never knowingly harmed a woman and had no desire to take one against her will. Granted, she didn't know that, but he'd just rescued her. Couldn't she at least give him the benefit of the doubt?

He took her arm, being careful not to bruise it, and led her along the hallway to put some distance between them and the fallen guard. They stopped near a torchlight, basking them both in its glow.

"What's your name?"

"Lady M-Margaret," she stammered.

"Who is your mistress?" he asked, although he already knew the answer. Unless he was mistaken, he'd seen the young female twice before in the company of the duke's sister-in-law.

"Lady Theda."

He needed more information. "Why are you wandering alone this time of the night, especially with one of the guards?"

"Our paths crossed when I was returning from an errand in town. I'd been delayed, and it was already dark when I started back. When he offered to escort me, I accepted, thinking I would be safer with him than alone."

She blushed and dropped her gaze. "I didn't realize until too late that he'd been drinking. Once we reached the great hall, he dragged me into that corner and demanded a kiss in payment for his services."

Lady Margaret would've been damned lucky if the guard had settled for just a kiss, but this was no time to berate her for her foolishness. He'd save his sharp words for her mistress.

"I'll see you safely back to Lady Theda's quarters."

She started forward. "I know the way."

He would have applauded the fact that she'd learned her lesson about blindly trusting a man she didn't know, but he wasn't in the mood. "I said I will see you safely back to Lady Theda. Let's go before anyone discovers your unconscious friend back there."

Without waiting to see if she'd comply, he started for the back staircase. It was a relief when she scurried to catch up, saving Kane from having to drag her along in his wake. At least she showed the common sense to keep quiet as they made their way through the darkened passages. At one point, he pulled her back into a corner and waited for a pair of servants to pass by.

Once they were out of sight, the two of them hurried up the steps that brought them to the second floor near Theda's personal quarters. At this time of night, she'd be more likely to be there than in her solar farther down the hall.

When he lifted his hand to knock, Margaret stopped him. "Let me."

She rapped her knuckles on the wood twice and then a third time after a brief pause. The door swung up almost immediately, the light from the room spilling out into the hallway as Lady Theda stepped into sight. Upon seeing Margaret, Theda latched onto her arms.

"Margaret! Where have you been? I've been so worried!"

"It was so awful, Lady Theda." Then without explaining what she was talking about, the younger woman collapsed against Theda's shoulder in tears. Her choking sobs echoed up and down that hall as she gave into the hysteria that Kane had been expecting since he'd rescued her.

He'd been standing in the shadows outside the pool of light, but now he eased closer. Unlike Lady Margaret, Theda showed no fear, only confusion at his unexpected appearance.

"What happened to her?"

Her tone stopped short of accusing him of being responsible for the tear in Margaret's dress. At least she hadn't dragged the girl inside the room and slammed the door in his face before giving him a chance to explain.

"She was foolish enough to linger too long in town. One of the guards escorted her back, but apparently he was only interested in saving her for himself. I got there in time to save her from suffering more than an unwanted kiss and a ripped sleeve."

Then he crossed his arms over his chest and waited to see what Theda had to say next.

Theda stared at the stony expression on Captain Kane's face and tried to discern his mood. His stance said he was angry. Fine, so was she.

"Captain, if you would be so kind as to wait a moment, I'll be right with you."

He jerked his head in a quick nod. Satisfied that he wasn't going to disappear, Theda led her young charge into her room but left the door open. "Lydia, please hand me a cloth for Margaret. She's been through a rough patch."

Margaret's tears had already slowed to a small trickle. Theda used the linen to wipe her face dry. "You're safe now. I think a small glass of wine is in order."

Before accepting the drink, Margaret turned back to face the grim warrior in the hall. "Captain Kane, thank you for coming to my rescue. I don't know what I would have done if you hadn't arrived when you did."

If Theda hadn't been looking at Kane at that exact moment, she would have missed seeing his eyes widen in shock. Why? Was he truly so surprised to have someone show a little appreciation for his efforts?

He nodded to acknowledge Margaret's thanks before turning his intense gaze back toward Theda. "I don't have much time, and we need to talk."

It was more of an order than a suggestion. Either way, his words sounded ominous as his deep voice rumbled along her nerves, although it wasn't exactly fear that had her clenching her hands at her waist. More like a heightened awareness of the man leaning against the wall outside of her bedroom door. What could he want to discuss this late at night? She picked up a lit candle before joining him out in the hallway and pulled the door closed behind her.

He straightened and looked up and down the hallway. "Is there somewhere more private we can go? I'd rather not be seen with you."

So few did, but his blunt statement still hurt. "Fine. My solar is close by."

Although perhaps she was being as foolish as Margaret had been in trusting a drunken guard to see her home safely. They walked in silence to the end of the hallway. She led the way into the solar, using her candle to light several more, driving back the shadows. Despite the flickering light, the man standing beside her seemed to carry his own darkness with him.

"We're here. What did you want to say?"

He frowned. "When I brought Lady Margaret to your door, she knocked twice, paused, and then a third time. Was that your idea?"

Where was he going with this? "Yes. I decided it was best that we find some way to know for sure who was on the other side of a door before we opened it. After the way you and Sergeant Markus strolled into my solar with no warning, I have also given my ladies orders to keep their doors locked at all times. The simple pattern will allow my ladies-in-waiting to know if it is safe to open the door."

"That was smart of you, Lady Theda."

Was that approval in his voice? She allowed herself a small smile. "Should I change the signal now that you know it?"

"That's your decision." He paced the length of the room and back. "This incident with Lady Margaret isn't the first, is it?"

Why would he care?

"No, but it's the most blatant."

Kane spun back to face her. "Yet you are the duke's sister-in-law."

"I am."

She left it at that. Despite Kane's rough kindness to Margaret, that didn't mean he was trustworthy. She wasn't about to criticize Ifre in front of his new captain. But rather than press her for more of an answer, Kane merely nodded as if her careful words confirmed something for him.

"If it happens again, let me know, but quietly. I trust your ladies will be more careful in the future about wandering alone at all hours. They would be safer traveling in pairs."

"I will relay your suggestion."

He shook his head. "I think it would be better to leave my name out of it, Lady Theda."

"For you or for me?"

Her question clearly made him angry. "Let's not play word games. I'll see you back to your quarters."

Before he could walk away, she reached out to touch his forearm. He hissed and jerked back as if her fingertips burned him. His pale eyes glittered with some powerful emotion, but she wasn't convinced it was anger.

"I'm sorry, Captain. I meant only to stop you long enough to thank you again. It has been far too long since someone showed me or my ladies this much kindness. It will, however, remain our secret. I will speak with both Margaret and Lydia."

Once again, he nodded. They walked in complete silence back to her room. He arrived a step ahead of her and softly knocked on the door in the proper rhythm. By the time the door opened, Kane had disappeared into the shadows at the far end of the hall. She stared into the darkness for a few seconds, almost certain he was still nearby watching her. Maybe more than that, he would be watching out for her.

In case she was right, she smiled and lifted her hand in farewell. Her mood oddly lightened by the encounter, she closed the door and turned the lock. Lydia and Margaret would both remain with her tonight. Some time ago, she'd had a couple of smaller beds added to her dressing room for just such times.

"Ladies, I think it is time we retire for the night."

When the last candle was extinguished, she stared up at the ceiling and waited for sleep to claim her. It was moments like this that she most often missed Armel and his warm touch in the night.

But for the first time since his death, it wasn't his handsome face that eased her mind. Instead, Kane's stern visage followed her over the edge into slumber.

Chapter 8

"*H*ob, I'm not sure I made the best decision about hitting that guard last night."

The gargoyle whined in sympathy and tunneled his head under Kane's hand for a good rub, the contact a comfort to them both.

Kane continued his monologue. "Yet I cannot bring myself to regret it. The bastard had it coming."

After leaving Theda's quarters, Kane had meant to retire to his own, but at the last minute he'd returned to where the drunken guard remained sprawled on the floor. Rather than leave him there, Kane had sought out two of the other guards and ordered them to drag their friend to one of the cells located near the barracks.

The fool, whose name was Gart, was to remain there to be dealt with when he sobered up. Kane had yet to decide what his punishment should be. It all depended on whether Gart remembered what he'd been doing when Kane had interrupted him.

Kane scratched his avatar's chin and smiled. It was certainly tempting to turn Hob loose in the cell with the fool. Seeing what was left of their compatriot after Hob finished with him would definitely discourage such behavior in the other guards.

However, Keirthan would see Kane's defense of the woman as a weakness, one he wouldn't hesitate to exploit. By the bastard's own example, the guardsmen all knew that Lady Theda and the others were not to be accorded the same respect as the wives and daughters of the visiting nobility and merchants.

Instead, Kane would fall back on military discipline. For his first official order, he would make it clear that public drunkenness would no longer be tolerated within the halls of the duke's home. It wasn't much, but at least he'd have grounds for punishing anyone else who dared to assault any female member of the household.

Time to start the day. "Hob, I have to send you back now."

The gargoyle shot him a reproachful look as he waddled over to where his shield stood against the wall. Kane murmured the spell that sent Hob back to rest on the curved surface of the shield. To anyone else, he looked like an especially detailed painting of a mythological creature. No one would suspect that he was real.

He wished he could let Hob join him in the practice fields, but that wouldn't be wise. Keirthan was already intrigued by Kane's past. If the blood mage learned that Kane's boon companion was straight out of the most distant myths, there was no telling how he'd react.

When Kane stepped outside of his office, Markus was waiting for him. The sergeant didn't look happy, no doubt having learned about Gart as soon as he went on duty. It would be interesting to hear what he had to say on the subject.

Kane walked past him without stopping. "I haven't eaten yet this morning. If you have something on your mind, we can talk as we walk."

As captain, Kane was within his rights to have his food brought to him, but he'd always found it useful to spend time in the common areas with those under his command. Markus fell into step beside him but didn't immediately speak. Fine. Kane would wait him out. He owed the sergeant no explanations.

They'd almost reached the door to the mess before Markus spoke. "Looks like Private Gart had a rough night."

"He did." More so than Markus knew.

When he spoke again, the sergeant's voice was completely devoid of emotion. "In the past, we would have dragged him back to his bunk to sleep it off."

"Since it's happened before, obviously that policy isn't working." Kane sat down at the table in the corner and signaled for a servant to bring food for both him and Markus. "The men are entitled to drink in their off hours. I do so myself. However, passing out on the floor where anyone can trip over them is unacceptable. It reflects badly on the duke and on our ability to maintain discipline among the men."

He broke off speaking until the servant set down their porridge and tea. "If Gart had staggered back to his bunk or passed out in the barracks, we wouldn't be having this conversation."

Markus flexed his fingers around his mug several times before speaking. "But, sir—"

Kane cut him off. "If you are not willing to enforce my orders, Sergeant, I will find someone who is."

The other man's chin came up, his hold on his temper slipping. "I will enforce the order, Captain, but the men won't like it."

Arching an eyebrow in mock surprise, Kane asked, "Do you always ask for approval from underlings before establishing rules and expectations? I hadn't realized that's how things were done around here."

When Markus didn't respond, Kane leaned forward, elbows on the table. "Make it clear that I am in no way restricting the men's access to the taverns in town, but I will not tolerate a bunch of stumbling drunks under my command. If they can't handle their drink, they are gone."

Having made his point, he backed away. "I will be participating in arms practice this afternoon. Have Gart there. I think he will make an excellent first opponent for me."

Markus shoved his bowl back untouched and rose to his feet. "If you'll excuse me, sir, I will post your orders."

"You're excused, Sergeant."

Markus started to walk away, but then turned back. "There was one odd thing about Gart, though."

There was note in Markus's voice that had Kane giving him his full attention. "And that would be?"

"The men said you found him lying facedown on the floor."

Where was he going with this? "That is true."

"Then why would he have what looks like a blow to the back of his head?"

"Peculiar, but you'll have to ask him about that." Kane turned his attention back to his meal, dismissing the sergeant and any more questions he might have.

Ordinarily, Theda had little interest in her brother-in-law's personal guard and even less in wasting her time observing the brutes bang swords and sweat. Today, however, she found herself standing alone on the balcony of her solar and watching the activity below.

She'd never admit to her friends that she was hoping to catch a glimpse of Captain Kane in action again, but she wouldn't lie to herself about it. He was definitely a man of contradictions, ones she didn't understand. So far, he hadn't yet joined the others on the field. Perhaps his administrative duties took priority.

As she started to go back inside, she spotted a bunch of small boys using sticks as swords to mimic the men-at-arms. Their laughter and shouts carried on the breeze, making her smile. When one troop succeeded in routing their enemy, they all took off running, only to have one of the smaller boys crash right into Kane as he walked out of the stables. He was wearing the same black leathers he'd had on during the night, emphasizing his fearsome appearance.

Their play faltered as they remained frozen in place, staring up at him in horror. But rather than snarl at the child, Kane steadied him on his feet. Then he dropped to a knee and said something that had the boy holding out his stick for Kane's inspection. From where Theda stood, it was impossible to hear the exchange, but it appeared the captain was admiring the makeshift weapon as if it were worthy of a great knight.

When he stood, the other children crept closer. Within seconds, Kane had them lined up and practicing their lunges as he corrected their stances. The whole encounter lasted only a short time, but clearly Kane had won over the entire bunch. As he continued on toward the practice field, the oldest of the boys took over barking orders at his friends.

For his part, Kane rounded the side of the stable and headed toward the cluster of guardsmen on the field. They all slowed to a stop at his approach. They watched him with trepidation, which he apparently did nothing to alleviate.

He barked an order and practice resumed as he studied the action. Finally, he called a halt to the proceedings as Sergeant Markus, accompanied by another guard, made his way onto the field. Kane watched their approach with what could be described only as predatory interest, his demeanor vastly different from what it had been only moments before with those children.

Markus stopped a few feet short of Kane, letting his companion continue on by himself. Everyone else formed a rough circle around the pair as first Kane and then the guard drew their weapons. At first their movements were slow and careful, but it didn't last long.

Badly outmatched, the guard was quickly in full retreat. Only a fool would have continued to stand against such an overwhelming onslaught, but apparently Kane wasn't interested in showing his opponent any mercy. If the match continued unabated for much longer, the guard would be lucky if he would be able to walk off the field without aid.

What had the man done to incur Kane's wrath? As soon as the thought crossed Theda's mind, she knew the answer. Without question, he was the drunk who had attacked Lady Margaret last eve. Kane knew punishing him for his actions would not sit well with Ifre.

No, canny man that he was, she bet Kane had found some other reason to make an example of him. Perhaps it was wrong of her to be glad to see the man bruised and bleeding, but she was. Once again she owed Kane for his actions on her behalf, although she suspected he wouldn't want her drawing attention to it.

The bout ended when Kane hooked Gart's sword and sent it flying through the air. The exhausted guard dropped to his knees. Kane stood over him, using the tip of his sword to lift the other man's chin up to look his captain in the face.

Whatever Kane said to him had him nodding despite the risk of being cut by the blade at his throat. Finally, Kane backed away and turned his attention to the other men. His entire demeanor changed again as he chose Markus as his next partner and ordered the others to pair off for more practice.

Where the first match had been meant to punish, this one was more akin to the match against the redheaded fighter days before. It was time for her to be about her duties, but she found it hard to walk away from the spectacle.

Once again, the dark warrior's actions brightened her day.

For once, Ifre had managed to slip outside without being noticed by his assigned guards. Taking refuge in the shadows of the trees near the practice field, he watched his new captain in action as Kane casually beat one of the guards into the ground. What had the man done to deserve such treatment? No matter. The guards were disposable. Even if Kane killed a few to make a point, so be it.

Right now he and Markus were crossing swords, testing each other for weaknesses as well as their strengths. The sergeant was putting up a good effort, but there was no doubt which of the two was the better fighter.

Ifre had definitely chosen correctly naming Kane as his new captain rather than promoting Markus, although Kane was not wearing his badge of office. Ifre didn't care if the men knew who was in command. Kane needed to wear that sigil if its power was to reach full strength. Until it did, Ifre would never break through Kane's mental shields.

And the darkness hungered to taste Kane's magic. Right now, its demands pounded in the back of Ifre's mind, no longer merely whispering its wants and needs. It was becoming difficult for Ifre to focus on anything other than the need to shed more blood and revel in the pain of his victims.

It was far too soon to give free rein to the darkness. He needed to bend another's magic to his will first or he'd risk burning through his own too quickly. He'd hoped to use Captain Terrick for that purpose, and failing him, Lady Lavinia. Kane was his third choice, but that didn't mean he was a lesser one.

No, every instinct Ifre had said that Kane's gift was a deep, dark pool of untapped power. Either the warrior was unaware of his own potential or he didn't care. It didn't matter which was true. Eventually, Ifre would chain the arrogant fool to his altar below the keep, and the world would tremble at what the two of them together would unleash.

Ifre had been out in the sunlight as long as he could tolerate it. Any longer and he'd need another pain draught before he'd be able to concentrate on his spells. Mixing drugs and complicated magery was never a good idea. He would return to the keep, partake of the midday meal, and then rest.

Once the sun went down, he could start the real business of the day. Earlier, he'd lured another servant down to his lair. Using a new spell he'd found, he'd rendered the man immobile but fully conscious. No doubt by now the man's own imagination had filled his mind with all sorts of terrible possibilities for what Ifre had in store for him.

He smiled. No matter how bad those thoughts were, they wouldn't even come close to what Ifre had in mind. He glanced up at the sky to gauge the time. His fun wouldn't commence for many hours yet, but as always, there was a certain pleasure to be had in the anticipation.

He took a more direct route back to the hall, the burn of the sun driving him inside as fast as he could get there. Before he reached the door, a movement above caught his attention. Lady Theda was just disappearing back into her solar. What had she been doing up there on the balcony? Shouldn't she be in the kitchen overseeing the final preparations for Ifre and his guests? If his meal was delayed, he would make her life even more miserable.

The guards on duty were visibly shocked to see Ifre approach without his usual retinue. It was doubtful anyone would dare attack Ifre so close to home, but it was always possible. Although he'd chosen to slip free of his guards, that didn't mean they wouldn't be punished if he'd come to harm.

They hurried to open the doors for him. He nodded as he passed by them. "Thank you, gentlemen. Please let your captain know that I enjoyed weapons practice today."

"Y-yes, Sire," the nearest one stammered.

Ifre had no doubt the man would do as he was told, which would accomplish two things. First, it would let Kane know that Ifre had taken a personal interest in his actions. But the real message was that the guards had been lax enough in their duties to allow their ruler to leave the keep unobserved and unprotected.

It would be interesting to see what Kane did with those two bits of news.

Chapter 9

"Captain, one of Sir Averel's dogs is approaching."

"Let him in," Gideon shouted as he and Murdoch ran toward the gate.

Sigil hung back, following more slowly. When the guard had shouted for the captain's attention, he'd started to answer himself, the reaction instinctive. He doubted Gideon or even Murdoch noticed, but it had left Sigil a bit shaken.

Were his memories returning? His new life as Sigil had only recently begun to feel normal to him as he developed a new store of memories and built new relationships based on the man he was now. If he were to recall what had come before, all of that progress could be destroyed, his friendships tarnished by the realities of who he'd been and what he'd done before an injury had stolen his memories.

"Sigil, are you all right?"

He realized he'd drifted to a stop halfway between the keep and the gate. He carefully schooled his features before turning to face Lady Merewen and her two companions.

"I'm fine, my lady." He gestured toward the gate. "The guard on duty spotted one of Sir Averel's dogs headed this way. I was just waiting to learn what news he has brought."

Merewen looked relieved. "Whatever the tidings, Gideon will be glad to finally hear something from Averel and Kane. The waiting has been hard on the rest of us, but him most of all."

They reached the gate just as the enormous black

beast came trotting in. It immediately dropped to the ground at Gideon's feet, panting hard with its tongue hanging out of its mouth.

Lady Lavinia stared at the animal in obvious shock. "What kind of dog is that? I've never seen another like it."

"Few have," Sigil answered with a smile. "It's one of a pair of battle dogs owned by another of the Damned. They are Sir Averel's avatars, much like Duncan's owl and Murdoch's mountain cat."

He noticed Lavinia flinched at his use of the word Murdoch and his four friends used to describe themselves. It was a reminder that her lover had been marked by the gods themselves, his life in their hands. It had taken Sigil himself a while to get used to the idea of men who measured their lives in centuries rather than years.

The deep rumble of Murdoch's voice caught his attention. "What does the note say? How do they fare?"

Gideon held up his hand as he read the paper that had been hidden in the dog's collar. "Averel found a position as a troubadour in a tavern in the city. He says the people speak in whispers of a terror that stalks the land, but no one dares criticize the duke openly."

He drew a sharp breath and looked up at Murdoch, obviously shocked at what came next. "It's Kane. I'm not sure if he's brilliant or if he's taken leave of his senses."

Merewen shifted closer to Gideon. "What's he done? Is he in danger?"

"He was fine when Averel sent this note. It seems that Kane was successful in finding a position with the duke's guard."

Gideon's cryptic remarks had them all leaning forward, trying to see for themselves what was written on the paper that had him so flustered. Murdoch snatched it from his hands and read it for himself.

When he was done, his face mirrored the same stunned look as Gideon's. "Kane is the new captain of the duke's personal guard. How did that happen?"

Gideon moved on to the second page of Averel's missive. "It seems Keirthan evaluates all of the men who are hired as guards. When he spotted Kane's mage mark, he took a personal interest in him."

Lavinia paled. "Your friend is mage-marked?"

Duncan spoke for the first time. "Yes. Kane's grandfather was a powerful mage, and his magic marked Kane while he was yet a babe in his mother's womb."

She rubbed her hands up and down her arms as if she were suddenly chilled. "Gideon, I understand why you want to spy on Ifre, but do you think it's wise to put a man with such power within his grasp?"

Now they were all frowning at her. It was easy to forget how little the Damned understood about the art of magic. It was Gideon who answered her query. "It is but a mark, Lady Lavinia, nothing more. Kane has no more love for magic than I do. He rejected his heritage long before I ever met him."

Sigil shook his head and found himself responding. "That wouldn't matter, Gideon. Mage marks are exceedingly rare nowadays, but my personal tutor spoke of them at length. Although Kane has not used his gift, it is still there. Picture Kane's magic as a pool of water that doesn't move and serves no purpose."

He felt the weight of everyone's stares as he continued. "But then a miller comes along to build his waterwheel and sets the water free to turn it, unlocking its potential. A mage with no scruples would have little trouble in releasing Kane's magic, with his cooperation or without it."

"And you know this how?"

Sigil realized the three warriors now surrounded him, crowding close. While they hadn't yet gone for their weapons, he suspected it wouldn't take much to stir them into action. Foolish him. He'd forgotten that he was still a prisoner under a sentence of death. Because of his memory loss, his execution had been postponed, not canceled.

He ignored Gideon and Duncan, choosing instead to

face Murdoch. "I'm not sure. The words j̶͟ ̶
though I have no doubt that what I said was

The big man now looked more worried th̶
"Your memories are returning."

It wasn't a question, but Sigil answered anyway. "No.
At least no more than what I just said and that my rank
might have been captain. Otherwise, my life still began
the morning I awoke four days after the battle."

He finally looked toward Gideon. "I swear this on my
honor."

To his relief, the captain nodded. "I believe you. If you
remember anything else, especially about magic, tell me
immediately. Is that understood?"

"Yes, Captain."

Gideon stared at him for another few seconds before
nodding, accepting his promise. That settled, Sigil was
only too happy to steer the conversation back to the
problem at hand.

"Lady Lavinia, do you agree with my analogy about
Kane's magic?"

"Yes, I do." She was clearly unhappy to be the bearer
of such dark news. "I understand the benefit of having a
spy in the enemy camp, Captain Gideon, but I would not
leave him there one second more than absolutely necessary. The longer your friend remains, the greater the
chance that Ifre will attempt to subvert Kane's magic to
his own needs."

"Thank you for your advice, my lady. I will send word
of your concerns to Kane. The dog will need to rest at
least until tomorrow before returning to his master."

Sigil needed some space to breathe now that the focus
was off him. "I'll take the dog and get him some food and
water."

"Thank you, Sigil. Meanwhile, Averel also included
approximate numbers of the duke's forces. Now we can
start making plans about how best to counter them with
the troops we hope to have at our command."

The three ladies excused themselves and headed

toward the garden as Sigil led the dog toward the stable. Before disappearing inside, he risked a look back toward the gate. Just as he feared, the Damned were staring in his direction, their expressions grim. While his past could be measured in but a few weeks, it seemed likely his future would be counted in days.

If so, all he could do was proceed as he had, trying to atone for the wrongs he couldn't even remember. He patted the dog on the head. "Come on, boy. Let's get you taken care of."

Even knowing it was likely too soon, Kane had stopped at Averel's tavern to see if the dog had returned from Lady Merewen's keep. Averel's avatars were coursers, but even one of them would have trouble traveling such distance that quickly. The dog could do so if necessary, but the effort would leave the animal weakened for days to come.

Already in the middle of a performance, Averel had answered Kane's unspoken question with a quick shake of his head. Kane had lingered long enough for a drink and to listen to a few songs to avoid drawing attention to himself by leaving too soon. On his way back to the keep, he saw few people out and about.

Even the taverns seemed quiet, as if most of the locals were staying home tonight. No doubt they thought they were safer that way. Perhaps they were. Kane knew in his bones that Keirthan continued to practice his dark arts, even though he didn't appear to prey on the townspeople.

So where was he getting his victims, and who was helping him? There was no way Keirthan was working entirely on his own. If Kane found out who his accomplices were, he'd do what he could to thin their numbers before he and Averel left to rejoin Gideon and the others.

Logic said Keirthan was using servants for his predations, but the steady supply of new ones had to be coming from somewhere. If not from the city, one or more of the nobles had to be furnishing them, the shortsighted bastards. What had the duke promised them for betraying their own people? Did they not realize that eventually Keirthan would turn on them, too? He was not the kind of man who was willing to share his power. Anyone strong enough to stand beside him would be seen as a potential rival, not an ally.

But troubling thoughts of the enemy were not the only reason that had Kane wandering the streets at such a late hour. Lady Theda's image haunted his every step. Did she think he hadn't felt the weight of her gaze following him each time their paths had crossed over the past few days?

She had questions about him, ones he had no desire to answer. He had other desires, though, ones that were inappropriate for a mere captain of the guard to be having for the widow of a duke.

And wouldn't Gideon have a good laugh over that idea? Especially after the way Kane had questioned the wisdom of his friend and leader sharing the bed of the woman they were both sworn to protect. The goddess herself had condoned the pairing, but that didn't mean she'd given all of the Damned free rein in such matters.

Regardless, his mission here was meant to be short-lived. Theda was not the sort of woman a man of honor would dally with, but the temptation was there. Rare was the person who didn't react to Kane's pale eyes and mage mark without flinching. Instead, Theda had treated him as a potential ally, even daring to touch him without fear.

The memory of the gentle brush of her fingertips against his skin remained sharp and clear even days later. It left him hungering for more of the same, which was insanity. So far he'd managed to control the urge to seek her out, but at night nothing kept his dreams of her at bay.

When he'd returned Lady Margaret to her mistress, Theda's hair had been down, tumbling in dark waves nearly the full length of her elegant back. He could only imagine what it would be like to have that dark silk spilled across his pillow, its scent filling his senses. He'd tangle his fingers in it as she whispered sweet words to him.

But unfortunately, it was a masculine voice speaking to him now. "Captain Kane? Is everything all right?"

He looked up, just then realizing that he'd reached the door of the keep. How long had he been standing there lost in a dream world?

"I'm sorry, Corporal. Did you ask me something?"

"Sergeant Markus asked me to let you know that he'd been called into town on business. He'll return before first light."

Meaning the sergeant and his friends were spending the night carousing in one of their favorite taverns in town. That was fine with Kane, although it might make weapons practice tough for them. He might even make sure of it.

On the other hand, the sergeant's absence made it that much safer for Kane to wander the halls of the keep without worrying about Markus spying on him.

"Thank you for relaying the message, Loman."

When he realized the young man was standing guard by himself, he asked, "Where's your partner?"

The youth swallowed hard. "He took sick, sir. Everything is quiet, so he thought it would be all right if he left an hour early."

He did, did he?

"Who was it? I need to know if he has something catching."

Loman clearly didn't want to answer, but he also knew he had no choice. "It was Gart, sir. He did look poorly."

Hungover again was more likely, but that was hardly Loman's fault. "How much longer until your relief is due?"

The guard's expression lightened as he looked past Kane. "They be here now, sir."

"That's good. Give them your report and then get some rest."

He clapped the young man on the shoulder and entered the keep. Inside, all appeared to be quiet, although not everyone had retired for the night. Servants clustered near the edges of the room, no doubt waiting for the few remaining nobles to seek out their beds so they could turn in for the night themselves.

He nodded at them as he passed by, ignoring the few who flicked their fingers in a pattern meant to ward off evil. Ironic that they felt that way toward the one man in the keep who was there to try to save them. He'd lived with such prejudice his entire life; most of the time he shrugged off their ignorant behavior.

But some nights, like this one, it still stung.

He continued on his tour of the hall before turning down the passage that would lead him toward the side door, which was normally kept barred after dark. A servant slept on a pallet nearby to open it if necessary.

Unusual to find it unlocked and the pallet empty. Yet another weakness in the duke's defenses. Or perhaps not. The servant, armed with a large cudgel, stepped out of the darkness behind him. As soon as he recognized Kane, he lowered his weapon back to his side.

Kane turned to face him, nodding toward the cudgel. "I was worried that the door was undefended, but I see I was wrong. What's your name?"

The servant patted his free hand with the cudgel. "Tom, sir. I'm waiting up for someone to return. No one gets by me."

Kane grinned in approval. "I believe that. I'll leave you to it."

He stepped out into the darkness, relieved to leave the heavy atmosphere of Keirthan's keep behind him for the moment. Tom hadn't mentioned whom he was waiting for; most probably one of the maids had slipped out to spend time with a beau.

Just in case, though, perhaps he would take a stroll through the garden and listen for the mystery person's return. He looked around. The night was still. Maybe it was safe enough to let Hob out for a while. The poor beast had been confined far too much lately.

Before Kane could return to his quarters to release the gargoyle, he caught a faint sound on the night's air and froze. Someone else prowled the paths that wound through the garden. He remained in the deep shadows under the trees as he studied the area. There, across the way, he caught a hint of movement.

Kane reached out with his senses, detecting a single heartbeat and the slow breath of someone strolling carefully in the darkness, most likely because he lacked Kane's enhanced night vision. The intruder was on the far side of the small clearing and heading in Kane's direction. Any movement on his part now would only draw unwanted attention.

A few seconds later, the unknown person left the shelter of the trees; the moon overhead bathed the clearing in its silvery light, revealing her identity at last. There was no mistaking Lady Theda despite the cloak she wore. Still oblivious to his presence, she stopped in the center of the clearing to push back her hood and smile up at the starlit sky.

Kane could have no more walked away at that moment than he could have quit breathing. The lady obviously had no fear of the night, not with that expression of simple pleasure on her striking face.

He must have made a noise because she gasped and looked right in his direction. "Who goes there?"

If he left without identifying himself, it would only frighten her more. He joined her in the light.

"Kane, my lady. I apologize for startling you. I only sought to enjoy the night air and didn't realize you were out here, too." He bowed his head slightly. "I will leave you to your walk."

She moved closer. "Please don't. Surely this garden is big enough for two. I wouldn't mind some company."

The poor woman must be desperate if she had to settle for him. He looked past her, not sensing the presence of anyone else nearby. "Where are your ladies?"

"I sent them to bed. They would be most distraught to find out sometimes I walk at night without them. I love them dearly, but at times their need to hover over me is a bit trying." She gave him a conspiratorial smile. "Please don't tell them I said that. It would hurt their feelings, and they mean well."

"Your secret is safe with me."

Theda stared up at him in the moonlight. "Shall we walk together?"

Kane offered her his arm, not sure she would accept it. But her hand immediately settled in the crook of his elbow with an ease that pleased him. He let her decide the direction of both their steps and their conversation. When she began pointing out some of her favorite flowers, he dredged up centuries-old stories from the times he assisted his mother in her herb garden. He shared one particularly vivid memory of when he'd mistaken one of her rare plants for a patch of weeds and pulled them all out by the roots. It had taken him hours to replant them all.

He liked that Theda found his story amusing, knowing how few reasons she had for smiling these days. He hoped that Tom didn't mind staying up for a while yet because Kane was in no hurry to return Theda to the keep. As he finished one tale, he launched into another.

Strolling in the night with the captain of the guard was scandalous, but Theda didn't care. Her reputation was no longer of any concern to her. The need for such worries had ended the day Armel died and his brother's reign of terror had begun. Besides, she liked Kane.

More than liked him, in truth. It had been a long time since she'd felt the stirrings of attraction for a man, but they were definitely simmering now. Perhaps it was the intoxicating scent of the flowers perfuming the night air that made her so daring.

Soon, her official period of mourning would end, and Ifre would auction her off like a prize horse. Once that happened, she would be at the mercy of whoever offered him the highest price.

"It grows late, my lady. I should return you to the hall. I'm sure your friend Tom will worry if you stay gone much longer." Kane sounded genuinely concerned about her.

She spied one of the clusters of benches that were scattered about the garden. "Would you mind if we sat for a few moments? Then I promise I will go inside."

He led her over to the nearest one and spread his cloak on the seat, which was damp from the dew. His courtly behavior seemed second nature to him, which made her wonder again how he'd come to be a mercenary. Despite the tales he'd shared with her, his past remained shadowed in mystery.

The bench was long enough for the two of them, but only just. The warmth of Kane's body seeped across the small space between them, making her want to curl in to his strength and let him hold the true darkness in her life at bay.

"Lady Theda—," he started to say, but she stopped him.

She cocked her head to the side to look up at him through her lashes. "I think under the circumstances, you could simply call me by my given name, Kane."

He frowned but nodded. "We're playing a dangerous game tonight, Theda. Despite the hour, someone might see us. I know for certain that some of the guardsmen will be returning from town before dawn."

They both paused to listen, but it appeared they still had the night to themselves. At the continued silence, he said, "We have lingered long enough for one night."

Her heart surged with hope. "So shall we share other nights like this?"

He studied her for several seconds before responding. Was he trying to find a gentle way to refuse her or fighting his own desire to spend time away from the tensions of the court?

Finally, he looked away. "You should know that I cannot stay here in the city for much longer. I have other commitments that have first claim on me."

His truth deserved hers in return. "And I have but a short time before Ifre will force me to marry one of his cronies. I'm not asking for anything you cannot give me, Kane, but only a few hours in the moonlight."

She was glad that the anger in Kane's pale eyes wasn't directed toward her. His hand sought out hers, cradling it with such aching care. "That man is a monster."

Then why did Kane serve him? She wouldn't ask the question when she might not like the answer. "So we have an agreement? A stolen hour here and there will surely cause no harm."

"I will meet you here in two nights' time if that's your wish. Now we should return. I will watch from the shadows to make sure you reach the door safely."

As much as she hated to admit it, he was right. But as she stood, he stepped in front of her, settling the reassuring weight of his hands on her shoulders.

"There is one more thing, my lady."

His cold anger had changed into something else, something hot and hungry. "What would that be, Kane?"

"This."

Then his stern mouth claimed hers with a fierce heat that burned and sizzled in the damp chill of the night air.

Chapter 10

Kane had never been one to give in to irrational impulses, but he could have no more let Theda walk away without kissing her than he could have stopped breathing. The hunger for her overwhelmed both his good sense and his honor, and he found himself taking what he had no right to want. If Theda had offered even a token protest, he would have stepped back, apologized, and escorted her to safety.

But she hadn't. Instead, as soon as she'd discerned his intentions, she'd smiled.

From the second Kane's lips touched Theda's, he was lost. She tasted of cool moonlight and the sweet spice of night-blooming lilies. He let his hands slide down from her shoulders, following the curve of her back, to settle at her waist. As much as he wanted to continue his explorations, willing or not, Theda was a lady and deserved to be treated as such. She was no wanton to be tussled within a garden, no matter how private the moment might seem.

Her hands fluttered up to circle his neck as he bent closer and deepened the kiss. Her lips parted without hesitation, moaning softly as his tongue swept in to sup deeply on her sweetness.

But even as he savored the way Theda fit in his arms, guilt was already pricking at his conscience. He didn't regret the kiss; he wasn't that noble. But the longer they lingered, even under the cover of darkness, the greater the risk that someone would happen along.

He broke off the kiss and tucked her head against his chest, holding her close and letting his touch say what he couldn't find words for. For her part, Theda melted against him, her curves playing sweet counterpart to all of the hard edges of his body and his life.

"Well, that was certainly unexpected."

Although he couldn't see the expression on her face, he heard the smile in her words. He pressed a soft kiss to the top of her head. "No regrets?"

She pushed gently against his chest, putting a small distance between them. Reaching up, she caressed the mage-marked side of his face with her hand. "None, other than we had to stop when we did."

Kane closed his eyes and savored the sweet touch of her palm against his cheek. "A regret I share. Now we really must get you back inside."

The night air felt far chillier without Theda's body pressed against his, but wisdom had to outweigh desire. He tucked her hand in the crook of his arm again.

"Come. I will see you to the door."

When they reached the edge of the garden, she stopped. "I will count the hours until we stroll in the garden again, Captain Kane."

He should tell her no, that this couldn't happen again, but he couldn't bring himself to refuse her. "As will I. Now go."

She spared another moment to smile and wave at him one last time before knocking on the door. Kane waited until she was safely inside before heading for his quarters. As he walked, he smiled up at the night sky and savored the knowledge that in less than two days he would once again walk in the moonlight with Theda Keirthan on his arm.

The afternoon sun beat down from above. Restless and unable to settle, Kane circled the small clearing where he'd met up with Averel. They'd scouted the location before entering the city of Agathia for the first time, knowing they might eventually need a place where they could talk in private. Hob kept pace with Kane, stopping occasionally to hiss at Averel's white dog if it got too close.

The younger knight looked on with bemusement. "You look like death walking, Kane. How many hours a day are you on duty?"

"I'm fine."

Averel gave him another pointed look. "No, you're not. You're not sleeping enough, or something else is making you tired."

He tried to ignore his friend's concern, but Averel wouldn't let it go. Kane wasn't about to admit what he'd been up to the night before last or that he hadn't been able to relax since. Not only did he wish to protect Theda's reputation, but if his young friend found out about her, he'd never let Kane live it down.

He was in no mood to be teased. Not about her, especially when his feelings on the subject were so raw. "I said I am fine. Let it go, Averel."

Instead of backing off, Averel came closer, and his eyes widened in shock. "I swear, Kane, you have the exact same expression on your face as Gideon did on the day we confronted him about Lady Merewen."

Enough was enough. "By the gods, I said let it go, Averel. Continue at your own peril."

Kane's hand strayed toward his sword. Averel's dog, trained to defend his master in battle, immediately lunged between them, his hackles up and a deep growl rumbling in his chest. Hob took umbrage at the dog's threat. He snarled and snapped back, his fangs dripping with venom.

"Whoa!" Kane shouted as he caught Hob by the neck and yanked him out of reach at the same instant Averel grabbed his dog by the collar and hauled him back a few steps.

As they both worked to settle their companions, Kane's face flushed with a painful mix of embarrassment and shame. "I apologize, Averel. My temper is unpredictable today."

His friend, always quick to forgive, waved him off. "I shouldn't have pushed."

Satisfied that Hob would behave, Kane closed the distance between himself and his friend. "I'm the one at fault here. This situation is hard on both of us. I shouldn't take my mood out on you." He stuck his chin out. "If you would care to take a swing at me, I promise not to hit back."

Averel laughed and gave him a soft tap on the jaw. "Where would be the fun in that?"

Kane sat on a downed log, the tension between them having eased. His bones ached with weariness, but perhaps it wouldn't hurt to talk about the situation.

"My position as captain has gone unchallenged. There are a fair number of good men among the guards. Others follow the duke's example in how they treat the members of his household."

He stared at his boots as he continued. "I've already drawn Keirthan's attention. If I were to openly object to their behavior, he would see it as a weakness to be exploited, perhaps putting those same people at greater risk."

Averel entertained his dog by throwing a stick for the misfit to fetch. That didn't mean he wasn't listening to what Kane was saying—and what he wasn't.

"Does this member of Keirthan's household have a name?"

What kind of stupid question was that? "Yes. And would you sit down? I tire of watching you caper about with that useless dog."

Averel threw the stick one last time before sitting down. "Keirthan's household is not the only one where servant girls are considered fair game. That doesn't make it right."

"True." Kane pulled out his knife and began flipping

it in the air. "But in this case, the females are noble-
women, not servants, including Keirthan's sister-in-law,
Lady Theda."

His friend watched Kane's blade twirling as he absorbed the implications. "And this Lady Theda, she is
deserving of better treatment."

Kane caught his knife and stabbed it into the log.
"She is. Unlike Keirthan, she cares about those in her
charge. He intends to wed her off to one of his friends as
soon as her official period of mourning ends."

A fact that had Kane wanting to gut not just the duke
but also the bastard who would eventually claim Theda
as his own. Kane could only imagine what kind of monster Keirthan would choose for her.

"You've developed strong feelings for the lady."

If Averel's tone had been anything other than gentle,
Kane would have gone on the attack again. Instead, he
offered up his truth.

"I have known her but a short time, but already she is
special to me in much the same way Lady Merewen is to
Gideon."

"And Lady Alina to Murdoch?"

Kane was surprised to find himself smiling. "Who
would have thought such a thing could happen to even
one of us, much less three at once?"

Averel shuddered. "I can only hope that I am immune
to such things. I am much too young to have my heart
entangled with another's."

Not to mention they were all running out of time. The
day would soon come when their mission was accomplished and they would return to the river to stand judgment before the Lord and Lady of the River. Regardless
of their decision, it would mean the end of the time the
five warriors would walk in the world, at least until they
were once again needed to stand against evil.

Although the other warriors all held hope each time
that the Lady would finally release them from her service, Kane held no such belief. They were too good at

what they did, and evil would always return. Besides, aside from his four friends, no one had ever valued Kane for anything other than his ability to fight. It had given him a purpose in life.

A small voice in his head whispered, *But Lady Theda saw you as a man, not simply a weapon to be aimed at the enemy.*

"Averel, I should return before my absence draws the duke's attention."

"How much longer do you think we should stay? Gideon will want to know."

"I have yet to find out who is giving aid to Keirthan, but someone is furnishing him with victims. Give me a week and then we'll leave regardless."

They both headed for their horses. "I'll let the captain know."

Before Kane could mount up, Averel caught his arm. "Be careful, Kane. I do not question your loyalty to the goddess, but your feelings for Lady Theda cannot help but muddy the waters for you. Now is not the time to lose focus, not when we have so little time left to bring down Keirthan."

"I have not forgotten where my duty lies, Averel, nor shall I. When the time comes for us to leave, I will ride out and not look back."

Even if it killed him.

Keirthan paced his office in frustration. Where was Kane? Right now, the connection between them was so faint as to be almost nonexistent. The sigil the captain wore allowed Ifre to track his every move. Kane had to have left Agathia, stretching the range of the magic to its limit.

What business could his captain have outside of the city walls? It was the first suspicious move the man had made since taking over command of the guard. If anything, Kane was doing too good of a job. Ifre had overheard grumblings about the newly instated schedule for weapons practice and the way Kane had of showing up at odd hours to check on his men.

Ifre himself had been unable to escape the building unnoticed since the day he'd observed Kane beating Gart bloody in a practice match. In fact, if he set foot outside of his office, Kane had a pair of guards waiting to haunt Ifre's every step. He supposed he should be flattered that the captain took his ruler's safety so seriously.

He wasn't.

It was damned inconvenient. How was he supposed to slip his latest victims down below with someone watching his every move? The darkness was hungry, demanding to be fed almost constantly now. If he didn't supply it with new blood soon, it might turn on him. Only when it was satisfied did it leave Ifre alone long enough to continue his studies.

He must have missed something in his reading, some detail that would help him strengthen his control over the weapon he'd created. He needed go back to the beginning and start over, comparing his notes to the original texts. Then he would—

A knock at the door interrupted his line of thought. "Come in."

Sergeant Markus stuck his head in the door. "Sire, Kane has returned."

Ifre threw his hands up in exasperation. "Don't hover in the doorway like a fool. Come in and make a proper report."

He waited until the sergeant closed the door before continuing. "Do you know where he was?"

Markus kept his stance relaxed, but all the same, Ifre sensed he wasn't happy to be there. "He left the city on horseback. He was gone for just over three hours."

Ifre stamped his foot in frustration. "I didn't ask how long he was gone, Sergeant. I asked where he went."

"I don't know, Sire. I made discreet inquiries of the guards at the gates, and all they could tell me was that he rode out alone and returned the same way."

"Did anyone else leave around the same time?"

Like someone who might be plotting against Ifre. He hadn't forgotten about the mysterious allies who had defended both Lady Merewen and Lady Lavinia.

"Only a young troubadour, but he left by a different gate and returned much sooner than did Kane."

Interesting. "This troubadour. What do you know about him?"

"Only that his name is Averel and that he arrived in the city within days of Kane. From what I hear, he draws a goodly crowd for all of his performances."

"If you learn more, report directly to me."

Markus bowed and backed toward the door. "Shall I tell Captain Kane that you are looking for him?"

There was a gleam in his eyes that told Ifre that the sergeant wouldn't mind seeing his new captain taken down a peg or two. "No. I'll send for him later. You may return to your duties, Sergeant."

When he was gone, Ifre sat back in his chair and stared at the ceiling. It was quite a leap in logic to assume it was anything other than a coincidence that the troubadour and Kane both picked today to ride outside of the city walls. Was it significant that they'd both arrived in Agathia at around the same time?

He'd let the matter go until he had more information. Once Markus reported back to him, he'd decide if the matter deserved any further action. Later, after he met with his petitioners for the day, he'd take a stroll through the hall and look for Kane.

It might prove interesting to see if the man mentioned his time outside of the walls on his own. Until then, Ifre would spend the rest of the afternoon studying potential suitors for Lady Theda's hand. He smiled at the thought. Once he pared the list down to the final few, he might even let her review his choices—not that he'd allow her to make the final decision.

It all came down to power and money. She would go to the one who would pour the most gold into Ifre's private coffers. Half of Theda's personal wealth seemed like a fair price. For a moment, he even considered taking her to wife himself. What fun it would be to strip her lands of everything of value.

And bedding her, knowing she hated him with every breath she took, wouldn't be a burden either. However, the intimacies of marriage would provide her far too many opportunities to cause him harm. After all, a man had to sleep sometime.

No. He'd have to settle for ensuring the rest of her life was miserable. Until that time, he would continue to control her strings and watch her dance. With that in mind, he headed for the door and signaled the servant who waited there in case Ifre needed something.

"Yes, Sire?"

"I find that I must work through the midday meal. Find Lady Theda and tell her to bring a tray to my office. Make sure she delivers it personally."

"It will be done."

Ifre closed the door. Of course it would be done. No one, not even his sister-in-law, would dare refuse Ifre anything. Not when he held their very lives in the palm of his hand.

Kane entered the hall, figuring to put in an appearance before retiring to his quarters. He'd been up for the past day and a half and definitely felt the lack of sleep. He stopped in the closest corner to study the room, which was filled with the usual collection of sycophants and servants. As he watched, he tried to convince himself he was there to do his job, not to look for anyone in particular.

Who was he fooling? Certainly not himself. So where was she? He scanned the room again, more slowly this time.

As a piece of iron is drawn by a lodestone, Kane's gaze was drawn to Lady Theda. At the moment, she was struggling to cross the crowded hall toward Keirthan's office while carrying a heavy tray. Kane had no doubt exactly who had ordered her to perform the menial duty herself. He also knew that for Theda the true burden wasn't the tray she carried, but all the attention she drew from the crowd as she walked through the room.

Which would she hate more? The sneers from those who curried favor with the duke or the pitying glances from the rest? A few had the audacity to snicker when she nearly tripped over the long train of a noblewoman's skirt, who stood her ground, forcing Lady Theda to walk around.

Kane couldn't stand to watch. He cut through the crowd, not caring if several of the courtiers nearly fell in their hurry to get out of his way. He stopped ahead of Lady Theda to avoid startling her by his sudden appearance.

He knew the moment she spotted him and guessed his purpose. She shook her head just enough to warn him off, making it clear that she wouldn't appreciate him making a scene. As much as he wanted to punish those who would deride her for merely doing what was commanded of her, he withdrew and let her continue on her way.

After she entered Keirthan's office, he waited until she reappeared a few minutes later before leaving himself. His temper was unpredictable at the best of times and only more so since he had been separated from the other Damned. As tired as he was at the moment, it wouldn't take much provocation to have him drawing his sword to teach this entire room of fools some manners.

It was a relief to step out into the sunshine. He nodded to the guards on duty, pleased to see that they were doing their job right. No slouching, no slipping off for a quick nap. He stopped to talk to the closest one.

"I will be in my quarters if anyone has need of me."

"Yes, sir."

On the way, he stopped at the stables to retrieve his shield, where Hob once again rested. As tired as Kane was, he could've sworn he was carrying Hob's true weight on his arm. As soon as he put the shield away, he would set aside all of his burdens in exchange for a few hours of sleep.

But when he reached his office, Sergeant Markus had taken up residence there. Kane's already foul mood worsened.

"Did we have an appointment that I've forgotten about, Sergeant?"

The chill in Kane's voice had Markus belatedly scrambling to his feet to stand at attention. "No, sir. I saw you were headed this way and thought I'd check to see if there is anything you need me to do."

Kane didn't believe that for a minute. As far as he could tell, the sergeant did exactly what was required of him, nothing more. Rather than call him on it, though, Kane laid Hob's shield on top of his desk, glad to be shed of its weight for a few minutes.

"At ease, Markus. Have a seat."

When the sergeant didn't immediately do so, Kane looked up to see what had captured Markus's attention. The guard stood staring down at Kane's shield in wonder. Finally, he glanced up.

"That's amazing artwork, sir. I've never seen its like before."

And never would again. Such gifts from the gods were rare. "It is special."

"May I touch it?" Markus asked, although he was already reaching out to run his fingertips over the surface of the wood. "Whoever carved this was a real artist. I can feel each individual scale."

Kane hid a smile. Little did he know.

Then Markus frowned as he studied Hob's picture from one angle and then another. "Is it supposed to be some kind of lizard? No, it has wings, too."

Kane took pity on the perplexed guard. "It's a gargoyle. In the old myths, they were thought to be related to dragons. It is said they had the forked tongues of serpents and venom that would kill their enemies quickly."

Markus finally leaned back in his chair. "Guess we should be glad they're only a myth. Can you imagine the terror even one would cause if it were turned loose in a battle?"

Actually, Kane didn't have to imagine it. "That would be something to behold."

He opened his desk drawer and pulled out a bottle along with two tankards. He poured each of them a fair-sized portion of mead and handed one across to Markus.

"I need something to wash the trail dust out of my throat."

Markus's eyes flickered with interest at Kane's comment, but his voice held only mild curiosity when he spoke. "I heard that you'd ridden out of the city."

Now, why would Markus be keeping track of Kane's movements? He didn't want to ask outright but waited to see if Markus offered the information on his own. "My stallion was growing restless. I took him for a long run to burn off some of his energy."

"I suspected it was something like that. I've seen your horse. He's a brute. Judging from the scars on his hide, he's been in more than his share of fights in his life."

"Rogue has saved my life in a battle or two, that's true." Kane sipped the mead, enjoying its sweet flavor, while Markus did the same.

When they both had finished their drinks, Kane put the bottle away. "I'm going to sleep until nightfall. Send someone to fetch me if the duke has need of me before then."

Markus stood up and straightened his uniform jacket. "He was looking for you earlier. I asked if he needed you for something specific, but he said no, just to let him know when you returned to the city."

"Have you told him?"

"Yes, sir, I did."

"Good. Now, if you'll excuse me, I'd better get some rest."

After Markus let himself out of the office, Kane sat staring at the door. So Keirthan had known Kane had ridden outside of the city walls. How? Right now he was too tired to spare much thought for it. He'd think about it later.

As he waited for sleep to overtake him, he thought about Lady Theda and how she had fared after delivering Keirthan's tray. He would ask her when next their paths crossed. He couldn't wait.

Chapter 11

Gideon had been sending out small patrols morning and night ever since Merewen's late uncle's attempt to regain control of the keep by force with the aid of Duke Keirthan's men. So far, there'd been no sign that the duke had made any move to try again. It was too much to hope the man had given up, especially when there had been more instances of the local farmers disappearing from their homes, leaving all of their possessions behind.

It could mean only one thing: The duke was using them to fuel the fires of his power. That thought haunted Gideon's dreams and left him too restless to stand the confines of the keep. He'd saddled Kestrel and ridden out before breakfast. He'd intended to visit some of the crofters near the foothills to the west, but the stallion had fought him every inch of the way. Finally, Gideon had given in and let the canny beast choose their direction.

They'd been riding hard to the east when Kestrel charged up the side of a low hill. At the top, he reared up, nearly unseating Gideon in the process. He managed to hold on as the stallion pawed the air before charging down the steep slope on the other side in a ground-eating gallop. A few seconds later, Gideon spotted the reason for the horse's strange behavior as an enormous ball of light flashed across the sky from the north to plummet down to the ground. Another quickly followed in its path. The resulting explosions rolled like thunder across the valley. Already smoke and flickers of fire were curling up from the field and spreading quickly.

Even with Kestrel's speed, by the time Gideon crossed the valley, the field was fully engulfed in flames. The farmers were doing their best to contain it by cutting down swaths of the immature crop and soaking the adjoining field with buckets of water. They wore wet rags tied across their faces, but still they coughed and choked from breathing in the thick smoke. Gideon cursed the duke's name and did the only thing he could to fight back. With his enhanced strength, he could make better time clearing the ground than the farmers. He dismounted and tossed the closest boy onto Kestrel's broad back.

"Ride hard for the keep and tell them what happened. Ask for Murdoch and tell him that Captain Gideon said to send men to help. Do you understand?"

When the boy nodded, Gideon slapped Kestrel on the backside and sent the stallion charging back in the direction of the keep. Then he demanded the use of a scythe and fell to work, swinging the curved blade hard and fast, all the time wishing it were his sword and his target the duke instead of a field of half-grown barley. Keirthan had a lot to answer for, and Gideon couldn't wait for the day they brought the bastard to bay.

Hours later, Gideon went in search of Duncan. He should've known he'd find him in the library. Since he'd seen Merewen taking Lady Lavinia into her workshop only a few moments ago, he figured Duncan would be alone.

"Have you counted our remaining days today?"

Duncan looked up from the manuscript he'd been studying. "No, I haven't, but what's the use? Counting them daily won't slow the passage of time."

Gideon prowled the room as if he were trapped in a cage. "True, but if we lose track, we could run out of days before we've accomplished our goal. We need to march upon Keirthan soon and therefore need to press our allies harder to send their men. I fear another fortnight is too long to wait. What if they change their minds?"

The other warrior didn't look worried. "Either they will send their warriors or they won't, Gideon. It wouldn't be the first time we five faced the enemy alone."

Slamming his fist down on the table hard enough to make Duncan's book bounce felt damned good. "Right now there are but three of us, unless you've forgotten. Averel and Kane are behind enemy lines."

Duncan placed a marker in his book and closed it. "I feel their absence as much as you do, Gideon, and I worry about them as well. If you'd like me to, I will ask Lavinia to scry to see what can be learned about their progress."

Even though Gideon found Lavinia's magic unsettling, it was tempting to ask her to make the effort. Gideon grew tired of fighting blind, of facing off against an invisible enemy who could strike at will across long distances. It had taken hours of hard work to limit the damage from Keirthan's latest attack to the loss of one field of barley. There had been no deaths, but destroying crops could lead to starvation over the winter.

"I appreciate the offer but not yet." Gideon searched for words that wouldn't offend his friend. "Are you truly sure the goddess herself does not object to the magic Lady Lavinia practices?"

No sooner did he speak the words than a cool breeze rippled through the papers on the table even though there was no open window or door to account for it. The air around them now tasted damp and carried the musky scent of river rocks. Gideon and Duncan immediately dropped to their knees, their heads bowed.

The sensation lasted but a few seconds as a soft voice whispered, "Tools aren't evil, my warriors. They are simply tools. It is the hand that wields the tool that determines whether its purpose is fair or foul."

Then the room warmed up and once again smelled of old leather and parchment. Gideon remained kneeling long enough to be sure the goddess had no more messages to deliver. He rose to his feet as Duncan returned to his chair. Both of them looked around the room, making sure they were alone. Or were they? Either way, they'd gotten their answer.

Duncan actually chuckled. Gideon was glad one of them found the situation amusing. "I'll leave you to your studies, Duncan. I'll be with Merewen."

Out in the hallway, Gideon ran in to Sigil. He had been avoiding the man ever since Sigil had admitted that bits and pieces of his life were coming back to him. Neither of them wanted that to happen, not with the stay of execution still hanging about Sigil's neck.

Yet the problem couldn't be ignored forever. Not with the days passing by so quickly. Rather than dance around the issue, Gideon made his decision and hoped neither of them would live to regret it.

"Have you had any more memories return?"

"No, not since we were discussing Kane's mage mark." Sigil offered Gideon a brief smile. "I am sorry that my presence only adds to your burden, Captain. Perhaps it would have been better all around if I had died from my wounds."

Gideon stopped to stare down at the great hall below. "There was a time I might have agreed with that assessment."

He rested his forearms on the low wall of the balcony. "But now I am convinced that the gods themselves have a greater purpose for you. Already you have helped save lives that could have been lost if you hadn't been there. Lives that are precious to me."

Sigil stood beside Gideon, staring at something only he could see, his expression solemn. "You honor me with your words, Gideon. I thank you."

"No gratitude is necessary. You have earned our respect. The five of us have been friends pretty much to the exclusion of all others for centuries. It is rare that any of us allow someone outside of our circle to get close. You have not only slipped past Murdoch's guard, a feat in itself, but I would trust you at my back anytime."

Before Sigil could respond, Gideon considered the goddess's words in the library. He'd assumed she'd been talking about Lavinia's ability to scry, but a man could be a tool in the hands of a god. Gideon and the Damned all knew something about redemption. Sigil had proven to be an honorable ally when given a mission worthy of a warrior.

"A man shouldn't have to live his days with the burden of an execution hanging over his head, Sigil. Some of Merewen's people might not like what I'm about to say, but they can come to me with their complaints. Whether your memories return or not, you are free of our judgment." He held out his hand. "Don't make me regret my decision."

Sigil grasped Gideon's hand with both of his. "I will endeavor to prove worthy of your trust and your friendship. Thank you for restoring my honor."

"You did that yourself, Sigil. Now go tell Murdoch to put you on the duty roster. You'll be standing guard along with the rest of the men."

"And if Lady Merewen's men object?"

As they well might. They'd lost friends and family to the forces that Sigil had led against the keep. "Tell him to partner you with one of us."

"I'll seek him out now."

Gideon remained at the top of the stairs and watched Sigil make his way across the hall below. The man moved with a new sense of purpose, clearly relieved to have the threat of execution gone. Murdoch would be pleased as well, as the two men had become close friends. Gideon turned back toward the library to inform Duncan of what he'd just done, hoping he'd approve as well.

At least now if their allies didn't send the troops that had been promised, the Damned would have one more sword they could count on. They would need it.

*   *   *

Theda stood at the window, admiring the fiery blaze of the sun sinking in the west. Night was coming and would soon blanket the world in deep shadows and the moon's cool light.

The contrast of the darkness with the light reminded her of the man who'd promised to be waiting for her in the gardens after the moon rose in the sky. With his jet-black hair and pale eyes, Kane seemed more at home in the shadows than in the light of day.

She could only imagine how her ladies would react to her choice of companions. Would they see the loyal heart that beat beneath his unusual appearance? She doubted it. Far too often people made the mistake of thinking a handsome exterior was a reflection of the man inside.

Her brother-in-law was a perfect example of how wrong that could be. Ifre was handsome and even charming when it suited his purpose. But he was also selfish, vicious, and totally bereft of even the smallest hint of decency. She hated him.

Kane stood in sharp contrast to Ifre. His looks were striking but harsh, especially with that odd mark on his cheek and his unusually prominent front teeth. She had no doubt that he was capable of great violence and that powerful body had been honed in the crucible of war.

But Kane could be charming when he chose to be, and his courtly behavior seemed to be second nature to him. He'd shown such careful restraint each time he'd kissed her, treating her as if she were . . . not fragile, but precious.

What would it take to make him lose control in her arms? She wanted to find out.

"My lady, are you sure you don't want any of us to keep you company? Perhaps I should stay the night in your room in case you need someone to fetch a draught for pain."

Theda had told her friends earlier that she planned to retire early because of a headache. She hated lying to them, but she couldn't very well tell them the truth. They'd never understand.

"Thank you for your concern, Margaret, but I will be fine on my own. My maid is drawing me a bath, which will help soothe my head."

Her young friend looked as if she wanted to argue, but Theda walked toward the door of the solar. "Please go now, so you can return to your room with Lydia. I don't have to remind you about the risks in walking these halls alone."

Margaret's fair skin paled at the memory. "No, you don't."

She hurried after her friend while Theda turned in the direction of her own quarters. She trusted her young friends would all use common sense and remain tucked safely inside their rooms until morning.

She had other plans, ones that were far more adventurous. This would be the fourth time she'd met Kane for a late-night stroll. Rubbing her hands in anticipation, she entered her room and began her preparations.

An hour later, Theda slipped down the back staircase, the one that came out near the storerooms at the back of the keep. If Tom was surprised to see her again so soon, he gave no sign of it.

"Be careful out there, my lady. The gardens might be deserted at night, but that doesn't mean they are safe for a lady such as you, especially alone."

She wouldn't be alone, but she couldn't tell him that. "Don't worry, Tom. I won't go far."

He rivaled Lady Margaret when it came to wanting to protect Theda. "All right, then, but if you run afoul of anyone, scream and I'll come running with this." He flashed his cudgel with a gap-toothed grin. "Never met a man yet who wouldn't listen to reason after I get their attention with it. Your late husband knew that for a fact."

Tom and Armel had been the same age. More than

once Tom had regaled her with stories about the scrapes the two had gotten into when they were little. Despite the vast difference in their birthrights, Armel had considered Tom a friend up until the day he died. She'd liked that about him.

But now she had another man waiting for her. Theda reached the edge of the garden without mishap. Sounds carried easily in the night, but she didn't hear anything that would give her cause for alarm. Where would Kane be waiting for her this time?

The answer was obvious. He'd be waiting at the bench; she just knew it. She lifted her skirts and quietly hurried in that direction. Turning the last corner, she smiled. She'd guessed right. Kane stood stone-still right where she'd pictured him.

A surprising surge of shyness washed over her. A woman of her station risked ruining her reputation by indulging in a romantic tryst, but Theda no longer cared about the rules of society. Even if she had, she doubted she would've been able to resist the temptation of spending time in Kane's company.

She stopped several feet short of her destination. "Good evening, Captain."

He sketched a small bow. "I wasn't sure you would come."

"I said I would. Would you doubt my word?"

"Never, my lady, but it has to be difficult for you to escape the keep unnoticed even once, much less four times in just over a week. I would not have your reputation called into question because of me."

Again, his first concern was for her. "And I fear what would happen if my brother-in-law were to catch you with me. Ifre is not given to sharing."

Kane walked a few steps toward her. "So we are both playing a dangerous game. The question is why you would risk so much."

She closed the last distance between them. "I have

spent my entire life playing by the rules, Kane, but no more. I cannot change my past; nor can I control my future. I will, however, spend these moments as I see fit."

She took his hand in hers. "I choose to spend them with you."

His smile was a bit sad. "I wish I had the strength to deny you that choice, Theda. It would be better for us both if I did."

Yet despite his reluctance, she thought her words had pleased him. "Now that we have that settled, shall we walk together after you offer me a proper greeting?"

At least she didn't have to explain what she meant. In an instant, his arms cradled her close to his body, his mouth claiming hers with a gentle kiss, so sweet in its intent. She wanted far more from him, and her belly was pressed against the hard evidence that he felt the same way. Even so, some moments were better savored slowly.

As they stepped back, a movement on the far side of the clearing caught her eye. Fear tasted bitter as she whispered, "Kane, we're not alone. There's something lurking in the shadows."

To her surprise, he smiled. "We didn't mean to frighten you, but I thought you might like to meet him." Then he patted his leg and said, "Come here, boy. It's all right."

She watched in stunned amazement as a large animal stepped out of the shelter of the bushes to waddle toward them. When it stepped into the moonlight, she gasped. What kind of beast was this? Her first urge was to retreat, but she sensed this moment and her reaction were important to Kane. She remained where she was and waited to see what happened next.

Kane waited until his friend reached his side before speaking again. "Lady Theda, this is Hob. He's been my friend and companion for most of my life."

When Theda stooped down to hold her hand out to Hob, letting him taste her skin with a quick flick of his tongue, Kane edged closer. "I would appreciate if you would keep Hob's existence secret. I have found that few people find a gargoyle's company to be entirely comfortable."

Theda laughed softly. "I cannot imagine why. He's quite the handsome fellow. May I pet him?"

Kane seemed to hesitate but then nodded. "He likes his chin scratched."

As soon as she started, Hob closed his eyes and pushed closer to Theda, clearly delighted with his new friend. She studied him, her eyes wide with wonder.

"A gargoyle, you say? I thought they were but a myth."

Hob's owner looked a bit sad. "They might as well be. As far as I know, he is the last of his kind. Hob was a gift from my grandfather, who never told me where or how he obtained him. Hob was but a hatchling at the time, so we grew up together."

Theda straightened up and took Kane's hand in hers. "Come. Let's all walk, and you can tell me more about the adventures that you two have shared."

They walked through the garden, their steps well matched despite the difference in their heights. Theda drew a deep breath, loving the heavy perfume of roses mixed with the sharp tang of Kane's masculine scent. Once again he wore his leathers rather than the showier flash of his guard uniform. Was it because black was harder to see at night or that he wanted nothing of his connection to her brother-in-law to taint their time together? Most likely both were true.

"Why haven't you brought Hob with you before?"

"I thought it best if he stayed in my quarters. He can be difficult to control if he thinks I'm in danger. If someone else were to enter the garden, we can hide easily enough, but Hob's not fond of strangers and might attack."

That surprised her. "Really? He's offered me no threat."

Kane cleared his throat. "He's, um, adept at reading my own feelings about people. He would've sensed that I felt protective of you and acted accordingly."

She gave his arm a small squeeze to tell him his words pleased her. As they continued on, a few drops of rain fell. She glanced up to see that the clouds had rolled in, blocking both the stars and the moon.

More rain fell, faster this time. Kane murmured something under his breath in a language she didn't recognize. Even so, she recognized disappointment and frustration when she heard it. If the rain continued, they would have to seek shelter.

The only question was where. Kane led her under the limbs of a towering tree, but its foliage did little to defend them from the increasing rainfall. He pulled the edges of his cloak around her, giving her one more layer of protection.

"I'll walk you back to the door before you are drenched to the skin."

Disappointment tasted sour. She'd looked forward to these stolen moments with too much anticipation to want them to end so quickly. What options did they have?

She peeked up at Kane. "How private are your quarters?"

His pale eyes gleamed down at her. "If someone came looking for me, it might prove difficult to slip you back out without being observed."

"Then we'll have to move to my quarters instead."

She held her breath, expecting Kane's protective nature to have him rejecting the offer out of hand. Instead, he held her close as he thought things through, clearly unwilling to rush into a situation without considering all the implications.

"I will return you to the door so Tom can let you in. After I return Hob to my room, I'll enter the keep by another route and make my way to your room, but only if I can do so without being seen. If I'm not there in half an hour, I won't be coming."

The thought of having Kane all to herself behind locked doors set Theda's heart to racing. "I'll be waiting."

Then, before he could change his mind, she lifted her skirts and ran for the door.

Kane knew better than to take unnecessary risks, and his focus should be on the goals of his goddess. But when it came to Theda, he had no self-control. If he could find a way, he was going to join her in her room.

Luck was with him. Once again Gart was asleep on duty, and his partner was nowhere to be seen. Kane opened the door only far enough to squeeze through and pulled it closed once he was in the clear.

Inside, the great hall was quiet, the duke's guests having retired for the night. Sleeping servants were scattered on the floor and tabletops, but no one stirred at his passing. Rather than taking the front staircase, he worked his way around to the smaller one off the back hall.

Again, the trip was uneventful, leaving him far too much time to wonder what Lady Theda had in mind by inviting him to her room. Did she really want to run such risks for mere conversation? It was probably sacrilegious to pray that she was thinking along the same lines as he was.

It had been centuries since he'd last sought pleasure in the arms of a woman, and he'd never bedded one who made him feel like Theda did. All she had to do was smile at him, and he trembled with need.

How did Gideon cope with having these feelings for Lady Merewen, knowing there could be no future for them? Kane had tried to warn Theda that their time together would be of short duration. If she pressed him for details, goddess forgive him, he would tell her the truth. She deserved that much.

He paused in the deepest shadows at the far end of the hallway to listen. All was quiet. If he'd heard even a hint of a sound that was out of place, he would retreat rather than risk damaging Theda's reputation.

As tempting as it was to sidle down the hallway, his back flat against the wall, that would only make him look more guilty if someone were to appear out of the darkness. Instead, he strolled down the center of the hall, moving with confidence, as if he had every right and every reason to be there. When he reached Theda's door, he lifted his fist, still hesitating.

Despite the thickness of the door, he could hear the rapid pounding of Theda's heart as she waited for him. She was as excited by their assignation as he was. How amazing that of all the men in the keep, she wanted him.

He rapped twice softly and then a third time. When the door opened, he knew the time for indecision was over. He'd always prided himself on being a man of action and wasn't about to change now.

Theda softly called, "Come in."

A heartbeat later, he was inside Theda's room. He locked the door before turning to face her. She stood but a short distance away, her back to the fireplace. One look and his ability to speak or think disappeared entirely.

In the interim since they'd parted ways in the garden, Theda had removed her cloak and even her dress. The room was dimly lit by the flickering light of the fire. But with Kane's sensitive eyes, he could see all too clearly that his lady was now clad in naught but a soft, billowy nightgown.

With the light behind her, the thin cloth did nothing to disguise her soft, womanly curves. The effect on his own body was profound. He could barely breathe.

Theda knew it, too. Her smile was temptation itself.

If he had any doubts what she was offering, they were dispelled when he noticed the bed was already turned down. By the goddess, he had to be dreaming because this couldn't be real. Feeling as awkward as a youth caught up in his first love, he wasn't even sure how to proceed. The lady deserved a gentle touch, not the rough hands of a warrior.

"Kane, are you going to hover by the door all night?"

The thread of laughter in her voice and the teasing sparkle in Theda's dark eyes gave him the final nudge he needed to spring into action. He tossed his cloak on a nearby chair before joining her in front of the fire. She stepped into his arms, right where he most needed her to be.

He stared down at her sweet face. "Know that I didn't expect this . . . that we'd . . . I would have been satisfied with conversation or even a game of chess."

That last comment earned him a ripple of laughter. "Truly? Chess is not the game I had in mind, but if you insist . . ."

He smiled down at her. "I am not that much of a fool."

Unable to restrain himself one second longer, he kissed her hard and fast. Laying claim to her mouth with his, he worshipped her body with his hands, touching, squeezing, learning what made her sigh with pleasure.

Her sweet face flushed with heat as she did some exploring of her own, tracing his shoulders, his chest. Then, in a bold move that stole his breath, she caressed his manhood, stroking it gently through the thickness of his leathers. He groaned as a raging hunger pulsed in his blood.

He stayed her hand. "Theda, if you have any doubts, we have to stop now before you tempt me beyond all reason."

Bless her, she didn't hesitate. Tugging her hand free, she placed it over his racing heart. "Kane, take me to bed."

He swept her up in his arms and held her high against his chest as he carried her the short distance to the four-poster. He set her down gently and then stood back to admire her, a feminine feast that he planned to savor for hours to come.

Theda scooted farther back onto the bed, propping herself up on her elbows to study him. "Black leather suits you, Kane, but I want to learn more of the man beneath it."

His body bore the scars of countless fights, but he suspected Theda would regard them as badges of honor from battles won and battles lost. He unfastened the lacing at his throat and tugged his tunic off over his head. After tossing it in the general direction of the chair, he removed his boots and then his trews.

Theda followed his every move. The tip of her tongue peeked out of the corner of her mouth, looking as if she were a cat and he were a saucer of cream.

Soon he stood before her clothed in nothing more than the firelight. She nodded and said, "Let down your hair."

"Only if you do the same," he agreed as he tugged on the leather thong that held back his shoulder-length hair.

She sat up and unplaited her braids, taking her time and slowly, so slowly, running her fingers through the dark waves to set them free. Each movement ate at Kane's control until he thought he would go mad with the need to tangle his fingers in all of that dark silk.

When at long last she was done, she leaned back again, the pose an invitation he could no longer resist. He joined her on the bed, kneeling beside her shapely ankles. Where to begin? The gown. It had to go. He needed to blanket her skin with his own.

Grasping the bottom edge of the fabric, he slowly eased it up the length of her legs. Theda lifted her hips long enough for him to free the gown, clearly as eager as he was to be shed of the last barrier between them. He tossed it over his shoulder, not caring where it landed.

He twined his fingers with hers and studied the marked contrast between them. Her skin was pale and smooth; his was rough and browned from the sun. Her hands were dainty, as befitted a woman of the noble class. His were a warrior's hands, callused from years of holding weapons.

Together, they were a perfect match.

"Kiss me, Kane. Let me feel the weight and strength of your passion."

He nodded, the need for words gone. He pressed her down onto the bed, settling over her, although it wasn't yet time to complete the union of their bodies. He captured her face between his hands and kissed her, taking his time to taste her fully.

She ran her hands up and down his back and wrapped her legs around his hips, bringing his shaft in direct contact with her core. He shifted his body to the side, moving away from the temptation of all that damp heat. Cupping her breast with the palm of his hand, he took its dusky tip in his mouth and suckled hard.

Theda bucked beneath him as she whimpered softly. He turned his attention to her other breast, savoring the rose-scented taste of her warm skin. As he continued to tease her nipples with soft kisses and gentle nibbles, he trailed his hand downward, following the curve of her waist, the flare of her hip, to slip between her legs.

Her slick folds left no doubt that she wanted him, that she was ready for him. He trapped her wandering hands over her head and stretched out full length beside her.

"Are you sure, Theda? There are more risks than someone finding us together."

She grew still, her expression solemn. "I am no untried maiden, Kane, but you make me feel as if I am. My husband was a good man, but he was chosen for me. Ifre intends to pick my next one."

Her mouth softened into a smile. "You, my captain, are a man of my own choosing, as are the risks. We deserve this time together."

Her words rang with such conviction that they burned away the last bit of his own hesitation. Kane moved over her, settling once again in the cradle of her body. When they came together, the fit was perfect.

He rode her gently, driving first her and then himself crazy with the slow slide of his cock within her welcoming heat. When he released her hands, she dug her fingertips into his shoulders, urging him ever faster, ever harder.

Everything beyond the walls of Theda's room disappeared. There were but two souls in this world, his and hers, joined together in a dance that was ages old and ever new. Kane had never known such hunger, such passion. She met each thrust eagerly, murmuring encouragements in breathless whispers. Finally, with a shout of triumph, he gave up all pretense of control and drove her right to the edge and then jumped off with her.

Chapter 12

*T*heda felt boneless and sated. Right now, Kane's weight above her. If he were to move off her too soon, she would simply float away. Right now, his face was buried in the curve of her neck, his breathing as ragged as hers.

He stirred, lifting himself up to look down at her. "Was I too rough? I fear I lost all control there at the end."

She brushed his dark hair back from his face. "I am no fragile flower, Kane. I am fine. More than fine."

His pale eyes studied her for a time, as if weighing the truth of her words. He leaned down to press a kiss on her temple and then rolled to the side. After tugging the quilt up to cover them both, he pulled her in close to his side. For a while, the shared warmth was enough.

Soon, though, she hoped they would rekindle the fire that had burned so brightly between them. Until then, she savored being surrounded by Kane's strength. She tipped her head up to study his face. It was the closest look she'd had of the mark on his face, which looked more like a brand than a scar.

"How did you get the mark on your cheek?"

As soon as the words slipped out, she wished she could call them back. Kane's expression hardened just enough to warn her that the question had caused him pain.

She brushed her fingertips along his cheek. "Never mind, Kane. Forget I asked. It matters not."

He stared up at the ceiling and answered anyway. "I was

born with it. My grandfather was a dark mage, one who wasn't above using his daughter in his rituals. He found that her blood was twice as potent when she was pregnant with me."

The note of pain in his words warned her the rest of his story would not be a happy one. How many people had shunned Kane because he bore the mark of a dark mage even though it was not one of his own choosing?

Rather than press him for details, she would see what she could do to distract him from the dark turn his thoughts had taken. She eased up over his chest, tucked her head under his chin, and stretched out along the length of his body. His arms immediately wrapped around her, cradling her against him.

As comforting as it was to be held in Kane's arms, she needed far more than the press of her body against his. She pushed herself upright, straddling his hips with her hands splayed over the powerful contours of his chest. She smiled down at her lover, rocking gently against the increasing evidence that his thoughts were traveling the same path as hers.

His big hands cupped her breasts, kneading them gently at first, and then just hard enough to ease the aching emptiness that was slowly building within her. She dropped down to kiss Kane, teasing him with quick forays of her tongue and then nibbling his lower lip.

For a while, he let her take the lead, encouraging her to have her way with his warrior's body. The sense of power that freedom gave her was intoxicating, but she knew the instant she shattered his control again.

And for a long, lovely time, nothing existed beyond the reach of each other's arms.

After the energetic night he'd spent, Kane had figured he'd want to cut weapons practice short. Instead, he managed to keep up his usual pace, working with one man after another. He concentrated his teaching efforts on those members of the guard he had judged to be good men, ones who served the realm out of a sense of duty and honor.

When it came to the others like Gart, Kane worked them to near exhaustion but did little to improve their skills. If they were going to shirk their duties, the least he could do was make sure they hurt too much to enjoy their free time.

The one real puzzle was Sergeant Markus. He treated Kane with the respect due his rank and followed orders without question. It was the man's habit of turning up in odd places and at odd times that was worrisome. While he couldn't exactly accuse Markus of spying, all too often Kane would feel the weight of his gaze during the day.

His real worry was if the man was also paying too much attention to Kane's activities during the night. He'd know if Markus were lurking in the garden when Kane and Theda were there. Certainly, Hob would sound the alarm if anyone got too close to them.

What did the man plan to do with any information he was gathering on Kane's movements? In a few more days, it would no longer matter. Averel had heard from Gideon again, and he wanted the two of them to rejoin him and the other Damned by the end of the next week. Kane had planned to leave sooner, but that was before last night.

In truth, he wanted to remain in the city as long as he possibly could. To leave Theda one minute before he had to was unthinkable. The idea made his chest ache with a pain that could not be assuaged.

"Captain, tell me I'm not the one who has put that look on your face, especially because I was hoping you'd have time to practice with me."

Kane blinked and looked around. All of the other men were still going through their drills, but Markus stood facing Kane just out of arm's reach. His stance was relaxed, the tip of his sword resting on the ground with his hands crossed on top of the pommel. If he'd wanted to kill Kane, he could have done so without Kane even having time to draw his weapon.

Rather than offer an explanation of where his mind had been, Kane nodded as he pulled his sword and picked up his shield. Of all the men, Markus was the closest to Kane's skill with a sword. Sparring with him took all of his concentration to make sure neither of them got hurt. Soon they were both grinning, each determined to find a weakness they could exploit in the other's defenses.

When Kane finally called a halt, they were both drenched in sweat and breathing hard. He sheathed his sword and offered his hand to the sergeant just as someone behind them applauded. The smile on Markus's face abruptly faded as all of the men snapped to attention, the only warning Kane had about who was standing behind him.

He turned and bowed just enough to acknowledge the duke's presence. "Duke Keirthan."

"That was quite a demonstration, Captain. Sergeant."

"You honor us." Kane handed his shield to one of the guards. "Did you have need of me?"

"Yes, I do." Then he sniffed in disapproval as he studied Kane's attire. "Clean up before you report to my office. I prefer my captain wear the uniform of his office, not the leathers of a common mercenary."

Keirthan walked away without another word, leaving the guardsmen staring after him in silence. Kane shifted his attention back to them, giving them all a long look before nodding in approval.

"That's enough practice for today. I posted the new duty roster. Check it for your assignments before you make plans for the rest of the day. Dismissed."

He picked up his shield and headed for his quarters. Markus walked along beside him in silence. From the way he was frowning, he clearly had something on his mind.

"Spit it out, Sergeant, before you choke on it."

Markus huffed in a rough laugh. "I just wanted to say I enjoy facing off against you. I'd hate to do it for real."

Then he walked away without a backward glance.

*   *   *

Ifre figured it would be at least half an hour before Kane reported to him. In truth, he didn't care about the guard uniform, but the arrogant bastard had better be wearing his captain's sigil this time. The connection between them was only slightly stronger now than it had been when he'd first promoted Kane to captain. Watching the man's uncanny speed and ability in combat made it all the more imperative that Ifre weaken the man's resistance as soon as possible.

Right now, trying to access Kane's latent powers would be too risky. If the link didn't enable him to break through the man's shields soon, he'd have to resort to more direct means. Considering not a single man in Ifre's employ could best Kane with weapons, trapping the man and dragging him down below would carry severe risks.

If he had unlimited time, Ifre wouldn't worry about it. Eventually the sigil would work. But lately he'd been aware of the hours passing, as if he were up against a deadline that was not of his own making. Danger lurked outside the walls of the city, and it was aimed directly at him.

Maybe it was the darkness pushing him along, demanding more and more blood, more magic for it to consume, but he didn't think so. He'd fed the beast well enough to make it sleepy. In the rare silence within his own mind, Ifre felt the press of those who would stand against him.

He considered sending more troops out into the countryside to find his enemies, to learn their weaknesses and their strengths. So far his efforts in that direction had failed. He also couldn't waste the energy it would take to bind the troops to him as fully as he had when he'd sent Captain Terrick out to recapture Lady Merewen's keep.

That ill-planned attack still rankled. Not only had he lost all the men he'd sent, but it had cost him Terrick. He missed his former captain, who'd supplied him with a constant supply of magic he could draw off of at will.

But also, if the news of Terrick's death ever became common knowledge, it would cause him problems with Lady Theda. Yes, she tolerated his shabby treatment out of her misguided desire to protect her two young friends. However, it was his overt threats to Terrick that kept her from finding some way to kill Ifre herself. He'd hinted that he had made arrangements that would ensure that if something happened to him, Terrick would die as well.

A knock at the door brought him back to the moment. "Come in."

Kane stepped through the door, wearing his uniform as ordered, his dark hair still damp from a quick bath. He crossed to stand in front of Ifre's desk.

"You wanted to speak to me about something, Sire?"

How best to play this? If he offered Kane a chair, he might relax his guard enough to let Ifre slip inside his thoughts, even if only briefly. On the other hand, forcing the man to stand at attention might keep him off center enough to accomplish the same goal. Decisions, decisions.

Before he could choose, his office door slammed open again. Stefan, his secretary backed in, obviously fighting a losing battle to keep Lady Theda from forcing her way inside. "The duke did not send for you, Lady Theda. He is with someone."

Stefan tried to angle his body to prevent her from getting past him. Theda got right in his face, "And we wouldn't be having this discussion if you had delivered my request for an audience with my brother-in-law when I asked you to."

This was most entertaining. His secretary drew himself up to his inconsequential height and glared right back at the woman. "I have better things, far more important things to do than deliver messages for you. I work for the duke, not the likes of you."

Before Theda could say another word, Kane took matters in his own hands. He picked Ifre's secretary up by the scruff of his neck and held him dangling in the air.

Stefan's face flushed red as he struggled to breathe, his feet kicking in the air as he tried to break free of Kane's grasp.

Ifre looked on in delight, finding the interchange fascinating.

Kane slowly lowered Stefan back to the ground without releasing his hold on him. "If you don't have better manners than that, I will be only too glad to teach you some myself."

When Stefan tried to turn his head in Ifre's direction, no doubt hoping to be rescued, Kane shook him like a dog would a rat. "Don't look at him, fool. I'm the one talking to you. In the future, you will not treat any woman with anything less than respect. Do I make myself clear?"

He gave Stefan a soft shove, setting him free to catch his breath. Finally, the secretary choked out, "She has no right to tell me what to do, and barging in here uninvited is not acceptable."

Kane took a step forward. "Did you deliver her request for an audience with the duke?"

Stefan turned pale, no doubt correctly guessing his answer wouldn't please his inquisitor. "Not yet."

"And when did she present her request?" Kane's question was said softly, sounding far more lethal because of it.

The secretary swallowed hard. "Two days ago."

Kane stepped closer again, looming over the smaller man. "And is part of your job deciding which messages will be important to the duke and which should be ignored? From my understanding, Lady Theda overseas the duke's household. I can imagine any number of issues she might need to bring to his attention."

It was time to intercede. Ifre stood up and walked around the desk. "That's enough, Kane. You've made your point. Stefan, return to your duties. In the future, please see that Lady Theda's messages get all the attention they deserve."

The woman in question finally spoke up. She shot Stefan a quelling look on his way past her, but gave Kane a wide berth as she planted herself in front of Ifre's desk. "I need to speak to you in private."

"Very well, Theda, but keep it brief." He jerked his head in the direction of the door. "Kane, we'll talk later."

Just before he left the room, Theda spared him a brief glance. "Thank you for your courtesy, Captain. It's a rarity around here."

Kane merely nodded and left. Ifre would listen to what his sister-in-law had to complain about this time. After she was gone, though, he would think hard about what had just happened. Kane's furious reaction to seeing a woman treated with disrespect was the first crack Ifre had been able to detect in the man's stern demeanor.

It might just be the opening Ifre needed.

Theda paced the garden, walking in circles but unable to outdistance her thoughts. What had Kane been thinking to attack Ifre's puppet like that? Even now, hours later, the memory kept her thoughts spinning like a child's top. Would he have reacted in the same way had another woman been seeking an audience with Ifre? Perhaps, but nothing would change that she'd been the one he'd defended.

She hoped that Ifre's thoughts on the matter hadn't run along the same path as hers. The last thing she needed was another life that he could hold over her head. The burden of her ladies-in-waiting and Terrick were already enough to weigh her down.

Kane wouldn't see himself as someone who needed protecting, but no one could stand alone, especially in the face of Ifre's evil. Over the past week, two more servants had gone missing. When she'd confronted Ifre, he'd brushed aside the problem with a wave of his hand. It was hardly his fault that farmers' daughters and sons found out that living in the city wasn't to their liking and skulked off in the night to go back home.

She didn't believe him for a minute. Even if she could prove he was killing them, who would she report him to? Kane might listen, but he was one man against all of the others.

Not to mention the man was late. If he didn't appear soon, she would have to return to the keep alone. Perhaps it would be better if she did. Margaret and Lydia were starting to wonder why she hadn't been seeking out their company at night.

She could plead a headache only so often before they'd insist on her seeking out medical care. It would hurt their feelings if she admitted that sometimes she preferred to be alone without the constant pressure of having to watch over her friends.

They certainly would never understand her involvement with the captain of the guard. They were still young and naïve enough to think that they would win the heart of some handsome, kind knight who would take care of them forever.

She'd been that foolish herself once. Yes, Armel had been handsome, and he'd been good to her. But his death had left her abandoned and at the mercy of a monster. In many ways, Kane was Armel's opposite, but at least he'd made her no promises he couldn't keep.

How soon would he ride away? She could barely stand the thought. What if he didn't have other commitments that required his presence elsewhere? Would he soon grow tired of her company? Or would he leave the minute Ifre decided which of his friends would be burdened with an unwilling wife?

For a moment, she allowed herself the small dream of what it would be like to belong to a man like Kane, one who would fight to keep her safe. But his strong sword arm wasn't the only thing about him that had her thinking along those lines. It was the way he treated her, both in bed and out of it, that had her sighing and wishing they could . . .

But then, why not? If Kane were to marry her, even if he had to leave, his name might offer her the protection she needed. He would also gain control of her fortune, which might aid him in his quest beyond the walls of Agathia.

"I wasn't sure you would still be waiting."

Kane appeared suddenly, solidifying out of the shadows. Hob waddled forward to stand at his side. She was grateful for the darkness, as it hid the blush that stained her cheeks. Her mind had been running wild, filling her heart with fey thoughts, dreams that were nothing more than wisps of smoke and dreams.

"I was about to go in, but I hoped that you would come." She stooped to pet Hob, not quite ready to face his owner. "I see you're wearing your captain's uniform. Am I keeping you from something?"

"I waited until it was safe to bring out Hob. He needs the exercise."

And perhaps Kane wanted his pet with them as chaperone. With Hob running loose, there was no chance Kane could risk following her back to her room.

The slight coolness in her words matched the chill of the night air. "Shall we walk, then?"

But rather than offer her his arm, Kane gently lifted her chin, forcing her to meet his gaze. Even in the darkness of a cloudy night, he seemed to see far too much.

"Have I done something to offend you?"

"Not at all. I suppose I am in an odd mood." Honesty had her adding, "And I will admit to being disappointed that we won't be returning to my quarters tonight."

Kane brushed a soft kiss across her lips. "Don't think it's because I don't want to, but I thought it wise not to take such risks two nights in a row."

"That's probably true, if disappointing." Which reminded her. "About what happened in Ifre's office. I know you're not going to like me saying this, but you shouldn't have interfered."

Kane's expression turned stony. "I would have done the same for any woman. That little worm had no right to treat you that way. I wanted to gut your brother-in-law for allowing such behavior."

She wrapped her arms around Kane's waist and laid her head against his chest. "And I am grateful. It has been a long time since anyone has been willing to defend me. I just worry that Ifre will see your willingness to put yourself between bullies and their intended victims as a weakness. Please be careful around him."

Kane rested his head beside hers. "I won't make promises I can't keep. My honor demands that I defend those who deserve it. If I could find a way to keep you safe from him permanently, I would do so."

Once again his words warmed her through, weakening her defenses. "Shortly before you arrived, it occurred to me that there might be one thing you could do. That is, if you are willing."

Kane stiffened, his hold on her still gentle. "What do you have in mind?"

She braced herself, hoping he wouldn't think she'd taken leave of her senses. It was tempting to hide her face against his chest, but that would be cowardly. Taking a steadying breath, she stepped back so that she could look into Kane's eyes, hoping he'd read the truth behind what she was about to say.

"You could marry me."

Chapter 13

Kane couldn't have heard Theda right. Marry her? What craziness was this? He stumbled back a few steps, turning away so that she wouldn't see how much her words hurt him. The idea of claiming her as his own stabbed through his heart, leaving him bleeding for something he could never have.

Something he wanted more than he wanted to draw another breath.

She kept right on talking. "You have proven to be a man of honor, Kane, one who treats me far better than any man Ifre might choose for me."

Theda followed him step for step, holding his arm as if she feared he would take off running. The gods knew he should. "Kane, please speak to me."

He refused to face her, looking back at her from over his shoulder. "What would you have me say, Theda?"

She already knew his answer. Her pretty face was ashen, her eyes huge and ashamed. "A simple no would suffice. I apologize for putting you in such an awkward position. I'll go now before I embarrass myself any further. Forgive my foolishness."

The catch in her voice warned that tears weren't far away. He couldn't let her walk away thinking he was offended by her proposal. Quite the contrary.

"Theda, wait."

She paid him no heed, instead quickening her pace. Soon she'd be close enough to the door for Tom to hear her coming. Three long strides and Kane caught up with her, blocking her way.

He caught her hand in his. "Let me explain."

"I don't need to hear your reasons, Kane. Forget I said anything." She fought to break free of his grip. To avoid the risk of bruising her delicate skin, he gave up trying to convince her to stay and simply picked her up.

"Put me down!"

He tightened his grip with one arm and used his free hand to cover her mouth. "Theda! Quiet! The last thing either of us needs right now is to draw attention to ourselves. Nod if you can control your voice."

She jerked her head up and down, but the fury in her eyes warned him that anything she did say was going to be dagger sharp. He carried her to the most distant bench, where he sat down and held her on his lap. Hob loped along in their footsteps, his tail swishing back and forth, sharing his owner's agitation. When they stopped, he looked from Kane to Theda and back again. Clearly he wasn't sure which of the two humans needed his protection.

"Hob, stand guard."

The gargoyle stared at Kane for a handful of seconds before slithering away into the shadows. No one would get by him, leaving Kane free to focus on the unhappy woman in his arms.

He cradled her head against his chest, glad that she'd allow him to offer her even that much comfort. Meanwhile, he searched for the right words to heal this wound between them.

He started off with the truth.

"Theda, I am honored by your words, but I am not a free man."

He paused, trying to gauge her response. She had been leaning against him, but she abruptly sat upright and looked at him in shock.

"What do you mean you aren't free? You would dally

with me knowing another woman waits for your return?"

All right, obviously now he was the one not making sense. "I have never been married, Theda, if that's what you're asking."

"Yet somehow you are not free?"

"You have never asked about the odd shade of my eyes, but they were not always this color. I was born with green eyes." He turned his face up to the sky, wishing he didn't have to go any further with his explanation.

"How can that be? Such a change is not possible."

"I would wager you've never seen anyone else with eyes like these." Kane turned his pale gaze toward her, letting her look her fill. "Nothing is impossible when one is dealing with the gods. I am sworn to serve the Lord and Lady of the River. There are five of us, known to some as the Warriors of the Mist. Others simply call us the Damned."

She drew in a sharp breath. He half expected her to pull away from him, and this time he would let her go. Instead, she surprised him again.

"I cannot believe how cruel people can be. If I were your goddess, I would smite them for saying such things."

Her outrage on his behalf soothed the pain in his heart. He caught her hand and brought it to his lips, pressing a kiss to her palm. "Thank you."

He leaned back, shifting Theda to make them both more comfortable. "I would tell you my story if you would hear it."

She nodded and settled herself more firmly in his arms. Once he started speaking, the words poured out until he talked himself hoarse. At least Theda allowed him to finish without interruption. He wasn't sure he would have found the strength to continue if he'd had to stop and start.

"So I have but a few days left before I must rejoin my friends."

She nodded as if he'd confirmed something she'd been thinking. "I knew from the first you were different from the men Ifre usually hires."

"Not so different. Before I was called to serve the goddess, I was a mercenary."

She held up a hand and counted off her reasons. "That first day when I passed you on the stairs, I sensed you didn't like how Sergeant Markus acted toward me and my ladies-in-waiting. You also apologized for barging into my solar without knocking. You saved Lady Margaret from that drunken guard and me from Ifre's fool of a secretary. And, finally, the children aren't afraid of you."

That last one surprised him. "What is that supposed to mean?"

She beamed up at him. "If you watch the children around the keep, they avoid drawing the attention of the guardsmen. I watched you from my balcony when you took the time to join in their games. Children can sense which adults offer them no threat."

She gave him an impish grin. "I'm betting animals trust you, as well. Who else could tame a gargoyle? And would I be right to guess that your horse is one that no one else could ride?"

If he had it in him to blush, he would have been bright red after listening to her assessment of him. He conceded the point about his horse. "My stallion's name is Rogue, and I'm the only one he has ever tolerated on his back."

As glad as he was that they seemed to have made peace, time was passing. Soon he must send Theda back inside.

Alone.

Before he could say so, he realized that she was caught up in her own thoughts, her eyebrows drawn down sharply in a frown. Her next words twisted the knife in his chest anew.

"I see no reason why we cannot marry, Kane, despite

your duty to the goddess. I understand that and promise to make no effort to divide your loyalties. All I need is your name to shield me from my brother-in-law's plans. You would, of course, gain control of all my wealth and my lands. Surely your cause could put that money to good use. Waging war on a man like Ifre is expensive."

She continued talking, evidently too caught up in the fool's dream she was weaving to notice how he was reacting. He carefully picked her up and set her aside. Lurching to his feet, he started to walk away, his thoughts scattering like dust in the wind. Once again Theda followed after him.

"Kane? I'm sure the local priest will perform the ceremony for us. He was a friend of my late husband's."

The last thing Kane needed at that moment was to be reminded that Theda had once belonged to another. He turned to face her, leaning close so she couldn't miss his fury.

"Were you not listening? I cannot marry you. By the summer solstice, I will be gone, perhaps this time forever, if the goddess chooses to release us from her service. Otherwise, I will once again sleep beneath the river for centuries. The only difference this time is that I will dream of you."

He kissed her, needing to claim at least that much of her for himself. It wasn't gentle, but she'd never doubt for a second that he wanted her.

When he broke it off, they were both panting as if they'd been running. In a sense, they had been. Running from the truth and from what lay ahead of them.

"But know this much." His temper made his next words cold. Sharp and jagged like his pain. "I don't want your lands or your wealth, woman. I want the one thing I can't have. I want your love."

Tears trickled down her cheeks as she smiled up at him. "But you already have that, Kane. Now and for always."

Her sweet promise was a balm to his weary soul. He

offered his own truth. "As you have mine. It changes nothing, but my heart is yours to keep."

When they kissed good-bye, he tasted her sweetness, her sadness, and his own grief.

Ifre was ready to retire for the night. He dismissed his manservant and climbed into bed, looking forward to a few hours of peaceful sleep. The day had been a long one, filled with the endless duties of running his realm. After the evening meal, he'd spent hours in his private chambers below the keep.

He'd fed his creation, using up the last of his captives to lull it to sleep. Free of its demands, he'd then pored over his books, looking for some way to strengthen his control over his spell. Afterward, for his own amusement, he'd burned up a great deal of the energy he'd built up to unleash his weapon again.

Over the past week, his courtiers had gossiped about outlandish rumors of bright lights that appeared out of nowhere to kill livestock and burn fields. Ifre had made all the right noises, outwardly looking concerned when inside he was howling with joy. Soon, when he had accumulated enough magic, the entire land would drop to its knees to obey his every command.

From there, his power would spread beyond the mountains. Yes, he had plenty to dream of when sleep claimed him. But as soon as he settled his head on the pillow, the acid-hot burn of magic had him jerking back upright and looking around for its source.

When he didn't detect an immediate personal threat, he waited until his pulse slowed to reach out with all of his senses to trace the source of the power. There. Just the barest wisp that tasted of his magic but carried the dark spice of another mage's power, one he didn't immediately recognize.

Gently, he latched onto the fading tendrils and followed it back to the source. Through the thick walls, down and down, and then outside. Where? Ah, the garden. The longer he was in contact with the magic, the more familiar it felt. Finally, he recognized the half that was his.

It was the sigil he'd constructed for Kane. He would have recognized it sooner, but the strength of the spell seemed to have increased by tenfold. It was already subsiding back to its original level, but he could hardly contain his glee.

Something had happened to weaken Kane's shields. By the time Ifre traced it all the way back to the captain himself, Kane had all of his protections back in place. Still, Ifre wanted to caper about the room in celebration. Kane might have repaired the wall, but the patches would be vulnerable once Ifre determined what had caused the breach in the first place.

Now wasn't the time to pursue the matter any further, not when he was already tired from his studies. But tomorrow the hunt would begin in earnest.

Sigil stood beside Murdoch on the rampart over the gate and watched another row of tents taking shape on the grasslands outside of the keep. From the way his friend was nodding, Murdoch found the sight satisfying. The first of the troops promised by their allies had arrived.

The big warrior glanced in Sigil's direction. "For Gideon's sake, I'm glad they are here. In truth, for all of our sakes, but I'll be far happier when Kane and Averel return. None of us feel at full strength without them."

Sigil had been counting under his breath. "If my numbers are correct, there are now close to a hundred men out there. It's a good beginning, but not enough to face Keirthan's forces."

Murdoch shrugged. "We've done more with less in the past. Never forget that we have the gods on our side."

Sigil envied his friend's faith. If the gods could end Ifre Keirthan's evil, why did they need mortals to wage the battle for them? The duke wouldn't hesitate to throw his own soldiers into the fray, not caring how many died as long as they kept the battle from reaching him. And

Keirthan would lob his weapons from behind the safety of his city walls, a coward's way of doing battle. Ifre had always been sneaky and weak.

The image of a handsome man with a slightly weak chin flashed into Sigil's mind. He tried to hold on to the picture, but it faded just as quickly as it had appeared. He had no doubt that it had been Keirthan himself. Another memory, another piece of Sigil's past, even if an unwelcome one. He didn't recall any details, but in his heart he knew he'd committed atrocities in the duke's name.

"Sir Sigil?"

He'd been too lost in the darkness of his own thoughts to notice that young Sarra had climbed up to the rampart to join them. Ever since their talk in the pasture, he'd spent a little time each day riding with her because she loved horses so much. So far, the voices that sometimes spoke through her had remained blessedly silent.

He lifted her up in his arms so she could see over the palisade to the grasslands beyond. "Hi, Sarra. Did you need something?"

As soon as he asked, he wished he hadn't. Her eyes glazed over, and her face had that stony look of when someone else was in control of her words. At least Murdoch had moved down to the other end of the rampart, so whatever Sarra had to say would be private.

"Captain, you are no longer the man you were when your memories were created. But as long as you fight their return, they still wield power over you. Do not let the past destroy your future."

As her words drifted away on the breeze, she wrapped her arms around Sigil's neck and gave him a hug. He closed his eyes, savoring the little girl's simple affection, and if she spoke for the gods, surely that meant there was hope for his salvation.

"Can we go riding today?"

He set Sarra back down. "Yes, little one, but it will have to be later. I'm on duty right now."

Her disappointment was obvious. "Promise me you won't forget. The horses miss us when we're not there."

Sigil leaned down to tap her on the tip of her nose. "I will not forget. You have my word."

Then Sarra skipped off down the rampart, pausing before she descended to the bailey below to smile at him one last time. He smiled back, his heart lighter than it had been since he first awoke to a world with no memories and a new chance at redemption.

Chapter 14

Kane saddled Rogue. He wasn't sure who needed a hard run more, him or the horse. As he rode through the streets, the close walls of the city pressed down on him to the point it was difficult to breathe.

Over the days he'd spent in the capital, he'd grown used to the pungent scent of Keirthan's magic tainting the air. But after leaving Theda last night, his sleeping hours had been plagued with dark dreams, ones that still shadowed his mood. It was as if a new layer of potent magic had blanketed the city overnight.

He'd planned to ride by himself, but he slowed Rogue as they passed near the tavern where Averel worked. Perhaps it would be better to see if his friend was available to join him.

After dismounting, Kane tied Rogue's reins to a fence post some distance from any of the other horses. The stallion's mood was a reflection of Kane's own, meaning he'd try to kick any horse that got too close.

Kane ducked inside the tavern and waited for his light-sensitive eyes to adjust to the dim interior. As soon as he spotted Averel, he headed straight for him, not caring if anyone wondered what kind of business the captain of the guard might have with the troubadour.

"Let's ride."

Without waiting for his friend to respond, Kane stalked back outside. Either Averel would join him or he wouldn't. While he waited to see which it would be, he stroked Rogue's nose and watched the ebb and flow of people passing by. Unless he was mistaken, more people were heading out of the nearby gate than were entering the city. Did they sense the growing darkness, too?

"What's going on?"

Averel came out of the back door of the tavern, strapping on his sword. His dogs tripped over each other as they hurried to follow their master out into the street.

Kane jerked his head in greeting. "We'll talk once we're outside the city. Do you need help saddling your mare?"

His friend rolled his eyes and walked into the stable alone. The dogs stayed with Kane, taking turns flopping in the dirt and then shaking hard to send up clouds of dust in the air. Once again Rogue's ears went back, but Kane thumped him on the shoulder.

"Hey, stop that. We'll be moving again soon enough."

The stallion chuffed, looking disgruntled until Averel reappeared leading his mare. As soon as they came into sight, Rogue's head came up, his ears flicking forward at the mare's approach, but she only ignored him. Clearly Kane wasn't the only one with woman problems.

He gathered Rogue's reins and swung up on his broad back. Averel followed behind, both horses moving at a brisk trot until they left the gates of the city. Once they were clear of the clutter of others on the road, Kane cut across country and kicked Rogue into a full gallop.

With the dogs running off to the side, Kane and Averel rode hard until they reached the same clearing where they'd met before. Kane dismounted and walked Rogue to cool him down before leading the horse to the small stream that ran along the edge of the woods. His young friend showed amazing forbearance by not demanding an explanation for the unexpected trip, for which Kane was grateful.

By the time they both sat down, he was ready to talk. Before he could say a word, Averel gave him a considering look and asked, "What did the lady do this time?"

Kane didn't bother asking Averel how he'd guessed

that Lady Theda was the source of his agitation. "She asked me to marry her."

The look of utter shock on Averel's face was worth the price of a bad mood and a bone-jarring ride. Kane waited to see what the younger knight would say once he recovered his ability to talk.

"Truly, she proposed marriage to you? What did you say?"

Kane's amusement faded away as quickly as it had appeared. "I told her about my past and about the Damned. I could not bring myself to lie to her about who and what I am. I owed her the truth."

Averel nodded, accepting the necessity of what Kane had done. "What drove her to propose to you? Surely that is not how these things are done, not with the widow of the former duke."

Kane leaned forward, resting his elbows on his knees as he stared down at the ground. "She thought if we were to marry, it would protect her from the kind of bastard that Keirthan would choose for her. In return, I would gain control of her land and wealth.

"Like that would matter to me." He picked up a stick and threw it for the dogs. "Even if I had a lifetime to live with her instead of the few weeks left before we face judgment again, I wouldn't care about such things."

"And I'm guessing your lady knows that. If she thought you were a greedy bastard like her brother-in-law or his friends, she wouldn't have let you touch her."

Averel gave Kane a sly look, his pale eyes twinkling with wicked humor. "And she has let you touch you, hasn't she?"

Kane shoved his friend hard. "Careful how you speak of her. Your listeners tonight wouldn't like how you'd sound with your nose broken."

Averel scooted farther away on the log, holding his hands up in surrender. "I meant no insult."

Kane backed off. "None taken. I've been edgier than usual since last night."

He rubbed his chest as he spoke, wishing the ache caused by having to refuse Theda would go away. "It nearly killed me to tell her we couldn't wed."

Averel stared at where Kane's hand rested on his uniform. "Why are you rubbing that emblem on your uniform?"

Kane looked down. "I'm not. It's my chest that hurts."

"All over or in that one spot?"

What was he getting at? "The pain radiates from there. Why?"

"Do you remember when the duke's guard saved Murdoch's life by throwing himself between Murdoch and Merewen's uncle? When Lord Fagan thrust his sword through the emblem the man wore around his neck, it released a blast of magical power."

Kane studied the badge of office that Keirthan had given him to wear. He grasped it with his right hand and closed his eyes. Sure enough, there was the barest hint of power flowing from the sigil. Worse yet, it carried the same taint as all of Keirthan's magic.

He jerked his hand away from the offensive symbol. "You're right, Averel. How could I have missed sensing the connection between this symbol and Ifre Keirthan himself?"

"I'm not sure." His friend leaned closer. "What do you think its purpose is?"

There could be only one logical answer. Kane touched his own cheek. "The duke must think this mark means I share my grandfather's gift of power. We already know that Keirthan consumes the magic of others along with their blood for his own foul purpose. Perhaps he believes he can gain access to the kind of magic this mark would normally signify."

"And can he?"

Kane had always assured his friends that he'd forsworn his family's magical heritage. While it was true that he'd never openly practiced the kinds of spells he'd learned as a youth, that didn't mean he'd necessarily shed himself of the potential to do so.

His gut twisted in a knot as he admitted, "I truly don't know. If I'm now sensing the effects of this device, there must be some possibility."

He ripped the emblem off his tunic and tossed it a short distance away to break the connection for the moment. If they were right, Keirthan would know if Kane destroyed the cursed thing. But how much longer could he risk wearing it?

Averel moved closer again, pitching his voice low, as if he feared being overheard. "Perhaps we should leave now right from here."

Maybe he was right. Who knew what Keirthan was capable of now? It was tempting to leave the emblem behind and ride hard for Lady Merewen's keep to rejoin the other three Damned, but he couldn't.

"I can't. I left Hob in my quarters because I didn't think I'd need my shield."

He rolled his shoulders in a futile attempt to ease the knots of tension that seemed to be his constant companion lately. "Mayhap I wasn't thinking at all, at least not about our mission back there in the city. Have we even learned anything that will be of value to our purpose?"

Averel looked no happier. "Just that the townspeople are restless and frightened. Yet few seem willing to point toward the duke as the source of their fears."

Kane stared out at the horizon. "What do they think happens when they hear rumors of people disappearing?"

"They don't say, and I'm leery of asking very many questions. People tend to forget that I'm sitting there, so they don't guard their tongues. If they were to realize I'm listening, it's less likely that I'd learn anything useful."

That made sense. "If you do hear about any townspeople missing, let me know. I'll pay a visit to their former dwellings to see if the same magic was used in their disappearance as on those abandoned farms on Lady Merewen's estate. Either way, though, we must leave soon."

The time with Averel had improved Kane's dark mood, but he couldn't afford to be gone for long. "I should get back to town. Thanks for coming with me. I hope being gone this long doesn't cause you problems at the tavern."

Averel stood up. "I'm not worried. The owner needs me more than I need him. Besides, it's a relief to simply be myself for a while."

That it was, especially when it came to Theda. No matter what happened from this point forward, at least she knew Kane's truth.

Something of his thoughts must have shown on his face, because Averel clapped him on the shoulder. "Don't give up completely, Kane. The goddess might ask a lot of her warriors, but she's not without compassion."

And yet how many times had she ordered the Damned back into the river to sleep? Had they not earned a respite from the endless cycle of non-death alternating with unrelenting battle? He held back his bleak thoughts from his young friend. Somehow Averel had managed to hold on to his good nature despite all the centuries of service to the goddess. His cheerfulness helped Kane balance his own tendency toward the darker emotions.

As they walked back to the horses, Kane stopped to retrieve Keirthan's sigil. He stared at the cursed thing before once again affixing it to his tunic. Feeling the sick chill of the duke's magic slither across his skin, he murmured, "I will continue to serve the goddess as I always have."

As they mounted up, a feminine voice whispered inside Kane's head. *"Have faith, my warrior. You do not carry your burdens alone."*

The unexpected message from the Lady herself startled Kane into jerking on the reins as he spun his head from right to left, looking for the source of the words. Rogue immediately picked up on his rider's agitation and bucked a few times. Averel kept his mare far enough away to avoid being kicked by the unpredictable stallion. "What happened to set him off this time?"

Kane wasn't ready to share what had just happened, not when he didn't quite believe it himself. "He's been skittish all day. I want to give him another hard run before we reach the city. When we get closer, I'll circle around and enter from another gate. I think it better that we avoid being seen returning at the same time, especially since we left together."

"Good thinking." Then Averel frowned. "But one more thing, Kane. I know you told Lady Theda about the Damned, but I'm guessing you didn't tell her about me being in the city as well. I think you should do so." He stared up toward the sky as he spoke. "If something should happen to alert Keirthan to our purpose in the city, he could attack you without warning. Someone should know to send for me."

"I will."

That is, if she wanted to see him again after last night. Another thought crossed his mind, one he kept to himself. It wouldn't hurt to show her how to call forth Hob. If something happened to Kane, she might need the gargoyle's protection from Keirthan or his men.

He braced himself in case the goddess had something more to say on the subject. But for the remainder of the ride, the thoughts inside his head were his alone.

"Where is Kane? Why is the link so weak right now?"

Keirthan walked circles around the fire pit in the center of his underground chambers. It was impossible to know if the sweat dripping down his face came from the heat of the blaze or from nerves. He'd already sacrificed two more to the darkness, but it wouldn't be satisfied for long, because neither of the victims had offered even a hint of magic.

Instead, the power he'd unleashed constantly hungered for blood laced with magic. Its demands pounded inside Ifre's head, leaving him unable to concentrate on anything but the thought of finding more power to feed his creation.

He glanced across the room to where an ebony cloud hovered and swirled right above the altar. Two days ago, his creation had surprised him by taking on a physical form. Just yesterday, it had been much lighter in color. Now it was thick and heavy with a new substance. Worse yet, it now watched him. More than once, he'd seen two eyes staring out of the darkness and following his movements. Once it even seemed to smile, its maw ragged and filled with dagger-sharp teeth.

He shuddered and kept walking. Was it really becoming sentient? Why had the books not told him that was even possible? The fear that he was losing control over it haunted his thoughts constantly. The only hope would be to either weaken it through starvation or increase his own personal power to the point he could ignore its constant hunger.

Right now, Kane was the closest Ifre had to a potential new source of power, one he desperately needed to keep for himself. But how was he supposed to utilize Kane's potential if the bastard refused to stay close enough for Ifre to strengthen his hold over him?

He paused at the far end of the pit, hoping the power of the fire itself would prevent the monster over the altar from tracking his thoughts. In his mind, he grasped the thread of magic that tied him to Kane. Earlier, the slender tendril had been stretched to the breaking point. When he'd tried to follow its path outward, it had suddenly snapped back, the connection to them broken.

This time, however, the thread was firmly back in place and far stronger than an hour ago. Kane was moving back in this direction. Good, but for how long? After all, the man was a common mercenary with no ties of loyalty to anyone, least of all Ifre himself.

Sooner or later the bastard would decide to leave. If Ifre was going to make use of Kane, he needed to do so soon. Should he strengthen the magic he'd infused in the sigil that marked him as Ifre's captain? To do so would weaken the mage-marked warrior's shields at a faster pace, but the stronger connection would carry its own risks.

If Kane were to figure it out, he might destroy the emblem, severing their connection completely. A movement at the other end of the room made the decision for him. The dark cloud had floated higher, giving it an unobstructed view of Ifre. Those eyes, now bloodred and flame-hot, stared at him with malicious intensity.

Ifre immediately bolted for the passageway that led to the keep above. When he reached the door, he waited until his pulse had slowed to normal. It wouldn't do to appear in the great hall looking shaken and fearful. At the first sign of weakness, his enemies would be on him like a pack of hounds on a hare.

They didn't think he knew they watched him, but he did. Once he reestablished control over his weapon, he'd unleash enough magic to track the bastards down and destroy them.

For now he'd retire to his office and reinforce the spell that would tie Kane to him with unbreakable chains. Ifre could almost taste the sweet flavor of the captain's magic. Feeling renewed, he strode across the hall, nodding to a few favored guests along the way.

Chapter 15

*T*heda made small talk as the servants cleared away the last of the evening meal. Ifre had chosen to eat in his office, leaving her to play hostess to his guests. She hated every minute of the time she had to spend with the courtiers.

Ifre made it all too clear that she had fallen out of favor with him, leaving her an easy target for their sly insults and superior smirks. Fools. Did they not realize that if Ifre was willing to treat a member of his own family this way, he wouldn't hesitate to do far worse to them?

As soon as she ensured the cook had the cleanup under control, Theda had every intention of retiring to her quarters until nightfall. Then she would seek out the darkest corners of the gardens in hopes of finding Kane waiting for her there. After the embarrassing fiasco of her impromptu marriage proposal, she wouldn't blame him for avoiding her.

But she had to believe that there was power enough in the feelings they had for each other to draw him back to her side. She truly hated that his time here in the city would soon come to an end. She could only hope that the knowledge he would take back to his allies would enable them to put a halt to Ifre's predations.

When she excused herself and left the table, Margaret and Lydia immediately joined her.

"My lady, shall we retire for the evening?"

She smiled and nodded. "Let me take one last look

around. It shouldn't take but another few minutes. You may go ahead if you'd like."

Margaret shook her head. "No, we'll wait. You are no safer walking the halls alone than we are."

And it was a sad state of affairs that Theda could not argue with her young friend's logic. "Very well. I'll hurry."

She made a quick stop in the kitchen to make sure everything was in good order. From there, she made one last circle around the room, nodding at one or two of her old friends who caught her eye with a friendly smile.

Satisfied she'd done her duty for the night, she cut across the hall, preparing to take her leave of the milling crowd. Margaret and Lydia rejoined her just as she reached the bottom of the staircase. She stifled a groan when she noticed Sergeant Markus standing nearby. She did her best to ignore him, but didn't expect her ploy to work.

His cool eyes raked over her from head to toe as he tipped his head in a brief bow. "Lady Theda."

His bold perusal was an insult of the worst kind. She returned his cool stare with an even colder one of her own.

"Sergeant," she said, tilting her head just enough to appear to be looking down her nose at him.

His face flushed hot. She savored the small victory, although she suspected he would find some way to make her regret it. Rather than dwell on the matter, she swept past him with her friends flanking her.

It had been too much to hope that he would simply let her leave. But no, he had to have the last say.

"If you see Captain Kane, please tell him that I was looking for him."

Was he dangling a baited hook in hopes he would catch something? As much as she wanted to simply ignore Markus, she couldn't. Pasting a smile on her face, she turned back.

"You've managed to misplace your captain, Sergeant? How very careless of you."

This time she kept walking, hoping to outdistance him enough to make her escape. Her calm demeanor as she followed her two friends up the steps was but a thin shell, ready to crack at any instant.

Had something happened, forcing Kane to leave the city? If so, she could hardly blame him for going. His duty took precedence, requiring him to serve his goddess alongside his friends. She had no real hold on him, but the possibility that he'd left Agathia without even a wave of farewell stabbed deep in her heart.

She headed straight through her solar to the balcony that looked out over the stable and the barracks where the guards lived. A quick look around did nothing to comfort her. The shadows were stretched out long and thin as the sun continued on its downward trip toward the horizon. Several of the guards were moving about, but Kane wasn't among them.

"Lady Theda, is there something wrong? You look worried."

"No. I'm fine, Lydia. Sometimes the walls seem to close in on me. Coming out here to watch the sunset helps to push them back out again."

She lightened her words with a smile. "Forgive me. I shouldn't be so gloomy when it promises to be a lovely night."

Lydia joined her at the railing, her pretty face reflecting the soft gold of the fading light. She drew a deep breath as if to calm herself.

"I should have told you sooner, but I did what you asked and wrote to my parents, asking that they let me return home. They are sending my brothers to accompany me back to the family estate within the week. They've also said that Margaret is welcome to come with me."

Lydia kept her gaze averted as she continued speaking. "I will be sorry to leave you, but I no longer feel safe here in the capital."

Theda wrapped her arm around the younger woman's shoulders and gave her a quick hug. "I will be sad to see the two of you go, Lydia, but I cannot find fault with your thinking. In truth, it will be a relief to know that the two of you are safely away from here."

Margaret, who had been hovering just inside the door, now joined them out on the balcony. "If you would prefer it, I can stay here and make the journey to Lydia's home later. I do not like the idea of you being alone."

"Bless you both for your friendship, but do not worry about me. I will be fine."

And even if she wasn't, her well-being shouldn't be a burden upon their young shoulders.

"Do your best to keep your preparations to leave quiet. It would better if my brother-in-law did not learn of your departure until after the fact. I don't know that he'd try to prevent your leaving, but his actions are difficult to predict." She considered the possibilities. "Pack only what you need for the trip. After you are safely gone, I will arrange for the rest of your things to be shipped to you by one of the trading clans when they come through."

"Only if you are sure, my lady."

Theda turned to face Margaret, placing her hands on the younger woman's shoulders. "I'm sure, and it will do you good to visit Lydia's family. As I recall, Lydia's brothers are quite handsome, as are several of her cousins. I'm sure they'll all be vying for your attention."

Margaret blushed prettily while Lydia rolled her eyes. "My youngest brother is a decent enough sort. The rest of them can be quite tiresome."

"Ah, but you're their sister, Lydia. They might behave differently around Margaret. You must both promise to write me long letters about what happens."

"We will."

After a quick exchange of hugs, she sent them back

inside. "I'll be just a minute. Lydia, if you'd like to play chess, set up the board."

When she was once again alone, she checked one more time for any sign of Kane. She was about to give up when a familiar figure rode into sight on the back of a huge stallion. Kane dismounted and proceeded to walk his horse in circles, probably to cool the enormous beast before returning him to the stable.

From what she could see, the two were well matched. The horse was heavily muscled but yet moved with the kind of grace that spoke of speed. In short, he was the perfect horse for a warrior.

It wouldn't do to get caught staring at Kane with such interest, so she headed back inside. As she did, she wondered once again why Sergeant Markus had sought her out to comment on Kane's apparent absence. What was he thinking?

Regardless of the risks, nothing would keep her from visiting the gardens again tonight. She had but a few more opportunities to be with Kane, and she wouldn't miss a single one if she could help it. And if they found a way to do more than simply stroll, so much the better.

Walking circles with his horse outside of the stable had done little to calm Kane's fury. After leaving Averel's company on the way back to the city, he'd taken the long way around, aiming for the gate normally taken by the caravans coming in from the east. Kane had been riding along lost in thought when Rogue stumbled over a sudden dip in the ground.

Startled by the sudden movement, Kane had sat up taller in the saddle and looked around. What was this place? He'd dismounted to study the unusual tracks on the dusty ground. A double set of grooves had been worn several inches deep in the dirt, too close together for a wagon to have made them. Most likely someone had been wheeling a handcart through the area on a regular basis. The tracks had led back toward the city of Agathia, but also stretched out in the opposite direction.

Considering how desolate the area was, the obvious question was why. First he'd followed the tracks back toward Agathia. They stopped just short of the city wall, where they circled around to the far side of a small hillock. The ruts stopped right at a small door set back into the side of the hill. From its proximity to Agathia, it had to be a secret way out of the city. The door was locked. No surprise there.

Having learned all he could from tracing the path to its source, he'd mounted Rogue and followed the trail back in the direction he'd come. A half mile farther on, it came to an abrupt end at the edge of a cliff. The flock of carrion birds soaring overhead warned of the horror he'd see when he dismounted again to look down into the canyon below.

Bodies. Lots of them in various stages of decay, all tossed away as if they were nothing more than trash. The stench had left him gagging. He'd found the first hard evidence of Keirthan's violence against his own people. It was also clear he'd had help, because the man wasn't the kind to clean up his own messes.

Kane bowed his head and offered up a prayer for the dead along with a vow to avenge their pain and suffering. He hated to walk away, leaving them to the scavengers, but there was nothing else he could do. If Keirthan's accomplice returned to find the bodies disturbed, he would sound the alarm. There was no telling what Keirthan would do if he panicked.

For now all Kane could do was tie his rope to a large piece of dry brush to drag behind Rogue, hoping to wipe out any sign of their tracks. The hour was growing late, but he took the time to also destroy any sign of his passing near the ruts left by the cart.

When he'd finished, he'd ridden hard back toward the city, entering from a gate some distance from the one he'd originally planned to use. If anyone had been watching for him, at least they'd have no reason to suspect where he'd been.

After walking Rogue, Kane turned the horse loose in his stall and headed for his own quarters. He had just enough time to change into a clean uniform before his late-evening rounds. As he stepped back outside, his eyes automatically went right to the balcony outside of Theda's solar.

It was empty now, but he'd been all too aware of her watching him as he'd cooled Rogue down after their hard ride. She should know better than to watch him where anyone could see her. He'd have to remind her of the danger — that is, if she joined him in the garden later for their nightly walk.

If he were a wiser man, he would end their trysts, not to mention any chance of sharing Theda's bed again. But he knew himself better than that. If there was a way for him to spend more time in her company without bringing disaster down upon both their heads, he would. There was so little time left for the two of them; he wouldn't waste even a single morsel.

Back in his room, he washed up and changed. Before leaving, he spoke to Hob even though the gargoyle was currently resting in Kane's shield.

"If I can, I will bring Theda here tonight. I plan to teach her how to call you herself." He rubbed his chest as he spoke. "I don't know why, but I sense that it's important. I fear for her safety, and she might need to call upon you for protection."

He could feel Hob's sleepy agreement in the back of his mind; he would come if the pretty lady called. Good. Hob's reaction to anything new was always unpredictable, and Kane felt better knowing his companion would look after his lady.

Of course, that would last only as long as Kane and Averel remained in the city. Once they left to rejoin the other Damned, there would be no one she could turn to, no one who would stand between her and the duke. The thought of riding out and leaving Theda to her fate made him furious.

If only he could convince her to go with him. But asking her to abandon those she cared about would be like her asking Kane to break his oath to the goddess and his friends.

Outside, he nodded at the first guard he passed by but didn't stop to talk. When he reached the front entrance of Keirthan's keep, he found both guards sitting on a nearby bench. The men were too busy talking to notice Kane's approach.

"Gentlemen, care to tell me who is guarding the door?"

His deep voice rang out, drawing the attention of several other people in the area. Normally Kane preferred to handle any problems with those under his command quietly, if possible. Right now he had no patience for such niceties.

"Get back to where you belong. And since you have obviously forgotten what is expected of one of the duke's personal guard, you will remain on duty through the next shift. If I catch you slacking off again, you will receive ten lashes each."

One hustled back to resume his proper position by the door, but his partner protested. "But Sergeant Markus said we could accompany him into town tonight!"

Kane smiled and stepped closer, stopping right before the man's face. "Well, that's different."

The man started to nod, happy that he'd made his point. Then he froze, finally realizing that he'd just made a major mistake. Too late.

"I can see why you'd prefer to spend the night carousing with your friends instead of pulling a second shift of duty."

Kane paused to reach out and flick a piece of imaginary dust off the man's shoulder. "I just hope you remember all the fun you had tomorrow when I tie you to the post out in the bailey and order your good friend

Sergeant Markus to give you fifteen lashes on your bare back."

Kane smiled one last time. "It's up to you how you choose to spend your night, of course, but I'll be waiting anxiously to learn of your decision."

When Kane walked away, his mood was vastly improved.

Chapter 16

*T*heda slipped out of bed and quietly got dressed. She put on a simple gown designed so she could fasten its laces without help, adding only her slippers and her darkest cloak. She felt a bit wicked about leaving her undergarments in a pile on the floor, but then she did have seduction on her mind. Somehow she thought Kane would be appreciative rather than scandalized.

All was quiet in the hallway, and Theda arrived at where Tom guarded the door without encountering another soul. He frowned at her, clearly not happy about her frequent nighttime excursions, but he opened the door without comment.

Out in the garden, the air tasted fresh and clean. She drew a deep breath, enjoying the scent of the roses and lavender. Finding the bench empty was a disappointment. Surely Kane would come to her. Too restless to sit and wait, she kept moving, strolling through the garden and watching the shadows for her lover. When he hadn't appeared by her third pass through the gardens, she swallowed her disappointment and made her way back toward the door.

She was about to knock to signal Tom she was back when a man's hand clamped down on her mouth and his other arm encircled her waist. Her first instinct was to fight, but then Kane whispered near her ear, "I'm sorry I kept you waiting."

As soon as she relaxed against him, he released his hold on her. She spun to face him, relieved and delighted that he'd come.

"I know it can't always be easy for you to take time from your duties."

He leaned down to kiss her. "My duties to the duke be damned."

Perhaps, but his other duties would soon take him from her. Shoving that unhappy thought to the back of her mind, she placed her hands on his chest, kneading his muscles like a contented cat.

"Can we find someplace more private?"

Her words sounded husky even to her own ears. Kane's eyes flared wide, clearly understanding what she was really asking.

He nodded. "It's risky, but I was hoping you would accompany me to my quarters."

"Gladly."

He'd mentioned before that his rooms were not all that private, but then taking him through the keep to her quarters offered its own risks.

"We shouldn't tarry in my room for long, my lady, but I have something we need to do that can only be done there."

He was already leading her in the direction of the barracks. She'd do whatever he wanted, but she decided to tease him a bit. "Are you sure you can think of only one thing we can do together in your room? I was hoping for so much more."

Kane usually moved with such predatory grace, but her question caused him to stumble. He caught himself and then turned those pale eyes in her direction. It was difficult to judge his reaction, but then he smiled at her.

"I will endeavor to ensure you suffer no disappointments, but we must be cautious no matter what activities we pursue."

They'd reached the entrance to the building. "Wait here while I make sure it's safe."

He was gone but a few seconds. Inside the building, it was completely dark except for the faintest hint of moonlight from a window farther down the hallway.

Kane tugged her along, holding her hand in his as he led her through a small office and into his private quarters. The room contained only a small table, a chest for clothing, and a narrow bed. His shield sat propped in the corner.

He had left a single candle burning. Its small flame provided just enough light to cast Kane's face in harsh relief. Her heart sang to see the same needs reflected in his eyes that coursed through her veins. He might have other plans for them, but she couldn't think beyond the driving compulsion to take pleasure in each other's arms.

She let her cloak drop to the ground. Next, she kicked off her slippers, leaving her bare feet peeking out from under the hem of her gown. Before she could reach for the lacings on her dress, Kane stepped forward to wrap her in the iron-hard strength of his arms.

His kiss tasted of the night, cool and shadowy and mysterious. His tongue thrust against hers, teasing her with the promise of what was to come.

As his hands wandered across her back and down to her bottom, he froze. "Theda, what are you wearing beneath this gown?"

"Nothing at all," she answered, letting the heat licking at her skin show in her smile. "It seemed foolish to put on all those layers only to have to take them right back off again." She pulled her laces loose, letting the dress slip down off her shoulders to settle along the top curve of her breasts.

Kane groaned, his eyes following the slow descent of the soft fabric as she tugged it down even farther, leaving her bare to the waist. He immediately took control, sending her dress tumbling down around her ankles. Then he lifted her high enough to suckle her breast and leave her gasping for breath.

She threaded her fingers into his hair, pressing him closer, asking for so much more. When he raked the tips of his canine teeth across the sensitive skin, she shivered with delight and cried out.

He froze, his pale eyes flashing red in the dim light. "We must be quieter, Theda. Voices carry in the night."

Her breath caught in her throat as she whispered, "Your eyes, Kane. They're . . . they're red."

He immediately shut them and set her down at arm's length from him. When he started to back away even farther, she followed right after him.

Taking his hand in hers, she tried to cross the divide that had opened between them. "Kane, just explain. Don't shut me out."

He still refused to look at her, but at least he stopped his retreat. After tugging his hand free from hers, he brushed his fingertips across the mark on his face.

"It is a sign of the magic that I was born with. I forswore the curse of my grandfather's bloodline when I was but a youth. That doesn't mean I could wash my blood free of its taint. Even though I don't practice dark magic, it has still marked me in several ways."

He finally opened his eyes again, and they were back to their usual color. "In times of high emotion or danger, a little of the magic breaks free of its fetters."

As he spoke, he bent down to retrieve her dress and held it out, still being careful not to touch her. "Perhaps it would be better if we focused on my original purpose in bringing you here."

He'd carefully banked the fire that had burned so brightly between them only minutes before. She missed that connection, missed its heat and the promise of where it could take them both. Kane obviously expected her to reject him, and clearly that had been his experience in the past.

Theda hated that others had been careless with his heart. She knew right down to her bones that the cool reserve Kane showed to the world was how he protected his heart just as he carried a shield in battle to protect his body.

"Kane, there will be time enough to show me what you brought me to see." As she spoke, she took her gown from him and carefully folded it before setting it down on the table. She tried to act as if it were perfectly normal to be walking around nude in a man's room. She might have lost courage if she hadn't felt the hungry weight of Kane's gaze following her every move.

She half expected him to hold out her cloak next, but he didn't. That gave her hope that the wound she'd unintentionally inflicted wouldn't prove fatal to their original plans.

"I apologize for my thoughtless outburst, Kane. I truly meant no insult. I was just surprised."

As she spoke, she moved back toward him, allowing him to look his fill and reveling in being able to rekindle the desire in this man.

He shifted restlessly, clearly having an increasingly difficult time holding on to his hard-fought control. "It was no insult, Theda, but an unpleasant truth. There is no denying I carry the taint of dark magic. You are right to be repelled by it."

"You have it wrong, Kane." She shook her head. "I am neither repelled nor attracted by the magic. There is no denying it is a part of you, but it's not what defines you. What I value is your honor, your courage, and your gentleness."

He actually snorted in derision at that last comment. "Don't make me out to be something I'm not, Theda."

"I won't if you won't. You would never raise your hand to a child or a woman. You have spent centuries serving at the side of your friends as a warrior who fights for the gods. How does that make you a bad man?" She smiled at him again. "The right answer to that question is that it doesn't."

By moving slowly and steadily, she finally stood close enough to him that only a breath of air separated them now. He stood rock-still as she wrapped her arms around his waist and leaned in to his strength.

"Please don't let my outburst ruin tonight for us."

She drew a deep breath, savoring the sharp, clean

smell that was all male. Her patience was finally rewarded when Kane's arms encircled her, holding her close as if she were something precious.

When he pressed a soft kiss to her temple, she raised her face to his, asking without words for more. He granted her wish, brushing his lips across hers, softly at first, but then gradually giving in to his hunger for her.

Oh, yes, this is what she needed. The tension that had been thrumming through Kane took on a new feel, a new purpose.

"Do you still want this?" he murmured.

She answered the question he was really asking with brutal honesty. "I still want *you,* just as you are. I don't care what color your eyes are or what that mark on your cheek means. You are not your grandfather."

"He would have hated the man I've become."

She started untying the laces on Kane's tunic. "Then he was a fool. Now, make love to me, Kane. I've waited long enough."

Kane stared down at the woman—no, the miracle—in his arms. He had done his best to explain what he was, but she'd have none of it. In the past, he'd known women who wanted him to bed them because they liked the taste of danger. He'd learned early on to avoid such females because he hadn't liked the way he'd felt after coupling with them.

But Theda wasn't like them. When she looked up at him, those dark eyes were filled with an honesty that was just as seductive as her beauty. He let her continue stripping away his clothing just as her words stripped away the layers of protection he'd built up over the centuries.

He should have felt raw, too exposed to remove those final layers between them. Right now, all he could think about was how sweet it would be to lay her down and show her with his body what he couldn't find the words to say.

When she freed his cock from his trews, she smiled

happily, as if greeting a friend she hadn't seen in a long, long time. He knew just how she felt. It had been but two nights since they'd spent hours tangled up together in her bed. It felt like an eternity.

He wrapped her in his arms, kissing her as he backed her directly toward his cot. He wished he had a more suitable place to lay her down, but right now proximity outweighed any other requirement in a bed.

He took great care in lowering her down to the narrow mattress, wanting her to never doubt that he cherished the gift of her trust. He lay down beside her, keeping his eyes closed and letting his other senses guide him. The warm silk of her skin was such a stark contrast to his, and its scent went straight to his head, like the finest wine. Kissing the fluttering pulse point at her throat, he smiled.

Theda captured his face with her hands. "Kane, look at me."

He knew what she was asking, but still he hesitated. The nearly white color of his eyes, which marked him as an avatar of the gods, was strange enough. He would not subject her to the red glow that was the curse of his grandfather's dark magic. For centuries his control over it had been unshakable.

He had no idea if it was the link Keirthan had been forging between them or simply the riot of emotions that Theda herself had unleashed in his heart that left him feeling as if he were tumbling down the side of a mountain. The cause didn't matter, only the outcome. But his lady was nothing if not stubborn.

"Kane, don't hide who you are from me." She brushed his hair back from his face and added, "Please."

He breathed in, doing his best to regain his iron-willed control. Not sure how successful he'd been, he did as she asked and looked down at her pretty face. She rewarded his efforts with one of her bright smiles, bathing him in the warmth of her simple acceptance.

"That's better," she murmured. "Now, where were we?"

Theda studied him, nibbling her lower lip as her hand

wandered down his body, as if searching for the answer to her question. When she encountered the evidence of his aching desire for her, she gave him a smug look and murmured, "Ah, now I remember."

He couldn't help but laugh, the last of his dark mood gone as he showed his lady that he, too, remembered.

Despite Kane's belief that they shouldn't tarry long in his quarters, they'd made love twice. The first time had been slow at the start, but hard and fast at the finish. The second time had been gentle and sweet. Both were perfect.

But as Theda laced up her gown and put on her shoes, she felt the press of time, the minutes and hours sliding by with no way to slow their passage. She hated it and not just because dawn was approaching. Kane felt the same even though he hadn't said so. It was there in his lingering touches and the way he stared at her as if memorizing every detail of her face.

Right now he was fussing with his shield. After setting it on the rumpled bed, he stood back to look at it. He made one last adjustment, angling it to face the room.

"I need to show you something, Theda."

His voice was deeper than usual, a clear indication that his emotions were stirred up. She accepted his proffered hand and stood at his side.

"This is my shield."

That much was obvious. What was special about it that he wanted her to see? She studied the image emblazoned on its surface.

"It's a painting of Hob." She chuckled. "I'm surprised you could get him to sit still long enough to pose."

Kane led her closer. "It isn't a picture of him. It's truly Hob himself. This is where he rests when he isn't with me."

At first she thought Kane was teasing her, even though the picture was incredibly detailed and lifelike. She eased close enough to touch the glossy finish of the shield. The white background was cool to the touch, but the image itself was surprisingly warm. She traced the contour of Hob's throat down to his chest.

"I can feel each scale, and his skin is so warm. I could almost feel him breathe." Which was impossible.

Although Kane was staring at his shield, she suspected he was actually looking beyond it to his past. "Back when Captain Gideon and the other four of us swore to serve the Lord and Lady of the River, we were each granted an avatar of our own. The gods taught me a simple spell to release Hob each time we leave the river to walk once again in the world. The same spell returns him to the shield."

Where was he going with all of this?

He squeezed her hand. "I want to teach you how to call Hob forth if you should ever have need of him."

"I am honored, Kane, but you plan to leave soon, don't you?"

"Yes, I do. Not even my friends know the words that would summon Hob from my shield, but I sense it is important that you learn them. I want you to be protected. You should also know that my friend Averel is the troubadour at the Broken Sword. You can turn to him for help as well."

Once again Kane's eyes flashed red before returning to their usual color. "Look, I know this all seems strange, but I trust my instincts. Perhaps you are in no greater danger right now than usual, but I'd rather not take the risk."

She shivered, his words settling like a heavy burden on her shoulders. Unlike her brother-in-law, she had no love of magic. In her life, it had done far more harm than good. Yet she couldn't find it in her to deny Kane this new connection between them.

"Teach me."

He handed her a piece of parchment with a series of words spelled out. "I've asked Hob to ignore his summoning until you have practiced the spell a few times."

She studied the sentences written in a bold, masculine script. "I don't recognize any of these words."

"No reason you should. They're written in the language of my birth, which hasn't been spoken in more centuries than even I can remember. Once you have mastered them, I'll have you call Hob for real."

She hated the note of sorrow in Kane's voice. How many generations had come and gone in his long life? He wouldn't want her to fuss over him, though, so she concentrated on the words themselves.

She read them through once and then again after Kane corrected her pronunciation in a few places. On the fifth time through, she managed to twist her tongue around the odd letter combinations.

"That is perfect." Kane traced the words on the page with his finger. "It is the first time I've heard another person speak even that much of my native language in centuries. You have a gift for it."

She enjoyed his praise. "Shall we see if Hob feels the same way? He may not respond to me no matter how well I say the words."

Kane chuckled as he set the shield up a little straighter. "I don't think you have to worry. Hob is loyal to those he chooses to call friend. Besides, I told him what I was going to do earlier, and he agreed."

Despite Kane's assurance that this was all real and that Hob would somehow appear out of the shield, Theda still wasn't convinced. There was only one way to find out.

She stepped back to give Hob all the room she could. Holding the paper in fingers that weren't quite steady, she rehearsed the words one last time in her head before speaking them aloud. As soon as the last word fell from her lips, a flash of light nearly blinded her. She squeezed her eyes closed and waited for the spots to fade. But as she did, she heard the scrabble of claws on the wooden floor and felt the familiar bump against the side of her legs as Hob brushed past.

To make sure she hadn't imagined it, she pried one eye open and looked down. Sure enough, the gargoyle was standing next to his master, his tongue flicking in and out of his mouth.

"It worked!" She stared in wonder at the shield, which now held only the outline of Hob's body. "Truly the gifts of your gods are amazing!"

Kane looked less than sure of that, reminding her that the price of their gift had bound him and the others into their service for centuries of fighting with no end in sight. He patted his friend on the head.

"The hour grows late, and the longer we tarry, the greater the risk that one of the guards will see you leaving my quarters." He started for the door. "Give me a few seconds to ensure that no one is around."

Theda caught him before he opened the door. "Thank you for tonight, Kane."

He kissed her softly. "It is I who should be grateful, Theda. You have reminded me what it is that the Damned fight to protect."

Then he disappeared into the shadows.

Chapter 17

*G*ideon watched the men-at-arms during their sword practice. The two opposing lines surged forward and back again and again, the rhythmic clang of blade against blade and shield forming a drumbeat in his head.

He wished Kane were with him. The dark warrior had a gift for bringing out the best in even the most inexperienced trainees. But in truth, there was a gaping hole at Gideon's side where Kane usually stood. If Averel and Kane didn't return soon, he'd have no choice but to start the long trek toward the capital city without them.

Murdoch joined him, making his own assessment of their patched-together army.

"No matter how good they are, there aren't enough of them if the duke throws his entire garrison at us."

He wasn't telling Gideon anything he didn't already know. "True, but then we never expected to defeat Keirthan on the battlefield, and the bastard won't lead his army himself. A man who would attack blindly, unleashing a weapon without regard to where it will land, is a coward at heart."

Murdoch glanced back toward the keep. "You're thinking it will take magic to finally defeat him."

There was no use in denying it. "I well know your feelings on the subject, Murdoch, but we cannot fight what we cannot see."

He pulled his sword and held it up to glitter in the morning sunlight. "Steel is no defense against magic. You know that as well as I do. We'd all prefer an honest fight, man against man. And my instincts tell me that we will play an important role in this battle, else the Lord and Lady wouldn't have sent us to defend Merewen and the people of Agathia."

At that moment a cloud passed before the sun, casting them both in a small pool of shade and stealing the shine from Gideon's sword. He immediately sheathed it, hoping that wasn't a harbinger of things to come.

The cloud moved on, taking its shadow with it. They'd reached the end of the row of men. Turning back again, Gideon said, "Kane and Averel will leave within the week to return to us."

Murdoch nodded as he stared at the horizon, as if hoping to see their two friends riding toward them. "It will be good to be back to full strength again. We've never been apart for this long. That's the only explanation I can think of for how long it has taken me to heal."

Gideon stopped to face his friend. "You still suffer from the effects of your wounds?"

Murdoch rubbed his side as if easing a lingering pain. "I don't hurt, at least not often, but I do tire more easily."

Gideon motioned for them to keep walking, not wanting to draw unwanted attention from the troops. "I worry that we are both being pulled in two directions. So is Duncan, for that matter. I do not question your dedication to the Lady of the River, but there is too much at stake for either of us to risk failing in our duty to her. For the first time, three of us have another lady who has a strong claim on us. I wish I knew if that claim is weakening us in some way."

They walked on in silence as Murdoch mulled over Gideon's words. Finally, he said, "I cannot believe that loving someone is a weakness, Gideon. If anything, it has strengthened our resolve to end Keirthan's tyranny. Even the Lady of the River said so. Leaving Alina when I return to the river will be the hardest thing I've ever done, but I will rest easy if I have made this world safer for her."

That his friend's words echoed Gideon's own thoughts eased the knot of tension in his chest just enough to let him breathe more easily. He could only hope that the return of Averel and Kane would bring all of them back to full strength. When they took the fight to Keirthan, they would need every bit of resolve and strength they could bring to bear.

"Have the men switch partners one last time and then let them rest. We'll practice again after the heat of the afternoon sun has eased."

"Where will you be?"

Gideon grimaced. "I have to go convince the cook to begin preparations to feed a small army for the long march to the capital city."

To his chagrin, Murdoch bellowed in laughter. "You do that. Personally, I'd rather face off against Kane in a bad mood than cross Ellie."

Gideon couldn't help but grin back. "Would you think me a coward if I asked Merewen to accompany me to the kitchen?"

The big man clapped him on the shoulder. "No, my friend. I would think you wise."

Was Markus up to something? Granted, he had every right to leave, since Kane's arrival in the great hall signaled the end of the sergeant's day. There'd just been something off about the way the man had gone out of his way to avoid speaking to Kane on his way out of the great hall.

Unable to shake his suspicions, Kane waited a few minutes and then left the keep by way of the side door near the garden. He strolled alongside the building until he reached the front entrance. No sign of Markus anywhere. Although he'd rather not alert his target of his interest in his activities, it would be simpler to ask one of the guards on duty which way Markus had gone.

Luckily, none of the sergeant's closest cronies were on duty. Kane kept his movements casual and relaxed.

"Did either of you see which direction Sergeant Markus went when he left?"

The guards both pointed toward the city. "He went that way, Captain. Do you want one of us to fetch him for you?"

"No, that's fine. I just wanted to review the new duty schedule with him. It can wait. If anyone asks for me, I'll be in my office."

Kane headed toward the barracks to give credence to his claim. The odds of anyone looking for him right now were minimal. The guards had all just started their shifts. If there'd been a problem, he would have already heard about it. If the duke had need of him, Stefan would've let him know as soon as he'd walked into the hall. That left him free to go after Markus, but he would need Hob's help to pick up the man's trail in the crowded city. The only question was whether it was worth the risk. He could only imagine the chaos if the fine citizens of Agathia were to get their first clear look at a gargoyle prowling their streets.

His instincts argued this would be his best chance to discover something to use against Keirthan and his magic. Kane's time in the city was growing short. Soon he and Averel would have to leave and return to Lady Merewen's keep to join the rest of the Damned in preparations for the battle to destroy Keirthan's hold over his people.

He slipped into the barracks through the back door and headed for Markus's desk. He needed something of the sergeant's to give Hob the man's scent. A piece of clothing would be best. Luck was with him because Markus kept an extra tunic in the top drawer. Kane wadded it up and stuck it inside his vest before heading down the hallway to his own quarters.

Inside his room, Kane quickly released Hob from the shield and gave the gargoyle a minute to stretch out the stiffness in his body from being confined for so long. Then he knelt down to face his avatar and held out the shirt. "We hunt, my friend."

Hob immediately buried his muzzle in the soft fabric and took several deep breaths. Then he grabbed it in his teeth and shook it like a rat, growling deep in his throat. Kane stood back to give the gargoyle more room to maneuver. In seconds, the tunic was torn to shreds.

Kane picked up the pieces and tossed them in the fireplace in the outer office. After checking the hall outside the door, he motioned for Hob to follow him. It was still too light to risk parading Hob through the city streets, which left them only one option. To follow Markus's trail, the two of them would have to take to the rooftops.

They skirted the edge of the practice field, staying just inside the tree line. While Hob kept his nose to the ground, Kane used his keen eyesight to ensure their passage went undetected. After a couple of close calls, they finally reached the alley that paralleled the first street crossing the route that Markus had taken when he'd left the keep.

Kane knelt down at his partner's side. "Can you find him?"

Hob's forked tongue flicked in and out of his mouth several times in rapid succession as he tasted the air. He waddled a few steps farther and turned his head from side to side, repeating the process. Kane watched, waiting for Hob to point the way. It didn't take long.

Interesting that this was the road that led to the same gate Kane had used to enter the city after his last ride with Averel. It was also the one closest to the secret tunnel he'd discovered. Could it be that Markus was headed there? It was almost too much to be hoped. But as they continued on, the scent grew strong enough for Kane to know they were on the right path. A few minutes later, they reached the wall that surrounded the city. The question now was how to get Hob out of the city without being seen. He'd have to create a distraction that would draw all of the guards' attention.

"Hob, stay until I whistle."

Satisfied the gargoyle would do as he asked, he

grabbed the back edge of the roof and dropped back down to street level. Once there, he studied the line of people and vehicles waiting to leave the city. The best prospect was a group of three horse-drawn wagons. He picked up a handful of small rocks and flung them one by one at the lead horse, putting all his considerable strength behind each throw. Although the jagged stones would sting, they would do no permanent harm to the animal. Just as Kane had hoped, the horse reared up, trying to get away from the uncomfortable barrage.

When it couldn't break free of its traces, the draft animal lunged forward, dragging the wagon right into the path of another caravan that had been cleared to enter the city. Within seconds, the drivers from both groups were down on the ground screaming at each other as the guards pushed their way into the argument. While they tried to sort out the tangled mess, Kane fell into step with a group of pedestrians as they walked out of the gate. He gradually fell back, letting the distance between him and his temporary companions increase. When they followed a curve in the road, he quickly cut back to the city wall.

Once he reached the safety of some scrub brush, he whistled three times, paused briefly, and then whistled one last time. Within seconds, Hob came flowing over the top of the city wall. Now that they were together again, Kane stepped aside to let Hob determine which direction Markus had gone.

The scent was strongest straight ahead on the trade road, which made no sense. Where would he be going out that way with no horse? It didn't matter. If he wanted answers, Kane had no choice but to follow. Past the next bend in the road, he found his answer. Markus had cut across country as soon as he was out of sight of the guards on the gate, heading straight for the hillock that held the entrance to the tunnel.

With Hob at his side, Kane took off running, hoping to close the distance between them and their quarry. As they ran, he watched the horizon ahead to make sure he didn't overtake Markus before he reached his destination. A few minutes later, he spotted him and immediately dropped to the ground when the sergeant abruptly stopped to look back. Was he sensing Kane on his trail or simply being cautious?

Kane remained where he was for several minutes, finally easing up slowly to look around. Markus was nowhere in sight, but there was little doubt where he was headed. Kane crossed the remaining distance at full speed.

He motioned for Hob to hang back as Kane cautiously approached the small hillock, listening hard for a sign of anyone in the area. The only heartbeats he could hear were his own and Hob's much slower one. Drawing his sword, Kane edged closer to the door and tried the handle. Unlocked. Good. It would save him the trouble of having to break in.

Inside the tunnel, the air smelled of fresh candle wax and smoke. Markus must have used the light to find his way through the tunnel. Despite the absolute darkness, Kane had no such need. That didn't mean Hob liked it. He bumped Kane's leg and whined.

Kane put his hand on the gargoyle's scaly shoulder. He never knew how much Hob actually understood and how much he picked up from the tone in his master's voice. Kane aimed for calm when he spoke. "I know you don't like being underground, boy, but I've got no choice. This might give us the answers we need."

Then he started forward, stopping every few feet to listen. Hob stuck close to his side, the flutter of his vestigial wings reflecting his increasing agitation, but he kept pace with Kane.

The tunnel stretched on ahead for some distance, gradually sloping downward, which came as no surprise. After all, it had to be deep enough to pass under the city wall and the streets beyond. Kane kept moving forward and down, focusing on his target. Like Hob, he'd always hated closed-in spaces, and right now he could feel the heavy weight of the ground above him pressing down.

It was tempting to turn back and wait for Markus to return. But Kane kept going, counting his steps to judge how far the tunnel traveled under the city, although he had his suspicions. It would be just like Keirthan to have a bolt-hole that would allow him to escape if the city came under attack. Kane was betting the tunnel led straight to Keirthan's underground chambers.

Once Kane knew for sure, he'd retreat and figure out how best to collapse the tunnel to permanently plug that hole. It would be the last thing he did before he and Averel left the city to rejoin their friends.

He moved forward, slower now, his movements more deliberate, with longer pauses between every few steps. If he was right about where the tunnel led, he had to be drawing close to its end. During one pause, he realized he was rubbing his chest, the pulsing ache a clear signal that he was approaching the center of Keirthan's power. When he started forward again, his cheek burned hot as his steps sped up with little regard for stealth.

He needed to slow down or, better still, retreat to safety, taking Hob with him. The danger that waited ahead could very well destroy them both. Inside his mind, he screamed an order for his feet to stop moving, but his body refused to obey. His face dripped with sweat as he fought against the relentless pull, his body no longer his to command. Hob planted himself in front of Kane, trying to block his way. It didn't work. The tangle of magic coming from ahead dragged him on and on.

The darkness was no longer absolute. The dim glow in the distance grew brighter even as the compulsion to hurry grew stronger. Kane struggled to break free of the invisible chains that held him in thrall before it was too late.

He focused all of his willpower on his feet, infusing the effort with only the smallest bit of the magic he carried in his bones. At best, its effect on slowing his forward progress was minimal. With his next attempt, he used more of the power he'd spent a lifetime denying. His body jerked to a stumbling halt; he even managed a step or two backward. The small victory wouldn't last long. He had to use what time he had to the best advantage, beginning with sending Hob back to safety. There was no way to know what would happen to the gargoyle if Kane were to die at Keirthan's hands, but his best chance for survival was back in the shield.

"I'm sorry, Hob. I hope we both live to hunt together another day."

He whispered the words to send Hob back. Nothing happened. He drew a ragged breath and tried again, this time saying the words with more force. A flash of light nearly blinded him, but when he opened his eyes, he was alone in the tunnel. "Thank you, Lady. Keep him safe for me." The effort left him winded, but this was no time to stop for a rest. He retreated another few steps. Each time took less effort, which scared him almost as much as the compulsion to move forward. Either way, the dark magic was in control. The only difference was in its source. Was it Duke Keirthan's or from Kane's own bloodline?

How could he fight against himself?

That single moment of doubt snapped the tenuous thread of control he had. Once again he lurched forward, the light growing brighter with each step. As the blackness clouded his mind, he managed one last prayer.

My Lady, I have failed you. Forgive my weakness and tell Gideon this was not his fault. Keep my friends safe and let them find peace. And if you have any fondness for me at all, watch over Lady Theda in my stead.

Chapter 18

*I*fre had been strolling through the great hall, allowing his nobles the illusion that he was actually concerned about their petty problems. Would they never cease their endless prattle? Did they truly believe that he cared about the quality of this year's wool or if their peasants had enough to eat for the winter?

He realized Lord Bacca was waiting for an answer.

"Have my secretary make note of the problem. If there's a way we can assist you, he will let you know."

Ifre walked away before the blustering idiot could do more than sputter, "Thank you, my lord."

Ifre looked around the hall for some sign of Theda. She'd always been better at diplomacy than he was. Perhaps he'd been wrong to do so much to destroy her credibility in his court. Mayhap he should do what he could to restore it, so that she could shoulder the burden of dealing with all of these fools. He toyed with the idea, deciding he liked it. The hunger of his creation called to him all the time now. It took nearly all of his time and energy to keep it fed.

It would help if he could improve the quality of the sacrifices he made, but those with even a hint of magic in their blood were growing increasingly rare. That left him no choice but to increase the quantity of the blood sacrifices.

The sound of feminine voices broke through his dark thoughts. Ah, yes, Theda's ladies-in-waiting were walking down the stairs for their nightly appearance in his court.

Their mistress wouldn't be far behind. She guarded over her friends with such fierce determination.

He allowed it because as long as she protected them, they would remain virginal. Their very purity made them valuable to him as potential sacrifices. After all, the blackness craved innocence as much as it craved magic.

Theda finally appeared at the top of the stairs. But instead of immediately joining her charges, she paused to look around the room from above. From the frown on her face, she was looking for someone specific. Who would that be? It clearly wasn't her young companions, because her gaze swept right past them. Had someone in the court actually befriended her?

Before Ifre could discern her intended target, she realized he was watching. Instantly, her face resumed its usual blank expression, the mask she thought hid her anger and hatred. He smiled at her, enjoying the small shudder of revulsion she couldn't quite hide even from that distance.

He raised his hand to summon her to his side. She nodded in acknowledgment and started down the steps. When she noticed her ladies were waiting for her, she waved them away. The crowd ignored her as she walked toward him. That would have to change if she was going to be of more use to him.

Perhaps all it would take was banishing the next person who openly showed her disrespect. That would serve the dual purpose of improving Theda's standing within his court and at the same time reminding his courtiers that their favor in his eyes could change in a heartbeat.

"You have need of me, my lord?"

Before he could respond, the darkness in the labyrinth below his feet flared hot and hungry. The power behind the surge left Ifre dizzy and disoriented. He managed to grab onto Theda's shoulder for support as he fought to keep his balance.

"Ifre, are you all right?"

Her words echoed as if coming from the bottom of a

deep well. What kind of stupid question was that? Of
course he wasn't all right. At the moment, he was blind
and nearly deaf. What was happening down below?

He was dimly aware of being led to a nearby bench.
When he felt it against the back of his knees, he gave up
all pretense of standing and sank down onto its cush-
ioned surface. As soon as he sat down, the floor settled
under his feet. Slowly, he fought the darkness back under
control until at last he could make sense of its babblings.

Someone had invaded his private sanctuary! Two people, actually, but the first one was Sergeant Markus, who
was supposed to be there. He would never be stupid
enough to bring anyone with him. So that meant he'd
been careless enough to allow himself to be followed.
The stupid bastard would pay for that.

But right now Ifre was more concerned about his uninvited guest. He needed to get down there. Now, before
his weapon lost all control.

"Ifre, sip this wine."

Theda shoved the drink into his hand and then actually guided it to his lips. He allowed it only because he
didn't have the strength to do otherwise. Gradually, the
darkness cleared, his vision returning. He blinked up at
Theda and then looked around the silent room.

"I am fine," he whispered, his voice little better than a
rasp. After another sip of the wine, he tried again, this
time his voice carrying across the room.

"I am fine. Quit staring and go about your business."

Everyone except for Theda and the guardsmen who
had rushed to protect him from the perceived attack immediately turned their backs and began talking among
themselves. As long as he sat there, he appeared weak
and vulnerable. He dredged up the strength to stand.

One of the younger guards remained in front of him,
blocking his view of the room. "Shall we help you to
your quarters, Sire, and fetch your physician?"

"No, and you may return to your posts." He reluctantly added, "Thank you for your concern. I will make sure Captain Kane learns of your prompt response."

The guard bowed and withdrew, leaving only Theda to deal with. He glared up at her. "What are you staring at?"

The note of concern he'd thought he'd heard in her voice was clearly gone. No doubt it had been a momentary weakness on her part.

She took the wineglass he held out to her. "What would you have me do? You had indicated you wanted to speak to me."

"That will have to wait. I have other business I need to see to right now."

He pushed himself up to his feet and was relieved to find the dizziness was gone. "For now, entertain my guests."

Normally, he would have taken a more circuitous route to the door leading down to the chambers below, but there was no time for subterfuge right now. The darkness could strike out at any second, once again leaving Ifre at its mercy.

His hands still trembled, so it took him several tries to get the key in the lock and open the door. He relocked it from the other side and then hurried down the passageway. He pulled up short of the entrance to the hall that housed the altar to school his expression into a blank mask similar to the one that Theda always wore around him. The hunger fed off Ifre's fear as well as anyone else's.

Taking one last deep breath, he started forward at a sedate pace. But as he walked, he prayed for strength. If he didn't somehow regain full control over his creation and soon, he might well be the next one to fall prey to its hunger.

Kane fought with everything he had, but still the dark compulsion dragged him forward until at last he stumbled out of the tunnel into a circular chamber with a high, vaulted ceiling. A movement over near a fire pit caught his attention briefly. It was Markus, not exactly a surprise. Neither was the cart loaded with dead bodies. But even with his sword grasped tightly in his hand, Kane was helpless to do anything but stare at the man.

A tangle of black threads streamed across the room to wrap themselves around Kane, head to toe. Their relentless pull had Kane moving toward a raised platform at the near end of the chamber. The bloodstained altar was bad enough, but the true horror was the malevolence hovering above it. Its red eyes flared wide as it smiled down at him. In a voice that grated on the ear, it rasped, "Lord Kane, welcome. I've been waiting for you."

A name arose out of the deepest recesses of Kane's long memory. He'd faced this enemy before, lending the strength of his inborn magic to his grandfather to bind the entity and send it back to the netherworlds where it belonged. He spat out the name as if it were poison.

"Damijan."

The crimson eyes blinked and the smile widened. "Ah, yes. The name your people gave me. I've been trying to remember who I am. That is not my true name, but it will do."

As Kane continued to struggle against the hold Damijan had on him, he hadn't forgotten about Markus. Right now, he was creeping across the stone floor, probably hoping to bolt for the passageway, while leaving the cart and its gruesome load behind. Coward. But before the sergeant had gone more than a few steps, Keirthan made his presence known. When had he entered the room?

"Sergeant Markus, stop where you are."

He'd made it almost to the tunnel, but he stopped short of his goal.

"Come here."

Keirthan's words were spoken softly yet carried across the room with amazing clarity. Still ignoring Kane, Markus circled around the fire pit to stand before Duke Keirthan. Damijan floated over to hover behind his master's shoulder.

"Yes, my lord?"

Keirthan gestured toward Kane, who remained frozen in place before the altar. "Would you care to explain to me how Captain Kane came to be here?"

Markus swallowed hard. "He must have followed me from the city, although I don't know how. I waited to leave the great hall until he was on duty. I never take the same route through town to the gate, and there's no way he could have followed my trail through the crowds."

The duke's eyes narrowed. "And yet there he is. How, then, do you explain his presence here?"

Kane almost felt sorry for Markus. By leading him to Keirthan's chambers, the sergeant may have signed his own death warrant.

"I cannot explain it, Sire."

The duke looked disgusted. "How did he act when he arrived?"

"He was moving strangely when he entered the room, as fighting a compulsion. I'm not sure he even realized I was here. At least not at first."

"Interesting." The duke started toward Kane, but paused to glance back at Markus. "Come here, and draw your weapon in case he decides to attack."

Markus did as he was ordered. Both men stared at Kane as if he were a piece of sculpture, not a warrior who would gut them both the second he broke free of these invisible bonds.

Kane focused briefly on the altar and then turned to meet Markus's gaze. Judging from the rank fear pouring off the sergeant, Kane knew his own eyes burned with flickers of red, and the mark on his cheek was hot and pulsing. Markus looked a bit sick.

Keirthan, by way of contrast, couldn't have looked more pleased. He leaned in close to Kane to study the mark. "Ah, Captain, I see that you do indeed possess your grandfather's gift for mage craft. How delightful! I suspected you had misled me about your inheritance from your grandfather. Perhaps you've thought it was of little value, but that's about to change."

The duke rubbed his hands together, looking more like a greedy child than the ruler of Agathia.

"You see, Kane, I was born with a lesser gift than either my father or my brother." He paused to point in the direction of the dark cloud over the altar. "But as you can tell, I have honed my gift razor sharp and strengthened my power a thousandfold. Imagine what I will accomplish when I add your strength to my own."

For the first time, Kane moved, shaking his head slowly from side to side. He growled, "I would die first."

"True, you will die, but not at first and hopefully not for a long time. I'm guessing my creation will find the taste of your blood quite satisfying. What did you call him? Damijan?"

"His name means 'death' and for good reason. And it will start with yours."

The memory of Damijan's name dredged up more of Kane's lessons from his grandfather. He'd rejected them, but right now they might be his only chance of breaking free of Damijan's hold on him. Kane turned his fury back on himself, twisting it around the blackest memories from his past to grasp a blade of magic. Screaming words of power, he shattered his bonds, the black threads snapping back at Damijan. Next he brought his fist up to connect with Keirthan's cheek, sending him flying backward to bounce off the altar.

He came close to gutting Markus, but he was still moving more slowly than usual. The sergeant belatedly blocked Kane's attack, dancing back out of reach. As it was, Kane managed to slip past his guard long enough to slice open Markus's forearm. The sergeant yelled in pain and charged right back, but just as the two of them collided again, the duke intervened from where he'd scrambled to safety on the far side of the altar.

"Sergeant, kill him and you'll take his place!"

Knowing it wasn't an idle threat, Markus once again retreated a few steps, still fending off Kane's blows.

Keirthan wasn't done interfering. "Keep him distracted long enough for me to ensnare him again."

Markus shot the duke an incredulous look as he continued to block Kane's blows. Unfortunately for him, Kane was picking up speed quickly.

"Let me past, Markus, and you'll live."

The guard shook his head. "You can't promise that, Captain. I won't die for you. Not down here."

And they both knew that was what Keirthan had planned for Kane, which was why he should be more intent on reaching Keirthan than on hurting Markus. By now, the duke was chanting, the words grating on the ear like two jagged stones rubbing against each other. Kane did his best to counter the spell, but with Damijan's help, the duke entrapped him again, leaving him frozen in place

"Take his sword and check him for weapons."

After Markus pried Kane's sword from his fingers and stripped him of his knives, the duke cautiously approached Kane. Markus stood back, his sword still at the ready in case Kane broke free again.

Damijan still hung over the altar, but now the black cloud was spinning and spinning. Yet even as it twirled in the air, those eyes remained fixed on Kane.

Keirthan's laughter rang out over the room, but Markus clearly saw no humor in the situation. For an instant, Kane thought maybe Markus was tempted to use his sword, but who would be his target? If he killed Kane to prevent the duke from using him, Markus would die screaming on that altar in his place. If instead he turned his weapon on the duke himself, there was no way to know how that malevolence by the altar would react.

Finally, he lowered his sword and stepped back. Keirthan smiled at the sergeant.

"A wise decision, Markus. I would hate to lose both you and the captain from my service at the same time."

Keirthan walked all the way around Kane, studying

him from every angle. "I will need your help lifting him up on the altar. Once we have attached the chains and stripped off his uniform, you can go about your business. Given Kane's strength of will, I doubt I will have need of your services down here for a good long while. I'm sure that pleases you."

Markus met Kane's gaze one last time and then did as the duke asked.

Kane awoke to the sensation of smooth marble at his back and cold steel on his ankles and wrists. Without even opening his eyes, he recognized the dread chill of Keirthan's blood magic. By now he'd grown accustomed to its oily stench, which permeated the entire keep, but he'd never been this close to the source of Keirthan's power. It washed over him in waves, lapping at his skin with greedy little licks and whispered promises of pain and death.

His instincts took over, leaving him straining against the heavy shackles. He threw his considerable strength into the effort, yanking and pulling against his fetters until his skin was bruised and dripping blood. His efforts got him nowhere, but he refused to surrender without a fight. To do anything else was a failure, an affront to his own personal honor.

A voice stabbed into his mind. *"Don't speak to us of honor, Lord Kane. You are nothing but a common mercenary, one who sells his sword to the highest bidder. You were a disappointment to your grandfather, and now you will disappoint your friends and your gods."*

"Lies! All lies!" he shouted back. "It is Keirthan who has no honor!"

The cloud above him stopped spinning as the eyes within it stared down at Kane. *"True, but he has power. All will bow before us once I drink in the rich gift of your magic and your blood. You've wasted the power you were born with, but I will put it to good use."*

Damijan laughed again, sounding like a greedy child. *"Keirthan has also promised me virgins. Their innocence*

*shall be mine to take. Their undoing will release me from
the chains that deny me entrance to this world even as
your shackles hold you down on my altar. Killing Keirthan's enemies will be a small price to pay for my freedom. See for yourself the future that awaits your friends."*

Images filled Kane's head of Theda's ladies-in-waiting
being led to the slaughter. Next he saw Gideon and his
friends fighting a leather-skinned monstrosity that howled
with joy as it cut them to pieces. Its eyes were the same as
the ones that now watched his every move.

No, there had to be another way. His faith in the
power of the Lady of the River and in the courage of his
fellow Damned ran deep, giving Kane hope. Remember-
ing the darkness fed off fear and anger, Kane smiled
back at his tormentor.

"Even with your help, the duke cannot, will not defeat
the forces that now gather to stand against him. He is a
coward, not a warrior. You've chosen your weapon badly
because he will snap like poorly tempered steel, sending
you right back to the netherworld that spawned you."

Kane believed that was true in the depths of his soul,
but his friends would need him at their sides when the
Damned finally brought the fight to Keirthan's gate. Even
more important, Theda needed him to protect her and
her friends from Keirthan's plans for them.

*"You are right, of course. Keirthan is a poor vessel,
one made of inferior metal, but he suits my purposes. If
I had chosen one such as you to build my path to freedom, it would have been a battle to take a single step.
Once I break free, I will drink his essence, swill that it is.
But you, Lord Kane, I will savor as a vintner does a rare
vintage."*

Suddenly, the hold on Kane's mind disappeared. He
blessed the silence, but the respite didn't last for long.
He'd been so intent on the words in his mind that he
hadn't heard the duke return. That explained the abrupt
end to their conversation. Obviously, the monster didn't
want his puppet to learn of his plans for him.

The duke grasped Kane's arm and studied it. "Ah, Captain, you have regained consciousness, but I see that you've managed to damage yourself. You shouldn't waste your energy or your blood, especially when I have pressing need for them both."

Kane ignored him, turning his eyes to the side to stare out toward the fire pit. The fool liked the sound of his own voice far too much.

"I'm surprised that you're not threatening me. Have you already surrendered to the inevitable? Don't tell me that the image you portray of a great warrior is nothing but posturing? That would greatly disappoint me."

Kane smiled at Keirthan, flashing his long canines, not caring if his eyes burned red or his mage mark pulsed with magic. "You know nothing of what it means to be a warrior and a man of honor. Regardless of my fate, you will face the judgment of the gods. When that happens, you will crawl on your belly and beg for mercy like the coward that you are."

Damijan laughed. Kane had no idea if his captor heard it and didn't care. Keirthan flushed red with fury and pulled a knife from his belt. He leaned down close enough that Kane could smell the wine on his breath.

"Do not think you can provoke me into killing you quickly, Kane. Your insults carry no weight, and your gods are helpless to save you."

He pressed the tip of the knife against Kane's chest. "You will bleed tonight, Kane, and you will scream even if you hold out longer than most. Watching you struggle to maintain your dignity and that honor you are so proud of will provide hours of amusement for me."

When he finished his taunt, Keirthan made a shallow cut in Kane's skin, a wound designed to bleed but not cause irreparable harm. When Keirthan laid the knife against the wound, it drank deeply of Kane's blood, turning the steel a dark crimson.

Kane's ability to heal slowly closed the wound, shutting

off the supply of blood to the knife. Instead of Keirthan getting angry over being thwarted, he smiled, clearly delighted.

"Lovely, Captain. I had no idea you had a talent for healing yourself. Think how much longer we'll be able to play together!"

As he made a second slash and then a third, the knife soaked up Kane's blood as the cloud that was Damijan pulsed darker and darker.

Theda circled the hall a fourth time, stopping to talk to a few people as she made her rounds. Her brother-in-law had returned briefly, only to disappear a second time through the door leading to his lair below the keep. She didn't miss his company, but she worried about what was keeping him occupied down there.

She was even more worried because Kane had yet to put in an appearance. When they'd parted company an hour before dawn, she was sure he'd told her he'd be on duty this evening. Even if she was wrong about that, he usually stopped by to make sure the guards were doing their job. And she liked to think he also came to see her, even if only from across the room.

Odd, though, that Sergeant Markus was also conspicuously absent. Normally, he was around if Kane wasn't. Had something happened that required the attention of both men? If so, surely she would have heard something. The courtiers lived to gossip, and she would've heard if any rumors were making their way through the crowd.

After slowly circling the room, she stepped outside to look around. The air was cool, and the sun hovered right above the horizon. Its fiery light painted the city crimson. On another day, in a different time, she might have found the sight beautiful.

Tonight it left her chilled and afraid. Was she jumping at shadows? She'd lived with fear as a constant companion ever since her husband's death, but right now it threatened to overpower her. Why? She studied her surroundings but could perceive no obvious threat. The guards were at their posts, scanning the area for danger. Their stance was attentive, not concerned.

So what was bothering her?

Experience had taught her that it wasn't wise to show too much interest in any particular individual because it gave Ifre another weapon to use against her. He'd already sent her stepson away from the city and refused to tell her where he was. In her darkest moments, she feared he was already lost. But until she knew for sure, she would do nothing to further endanger him.

Margaret and Lydia would soon leave the city. She prayed nothing happened to interfere with their plans. Ifre grew more unstable with each passing day. Soon no one would be safe within the city walls, and she wanted her young friends as far from danger as possible.

But for Kane's sake, she was willing to take the risk of drawing Ifre's attention to her interest in the captain. She studied the two guards briefly. She picked the younger one to approach for no other reason than he nodded as she passed by.

When she walked toward him, his shoulders snapped back to attention. "Is there something you needed, my lady?"

The respectful greeting surprised her. He certainly hadn't learned that from Markus. "Yes. I was wondering if you had seen either Sergeant Markus or Captain Kane. I need to talk to one of them."

Preferably Kane, but it was better the guard not know that.

"I saw Sergeant Markus come out of the hall and walk toward the city some hours ago right after Captain Kane came on duty. The captain himself came out shortly after that and asked after the sergeant. When I told him where the sergeant had gone, he went to his office to work. Shall I send word that you have need of him?"

"No. That's not necessary. The matter can wait until I

see him tomorrow." She smiled at the young guard. "Thank you for your help."

She returned to the great hall, not sure what she should do next. It appeared that everything was as it should be. If Markus was off duty, he was entitled to spend time in the city.

It seemed odd, though, that Kane had been looking for Markus when they'd both been in the hall only minutes before. Knowing she wouldn't rest easily until she knew for sure Kane was safe, she made her way to the side door by the garden. She stopped short of her goal, realizing it was too early for Tom to be there.

If she walked outside now, she'd have to pass by another guard, who might report her movements to Ifre, but it was worth the risk. It was imperative that she find Kane immediately, even if she was unsure why the compulsion to do so was so strong. After all, he was a warrior and capable of defending himself.

But her mind kept turning back to the previous night, when Kane had felt compelled to teach her how to call Hob from his shield. At the time, he'd thought she might need Hob for her own protection, but what if he had it backward? What if his goddess had sensed he was the one who would be in danger, and Kane had misunderstood?

If he was fine and simply doing paperwork, well, she'd live with the embarrassment. Theda drew herself up and walked out the door without hesitation. Just as expected, there was a guard standing slouched against the wall to the right of the door.

He barely acknowledged her, a reaction typical of the men Ifre hired to protect the keep. She swept past the guard, ignoring him in return.

Rather than heading directly for Kane's quarters, she took a more indirect route through the garden. Once she was out of sight, she lifted the front of her skirts and ran, slowing only when she reached the far edge of the garden.

There, she paused to study her surroundings. Two

guards were just leaving the stable, forcing her to retreat a few steps until they were gone. Drawing a deep breath, she started forward again, constantly on the lookout for anyone in the area. She made it as far as the door Kane had taken her through last night.

Thank the gods, it was unlocked, and she hurried inside. Once again, luck was with her. The hallway was empty even though she could hear men talking in the distance. By the time she reached the door to Kane's office, her knees were shaking.

He wasn't at his desk, and the candle was cold, making it unlikely he'd been there recently. Pressing her ear against the door to his bedroom, she heard nothing but more silence.

What if he was merely sleeping? Rather than barge in, she knocked softly on the door, calling, "Kane? Are you in there?"

No answer. She cracked open the door and looked in. The room was empty, the bed neatly made. Kane's shield hung on the wall, and Hob had returned to rest in it. Rather than immediately retreat, she walked over to the shield and reached out to caress Hob's head.

"I wish you could tell me where your master is, Hob. I'm worried about him."

As soon as her fingers touched the warmth of Hob's image, a jolt of dizzying pain burned up her arm, sending Theda to her knees. She held her burning hand against her breast and struggled to make sense of what had just happened.

It wasn't her pain she'd felt; nor did it make sense that it was Hob's. That left only one horrifying alternative: It was Kane's, and the gargoyle was feeling it through his connection to his master. Wherever Kane was, he was in agony.

Her worst fear had come true. Ifre had captured Kane and now held him prisoner in the chambers below the keep. He couldn't have been there long—a few hours at best. A warrior like Kane wouldn't break easily. What had her bastard of a brother-in-law done to him in such a short time to leave Kane screaming like that?

She rocked in grief, her soul sick with the idea. Her distress had her stomach churning until she started retching. After losing her dinner, the dry heaves kept her bent double for a long time. It seemed forever before the waves of nausea abated.

Ifre had already taken too much from her. She would not let him take Kane, too. Rising to her feet, she sat down on the edge of the bed, taking comfort from the memories they'd created there only hours before. Thinking about Kane helped to calm her mind; she'd have to have a clear head if she was going to find a way to free her lover from Keirthan's clutches.

The first step would be to figure out the best plan of attack. She rose to her feet, ignoring her fear and concentrating on what had to be done.

On her way out, she once again paused to offer Hob the comfort of her touch. "Hob, tell Kane to hang on. We'll be coming for him soon."

And although she was raised in a different faith, she added a prayer. "Dear Lady, please watch over your warrior and give me the strength to do what needs to be done. He deserves better than to die at the hands of a coward like Ifre."

Maybe it was only her imagination, but as she stepped out into the gathering darkness, she could have sworn she heard a woman's voice whisper in the back of her mind, *"That he does, Lady Theda, but hurry. Time grows short for all of the Damned."*

Chapter 19

Gideon jerked upright, gasping for breath. His chest was covered in chevrons of shallow cuts, and his blood poured down his rib cage to drip on the marble surface beneath him. He spread his hands on his chest in a futile attempt to stanch the flow of his life's blood.

He struggled to make sense of the confusion. His skin was hot to the touch, but whole and dry. Gideon held his palms up to his eyes to make sure. No blood. No open wounds. No marble surface either, but a soft mattress. Had it all been a dream? If so, he'd never experienced one so real.

Merewen stirred and blinked up at him sleepily. "Is everything all right?"

"I don't know."

Before he could explain, there was a knock at the door. "Gideon, are you awake?"

Hearing the worry in Murdoch's voice deepened Gideon's own growing sense of dread. "Stay here, Merewen. I'll explain when I can."

He reluctantly left the bed. Without bothering to grab his clothes, he yanked open the door to find both Murdoch and Duncan waiting there. Both were barefoot and wearing nothing but their trews. Like him, they were breathing hard, as if they'd been running long distances over rough ground. They also had matching sets of red welts on their chests. He glanced down to verify that his skin bore the same marks.

He asked the obvious question, needing to hear the

truth from his friends. "Did you both feel as if your chest had been sliced open, and you were bleeding?"

Murdoch merely nodded, but Duncan said, "I woke up screaming. I terrified Lavinia."

"It has to be Averel or Kane." There would be no more sleep for any of them now. "Get dressed, and I'll meet you down in the hall."

Gideon returned to Merewen. She was sitting up and waiting for him. "What's wrong?"

It was easier to show her than explain. Already the marks were fading. "Something has happened to Kane or maybe Averel. We've never experienced anything like this."

She pressed her palms against his chest, murmuring softly under her breath. The marks and the last ghosts of pain disappeared, allowing him to think more clearly. He took her hand and brushed a kiss across her knuckles.

"Go back to sleep. I'll be fine. I'm meeting Duncan and Murdoch downstairs."

The urge to be with all of his friends, not just Murdoch and Duncan, was riding Gideon hard. He wished to the gods that Averel and Kane weren't half a realm away. None of them would feel complete until they were all together again.

"I'll join you as soon as I get dressed." Merewen held up a hand before he could protest. "Don't bother to argue, Gideon. They are my friends, too. I suspect Alina and Lavinia will be there as well."

A wise warrior knew when to surrender, especially when it was a battle he didn't particularly wish to win. "On one condition."

"Which is?" she prodded.

Despite his worry for his friends, he managed a smile for his lady. "You three are the ones who stage a raid on Ellie's kitchen for food and drink for all of us. She might come after one of us with her sharpest knife, but she likes you."

Merewen smiled, which was his intent. "Agreed."

*   *   *

An hour later they were no closer to understanding what had happened. In all the time Gideon had known Kane, he had never once deliberately used the legacy he'd inherited from his grandfather. But what if Keirthan had subverted Kane's resistance to dark magic? In his pain, could Kane have somehow found a way to reach out to them across the miles? If so, why were they no longer feeling his pain?

Gideon exchanged looks with Murdoch and Duncan. Just as he'd feared, they'd all jumped to the same painful conclusion: Kane was no longer screaming because he couldn't. A fist-sized ball of pain caught in Gideon's throat, making it impossible to speak, his attempt nothing but a deep rumble in his chest. It was becoming clear that someone, most likely the duke himself, had captured Kane for the purpose of working dark magic.

Death had been their constant companion for centuries as they rode into battle. That was true for any warrior, but for Kane to suffer and perish alone was beyond bearing.

All three men clutched their knives, hunting in vain for a suitable target for their pain. Frustrated when he couldn't find one, Gideon picked up the ewer of ale and heaved it across the room to shatter against the wall.

Merewen caught Gideon's wrist with both hands. "Be calm and think. I am convinced you would sense if he was dead. Remember, too, you told me Kane is the strongest man you know."

She was right, although Murdoch looked mildly insulted by her words. Merewen was still talking.

"You are right to be worried about him, but allowing your anger to rule your thoughts will not help Kane." Her dark eyes were sympathetic. "Think about what we know for certain. Perhaps then we can figure out what can be done to help him and Averel."

Merewen meant well, but none of the information they had was at all useful. He listed the few facts they had. "We know Kane was hired as the captain of Keirthan's personal guard, and Averel has been working as a troubadour. In the last message the dogs brought, Kane and Averel were planning to return to us in a matter of days.

"Did I forget anything?" He paused to look around the table and then answered the question himself. "Oh, yes, we all awoke in agony because one of our friends is being tortured."

Gideon and the other two men sat in stony silence while the three women exchanged glances. Just as Gideon expected, no one had a single helpful suggestion.

Merewen was the first to speak. "You three should ride for the capital and rescue Kane. I'll call for spare horses for the three of you, so you can change off mounts on the way."

As much as Gideon appreciated her offer, he shook his head. "Our duty is here with you, my lady, until we are ready to march against Keirthan. We are still awaiting the arrival of additional men. Rushing our plans will only increase the likelihood of failure."

She immediately protested. "But you need Kane and Averel to be the most effective against the duke and his men."

Murdoch spoke for the first time. "My lady, even if we were to ride for the city this very moment, there's no guarantee we would reach Kane in time to save him. We would also run the risk of all of us being captured or killed. The goddess would not soon forgive us for failing you in order to save one of us. In truth, neither would Kane."

Merewen turned to Gideon, probably hoping he would deny the truth of Murdoch's words. "But we can't just let him die!"

The hall held a chill more akin to a winter night than to an early-summer morning. The truth was painful, but it was still the truth. "Murdoch has the right of it, Merewen. And remember what our failure would mean to you.

I won't have you wandering the afterlife forever alone and cold. I will not risk that, not even for my friends."

This was getting them nowhere. He needed guidance, the kind that his friends could not provide. Only rarely over the centuries had he risked a trip back to the river to ask the Lord and Lady for advice. Mayhap it was time to do so again.

"I will go to the river." And before his friends could react, he added, "Alone."

Duncan's fist came down hard on the table in a rare show of temper. "No, Gideon. You will not do this by yourself. Kane and Averel are our friends, too. Your duty is our duty. If we need to approach the Lord and Lady, we go together."

"No. We cannot all be gone at the same time. If I don't return, Lady Merewen will need the two of you more than ever."

Lady Lavinia rose to her feet, drawing everyone's attention to her. The men immediately fell silent. No matter what she was about to say, Gideon was grateful for the distraction. The memory of Kane's agony had all of them short-tempered and ready for a fight.

If Duncan had any idea what his lady was up to, he gave no sign of it. She gave him a small smile before looking first at Gideon and then Murdoch.

"I well know and understand how the Damned feel about the practice of magic. However, Captain, I would offer you an alternative to journeying to the river. I could attempt a scrying. Your goddess has already spoken to me once before. Perhaps she will do so again."

To everyone's surprise, it was Murdoch who immediately agreed. "If you think it will present no danger to anyone here in the keep, I would appreciate your offer to check on our brother for us."

"I do not control what the gods choose to reveal to me, Sir Murdoch, but I am willing to ask for their guidance."

Gideon glanced around the room, noting the servants

were now up, preparing to serve the morning meal. Soon the hall would be crowded, offering no privacy for what they were about to do.

"Lady Lavinia, I would greatly appreciate anything you can do to help, but I suggest we seek out a more private spot."

Then it occurred to him to ask, "Is this something we can all observe, or would our presence be an unwelcome distraction?"

He liked that she gave the matter some thought before answering. "I've had success scrying with Duncan at my side as well as a near disaster. I am willing to have you there as long as you understand it may not work with an audience."

"Of course. Where would you prefer to set up your scrying bowl? In the library, perhaps?"

Duncan answered as he caught Lavinia's hand in his. "The garden would be better. Is that right, my lady?"

Lavinia stared down at their joined hands. "There's nothing written that says that I have to be outdoors, but I find it easier to concentrate in the quiet of a garden."

Having a plan of action, however tenuous, gave Gideon the first glimmer of hope since he'd awoken in pain. "Then that's what we'll do. Shall we gather in there after the guards change shift? I would like Sigil to be able to join us as well, and he's still on duty."

Their plans made, they all scattered to take care of their usual morning duties. As Gideon joined Merewen in her early-morning stroll through the newly rebuilt stable, he prayed that the gods could offer their avatars some badly needed help. He'd already made the decision to send out Scim to seek Averel and Kane if Lavinia was unable to discover what was happening with them. If their friends were lost, the rest of the Damned knew their duty and would see it done.

The sky overhead was blue, the sun warm. Sigil trailed along after Murdoch and the others as they walked toward the garden. Gideon had ordered everyone else away from that side of the keep, even the guards who were patrolling on the rampart along the top of the palisade.

Sigil couldn't exactly say that he was looking forward to watching Lady Lavinia scry. Magic was nothing to be taken lightly, but it would be beneficial to see what advice the gods might have to offer to aid their avatars. Soon the Damned and their allies would all march into battle. After all, Gideon and company had to finish this fight before the solstice.

He would ride at their side, willingly offering up his life if necessary to support their cause. He had no past and perhaps no future. What he did have was this one chance to redeem his honor. For that, he was grateful.

He joined the others in forming a circle around Lavinia and Duncan. She set a deep green glass bowl on a small table. When she had it arranged to her liking, she motioned Lady Alina to bring forward the pitcher she was carrying.

Lavinia drew a deep breath and slowly filled the bowl to the brim before she handed the pitcher back to Alina, who set it on a nearby bench before rejoining the circle. When she was back in place, Lavinia and Duncan stood on opposite sides of the bowl, their hands clasped as she bowed her head.

Without looking up, she said, "You may all approach now."

The rest of them took slow steps forward until they stood shoulder to shoulder an arm's length from Lavinia and Duncan. From where Sigil stood, he could see the surface of the water in the bowl, but he noticed that Murdoch had positioned himself so that Duncan blocked any view of the bowl. No surprise there, given his particularly strong feelings about magic.

As Sigil watched, Lavinia murmured a few words, their meaning unknown but their sound and rhythm soothing to the ear. After several repetitions, she fell silent. At first he thought perhaps she had given up, but then he realized the water, which had been still, was now rippling.

Lavinia and Duncan leaned in closer, their expressions rapt. He wished he was close enough to see into the depths of the bowl, but Lavinia would explain her vision soon enough.

As they watched, the water continued to ripple and then grew still. Finally, a pair of small figures rose up out of the water, one male and the other female. Despite being made of clear water, there was no doubt they were alive and aware of those crowded around the bowl.

Duncan's eyes flashed wide as he looked around to find Gideon in the circle. When three warriors dropped to their knees, Sigil followed suit, as did Lady Alina and Lady Merewen. Lavinia remained standing, but bowed her head to the gods who had now grown in size to reach her eye level. How was that possible? There couldn't be that much water in the bowl. Now wasn't the time for such thoughts. Sigil forced his attention back to Gideon.

"My Lord and Lady." Gideon spoke for them all with great solemnity. "Thank you for answering your servants' call."

The gods turned to face their captain. "Rise up, Warriors. We have much to say and little time to do so."

Once again everyone crowded close to the bowl and waited to learn what they had to say.

It was the Lord of the River who spoke for the pair. "Your friend suffers greatly, Captain, but know he also has an unexpected ally. For your efforts to succeed, you must trust that Lord Kane will find his own way out of the darkness."

The Lady spoke next. "Sir Murdoch, set your doubts aside. They weaken you all. Victory will come only if everyone is free to use their gifts."

Murdoch nodded, his face flushed red.

"Sir Duncan, when it comes to the final battle, your lady will need you at her side."

"Yes, my lady."

Everyone stood frozen as the gods spoke to each of the Damned in turn. But instead of disappearing back into the water, they both turned to face Sigil directly. Speaking as one, they said, "Captain, we accept your unspoken pledge to serve our cause. Adding your strength to that of our chosen avatars will help turn the tide against your former master. Serve us well, and what was done in his name will be washed clean from your soul."

At first Sigil could do naught but stare at the two shimmering figures and nod. Finally, he found his tongue. "Thank you, my Lord and Lady, for allowing me the honor of serving with your warriors. I will proudly stand with them and share their fate, whatever it may be."

Someone gasped; he thought it might be Murdoch, but he could be wrong about that. Perhaps the Damned thought him foolish for offering to stand judgment with them at the end of their service on the solstice, but he meant every word. Despite the huge gaps in his memory, he knew he'd never served with men more deserving of his loyalty and friendship.

The Lady spoke again, "Captain Gideon, do you formally accept this warrior as a Warrior of the Mist?"

Gideon's pale gaze met Sigil's head-on. "I do, my lady, and am honored to so."

She tipped her head to the side in acceptance. "Then so shall it be."

The Lord had the last word. "Time grows short, Warriors. May your swords win the day."

His words seemed to hover in the air even as the pair slowly disappeared back into the rippling water in the bowl. Everyone remained where they were until Lady Lavinia finally stepped back from the bowl. She picked it up and carefully carried it over to pour the water on the nearest rosebushes.

When she was done, everyone else started moving again. The three ladies took their leave, perhaps sensing the four men needed a few minutes alone. Sigil didn't know about the other three, but right now he needed to sit down, the import of what he'd just done hitting him hard.

He tried to walk with dignity but wasn't all that steady as he headed for the nearby bench. As soon as he sat down, Gideon drew his knife and held it sideways in front of Sigil's eyes. What was he doing? Then he realized the man was offering the blade as a mirror.

Sigil stared at the reflection of his own face, familiar in all but one aspect. His eyes were now a match to the three pairs of pale-as-death eyes staring down at him with an odd mix of pride and sympathy in their depths.

He needed to say something, anything, but what? He settled for, "Someone has to keep an eye on Murdoch. I figured it might as well be me."

For the first time all morning, the other three Damned grinned, even Murdoch. Gideon held out his hand to Sigil. "Thank you for taking on that particular chore. It's been quite a burden for the rest of us all these years."

Sigil was at a disadvantage, sitting down with the three warriors towering over him. He shook Gideon's hand and then stood up. "Mayhap I should rethink my offer."

Murdoch's smile took on a harder edge. "Too late, my friend. Go get some sleep, and this afternoon the four of us will learn during sword practice which of us is the real burden to the group."

Feeling prouder than he had in a long time, Sigil agreed. "I look forward to it."

Still feeling a bit shaky, he made his way to his quarters, hoping to catch a few hours of sleep. As soon as he stepped into the room, he sensed something was different. The air smelled fresh and damp, as if he were standing beside a mountain stream rather than in a small room inside a stone keep.

But even more amazing, there was a shield on his bed, a match for the ones Murdoch and the others carried. He cautiously approached the bed, the tingle of magic growing stronger with each step he took.

A feminine voice whispered in his mind. *"Warrior, this is our gift to you as one of our avatars. His name is Otsoko. He, too, has the fierce heart of a warrior who needs to redeem himself."*

Then she added a few words, ones that rang with power. When she repeated them a second time, it felt as if she were carving them into Sigil's skull with a dull knife. The pain faded as quickly as it had come, but the words remained shiny bright in Sigil's thoughts. He knew without asking that the Lady had gifted him with the means to call forth his new companion.

He whispered the words, careful to say each one just as the goddess had. He knew not what language they came from nor the meaning behind any of the words. All that mattered was that their magic worked. When nothing happened, he tried again, this time speaking them with more confidence.

A flash of light had him belatedly throwing his arm up to shield his eyes. He kept his eyes closed as he waited for his vision to clear. In the meantime, the bed creaked as something heavy jumped down onto the floor.

He immediately opened his eyes, his heart pounding hard. An enormous gray wolf stood staring back at him with bright amber eyes. Under other circumstances, Sigil would have been terrified, but his heart knew this animal was no threat to him.

He knelt down, bringing himself down to eye level with the wolf. "Hello, Otsoko. I am called Sigil."

When Sigil held out his hand, the wolf took a step forward to first sniff it and then gave it a quick lick. That small success had Sigil feeling more daring. He stroked the thick fur on the wolf's neck and back. Evidently he was doing something right because Otsoko immediately turned to give Sigil easier access.

After giving his new avatar a good scratching, Sigil pushed himself back up to his feet. "I'm sorry, my friend, but I've been up for far too long and need to sleep. Once

I've rested, I'll show you around the keep and introduce you to the goddess's other warriors."

The wolf actually nodded, as if understanding every word. Sigil carefully set the shield aside and stretched out on the bed. Otsoko waited until Sigil was settled and then jumped up to curl at his feet.

What an eventful day! Seeing the gods appear in the water. Swearing an oath to them that made him one of the Warriors of the Mist. His eyes changing colors. And now, most wondrous of them all, he had his own avatar. The warmth of the big wolf's head on his ankles soothed away the last bit of Sigil's tension, and he drifted off to sleep.

Chapter 20

*T*heda watched Ifre closely. He was clearly agitated, his gaze never lingering on one person for more than a few seconds, his hands constantly in motion. His excitement only confirmed her worst fears. The bastard was acting like a small child gloating over a new toy, one he didn't want to share.

She wished he would drop dead right where he sat at the head table. If that was evil of her, she didn't care. Tonight she would do everything she could to snatch at least one victim from Ifre's clutches.

Once the evening meal was over, she would bring Ifre his last drink as she always did. She already had it poured and ready to serve. An hour after he consumed it, he would get a headache that would render him unable to do more than crawl into his bed for the night.

Everyone knew the duke was given to such episodes; no one would question him succumbing to yet another one. Her only fear was that somehow his magic would warn him that his wine had more than the usual spices in it.

"What about your brother-in-law has captured your attention tonight, Lady Theda? Normally, you ignore him as much as you possibly can."

She glanced at Markus with disdain. "I am merely waiting to serve him his favorite wine, not that it is any of your business. He doesn't like to be kept waiting."

"It is wise of you to avoid provoking him. He is not a man I would willingly cross."

The sergeant's response surprised her. Normally he

would have taunted her and treated her with casual disrespect. Instead, he looked particularly grim as he stared across the room to where Ifre sat laughing with one of the nobles. What had happened to change his attitude toward the duke?

Could it be that he knew something about Kane's fate? Not that it mattered. Even if he did, he would never do anything to help. She noted the servants had started to clear the tables. That was her signal to serve the spiced wine.

"If you'll excuse me, Sergeant, I have duties that require my attention."

"Lady Theda," Markus called after her.

She looked back over her shoulder. "Was there something you needed?"

He started to speak but then shook his head. "It is nothing."

Then he walked away, disappearing into the crowd. How very odd. But rather than pursue the matter, she picked up Ifre's wine and put her plan into motion.

The gods were with her. It had taken longer than she expected for the spiced wine to take effect, but finally Ifre had withdrawn to his quarters. His manservant had been dispatched to fetch the physician, who arrived promptly and then left again within minutes. She hoped that meant that no one was questioning the source of Ifre's pain.

Next, Ifre's secretary had made a general announcement that the duke was going to spend the evening in his quarters. With luck, that meant the doctor had dosed Ifre with a pain medication that would keep him abed until morning.

Praying she was right, Theda had sent her ladies to their rooms with orders for them to remain there until morning. Having done what she could to keep them safe, she had retired to her own quarters to wait until she could safely escape the keep without drawing unwanted attention to herself. To occupy her mind while she waited, she put together a small pack of bandages and salves. If Kane was injured, he would need his wounds tended to before he could ride for freedom.

Wearing her darkest gown and cloak, she made her way to the garden. How she wished Kane would appear, safe and sound, but that wasn't going to happen. At least, not without her help. She headed for his quarters, hoping and praying that she would be able to call forth Hob without trouble.

Creeping from shadow to shadow, she approached the barracks and slipped through the door. Inside, all was quiet except for the pounding of her heart. She prayed it wasn't as loud as it sounded to her, but there was nothing she could do to control her racing pulse or the fear that followed in her footsteps.

The shield was right where she'd last seen it. She quickly packed up Kane's few possessions in the saddlebags she found stashed under the bed.

He'd want the shield, but she would need to drape it with his cloak to hide its bright white surface after she called Hob. The packing done, she wiped her hands on her skirts and pulled out the small piece of paper Kane had given her with the words of the chant written down. She traced the words with a fingertip, savoring the small connection with the warrior.

The night was quickly passing. If she was going to do this, now was the time. She read the words aloud. As soon as she said the last one, she shaded her eyes against the light and waited until she heard Hob snuffling around the room before opening them again.

"Hob, we have to find him."

But before going after Kane, she had to saddle his horse so he could make his escape. She gathered up the saddlebags and the shield and led Hob to the stable. Once they were inside, Hob headed right for a stall in the far corner. Inside was the enormous gray stallion she'd seen Kane riding. The horse stirred restlessly as she approached until Hob scooted underneath the door to exchange sniffs with him.

The stallion immediately calmed, evidently accepting her as a friend if Hob vouched for her. She set Kane's packs and shield down inside the stall before quickly backing out. "I'll find your tack."

Hob came with her. It was impossible to see anything in the tack room. "How am I supposed to find Kane's saddle?"

She had directed the question to Hob, but it was a man who materialized out of the shadows who answered. "It's the one right in front of you."

He quickly clamped his hand down over her mouth before she could scream. Hob growled low but made no move to attack.

Her captor snarled right back. "Shut up, Hob. I have enough problems right now without arguing with you."

The stranger knew Hob? Was he here also hunting for Kane? She forced herself to relax, hoping he would interpret it as a signal that she wouldn't do anything that would draw unwanted attention to them.

"Good. I'm going to release you now."

As soon as he did, he stepped back and lit a nearby lamp. "I would know your name."

Hob immediately sat down at her feet. She reached down to pat his head, drawing comfort from his staunch support. "I am Lady Theda. And you are?"

"Averel, a friend of Kane's." He glared down at the gargoyle. "I can't believe that miserable beast is letting you pet him. He's not a trusting soul."

"Kane introduced us." She took a chance and added, "He also taught me how to call Hob from his shield."

That clearly shocked Averel. "I didn't even know that was possible. Where is Kane? How badly hurt is he?"

She still wasn't quite ready to trust this man. "How did you know he was hurt?"

When he raised his tunic, she gasped. His chest was covered in faint red streaks. "What happened to you?"

"Nothing, and that's the problem. They've faded, but when I woke up this morning my body was covered with painful welts. Somehow I was feeling everything Kane was."

She should have guessed the young knight and Kane were more than merely friends. "You're not a simple troubadour at all, are you? You're a Warrior of the Mist just like Kane."

"He said he'd told you about us." Averel smiled at her, apparently not upset by Kane's decision to reveal their secrets.

It was time to tell him everything. Her eyes burned with tears. "My brother-in-law, Duke Keirthan, has captured Kane and taken him to his private chambers below the keep. Hob and I are going to break Kane free."

"Let me get Kane's horse saddled first, and then you show me where the duke's chambers are. We'll need to be ready to leave as soon as he's free."

Averel pulled the saddle down and headed back toward the stallion. "This won't take long, provided Rogue cooperates. Kane likes to surround himself with contrary beasts."

The disgust in Averel's voice finally convinced her that he was indeed the troubadour Kane told her about. Despite the seriousness of the situation, she couldn't resist tweaking the young knight a bit. "Hob, I think we've just been insulted."

Averel looked horrified. "I was talking about Hob and Rogue, my lady, not you."

When she laughed, he looked chagrined but smiled back. "All right. I suppose that did sound bad. My apologies."

As he finished tightening the cinch on Rogue's saddle, it occurred to her that one horse couldn't carry two grown men very far. "Do you have your own mount? If not, you are welcome to take mine."

Averel patted Rogue on the shoulder as he left the stall. "My mare is saddled and waiting for me not far from here. I didn't want to risk drawing the attention of the duke's guards by riding here."

Good. She liked that he was thinking ahead. She'd been worried about how Kane would fare if he was badly hurt and had to ride out on his own. Hob would be able to stand guard, but Kane might need continued care if he was going to make it back to his friends.

"We should go if we're going to get Kane away before daylight."

When she picked up her pack and started for the door of the stable, Averel stopped her. "Lady Theda, Lord Kane would not soon forgive me if I allowed you to walk into danger for his sake. Show me the entrance to this chamber you spoke of, and I will see to his release."

Theda's temper flared. "You have no right to decide what I am allowed to do. You may accompany me, but you will not be going alone. I will remind you that Hob and I were doing fine on our own. We had Kane's gear packed up and waiting, and I would have saddled Rogue as well."

Then she played her winning card. "Besides, you have no idea where he is being held and cannot enter the keep without fear of rousing the guard. I can."

She expected an argument, but Averel held up his hands in surrender, although he was clearly not happy. "As you said, the night grows short."

She led the way back through the garden. At the edge, she studied their surroundings. All was quiet. "A friend will let us in that door. From that point, we'll have to tread carefully through the great hall to reach the entrance to Ifre's private chambers below the keep."

Averel drew his sword but kept it down at his side. As soon as she knocked on the door, Tom opened it.

"I wondered if you were outside — ," he started to say but stopped when he spotted Averel standing behind her. "Who is he?"

"A friend, Tom. One who will not be staying long. It would be safer for all of us if you never saw him."

She held her breath, hoping their friendship stretched far enough for Tom to turn a blind eye to an unknown warrior sneaking into the keep. It was asking a lot of him when it could cost him his life if anyone found out.

Finally, he nodded. "As long as you promise he'll be gone before dawn."

"He will be. Thank you, Tom."

Her friend walked away, disappearing into a nearby room. As soon as he was out of sight, she motioned for Averel and Hob to follow her. She took a roundabout route to the great hall, noting her two companions moved with the same predatory stealth as Kane.

When they reached the last turn before the passage opened up into the great hall, she motioned for Averel and Hob to wait while she scouted ahead. The two males clearly weren't happy to be left behind, even for that short time, but she'd have an easier time explaining her presence if she were to encounter anyone.

All was blessedly quiet, but then she noticed movement over near the front door, which should be locked this time of night. Sure enough, one of the guards was walking along the perimeter of the great hall and heading straight for her.

She retreated to where Averel stood waiting impatiently. "A guard," she whispered. He nodded and followed after her.

The guard made no effort to move quietly, his boots ringing on the stone floor as he circled the room. She held her breath when he passed by the passageway where she and Averel stood. He paused briefly, cocking his head to one side as if listening to something. After a few seconds, he started forward again, his steps still methodical and slow.

How were they to reach the doorway without him noticing? It wasn't far, but the torches cast enough light to banish all but the darkest shadows. There was no way he could miss them if they were to dart across the last distance.

Then he stopped and pulled out a wineskin and took a long drink. Averel caught her arm and leaned down to whisper, "I'll take care of him when he passes again."

What could she do but nod, even though the man had done nothing to deserve death on this night?

He was coming around again. As soon as the guard passed by, Averel ghosted after him, wrapping his arm tightly around the man's throat. The guard struggled for several seconds, but then his body went slack.

Averel dragged him far enough into the passageway that he couldn't be easily seen from the great hall. He was still breathing. Good. If one of the other guards were to check on him, she hoped they would simply assume that he'd left his post to pay a visit to the garderobe. Averel arranged the guard's body to look as if he'd fallen asleep sitting down with his back to the wall. After spilling the wine, he returned to where Theda stood.

"Are you ready?"

She nodded and cut straight across to the door that Ifre was always careful to lock. He'd evidently forgotten that the former chatelaine of the keep had a set of keys to every door in the keep. Until now, she'd never been tempted to explore the labyrinth, but her late husband had told tales of him and Ifre exploring it when they were children. It had only been since Ifre had come to rule that the place was used for foul purposes.

The key worked, but the passage beyond it was shrouded in total darkness. Averel left her side long enough to fetch one of the torches burning in the hall. It did little to hold the shadows at bay, but her companions strode forth with no hesitation. She hurried after them, not wanting to be left behind.

Averel stopped a short time later to take a deep breath. He muttered something vicious under his breath, and the gargoyle growled softly. She didn't know what made them so angry, but she was glad their tempers weren't aimed at her.

The young troubadour looked back at her, his eyes glittering in the half-light. "This place reeks of blood magic and death. Duke Keirthan has much to answer for."

When he started forward again, his long legs moved at a pace that was nearly impossible for her to match. The floor beneath their feet sloped steadily downward with no railing at the side to offer her support. She reluctantly put her hand on the wall as she walked, holding up her skirts with the other. Still she fell further behind.

"Averel, please. I cannot keep up."

He immediately stopped and looked back apologetically. "My pardon, Lady Theda. It is only concern for my friend that drives me so hard."

She hurried the last few steps to where he stood studying the way in front of them. "It flattens out shortly, which should make it easier for us both."

She squinted, trying to see ahead but with no luck. How could he know that from where they stood? But then, Kane had also seemed to be able to see in the darkness far better than she did.

Rather than waste her breath on responding, she put her hand on Hob's shoulder and concentrated on keeping up. Just as Averel promised, their path soon leveled out. Hob left her side to range out in front of them, his nose to the ground as he tasted the scents with his tongue.

Her fear about what lay ahead worsened. What if the combination of her potion and the pain medication from the doctor hadn't kept Ifre abed tonight?

"Can you hear anything?" she whispered when Averel stopped for a second time.

"One heartbeat, but there's something else." He stared toward a dim glow in the distance. "Something dire and dangerous lies in wait."

He glanced in her direction. "It is not too late for you to turn back, my lady."

It was tempting, but she would not act the coward when Kane's life might depend on the two of them. "Kane may need my help. I will not abandon him now."

She must have convinced Averel because he started forward again. Before they reached the room at the end, he handed her the torch. "Hold this. I may need both hands free to fight."

The passageway they'd followed had been dank and cold, but as they crossed into the enormous chamber at its end, they were hit with a wave of heat that rivaled the hottest summer day. The air was heavy and difficult to breathe. The stench of drying blood and death left her gagging.

"Breathing through your mouth may help with the smell." Averel looked a little queasy himself as he glanced around the room. The ceiling vaulted high overhead. The fire pit in the center of the room accounted for the heat, but the most prominent feature in the place was the altar sitting on a dais at the far end of the room.

The bloody body displayed there belonged to Kane. He was naked, his arms and legs hanging limply from chains attached to four pillars at the corners of the altar. From where she stood, it didn't appear there was a single inch of his body that hadn't been sliced with a knife. He wasn't moving, perhaps not even breathing.

"Kane!" she called and started forward.

Averel caught her arm and pointed toward the ceiling above Kane. "By the gods, what horror is that?"

Theda followed his line of sight and gasped. A black cloud about as wide as her arm span hovered high in the air directly over Kane's body. Although it looked to be the consistency of oily smoke, her instincts told her there was far more to it than that.

"It's either the source or the product of Ifre's blood magic." She had no gift herself, but her late husband had taught her enough that she knew she was right. "Whatever it is, we are in the same grave danger as Kane."

She took a tentative step forward. "Do you believe Kane to be alive?"

Looking even more grim, Averel nodded and rubbed his chest. "I would know if he wasn't."

The conviction in his words gave her the courage to continue forward. When they were but a few feet from the steps leading up to the dais, the black cloud moved, drifting downward. Averel shoved Theda behind him, planting himself firmly between her and any danger the darkness might represent.

Averel called out, "Kane, can you hear me?"

A soft moan was their only answer, but it was enough to send Theda bolting past Averel toward the altar.

"Lady Theda, stop where you are!"

Averel charged after her. She wanted to ignore him, but then she realized that the heavy cloud was slowly spinning faster now and had dropped several inches closer to Kane. She slowed her approach, but nothing was going to keep her away from her warrior lover.

"Let me distract that thing before you get closer."

Theda didn't want to delay another instant, but Kane would not be well served if she were to run afoul of Ifre's dark magic before she could set him free.

As soon as Averel plucked a burning torch from the wall and brandished it and his sword at the hovering darkness, the dark cloud spun around and drifted back away from him. Two red orbs appeared in its center. What kind of horror was it?

"Come on, you!" Averel taunted. "I'm guessing you're only brave when your victim is chained down."

Hob joined Averel's efforts, his muzzle pointed toward the cloud as he spit venom and snarled his own brand of insults. He leapt off the ground and succeeded in hitting his target with a heavy spray of venom. The cloud shuddered and faded in color as it retreated farther from the altar. When they'd driven Ifre's monster to the far end of the dais, Theda climbed the few steps, keeping a wary eye on the hovering mass. The young knight and Hob drove the cloud toward the fire pit, its movements growing more sluggish.

Despite the heat near the fire in the center of the room, the air around the dais was cold enough to make her breath visible. If she was chilled fully dressed and wearing a heavy cloak, how cold must Kane be?

She pulled out the pin that held her cloak fastened and took it off. Sidling along the front edge of the platform, she reached the altar. Her first close-up look at Kane broke her heart. What skin wasn't cut and crusted with dried blood was nearly blue with cold. She ignored the pain it caused her, but at that moment, she couldn't imagine hating anyone as much as she hated her brother-in-law.

Having lured the cloud away for the moment, Averel joined her on the dais while Hob kept watch, ready to sound the alarm if the cloud moved back toward them. The young warrior stood beside her, staring down at his friend in absolute fury.

After covering Kane's body with her cloak, she said, "Promise me Ifre will pay for this."

Averel began working on releasing the chains from Kane's wrists, still keeping a wary eye on the cloud. "Upon my oath, Keirthan will die."

She believed him and drew comfort from the knowledge.

Chapter 21

$\mathcal{B}$y the Lady, Kane hurt. His skin was on fire, and his bones ached. He'd been passing in and out of consciousness for hours, maybe even days by now. Trapped down here in Keirthan's private torture chamber, time was meaningless. Only the precious respites from the bastard's games mattered.

Something had woken him up, but what? Ah, yes, someone was moving around nearby, which meant the bloody games would soon begin again. Kane had always been grateful for the gift of healing from the Lord and Lady of the River. But here, in the eternal darkness of Ifre Keirthan's chambers, it only made the torture that much worse.

In Kane's few lucid moments, he knew that death would have already claimed a normal man, but there was nothing normal about any of the Damned. That was especially true for him. The strength of his forsworn legacy combined with the gifts from the Lady ensured that Kane would suffer a long, long time before he'd be granted the sweet release of death.

"Kane, can you hear me?"

His mind was playing with him because that sounded more like Averel than Keirthan. He tried to answer, but a moan was the best he could manage with his throat nearly ruined from screaming.

Footsteps that couldn't belong to Averel grew closer. Too light. Too quick. Feminine. The air above him stirred as a soft blanket settled over his body. He moaned again, soaking in its soothing warmth. It smelled of roses, a nice change from the stench of his own blood, vomit, and sweat. Who would do such a thing? Then his pain-fogged mind recognized the scent.

Please, Lord and Lady, tell me it isn't Lady Theda standing over me!

The touch of her soft hand cupping his face confirmed his suspicions. Gathering up the tattered remains of his strength, he strained against his chains. He'd long ago given up trying to break free of them, but he had to protect her. If Keirthan caught Theda here, he'd feed her to Damijan.

"Kane, stop fighting us! We're here to get you out of here, but you need to hold still."

We? Who was with her? There was no one in the keep that he would trust with his life, much less hers. Finally, a male voice entered the discussion.

"Stop thrashing around, Kane. You're opening your wounds again. I'll get the chains off if you'll hold still."

"Averel?" he managed to whisper.

"Yes. Hob's here, too."

He had to warn them. "Monster. Death."

"We know. Hob weakened it with his venom. He will warn us if it comes closer."

While he spoke, Averel pulled on the chain attached to Kane's right arm, unleashing an agonizing fresh wave of pain. Kane bit back a curse and fought off the dark oblivion that had provided his only relief when Keirthan had been the one standing beside the altar.

He forced his eyes to open, staring up at Theda and drinking in her gentle beauty. She shouldn't be there, but a selfish part of him was glad she was. He hadn't thought he'd live to see her again. As Averel struggled to break open Kane's shackles, Theda poured water from a flask onto a cloth and sponged Kane's face. It felt wonderful, especially on his cracked, dry lips.

"I'm going to lift your head so you can sip some water. Go slowly so you don't choke. Understand?"

He managed a small nod. She eased her hand under the back of his neck and raised his head up a few inches. The water trickled into his mouth with almost as much spilling down his chin. He swallowed once, the cool liquid stinging his throat. The second sip felt better, the third better yet.

She lowered his head. "We'll give it a minute and try some more."

Averel was muttering something about hunting down the smith who'd made the shackles for Keirthan and gutting him. Hearing his normally cheerful friend talking that way made Kane laugh, a big mistake considering how much he hurt.

"You think this funny, Kane? If I'd known you were enjoying yourself down here, I wouldn't have risked my own hide trying to rescue you."

Theda interceded. "That's enough, both of you. Nothing about this is funny."

The fear in her voice silenced both men quickly. She held out a long pin. "Perhaps this will work better than your knife to open the lock."

Averel went to work with the pin. His efforts were rewarded a few seconds later with a soft click. Kane's arm hit the table with a thump. It had been numb from hanging over his head for so long, but now feeling came rushing back with a vengeance. Fine. He needed to regain full use of it and the sooner, the better.

When Averel unfastened the second lock, Theda caught Kane's arm and lowered it to the marble surface of the altar. They unlocked his ankles next. Free at last, he tried to sit up, but failed miserably. Could he appear any weaker in front of his woman? His mind argued it didn't matter; he had no right to lay claim to her that way. His heart felt differently.

"Catch your breath, Kane, and we'll help you up."

The rough sympathy in Averel's voice was only slightly easier to take than the sheen of tears in Theda's eyes. He closed his eyes briefly, hating their pity and wondering how bad off he must be to have both of them looking that way.

"Get me up. He'll be back."

"Not tonight," Theda said, shaking her head. "I added a potion to his spiced wine to give him a headache. His physician came and gave him something to help him sleep through it. That doesn't mean we can afford to linger. The servants will be stirring soon, and we can't risk being seen in the great hall."

Finally, something he could do to help himself. "Another way out. Comes out beyond the city walls."

Averel looked relieved. "Good. We'll all go that way."

Theda started to protest, but Averel stopped her. "No, we can't go back the way we came. If anyone has discovered the guard, there could be swarms of guards prowling the hall now."

She quit arguing. "Very well, but the longer I'm gone, the greater the chance of discovery."

That alone gave Kane the strength to sit up. He managed the feat on his own, which went a long way toward restoring his pride. As soon as he did, the cloud spun around and headed straight for them.

"Get down!" he croaked. "Get Theda out of here! I'll follow when I can."

"But—," she protested even as Averel dragged her down off the dais.

Kane trusted his friend to keep Theda out of harm's way. Meanwhile, his mage mark was throbbing. If he wasn't careful, Keirthan's creature would latch on to him like a leech to feed on the magic he'd been gifted with at birth. The choice was simple: He could use the magic or it would use him.

He brought his hands up and began chanting, the words dragged up from the farthest reaches of his memories. By now his mark burned as if a hot branding iron had been laid against his cheek. He ignored the pain even as he ignored every wound that Keirthan had left upon his body.

Nothing mattered as long as Theda and his friends made it to safety. At first the flow of the magic was but a small trickle, barely enough to do more than make his fingertips tingle. But he repeated the words over and over, taking pleasure in speaking in his native tongue.

Then, as if a dam burst, the power poured through him to mend his body, banishing his pain and exhaustion. When he was back to full strength, he turned the wave of power against the whirling blackness. Revenge tasted sweet. At first the pool of darkness overhead resisted his attack, but slowly Kane forced it to retreat.

He jumped down off the dais, following after his nemesis. The cloud no longer spun; the pair of red eyes were blinking in and out, as if it was having a hard time holding on to its consciousness. One more little push and even the color was fading. No longer black, it rapidly faded through all the shades of gray.

But the pool of magic Kane had called upon was not limitless, and already the stream of power he channeled grew weaker. He could sense his friends were waiting for him only a short distance down the passageway. They wouldn't leave until he joined them, so he held back enough of his strength to follow after them.

He took little comfort in knowing he'd badly weakened Keirthan's spells. The bastard would only rekindle their power when next he returned to the labyrinth. Kane picked up Theda's cloak and retrieved his weapons from the corner where Markus had dumped them. They'd cut off Kane's jerkin in pieces, but his trews were more or less intact, making them better than nothing. He strapped his sword at his waist and retreated toward the passageway. About halfway there, he stopped. Maybe there was one more thing he could do, but only if he hurried.

Turning his attention to the altar, where so many innocents had died, he began chanting again. He'd probably regret expending the energy necessary to accomplish his goal, but he wasn't going to stop now. When he said the last word of the spell, he brought his fist down on the marble with all the fury he could muster.

A crackling sound echoed through the room as first the columns that held the chains and then the altar itself crumbled into pieces. He raised his voice in one final shout, and the entire structure burst apart.

He wished he could be there when Keirthan returned, to witness the fool's reaction firsthand. Instead he'd have to be satisfied with the knowledge that he'd struck the first blow at bringing Keirthan's reign to an end.

The passageway seemed much longer going out than it had when Kane had followed Markus to Keirthan's chamber. He sent Hob ahead to scout for them. Taking Theda's hand in his, Kane followed after his avatar, holding his sword at the ready. It was doubtful they'd run into anyone, but he didn't want to walk into a trap unprepared.

Averel brought up the rear, still keeping a wary eye on the path leading back to Keirthan's chambers. "Kane, what was that noise at the end?"

He really didn't want to explain about his newfound abilities with his magic, but he wouldn't lie to his friend. "I shattered Keirthan's altar."

"Wasn't it solid marble?"

Kane didn't bother to deny it. "Yes, it was. I'll tell you more later, but right now lengthy explanations will only slow us down."

He picked up the pace. He knew he was pushing them all hard, but it was necessary they put as much distance as possible between them and the center of Keirthan's power. Once they were out in the clean, fresh air, he'd feel better. They all would.

Hob was waiting for them at the door. Kane pressed his ear against the rough surface but could hear nothing at all through the thick wood. He released Theda's hand.

"Wait until I check outside."

Averel shoved himself between Kane and the door. "I'll go. You've made a remarkable recovery for someone who was more dead than alive a few minutes ago, but we can't risk you collapsing again."

Averel was right. The magic had restored some of Kane's strength, but it wouldn't last for long. Besides, he'd rather be the one to stay with Theda. At the same time, he wished he could protect her from what he needed to tell Averel next.

"Outside of this door is a narrow trail that leads around to the far side of this small hill. From there, it heads straight toward a deep canyon where Sergeant Markus has been dumping the bodies Keirthan was done with."

He wrapped his arm around Theda's waist and pulled her close. "I doubt Markus is out there right now, but there's no way to know for sure. He's a good swordsman, Averel, but not as good as you are. Before I learned that he was in league with the duke, I wouldn't have wanted him killed. Now I don't care."

Theda shuddered but made no protest. Good, but then he shouldn't be surprised. Markus had certainly done nothing to ingratiate himself with her or her friends.

Averel opened the door just far enough to squeeze outside. While he was scouting the area, Kane took advantage of the opportunity to enjoy the time alone with Theda. The press of her face against his bare chest soothed his weary soul.

"Kiss me, Kane."

He didn't need to be asked twice. She tasted so very sweet, but she demanded as much as she gave. He fought to keep his driving need for her under control. This was neither the time nor the place to fan the flames of his desire for her.

If he hadn't recognized that fact for himself, Averel's return would have reminded him.

The young knight immediate backed away and started to close the door again. "Oh, sorry. Maybe I should go take another look around."

Theda buried her face against Kane again, her shoulders shaking. No doubt Averel thought she was embarrassed at having been caught, but Kane knew his lady better than that. Right now, she was laughing and didn't want the young knight to know she found his reaction amusing.

"We'll be right behind you."

Averel immediately retreated, leaving Kane with Theda. She finally looked up at him. "Were you ever that young?"

He chuckled. "Not that I can remember. We are all constantly amazed that he has held on to his ability to blush despite spending centuries with the rest of us. Don't tell Averel, but in some ways I've always envied him."

He briefly touched the mark on his cheek. "I was born knowing there was great darkness in the world."

Theda's fingertips followed after his. "Awareness of that darkness does not mean you are part of it, Kane, only that you are better prepared than most to fight it."

He had no words to express his gratitude, so he let another kiss do his talking for him. Her faith in him was an amazing gift, if a bit misplaced. Giving in to using magic after centuries of forswearing his grandfather's teachings had left him badly shaken, even if the circumstances had warranted its use. What if on some level he'd only been waiting for the right excuse? Would he give in to it more easily next time?

And what would the Lord and Lady think of his actions? If they disapproved, he wasn't the only one who would suffer for his poor choices. Yet now wasn't the time to worry about it. He released Theda and stepped back. "We need to go."

Averel waited for them a short distance away. "We must hurry if we're going to get out of the city before

Keirthan learns of your escape. My mare is saddled and ready to go. I brought supplies as well, so we can leave immediately."

"Good thinking. We should leave before the sun comes up."

As they cut across country, Kane kept Theda's hand in his. Helping her find her way in the darkness was only the excuse; the real reason was that he needed her touch. The pace he set kept all of them moving too fast for much in the way of conversation. At Kane's order, Hob ranged out in front and occasionally circled around behind them to make sure that their presence had remained undetected.

When they were within sight of the gate back into the city, Averel stopped.

"I'll go on ahead while you stay here with Hob. One man alone will draw less attention than the three of us together would, especially in your condition, Kane. Be ready to ride, though, because my leaving the city with two horses under saddle besides my own won't go unnoticed."

Kane started to protest that his condition was much improved. Then he realized that Averel was referring to him being bare-chested and still covered with dried blood.

Instead, it was Theda who argued. "I must come with you, Sir Averel. I cannot remain out here long enough for you to return. I have duties I must see to before my absence is noted."

A sick feeling stirred in Kane's gut. "You're coming with us, Theda."

But the truth was there in her dark eyes. "I cannot, Kane, no matter how much I want to stay with you. Right now Ifre has no reason to suspect that I helped you escape. If I leave now, it will be obvious I was involved, and his vengeance will know no bounds."

Theda stared up at the night sky, anguish and fear etching their marks in her beautiful face. Finally, she turned her gaze back to Kane. "He will execute my stepson and sacrifice my ladies-in-waiting to his blood magic. They are leaving the city soon, but they are in danger until then."

Averel walked a short distance away and turned his back to them. Kane appreciated his attempt to offer the two of them some small bit of privacy. He wanted to rail at the woman. Or better yet, hold her prisoner until Averel returned with the horses and then throw her over his saddle and lead the charge back to Lady Merewen's keep.

That wasn't going to happen. Theda would never forgive him for such a selfish act if those she cared about suffered for it. They both knew he wouldn't abandon his own friends; he couldn't ask her do so.

"Theda, I cannot stay."

"I know, Kane. You've never lied to me about that." She smiled through the tears streaming down her face. "I am so glad that we met, that we . . ."

Her words trailed off as she glanced in Averel's direction. That was all right. Kane knew what she meant. The short time they'd spent in each other's arms were the best hours of his long life. He wished he had Duncan's gift for words, but he'd never mastered the language of the poets.

"I will return. My gods have sent the Damned to destroy Keirthan's evil, and I will see that duty done or die in the attempt."

He tangled his fingers in the dark silk of her hair. "Theda Keirthan, know that even as I ride away, my heart will remain here with you."

She hugged him close. "And mine will be yours to keep, Kane. Now and for always."

Their kiss was infinitely sweet and far too brief. Kane wanted to hold her close until the end of his days, but she had to leave now or risk discovery.

He stepped back. "Go and be safe. We will return by the solstice. May knowing that give you hope."

Her smile was incredibly brave. "I'll be waiting, Kane."

She hurried after Averel. Kane watched long after they disappeared into the darkness, the pain in his heart far worse than anything Keirthan had inflicted upon him.

Chapter 22

*A*verel escorted Theda all the way to the door. In part he wanted to make sure she was safe, but he'd also not given up on getting her to leave with them.

"Are you sure you won't come with us, my lady? It does not sit well with either of us to leave you alone to face the wrath of your brother-in-law once he discovers Kane has escaped. He will know he had help. Kane will not forgive himself if you were to suffer because of him."

She dug her nails into the palms of her hands as she struggled to refuse his offer. It was so tempting to allow Averel and Kane to whisk her away from the capital. Anything was better than living day after day with Ifre's evil. She was soul weary and scared, but neither could she abandon her friends.

She studied the young man standing in front of her. "Tell me that you know Kane's true worth, Averel. That you see past the surface to the man inside."

Averel stared down at her, his expression so earnest and young. "Lord Kane has been my friend and companion for centuries, my lady. There is no one I'd rather stand beside in battle. I know full well his worth as a warrior and as a man." Then his stern expression softened briefly. "I cannot believe the gods would bring you into his life for only such a brief time. He deserves more. I will do my best to return him to your side."

"Watch after yourself as well, Sir Averel."

She rose up on her toes to quickly kiss the young knight's cheek. "Now, go. I'll be fine."

She hoped. But the longer she lingered outside of the keep, the more danger Averel and Kane would be in. She knocked on the door and was relieved when it was Tom who let her in.

"Thank you, Tom."

The big man pulled the door shut and locked it. "I'm glad you're back, my lady. Things have been quiet."

"I am glad to hear that. Now get some rest."

Theda hurried down the hall to the back staircase. The gods must have been looking out for her because she reached her quarters without encountering anyone else. Soon the sun would be peeking up over the horizon, and the servants who helped with the morning meal would be stirring.

She quickly stripped off her gown, wincing when she realized it reeked of Kane's blood. Had Tom noticed? It was doubtful, considering the dark color of the cloth and the dim light in the hall by the door. For the moment, she hid it in the bottom of a chest.

She looked longingly at her bed, but she was due downstairs in less than an hour. Oversleeping would increase the risk of drawing unwanted attention from Ifre. Once he discovered his prisoner had escaped, he'd be looking for a handy target for his rage. She had no regrets about the part she played in the night's activities. That didn't mean she wanted to take Kane's place in offering up her blood to feed Ifre's magic.

Once she made it through the morning routine—if she made it through—she could return to her room for a long nap.

Where was Kane now? She had to believe he and Averel had gotten away safely. And when they returned, it would be in force. May the gods see that they were victorious.

She hated that good men of Agathia would die defending the capital, fighting in the name of a ruler who did not deserve their loyalty. But she knew Ifre well enough to know he wouldn't surrender easily. No, he'd hide behind the gates and let others do all the dying.

The gates! Once he discovered Kane's absence, he'd order them locked, hoping to trap Kane within the city. That wouldn't happen, but others could be caught up in the net, specifically Lydia and Margaret. She had to get them up and out of the keep before that happened.

The plan had been for one of Lydia's brothers to approach the keep alone as if simply stopping by for a visit. The rest were going to stay at an inn near the gate to the city. He was supposed to have sent word of his arrival last night. She hoped he had. If they hurried, her friends could be gone before Ifre had time to start issuing orders. She needed to warn them.

Lydia answered on the second knock. "Lady Theda, what's wrong?"

Theda pushed past her into the room. She was relieved to see Margaret was already with her. "There is no time for explanations, but you need to leave here immediately. Go out through the side door and don't stop until you reach the inn where your brothers are staying."

The two young women were already changing clothes. Theda gave each of them a quick hug. "Your friendship has been a true gift in my life, but do not return to the capital for any reason. Lydia, warn your father that dark times are upon us. I can say no more."

As tempting as it was to linger long enough to see them off, that would be a break in her usual routine. Now more than ever she needed to maintain normal appearances.

"Keep safe."

Lydia stopped her. "Will you not come with us, my lady? There will be plenty of room in the coach."

For the second time, Theda refused a chance to escape. "I would only draw more danger in your direction. I will be fine."

After one last hug, she headed for the kitchen. Each

step of the way she prayed for those who had escaped Ifre's stronghold and even more for those who hadn't.

Sigil scanned the horizon, watching for any sign of movement. The rest of the troops the nobles had promised to Gideon were due today. But the men-at-arms weren't the only ones Sigil was watching for. Averel and Kane had yet to return to the keep. The other Damned were restless and edgy as their worry about their safety grew stronger with each passing hour. At least last night none of them had awoken screaming.

Gideon and Duncan both professed to believe that meant Kane was all right and on his way back. Murdoch, ever more pessimistic than his two companions, remained silent on the subject. The big warrior spent hours upon hours on the palisade, staring into the distance with a stony expression on his face.

Right now Sigil was off duty, but he was too restless to sleep. As tired as he was, he was still in better shape than his friend. Alina had looked particularly grateful when Murdoch had agreed to stand down for several hours, trusting that Sigil would send for him at the first sight of the two missing Damned returning to the fold.

If Sigil remained stationary there much longer, though, he'd fall asleep standing up. He rubbed his tired eyes and walked across the width of the gate and back to stir his blood again. As he made the turn a second time, he scanned the horizon. Wait! What was that?

Blinking twice, he looked again, staring hard at the farthest ridge in the distance. Nothing. He was about to give up when he saw it again. One—no, two—riders coming this way. It was too soon to sound the alarm, but his gut told him that it was Kane and Averel out there, riding hard for the keep.

As he watched them draw ever closer, it occurred to him that before he'd become one of the Damned himself, he wouldn't have been able to see the two warriors until they were much closer. His excitement growing by the second, he shouted down to one of the guards.

"Send for Captain Gideon, Duncan, and Murdoch. Make sure they know it's good news!"

The man nodded and took off running. Satisfied his message would be delivered, Sigil climbed down off the palisade. Someone had to ride out to meet the warriors. None of the assembled troops camped out on the grasslands had ever met Averel or Kane. There was no telling how they would react when two heavily armed warriors came charging through their encampment.

He ran for the pasture and threw himself up on the first horse he found. Rather than wait for someone to open the pasture gate, he urged the mare to jump the fence. One of the guards smartly had the main gate open for him.

Gideon and the other two warriors were already there.

"They're back!" Sigil shouted on his way out. "I'll provide escort through the troops."

By rights, it probably should've been one of the other three who rode out to meet the returning warriors, but they didn't argue. The sentries posted out on the grasslands let him pass without question, but he slowed enough to tell them he was meeting two more of Captain Gideon's men.

After that, it was a short ride to meet Kane and Averel. One look at the dark warrior, and Sigil was glad he'd been the one to come. Both men looked haggard, grim, and ready for a fight.

They slowed to a stop and waited for him, their horses sweaty and breathing hard. Man and beast were both clearly exhausted. Even so, Kane immediately noticed the change in Sigil's eyes.

"You must be Sigil, the one Gideon told us about in his message." Kane's voice was hoarse and rough. "You're one of us now? How did that happen? Keep in mind right now I'm in no mood for long stories."

Sigil kept it short. "The Lord and Lady of the River accepted my offer of service. It seemed like a good idea."

Averel immediately maneuvered his mare closer and held out his hand to clasp Sigil's arm. "Welcome, brother."

The gesture meant a lot. "Thank you. I'm still trying to come to terms with it. We can talk more later, but I left Gideon and the others waiting at the gate. I came because I wanted to make sure you didn't run into any problems riding through our assembled forces."

Kane stood up in the stirrups to scan the area. "Not as many men as we really need but more than I expected to answer the call."

He was right. "We're hoping more will arrive by tomorrow, but we can only wait and see. For now, let's get you to the keep. Welcome back."

Only pure hardheaded stubbornness was keeping Kane upright and moving. He hurt, the pain due in part to riding hard and fast for Lady Merewen's keep. They'd stopped for only a few hours to rest the horses, driving both themselves and their mounts hard.

But his agony stemmed from another source. Every mile they'd ridden had taken him that much farther from Theda. He cursed her stubborn nature, which had kept her from coming with him even as he respected the reasons behind her decision.

And not knowing her fate was the worst part of it. He'd give anything to know what had happened once Keirthan learned of Kane's escape. How many had suffered because of it? There was no way that bastard would accept defeat easily. No. Once he got over his initial anger, he would have begun rebuilding his power.

That made it all the more imperative that the Damned marshal their forces and begin the forced march back to the capital city. The longer they dallied here in the safety of Lady Merewen's keep, the stronger Keirthan would be when they faced him and the more innocent deaths would be on Kane's conscience.

He hated knowing people he cared about were in harm's way. Lady Theda was the most important, but by no means the only one. There were several of the guards he would hate facing in battle, knowing they would likely die protecting a man who didn't deserve such a sacrifice. And what of Theda's ladies-in-waiting? Had they made it away?

After reaching the keep, his friends had kept the reunion celebration blessedly short. Gideon had ordered him and Averel to eat a good meal and get a good night's sleep before he'd even consider discussing their plan of attack. He was right, but that hadn't meant Kane was happy about it.

Kane had awoken before first light, restless and ready to talk. So far, none of the other Damned had dragged themselves out of bed. If they didn't do so soon, Kane would hunt them down himself.

Of course, if Theda were here with him, he wouldn't be all that eager to leave his bed either. Gideon, Murdoch, and now even Duncan slept with their women safely tucked in next to them. On one level, Kane was happy for his friends, but on another, he secretly railed at the gods for the unfairness of it all. Why had they let this happen?

But maybe he already knew the answer. Gideon and the others weren't the ones who had broken a centuries-old vow to forswear the use of dark magic. Had the gods been testing his resolve? If so, he'd failed. Had he leapt at the first excuse to unleash his power?

Even now, his cheek throbbed where his mage mark pulsed hot and hungry. His worry over Theda's fate wasn't helping his already weakened control. Being this close to so many people left him feeling boxed in and on the edge of violence. Perhaps it would be better if he saddled Rogue and left the keep, waiting at a distance for their makeshift army to ride out. He'd never forgive himself if he struck out and injured one of his friends or another innocent. It wasn't their fault that he was so close to raging out of control.

A knock at the door came at last.

He backed into the corner farthest from the door, feeling better with his back to the wall. "Come in."

Sigil stepped into the room. Despite having spent some time with the man yesterday, it was still jarring to see his eyes a match to Kane's own.

"The others are coming."

The warrior came around the table to sit down, taking a chair that made it possible for him to keep a wary eye on Kane, but he took no offense. Maybe talking would help him maintain control.

"So the Lord and Lady accepted your oath."

Sigil nodded and leaned back in his chair. Kane was willing to bet he wasn't nearly as relaxed about that change in his circumstances as he pretended.

Staring past Kane at a sight only he could see, Sigil said, "They did. The Lady said that my service to them and their cause would help erase what I did in the name of the duke."

Curious, Kane said, "I thought you'd forgotten your past."

Sigil's eyebrows drew down low over his eyes. He looked frustrated. "I remember a few things, like I held the rank of captain in Keirthan's service, and I have some knowledge of magic. No real details, though. So that much hasn't really changed."

Then he smiled. "The gods gave me my own avatar. He's a monster of a wolf named Otsoko. I'll have to introduce you and Hob to him when you have time. Averel's dogs, too."

Kane snorted. "That should prove interesting. Dogs like Averel's were bred to hunt wolves."

"Otsoko could hold his own against them, but I'm hoping it won't come to that. He and Shadow have managed to make peace. If she can tolerate him, maybe the dogs will, too. How about Hob? Think there'll be a problem?"

Kane tried to picture the meeting in his mind. Every

scenario that he came up with ended badly. "Hob has made stranger friends over the years."

Footsteps out in the hall had them both watching the door. Gideon led the procession into the room. He provided introductions between Kane, Averel, and Lady Lavinia. She gave Averel a bright smile, but when she turned to greet Kane, Lavinia hissed and backed up several steps.

He made no comment, but neither did he look away from her sharp gaze. The woman carried her own heavy dose of magic, although it lacked the dark flavor of his own. He couldn't change what he was. She would accept him or not.

But perhaps he'd underestimated her. She took a cautious step toward him. "Lord Kane, I'd been warned that you bore the mark of a high-ranking mage, but no one told me that it was so powerful. Please forgive my reaction."

Well aware the other Damned were watching him closely, most especially Duncan, Kane allowed his own anger to drain away.

"No apology is necessary, Lady Lavinia. It isn't often that we encounter mages of great power, regardless of the source of their magic. Considering the actions of your half brother, it is understandable that you would have concerns about another whose gift is from the same end of the spectrum as his."

Her dark eyes conveyed a wealth of sympathy. "I'm sure that, like me, you find your gift to be more of a burden."

"It has ever been that."

He didn't know which of them he surprised more with that admission, but he didn't regret sharing his truth. They would need to work together if they were going to defeat the duke. To do so, they needed to trust each other, which had to be built on a firm foundation of honesty.

They needed to know what had happened to him

while he'd been in the service of the duke, and the telling wouldn't get easier by delaying. Drawing a deep breath, he met the gaze of each person in the room.

"Averel and I will explain what we experienced while we were in the capital. Afterward, you can tell us all that has transpired here."

Before he sat down himself, he added, "I know time is growing short for us all and that you will not delay our attack needlessly. I would ask you to remember that innocent lives depend on our actions, and one life in particular. If my lady comes to harm because we fail to act quickly, the gods themselves will not stand before my fury."

Chapter 23

*I*fre lay staring up at the ceiling, trying to decide what was different. Ordinarily, his manservant would have awakened him by now, but he'd left orders that he was not to be disturbed. That headache last night had been the worst one yet, but the tisane the physician had given him had helped lessen the pain. But only at first.

Shortly after he'd taken to his bed, another blast of pain had left him writhing in agony, tangled up in his blankets and fighting to even breathe. When the worst was past, Ifre had stumbled from his bed long enough to take two more doses and finally managed to fall asleep.

In the past, the medicine had left him feeling groggy and sick the next morning. Not this time. In fact, he felt better than he had in weeks. He threw back the covers and got out of bed. A glance out the window confirmed that the morning was already mostly gone.

He rang for his manservant. After getting dressed, he would join his courtiers in the great hall. No doubt there was another long line of petitioners hoping to speak to him. Well, they could wait until after the midday meal. Then he'd make a token effort to listen to their whining. He had important work to do down in the labyrinth.

For the first time since waking up, he thought about his special guest and smiled. How had Kane fared since Ifre had finished with him last night? He'd never had quite so much fun bleeding a victim as he had working on Kane. He loved that the captain healed almost as soon as the wound was inflicted. It had been amazing to watch. By now, surely Kane had recovered completely from their first encounter.

Ifre's creation had enjoyed the session as well, lapping up all that delicious blood and energy with such glee. Odd that Kane would have recognized it by name. Something else to question him about.

By the time Kane had finally lost consciousness, the cloud had been soot black and pulsing with power. Damijan had wanted more, but then it always did.

Except right now it was quiet.

In fact, Ifre hadn't heard a single sound from that direction since he woke up. The first flicker of concern had Ifre opening his door and shouting for his manservant to hurry. Where was the fool? If he didn't appear quickly, Kane would have a new companion by nightfall.

Finally, at the sound of running feet, Ifre returned to the window. His servant appeared in the doorway. "I'm sorry to keep you waiting, Sire. I wanted to make sure Lady Theda knew to hold the midday meal until you were ready to be seated."

All right, he would forgive the man this time. "Thank you for your consideration. Now, lay out my clothes. I have pressing business to attend to."

Such as finding out what had happened to quiet his creation, but that would have to wait until after Ifre ate. He'd need to be at full strength to face whatever waited for him down below. His real fear was that Damijan had finally gained enough strength to break free of Ifre's control altogether, a frightening possibility, to say the least. That didn't seem likely because he'd always suspected the first person Damijan would come after was Ifre himself.

So perhaps he had underestimated Kane's magical strength. The warrior's pulsing mage mark and those elongated teeth made it clear that Kane had much in common with the mages of old described in the forbidden manuscripts. According to the legends, mages of that strength had eventually been hunted down and destroyed centuries ago, along with all their blood kin. Was Kane some kind of throwback to the days when those mages had commanded great power?

Had the bastard done something to weaken the connection between Ifre and the power he'd worked so hard to build? If so, Kane might think he'd suffered before, but he would soon learn differently. Night after night, Ifre would bleed the mage warrior near unto death, let him heal, and then start all over again. The game the two of them played could continue for days, weeks, perhaps even months.

Having made his plans, he headed down to greet all the fools waiting to see him in the great hall.

Ifre hated the leeches who craved his attention. It had taken him until after sunset to finish hearing petitions. How he looked forward to the day he could simply turn his back on their endless clamor for more money, more attention, more of everything. If he didn't need their cooperation, he would have ordered his guard to round those pathetic nobles up like sheep and lead them to the slaughter.

There was plenty of room for more corpses in the canyon where Markus had been disposing of Ifre's previous guests once he was finished with them. He unlocked the door and started down the steep passageway. He'd gone but a few feet when he realized something was wrong, something far worse than he'd even imagined. Panic wouldn't solve anything, but he ran until he reached the floor below.

In the distance, the glow of the fire pit was far dimmer than normal. But it wasn't the dying fire that sent a chill right through him. No, it was the absolute silence. At the very least, he should be sensing the hum of his creation in the back of his mind. Earlier, he'd worried it had broken free or that Kane had usurped Ifre's control. Even if one of those two things had happened, he should still be able to sense it this close.

He crept forward, unsure what would be waiting for him when he crossed the threshold into the chambers ahead. Fear mixed with worry, leaving his hands trembling and his knees unsteady, but he knew better than to show weakness. Drawing himself up, shoulders back, head held high, he strode forward, ready to confront the enemy.

With dawning horror, he slowly made sense of the scene in front of him. Nothing was left of his beautiful altar except gravel and dust. Damijan, his beloved creation, was pale gray as it hovered but a scant few inches over the floor, its power drained.

And worst of all, Kane was gone.

Ifre forced himself to approach the dais. One of the shackles lay on the top step, perfectly intact except for a few scratches on the lock. Kane's possessions were also missing. He picked up a chunk of the broken marble and threw it as hard as he could. The action gave him no satisfaction.

Finally, he walked around his creation, his heart aching to see it so listless, so lifeless. Damijan barely stirred, drifting on the slight disturbance caused by Ifre's movement. No eyes, no mouth, no hunger. Right now his weapon was impotent, Ifre's enemies safe from his retribution.

It all added up to one thing: betrayal. There was no way Kane, even with all his mage-given power, could have broken free of his chains alone. The lock had been picked, not broken.

Somehow the enemy had managed to infiltrate Ifre's stronghold undetected. How was that even possible? There were only two entrances: the way Ifre had just entered the chambers from the great hall and the way Markus used to come and go that led beyond the city walls.

Had the sergeant betrayed him? No, that didn't make sense. The man was smart enough to know that he'd be the first one Ifre would suspect. For now Ifre would give him the benefit of the doubt.

So whom did that leave? Did Kane have any special friends? There was that troubadour that Markus had mentioned. Maybe it had been accidental that the two had gone riding outside of the city on the same day, but he wouldn't discount the possibility that the two were connected in some way.

There was one way to find out for sure. His first order of business would be to send Markus to see if the singer was still at the tavern. Ifre stared at his creation. It would need to be fed and soon. No one would miss a wanderer like a troubadour, and his gift for music might lend special power to his blood. If the man was innocent, well, too bad.

Ifre trudged back up the ramp to the door to the great hall. Ignoring the few nobles still scattered about the place, he headed for the nearest guard.

"You there, fetch Sergeant Markus for me. Tell him to meet me in my office in fifteen minutes. If it takes any longer than that, I will not be happy."

That's all it took to have the man running for the door. Satisfied that the sergeant would appear in short order, Ifre crossed the room to wait in his office. The last thing he wanted right now was to get caught up in some inane conversation with some self-important noble trying to curry his favor.

The knock on the office door came right on time. Ifre called out, "Enter."

Markus looked curious, not worried. "You sent for me, Sire?"

"Yes, I did, but we will not talk here. You will accompany me below immediately."

The sergeant paled, but he didn't question Ifre's orders or hesitate to follow him. Every eye in the hall followed their progress across the room. No one was foolish or brave enough to intercept them. Considering the mood Ifre was in right now, any such action might have ended in bloodshed.

As soon as they were safely down the ramp and approaching his chambers, Markus finally found his voice.

"Is something wrong, Sire?"

Ifre spun around to face him. "Not just something, Sergeant. Everything. But I'll let you see what has happened for yourself."

He hurried into the chamber ahead of Markus, positioning himself to watch the guard for any sign that he already knew what was waiting for them. But no, the shock on Markus's face was too real. So was his fear. For the first time, the ghost of the cloud stirred, no doubt supping from the tension and worry that poured off Markus in waves.

Looking bewildered, the sergeant stared at the shattered remains of the altar. "By the gods, what happened here, Sire?"

"I would think the answer would be obvious. Someone freed Kane from his fetters and helped him escape. One of them, most likely Kane himself, drained my power and then used it to destroy my altar."

Ifre clenched his hands into fists, wishing he had a handy target for his vengeance. "I need to know how they got in, how many of them there were, and where they are now. I'd suggest you start by checking on that troubadour again."

"Yes, Sire."

Ifre stared hard at the sergeant. "Bring me those answers, and you will be my new captain."

Markus immediately brought his right fist up to his chest in a salute. "It will be my honor."

Or it will be his death, Ifre added to himself. No use in scaring the man any more than he already was.

"For now we will search together for any evidence my enemies might have left behind. I've already discovered that someone picked the lock on Kane's shackles. That's how I know he had help."

Hoisting a torch, he led the way down the passage that Markus normally used. The cart was right where it should be, so either Kane walked out on his own or his rescuers had carried him. With no way to know for certain, that bit of information was useless.

The stone floor of the passage offered up no clues. No tracks, no drops of blood, nothing that hinted at how many people had trod its surface recently. The door at the far end was locked. He held the torch close to the mechanism.

"No fresh scratches, so either they had a key or else they only left by this route." He glanced back at Markus. "Assuming, that is, that you still have your key."

Markus immediately produced it. Again there was no sign of guilt in his expression.

"Put it away. If they didn't come this way, it would appear they somehow infiltrated the keep. How could they have entered through the hall above without being seen?"

Based on the evidence, that seemed to be the most logical approach for them to have used. The idea of an enemy being able to pass through Ifre's own stronghold unheeded was frightening. But then Kane had done exactly that from the beginning, hadn't he?

Markus said, "I will see who was on duty last night and determine if there were any irregularities that have not been reported. After that, I will go after the troubadour."

"Do that. I want to know anything you learn, no matter how trivial it may appear."

They walked back to the chambers. "Add wood to the fire while I look around one last time."

Marcus started tossing chunks of wood into the pit, sending up a shower of sparks. It didn't take long for the room to warm up. The heat did little to relieve the bleak chill that had settled over Ifre's mood.

"Bring that troubadour to me by morning. If he's not to be found, I will need two—no, make that three—new subjects."

"I will not fail you, my lord."

Ifre fluttered his hand in the air in a gesture of dismissal. "I know you won't. Now go."

The sergeant left the room with impressive speed. Relief did that to a man. For now there was nothing more to be done. Tomorrow they would clean up the mess Kane and his fellow conspirators had left behind. Ifre would also order the stone mason to make him another altar. One benefit of being the duke was prompt service.

Alone again, he returned to study his creation. "I'm sorry this happened, Damijan. When I have Kane back under my control, he will be my gift to you, and he won't have a drop of blood or magic left when we are finished with him."

The memory of Kane screaming until his voice was ruined flared bright in Ifre's mind. "That warrior will die, but not before he watches his friends bleed out in front of him."

The cloud stirred again, just enough to reassure Ifre that he wouldn't have to start over from the beginning to re-create his weapon. Once it was back at full power, he would strike out at those who stood against him. They would beg for mercy before he was finished, but they'd soon learn that mercy no longer existed for the people of Agathia.

Chapter 24

"*H*e's suffering."

Merewen hadn't told Gideon something he didn't already know. Kane's pain was obvious, especially to anyone who knew him well. Since his return, the warrior barely slept, rarely ate, and snapped at anyone who came too close, Gideon included.

Merewen's dark eyes stared down at Kane, who was busy taking his bad mood out on those foolish enough to face him in weapons practice. In a few minutes, Gideon would go down and challenge him himself. At least he had a fighting chance against Kane's twin swords. The purely human soldiers only ended up bruised and hurting.

"Is there nothing else we can do to ease his mind? I hate seeing him like this."

Kane paused for a moment to glance up to where they stood watching him. Did he sense they were talking about him? Probably, considering the angry look he shot directly toward Gideon.

"I'd act the same way if it were you trapped inside Duke Keirthan's keep beyond my reach. Add to that knowing that others will suffer and die because of Kane's escape, and you can understand why he is nearly out of his mind with worry and guilt."

Gideon walked back into their room from the balcony. "The day after tomorrow, we will march toward the capital. Kane will be better once we are on the move. The waiting is always the worst part."

Well, that and the actual fighting and dying that would follow. Images of past battles came flooding back, the memories never far from Gideon's mind. He could see it all too clearly: blood, screams, and death. And even when the Damned walked away victorious, the battlefield was still covered with the dead and dying from both sides.

Merewen brought him back to the moment at hand. "You do know that I'll be coming with you when our forces march, Gideon."

He closed his eyes and tried not to lash out. She meant well, but how was he supposed to fight knowing she was anywhere close to the battle?

"No, you're not."

It came out as a growl, the words harsher than he meant them to be. He reached out for her, pulling her close, hoping she would let it go. He should've known better.

Everything about Merewen showed her mind was made up. "This is as much my fight as it is yours, Gideon. My fate is tied up with yours, and I will not huddle here inside these walls and wait for news."

When he finally tried to speak, she shushed him. "I know what you're going to say, and I even understand, Gideon. Remember, I love you, too, and would keep you out of harm's way if I could. We both know that is not possible. You will do whatever it takes to defeat the enemy."

She hugged him tight. "I may not be a warrior, but I am a skilled healer. Do not tell me that I cannot be of use once the fighting starts. You cannot leave Lavinia behind, either, although we both know Duncan doesn't want her to face the duke's magic in battle."

Then Merewen chuckled, although he could not imagine how she could find anything about this impending disaster amusing. "Alina offered to assist me in caring for the injured, and I said yes. When Murdoch bellowed and tried to change her mind, she told him she was done cowering in her room."

What could Gideon say to that? It wasn't as if he had any better luck controlling Merewen. Murdoch was on his own.

A wise leader knew when to retire from the battle to fight another day. "Let's not argue about this now. I need to go distract Kane before he works his way through all of our troops. Maybe he'll listen if I point out that it will only delay things further if we have to give them all time to recover from his lessons."

He was pleased when Merewen laughed again. Right now, there was precious little to smile about in any of their lives. The summer solstice was nearly upon them. He didn't want to spend what time he had left fighting and listening to the screams of dying men. No, he wanted every last second with this woman in his arms, in his bed.

He pressed a kiss against her temple. "I love you, Merewen. Never forget that."

Never forget me, although that last thought was pure selfishness on his part. A better man would want her to move on, to find happiness with someone else after the Damned stood judgment and learned what their fate would be this time.

Please, Lady, let this half-life end for me and my friends. Our souls grow weary of the battle.

In truth, he wasn't sure he could face more centuries in the cold chill of the river only to return to a world that wouldn't have Merewen in it.

To his surprise, the Lady answered. *"Have faith, my warrior. Stand strong and you shall know peace."*

Kane needed to get away. Now, before he hurt someone seriously. He settled his shield on his back and threw himself up on Rogue's broad back. As soon as they left the stable, he started cursing. The guard he'd ordered to open the front gate for him was nowhere in sight. He should've known he wouldn't be able to escape without someone interfering. At least it was Gideon, who stood the best chance of defending himself against Kane if he lost control.

Which could happen at any second.

"Get out of the way, Gideon. I have to go. Hob and I need to hunt."

His friend nodded. "I guessed as much. We leave tomorrow by midday. If you don't return by then, catch up when you can."

"I will."

Gideon hadn't asked him to explain why he was leaving just when there was so much work to be done. He gave one anyway.

"I can't be near people right now. Keirthan did something to me, to my control. Right now I'm not safe to be around."

He finally met his friend's gaze. "I can't stand knowing that I just left her there, Gideon. I could have overpowered her. Rogue could've carried us both to safety, but I didn't do any of that. I abandoned the woman I love for my duty."

"But the gods—"

His grief became rage. "Damn the gods, Gideon. No matter what we've done in their names, no matter how many centuries we have answered their call, they didn't protect the one person in all that time who matters to me."

He expected anger from Gideon. Hoped for it, knowing it would give him a handy target for his frustration. Instead, the sympathy in Gideon's expression was almost his undoing.

"Kane, we both know the gods don't work that way." Gideon patted Rogue on the neck as he spoke. "I grant that you have the worst of it right now, but it's not easy for any of the rest of us, knowing our women will ride right into the same danger as Lady Theda."

Kane knew that. It didn't change anything. "Open the gate, Gideon. Please."

As he charged out of the keep, he hoped Gideon recognized that last word was meant as an apology.

Kane had no destination in mind other than to get away from the keep and everyone in it. All he was aware of was the pounding of Rogue's hooves as the big stallion loped across the grasslands at a ground-eating pace. As the two of them put some distance between themselves and the crowded keep, Kane gradually became more aware of his surroundings.

The sun was low in the sky, the growing darkness soothing him even more. Soon he'd have to rein Rogue in. It wouldn't be fair to risk the horse taking a tumble because Kane's own demons were riding him hard.

As if sensing Kane's improved mood, Rogue slowed on his own. It was then Kane realized they'd run out of grassland. He signaled Rogue to stop completely. The path ahead led straight up the mountainside. At the top lay the deep pool that had been the home of the Damned since the day they'd sworn service to the Lord and Lady. How had the horse known to bring him there? He certainly hadn't guided Rogue there. Or maybe he had.

Gideon wasn't the only one to whom Kane owed an apology. He was also guilty of far more than simply cursing the gods themselves. Resigned to his fate, he dismounted and stood his shield against a nearby boulder. Next he stripped off Rogue's bridle and saddle.

Patting the big horse on the nose, he rested his head against Rogue's neck. "I'm going up the mountain to have a conversation with the Lord and Lady. I don't know how that's going to turn out, but I suspect it won't end well. If I'm not back by morning, find Lady Merewen and let her know what's happened."

The horse nodded and shook his head. Kane laughed and patted him again. "I'm going to set Hob free, too."

He chanted softly, closing his eyes briefly against the

flash of light. Kane smiled as Hob stretched before exchanging a quick sniff and snort with his equine friend.

"I'm going to the river, Hob. You stay with Rogue. This is a journey I must take alone."

He rubbed his scaly friend's head and walked away. He hadn't gone but a few steps when he heard not just Hob but Rogue following in his footsteps.

"No, you two stay here. That's an order."

Despite Kane's command, the contrary beasts ignored him. Finally, after another attempt, he gave up and let them do as they pleased. They would anyway.

As the climb grew steeper, he slowed down, not for his sake but for Rogue's. This trail was never meant for horses, but the stallion was nothing if not stubborn.

Eventually, Kane found himself encouraging his friends. "It's only a little farther. At the top, you'll be able to get a drink of water and rest."

Ahead the trees thinned out, giving way to the rocky shoreline of the river. It was all painfully familiar. Despite Kane's dread of the place, the cool night air and quiet murmur of the water eased him. Rather than approach the black mirrored pool right away, he took a seat on the ground and leaned back against a boulder.

Rogue wandered to the river's edge and took a long drink. Hob joined him, his forked tongue flitting in and out of his mouth as he slurped up the water. They were an odd pair, the scarred stallion and the gargoyle, but then Kane wasn't exactly normal himself. Hadn't been even before the gods had claimed him as their warrior.

At least up here on the mountain, far from everyone else, he could breathe and his skin no longer felt as if it were a size too small for his body. He stared up at the stars overhead, enjoying the simple beauty of the night sky. Gradually, his eyes grew heavier, until he could no longer hold them open. Maybe a brief rest would be a good idea before he approached the gods. His temper, always unpredictable, was worse when he was exhausted.

Since leaving Theda, he hadn't slept for more than a couple of hours at a stretch.

He settled back and let his mind drift. As soon as he gave up control, the air around him changed. No longer did it carry the scent of damp rocks and pine. Instead, he smelled . . . what? Then he knew: roses and night-blooming lilies. He'd never paid much attention to flowers. They had little to do with the life of a warrior. But the first night he'd strolled through Keirthan's garden with Lady Theda, she'd pointed out her favorites.

At the moment, he didn't know if he was dreaming or simply imagining that he no longer sat by the river. Instead, he was sitting on a familiar bench, the one he'd shared with Theda in the garden. As he looked around, everything seemed so very real to him. The smooth texture of the stone seat. The bushes stirred in the night breeze, surrounding him with the heavy scent of roses.

Noises were real, too. In the distance, one of the guards shouted at another to hurry up and relieve him. But the sound that had Kane lurching to his feet was the soft sweep of a lady's gown across the grass.

"Theda?" he whispered as the lady herself came into view.

Her face paled in shock, standing out in stark contrast to the thick darkness around them. "Kane, is that you? What are you doing back here?"

Then she looked around them. "Am I only imagining you? I remember going to bed."

"If you are dreaming, I am as well. I sat down and thought to rest but a short time before calling upon the Lord and Lady of the River."

As he spoke, he eased closer to Theda, terrified she would fade out of sight if he moved too quickly and jarred himself awake. This might be a dream world, but it was one he was in no hurry to leave.

She stared at him in wonder. "This feels real to me, Kane. As if I could reach out and touch you."

Theda slowly raised her hand, moving as cautiously as he did. Finally, their fingertips touched, blessedly solid and warm. He brushed his hand over hers, lingering there briefly before taking another small step closer. Since when in a dream could a man feel the warmth of a lover's skin and the soft flutter of her pulse?

Rather than question his good fortune, he enfolded Theda in his arms, cradling her gently against him and savoring the simple joy of the moment. Holding her was a balm to his ravaged soul.

"I should have taken you with me. I can't breathe for knowing you're here where Keirthan could turn on you at any moment."

She smiled up at him, her eyes shiny with tears. "You'll be back soon enough. Know that I am counting the minutes until you return."

It would be days yet, and she was smart enough to know that. Armies, even one as small as theirs, moved at a crawl. "How did Keirthan react to my escape?"

"I don't know. He went down to his chamber only a short time before I retired for the night. He spent the whole morning sleeping and then heard petitions for most of the afternoon."

That made no sense. "But I've been gone for four days, Theda."

She looked up at him in confusion. "That can't be. It was just last night that you and Averel left the city."

He didn't understand what was happening any more than she did. "Perhaps in dreams time doesn't move the same way. But I am not going to question this gift the gods have given us."

Already he could feel himself fading, their surroundings growing more indistinct. Rather than fight to hold on to the moment, he concentrated on the one thing he knew was real. He captured Theda's sweet mouth with his, kissing her hard and deep. Her lips smiled against his, and she sighed with contentment as she twined her arms around his neck.

He wanted so much more, to lay her down on the soft grass and make love to her, to once again claim her as his own. There was no time for that. Not with the world around them going black.

"Theda, I will come for you."

She cupped the marked side of his face with the palm of her hand, her touch a blessing he needed so badly. "I know you will."

"I love you."

As soon as he said the words, she disappeared from his arms. No longer in Keirthan's garden, Kane was back sprawled on the damp rocks on a moonless night. Had Theda heard him? Or had he simply imagined it all? He rubbed his mage-marked cheek, missing Theda's touch.

As if sensing Kane's pain, Hob raised his nose to the sky and howled, his eerie call echoing off the rocky bluff above the water. Kane considered joining in as he often did when the two of them hunted together. Not tonight, though. He had other business to attend to before he could return to the keep.

He approached the water, aware of Hob and Rogue moving to stand on either side of him. If he thought it would do any good, he would have ordered them to leave. He was the only one who should have to stand before the gods this night.

However, he trusted the gods to not punish his companions for their loyalty to him. He knelt on one knee, head bowed. He remained in that position for several minutes, silent and penitent. When he finally spoke, his voice was rough and low as his emotions welled up and threatened to choke him: regret, anger, hatred, and most of all his love for his friends and Lady Theda.

"My Lord and Lady, I stand before you to confess my failures."

It was the Lady who answered. "And what failures would those be, Lord Kane?"

She knew full well everything her warriors did, but he

would list his transgressions aloud if she needed to hear them.

"I used the magic my grandfather forced upon me, breaking my vow to forswear it. In anger, I cursed your name. And I have let my emotions cloud my judgment. If I could've convinced Lady Theda to leave with me, I fear I would've forsaken my friends and duty to you."

"Your anger is forgiven, Lord Kane. It was your love and worry for the woman who has claimed your heart speaking. We know you will stand strong when we need you the most. As for your magic, it is part of you, not something that can be tossed aside or shoved into a box. You wielded it to save your life and to weaken the enemy. Where is the wrong in that?"

A soft breeze toyed with Kane's hair, as a mother would pat her child on the head.

"Your four-footed companions stand with you because they, too, know you for a man of honor. Now rise and return to the captain and your friends. Time grows short and the battle the Warriors of the Mist must fight grows near. One more thing, Lord Kane. The dream was real in your mind and in your heart, as it was for Lady Theda. She heard your words. Take comfort in that."

"Thank you, my lady."

Kane rose to his feet, bowed toward the river, and led his companions back down the mountain.

Chapter 25

"*H*ow much farther?"

Kane let Averel answer Gideon's question. His memory of the route from this point on was a tangled mess. On their journey to the capital, he'd taken a different approach to the city gates, one that didn't pass through this area. When he and Averel had escaped, he'd been too caught up in the pain of leaving Theda behind to care about the landscape.

Averel stood in his stirrups to look ahead. "The city is less than an hour's ride beyond that farthest ridge. This road winds around to the east end of those hills, where it joins up with one of the main trade routes."

It was time for Kane to contribute something to their effort. "If I'm correct, there's a small river just west of here that cuts through the forest. I suggest everyone set up camp there for tonight. While you get everyone settled, I'll take the scouts out to reconnoiter."

Murdoch joined them. "Sigil and I will hunt. We could all use some fresh meat."

Gideon glanced behind them, his mouth set in a grim line. Kane followed Gideon's line of sight back toward the women stopped a short distance away. Not one of the three had uttered a single word of complaint over the long, hard ride that had brought them to this point, but their near exhaustion was clear.

The captain's decision wasn't long in coming. "Averel, tell the men to ride for the river and set up camp. Post a double circle of guards, one near the camp and the other at the outer edge of the forest. Murdoch, hunt but don't stay gone long."

The big knight nodded and rode away, waving for Sigil to join him. That left just Kane and Gideon. He shifted in the saddle as he waited for his friend to finish giving orders.

"Send out the scouts, but I want you with me. We have plans to discuss, and I want your opinion. After we eat tonight, I plan to hold a war council and to present a united front to our allies. If we're going to argue about how we're going to do this, I'd rather do so in private."

What did Gideon have in mind that he thought Kane might object to? "I will join you as soon as I've given the men their orders."

"I'll be helping Merewen get our camp organized." Gideon kept his eyes on the horizon, a clear sign he was uncomfortable with what he was about to say. "I understand why you've been more at ease sleeping away from the rest of us. But now that we're this close to the capital, I'd rather you stay in camp." When Gideon finally looked toward Kane, he wore a puzzled look. "Are you all right?"

That's when Kane realized he'd been rubbing his chest right over the spot where he'd worn the symbol of his office as captain of the duke's guard. He jerked his hand back down to grab Rogue's reins. Surely that connection to Keirthan had been broken when Kane quit wearing the duke's sigil. Was the ache real or memory?

Either way, he owed Gideon an explanation. "When the duke made me captain, he gave me an emblem to wear that showed my new rank. I didn't realize at first that he'd infused it with some of his magic. I suspect now that it was what enabled him to override my magic and imprison me. It weakened my resistance to magic of all kinds."

Gideon maneuvered Kestrel closer to Rogue. Other than flicking their ears back and forth, for once the two stallions remained calm. "I'll ask again. Are you all right?

If there's a chance you're still connected to him in some way, we need to know that now."

Kane wanted to deny even the possibility, but he wouldn't lie to Gideon. "It didn't interfere with my efforts to weaken the store of magic he'd poured into Damijan, that abomination he created. It was definitely my own magic that crushed his altar."

He closed his eyes, turning his senses inward. If there was something foreign inside of him, he couldn't sense it. That didn't mean much.

"Gideon, I cannot swear that I am completely free of that bastard's influence. If at any point you have doubts about my loyalties or my actions, don't hesitate to act. Your duty is to protect Lady Merewen and her people."

"You don't need to remind me of my duty, Kane," Gideon snapped.

Kane leaned in close enough to grasp Gideon's sword arm. "Swear by the goddess that you won't fail to do what's necessary if I'm the source of the danger. I would rather die than dishonor all that we have done."

It was his captain who slowly nodded, accepting the burden of the vow. But it was his friend who took Kane's hand in his own and said, "Your honor is my honor, Kane. You have never failed me in all our time together. I will not fail you in this."

His words lifted a weight off Kane's shoulders. "I'll send out the scouts and then find you. And, Gideon, if you still want me to, I will pitch my tent next to yours. With the battle soon upon us, I would spend these last hours with my friends."

Gideon smiled. "I would have it no other way."

Ifre wasn't used to manual labor, but he didn't want anyone other than Sergeant Markus to know Kane had succeeded in destroying his altar, the symbol of Ifre's power. It would be seen as a sign of weakness by anyone who thought to stand against him.

Markus had made inquiries about the troubadour.

Just as expected, the man had disappeared. The sergeant had verified the man's belongings, his horse, and dogs were all gone.

Ifre swept up another shovelful of broken rock and dust. If he didn't hate Kane so much, he would have admired the warrior. Whatever the man had used to shatter the altar, he'd done a thorough job of it. Perhaps he'd had help. Was the troubadour a mage as well? If so, he would've left behind some trace of his magic. Ifre muttered a curse. Why hadn't he thought to check earlier? By now even the residue of Kane's powerful magic had faded. Ifre held his hands over the pile of rubble, his fingers spread wide as he chanted softly under his breath.

Nothing. Not even a faint tingle other than the familiar feel of Kane's magic. That was reassuring. Having one powerful mage set against Ifre was bad enough.

Picking up the broom that the sergeant had left for him, Ifre started on the far side and swept the dust toward the area where the altar had stood. As he worked, something sparkled in the pile of dust. He used the broom to clear away the dust, revealing a piece of gold wire. Reluctant to touch anything Kane might have left behind, he bent down to study his find.

It was a pin, and judging by its length, the kind used to fasten a cloak. He held his hand over it briefly, but sensed no magic attached to it. Even so, he used a bit of rag to pick it up and carried it over toward the fire pit, where the light was brighter.

Just as he suspected, it was a stick pin, one he recognized. The pin used to belong to Ifre's own mother, part of the jewelry that was handed down from one generation to the next. His brother, Armel, had gifted his wife with the collection on their wedding day.

So this pin hadn't belonged to Kane or the troubadour. It was Theda's. All the pieces fell into place, solving the mystery of how Kane's friend managed to infiltrate Ifre's stronghold without being caught. Clearly she'd led him through the great hall and then somehow unlocked the door to the labyrinth for him. Most likely they'd used her pin to pick the lock on the shackles and lost it in their hurry to escape.

The only question that remained was why Theda would risk so much for a man like Kane. But the answer was obvious. Somehow she had subverted Kane's allegiance to Ifre for her own purposes. Had she betrayed Ifre, thinking to win her freedom? If so, why had Kane left her behind? She should have known better than to trust a common mercenary. If he would betray Ifre, then why not her?

None of that mattered. Her actions would cost Theda dearly, starting with the blood and lives of her friends. Their virginal blood would restore the strength of his magic. They'd die screaming as Theda watched, helpless to do anything to relieve their suffering.

Then Theda herself would learn the feel of his knife and the depth of his vengeance.

Markus's arrival interrupted his thoughts. Ifre shoved the pin in his pocket, looking forward to the moment he confronted Theda with her crimes.

"Ah, Sergeant, I'm glad you're here."

Markus saluted Ifre. "Sire, I have news."

The sergeant was careful to keep the entrance to the tunnel to his back, so most likely the news wasn't good and Markus thought to escape Ifre's wrath. Did the fool really think he'd be able to reach safety that way? He'd seen what had happened to Kane when he'd tried to escape Ifre's control. Markus would stand no chance at all against Ifre's power.

"Well, I'm waiting."

Markus drew a deep breath before speaking. "One of my men confessed there'd been a problem when he was assigned to guard the hall. The fool had a skin of wine that he stopped to drink from when he thought he heard a noise. The next thing he remembers is waking up sprawled in one of the hallways stinking of wine."

"Has his drinking been a problem before?"

"No, Sire. He's one of my most dependable men, which is why I assigned him to this particular duty. I believe he was rendered unconscious and dragged to that hall." The sergeant sounded defensive, as if he knew how improbable the guard's story sounded.

"I believe him, too, Sergeant. I have found evidence that we have a traitor in our midst, but it wasn't a member of my personal guard. Despite Captain Kane's treachery, you and your men are above reproach."

Markus looked marginally happier, but then he frowned. "Then you know who the traitor is?"

"I do."

He immediately unwrapped the pin and held it out for Markus's inspection. The sergeant stepped forward to stare down at the piece of jewelry.

Recognition wasn't long in coming. "It bears your family crest, Sire. Are you saying Lady Theda is the traitor?"

Ifre returned the damning piece of evidence to his pocket, his expression grave. "That's exactly what I am saying, Sergeant. For the moment, I do not plan to accuse her of crimes against the crown. Once I have restored my altar, though, she will answer for her betrayal. When I am ready, you will deliver her and her ladies to me here."

For a brief second, Markus looked shocked, but it didn't last long. The man was nothing if not pragmatic. He knew full well that he would have to produce the women or take their place.

"Yes, Sire. Until that time, is there anything else I can do to assist you?"

"Empty the cart and then return to finish the rest of the cleanup. The stonemason assured me that my new altar will be ready by tomorrow at the latest."

As Markus trudged back down the passage with the heavily laden cart, Ifre picked up the broom and went back to work. By this time tomorrow, he would begin the arduous process of rebuilding his power. Once Damijan was up to full strength, he would unleash it upon his enemies.

And then maybe upon his friends.

Theda watched her brother-in-law from afar. He'd been remarkably calm since losing Kane, which was far more disturbing than if he'd exploded with fury. He hated being thwarted in any way, and this had been a major defeat for him. Why was he taking it so calmly?

A chill of dread washed over her. He wasn't calm. He was plotting. With Kane and his friend safely out of reach, that meant Ifre had another target in mind for his revenge. The possibilities were limited, each one worse than the next.

There was the guard that Averel had rendered unconscious. Had the man regained his memory of what had happened? If he claimed to have been attacked, would Sergeant Markus believe him? As far as she knew, the man hadn't seen her at all, so at least he couldn't point a finger in her direction.

Then there was Tom. There were only so many ways into the building. Had Ifre or Sergeant Markus figured out Averel had come in through that door? She'd known she was putting her friend at risk, but her need to help Kane had left her no choice.

Should she warn him? Yes. Tom needed to disappear before it was too late. He would resist leaving, but she wouldn't let him die because he'd remained her friend. If Kane and his friends were successful, he would be able to return to the city soon. If they weren't, the capital wouldn't be a fit place for anyone to live.

That left her. Ifre had always had plans for her once her mandatory time of mourning was over. She still had a month left before custom declared she could remarry. If Kane had been willing, she would have ignored the tradition, but she was grateful for the scant protection it had offered her from Ifre.

If Ifre somehow connected her to Kane's escape, nothing would save her. They'd been so careful, and she'd returned to her quarters without being seen. She'd hidden her bloody dress and then later destroyed it. Her slippers, too. The only thing she'd kept was her cloak. After washing it clean of Kane's blood, it was as good as new.

"Are you all right, Lady Theda?"

She'd been so lost in thought, she hadn't noticed Sergeant Markus's approach. He offered her a cup of wine.

"I noticed you were looking a bit pale and thought perhaps a drink would help."

She had no choice but to accept the wine. To refuse in so public a place would draw too much unwanted attention to them both. Although she hated to admit it, the wine did taste good to her.

"Thank you, Sergeant. I appreciate your thoughtfulness."

Then she noticed the emblem pinned to his tunic. "Forgive me for not noticing sooner. Congratulations on your promotion, Captain Markus."

He tilted his head in acknowledgment. "Thank you, my lady. I was honored when Duke Keirthan offered me the position."

She took another sip of her drink. "I hadn't heard that Captain Kane had resigned."

"The duke chose not to make a formal announcement about his departure. It was rather, shall we say, unexpected."

"You have served the duke well, Captain. I'm sure he will reward you for your loyalty."

She started to excuse herself when the first wave of dizziness hit her. By the second wave, it felt as if the floor beneath her feet was rolling. She latched onto Markus's arm for support at the same time a small voice in her head screamed that this was his doing, that he'd drugged her.

"My lady, you don't appear to be well. Please allow me to escort you from the hall."

She wanted to refuse, wanted to do anything but let Ifre's lackey lead her away from the relative safety of the crowded hall. Her feet wouldn't obey her, and her throat refused to give voice to her growing terror.

With her mind under the control of whatever drug Ifre had ordered Markus to give her, she couldn't trust anything she saw or heard. But as Markus unlocked the door that led to the labyrinth below, she could have sworn she heard him whisper, "I'm sorry."

Chapter 26

*T*he wood smoke trickled up through the trees overhead. The women had yet to join them, so for the
moment it was only the six warriors seated in a circle
around the fire. Kane knew it wouldn't last, but he would
enjoy the few minutes of peace with his friends. No one
seemed moved to talk, but men were often quiet on the
night before a battle. As he sipped his tea, Kane studied
each of the men who had been his friends for more life-
times than he could remember.

Of all of them, he hoped young Averel would be released from the Lady's service and allowed to live a long
and full life. Despite everything that had happened to
them in the service of the gods and even before, Averel
had managed to hold on to his good nature. As if sensing
Kane's scrutiny, he looked up from tending the fire and
grinned.

Kane nodded in response before turning his attention
in Duncan's direction. He was the second one who deserved far better out of life than he'd been given. With a
mind like his, he should have been a renowned scholar,
not sitting in the dirt honing a sword.

Murdoch and Sigil sat side by side, their odd friendship a surprise to them all. The big man's gaze was never
far from Lady Alina, another odd pairing, but perhaps
not. Murdoch rarely spoke of his youth, but it was obvious that it had been as brutal as Alina's marriage to her
late husband. Clearly, the petite woman and the giant of
a man had found solace in each other's arms.

Sigil was a puzzle. He seemed to possess a strong sense of honor, yet he'd served that bastard Duke Keirthan. Of course, so had Kane for a short time, so who was he to judge? The Lord and Lady had seen fit to accept the man into their service. That was good enough for Kane. He just hoped Sigil didn't come to regret his decision to become one of the Damned.

That left Gideon, the first friend Kane had ever made. Few had ever bothered to look past the mark on Kane's cheek and his dark looks to the man inside. Back in his youth, the world had been such a superstitious place. People assumed that because he'd been marked by dark magic on the outside that he carried its taint on his soul.

Gideon had dismissed the common belief and had given Kane a chance to prove himself. Through the captain, Kane had gained this circle of friends. Kane would die for Gideon and the others. Had, in fact, and wouldn't hesitate to do so again. A man could do no less for his brothers, a family born out of blood and pain and held together by loyalty and honor.

Gideon poked at the fire with a stick, sending up a shower of sparks. "We need to discuss plans."

As he looked around the circle, everyone went from relaxed to alert. "We cannot hide an army for long, not even a small one such as ours. We have to be ready to fight by tomorrow morning."

Frowning, he stared into the flames. "The scouts encountered at least two patrols of Keirthan's forces in the area. It's only a matter of time before they cross our trail."

So far, nothing he said accounted for why Gideon was holding that stick in a white-knuckled grip. If Kane had to guess, the true source of his friend's tension could be laid at the feet of the three women headed their way. Kane sympathized, but it was too late to send them back to safety even if they were willing to go.

The men made room for them around the fire. Gideon waited until everyone was settled again before continuing. "As much as I hate to divide our efforts, we will face Keirthan's forces on three fronts. He is a coward and will send his men to die upon our swords while he remains hidden behind the thick walls of his city."

Kane spoke up. "And his weapon, if he has brought it back to full strength, can be fired without him ever leaving his underground chambers."

"Which is why we need to attack from three directions." Gideon used the stick to draw a rough diagram in the dust. "Murdoch and I will lead our forces on a direct assault, hoping to draw Keirthan's troops out of the city. Barring that, at least we will hold their attention. At first light, Murdoch will take half of the men and circle around to come in from the east. Once they are in position, the rest of our forces will attack the southern gate."

He reached for a pair of rolled-up parchments that Merewen had brought out with her. "These are the maps that Kane and Averel have drawn for us of the surrounding area as well as of the city itself."

He tossed one to Murdoch. "After we're done talking, commit that to memory."

"This next one is for you, Duncan."

The scholarly warrior unrolled it. His face paled when he realized what Kane had drawn out for him. "This is Keirthan's keep."

It wasn't a question, but Kane answered anyway. "We'll be entering from outside of the city walls through a tunnel that leads straight to where Keirthan practices his dark arts."

At first, Duncan looked confused. "But the goddess said I was to remain at Lavinia's side during the battle. I can't do that if I'm inside the city."

The lady herself spoke up. "I will be going with you, Duncan. If I'm to counter Ifre's magic, I need to be close to its source. Otherwise, I'm striking out blind and could do more harm than good."

Duncan, usually slow to anger, exploded. He tossed the parchment back at Gideon. "Keep this. I'm not letting Lavinia anywhere near Keirthan. He's been hunting for her for months and knows full well she'll never join his effort. He's already tried to kill her three times. If Keirthan were to capture her, he'll fuel his magic with her blood. She stays here with Merewen and Alina."

Lavinia restrained Duncan when he started to rise. "I'm sorry, Duncan, but this is my decision to make. You reminded me back at the abbey that it was my duty to protect our people, and that's what I'm going to do. And before you yell at the captain again, you should know that I volunteered to go. He argued long and hard against the idea."

Kane looked up from honing his throwing knives. "The two of you won't be going alone, Duncan. Averel and I have been in Keirthan's chambers before, and we both know the city. Sigil will be coming along as well. Between the four of us, we will keep your lady safe."

"You have no idea what you're asking of her, Kane." Duncan turned his frustration in Kane's direction. "You can't promise that she'll be safe. By the gods, you almost died in those chambers yourself. I won't put her at such risk."

"Do not presume to tell me what I understand, Duncan." Kane jerked upright and stabbed his knife deep into the ground to resist throwing it at his friend.

From the way Lavinia was staring at him, he suspected his eyes were glinting red and his long canine teeth were on full display. "Lady Theda risked her own life to save mine even knowing Ifre Keirthan murdered her husband, his own brother. She lives every minute of every day in his presence with nothing but her wits to keep her safe."

Breathing hard, he retrieved his knife and wiped the blade clean on his leathers. "If Lavinia cannot stop Keirthan, Duncan, no one will be safe. No one. And we, the Damned, are almost out of time. Caution is a luxury we can no longer afford."

Duncan clearly wanted to argue more, but Gideon

stepped in. He held out the parchment again. "The decision has been made, Duncan. Murdoch and I will draw the duke's attention in our direction. Kane, Averel, and Sigil will accompany you and Lavinia to attack the duke directly. Right now, I'd suggest you learn everything you can from Kane and Averel about Keirthan's private lair."

Lavinia took the parchment from Gideon and set it down beside her when Duncan made no move to take it. Kane knew his friend well enough to know that when the warrior calmed down he would memorize the drawing and then grill both Kane and Averel until he'd wrung them both dry. No detail would be too small or insignificant.

Merewen took over the discussion. "The scouts located a large clearing a short distance from the city. Lady Alina and I will move our wagon there in the morning and prepare to treat the wounded."

Kane was impressed Gideon wasn't demanding that she and Alina move their wagon farther away from the anticipated battle. He'd probably already lost that argument, too. They all knew that a greater distance would cost lives that might have been saved if the wounded had reached Merewen sooner.

Gideon picked up the remaining parchment. "I think that's everything. After we eat, Murdoch and I will meet with our allies."

There was nothing Kane could add to the conversation, and he needed some time alone. "I will return shortly. I want to check on the horses."

He walked away before anyone questioned his excuse. As much as he cared about his friends, right now all he could think about was Theda. In their dream meeting, she'd been fine, but by her reckoning, Keirthan had barely had time to learn of Kane's escape. There was no telling what had happened to her since then. Worry had burrowed deep inside his heart, leaving him restless and wishing the battle was minutes, and not hours, away.

Rogue stopped grazing to watch Kane approach. At

the last second, he let the animal eat in peace; they would both need all their strength to face what was to come. Veering off his intended path, Kane headed toward the edge of the woods.

He stared up at the dark sky, a reminder that the hours were passing by all too quickly. Soon the gods would know if their warriors had succeeded in their calling.

Then the Damned would have little time left to set their affairs in order before making their way back up the mountain. When they climbed the path, they would set their avatars free to roam one last time before recalling them back to the shields. Then the five men, now six, would stand at the edge of the river.

While they waited for the Lord and Lady to appear, they would speak of things that men rarely felt comfortable discussing: loyalty, honor, and friendship. Soon the water would ripple and roil, signaling the presence of the gods, and the warriors would stand shoulder to shoulder as they waited to learn their fate.

Each time they hoped to move on to the afterlife and the promise of peace. Failing that, they prayed to once again be sent to sleep beneath the river, the bitter taste of disappointment their last memory before sleep overtook them. So far, they'd never once failed the gods. But if this continued, one day they would, and they'd all pay the price. Each of them would wander alone and soulless in the darkness of the netherworld. If that weren't horrific enough, the petitioner they'd sworn to serve would suffer the same fate. Lady Merewen's face filled his mind.

He prayed it wasn't this time, not when each of them had people they cared about. Even loved.

Sunrise was an eternity away. It was hard not to mount Rogue right that moment and ride hard for the secret entrance to Keirthan's chambers. He forced himself to stop and think, not just react. They had a plan, and he would follow it. For now he offered up a simple prayer to the gods who had guided his footsteps for so long.

"Please watch over Lady Theda until I can do so myself."

Then he bowed and walked way. For tonight, he would sharpen his weapons and prepare for battle. He hoped Ifre Keirthan enjoyed his last few hours of life, because come tomorrow, anyone who stood between Kane and Lady Theda would die.

The pale light to the east hinted at dawn's arrival. The battle for Agathia would soon begin, but for now everything was quiet. Kane kept his mind occupied with small things. Before saddling Rogue, he'd given the horse a thorough brushing, finding solace in the rhythm of the strokes. He was checking the stallion's hooves when he sensed Sigil's approach. He set down Rogue's forefoot and moved on to the next while he waited for Sigil to state his business.

"Did you sleep at all?" As Sigil spoke, he adjusted the bridle on his mare.

Kane straightened up. "I didn't even try. Did you fare any better?"

Sigil shrugged and patted his horse's neck. "I'm always restless the night before a battle."

Interesting. Kane walked around to Rogue's other side and lifted the horse's foot. "Something else you've remembered about your prior life?"

The warrior rolled his shoulders several times as if trying to shrug off some tightness. "No, just another fact I believe to be true without knowing the reason why."

Sigil fell into silence as he checked his own weapons and then the cinch on his horse's saddle. Finally, he met Kane's gaze head-on. "Are you all right with me accompanying you, Kane? Especially not knowing what effect returning to the capital will have on my memory?"

A fair question, one Kane didn't answer immediately. Sigil deserved his honesty. After all the centuries of being one of five, how odd to now be one of six. In the end, the answer was easy. Sigil may not have been one of the

Damned for long, but that didn't mean he was any less deserving of Kane's trust and loyalty.

"You will not betray us, Sigil, with your memories or without. Now, mount up. I told Duncan we would scout ahead to make sure Lady Lavinia doesn't ride into a trap."

Murdoch's forces were already on the march as Kane and his companion rode out. Gideon held out little hope that their presence would escape notice for long. He had scouts ranging back and forth in the area, watching for Agathian patrols and ready to sound the alarm.

Sigil kept glancing back toward the marching troops, his expression increasingly grim. "Too many good men will die today."

Kane couldn't disagree. "That is the way of war, and I regret that your people fight on both sides today. Most of the guards I met in my brief service to Keirthan were good men and deserve better than to die defending a villain like him."

He urged Rogue into a fast trot. The sooner they ensured the path ahead was safe, the sooner the battle to take down Keirthan could begin.

Theda was bone cold and scared beyond reason. Ifre had yet to visit her since he'd ordered Captain Markus to drag her down to his private chambers. She'd been too drugged to remember much of what happened between drinking the wine and waking up sprawled on the stone floor. With her hands and feet bound, it had taken her several attempts to sit upright, which had helped with the nausea left over from the drug.

She didn't have to guess what lay in store for her, not after seeing the pain Ifre had inflicted on Kane. Even though Theda lacked her late husband's gift for magic, she sensed the nearby presence of pure evil. The terrifying chill was coming from the hall that led back to the keep above.

Right now, Markus was helping an older man set up a

new altar on the dais at the far end of the chambers. Before bringing the artisan in, Markus had dragged Theda over to the darkest shadows at the far end of the room behind the low wall surrounding the fire pit. He'd gagged her, warning Theda that if she made a single noise, the stonemason would die.

What had happened to the original altar? It had been intact when she and Averel had left the chambers behind. Had Kane found a way to destroy it, or had Ifre done it himself when he'd found his prisoner had escaped?

In the long run, it didn't matter. Old altar or new, she would die.

Before leaving, Markus had paused to glance back in her direction. Looking disgusted, he said something to the stonemason and walked back toward her.

He'd untied her gag and tossed it aside. Then he surprised her by cutting the rope that had bound her ankles. As tempting as it was to plead with Markus, to beg him to take her out of this place, she didn't even bother to try. There was no way he would cross Ifre. This time he walked away without looking back.

She leaned against the wall and rested her eyes, ignoring the tingling pain as life returned to her feet and ankles. Her hands were tightly bound, but she tried to untie the knots with her teeth. There was little chance she'd break free, but she refused to give up. Ifre was a coward at heart; maybe if she went on the attack, he'd back off.

"Ah, Theda, there you are. I wondered where Markus had left you."

Her eyes popped open. She stared up at her grinning brother-in-law in horror. How had she missed hearing Ifre enter the chambers? And right behind him was that same cloud that had been hovering over Kane when he'd been tied to the altar. She shivered, recognizing it as the source of the dread chill she'd been sensing.

Its red eyes stared down at her from over Ifre's shoulder. She couldn't hide either her revulsion or her fear, which had her brother-in-law laughing in obvious amusement.

Then his expression hardened. "I regret that you've taken sick and will not survive to wed the husband I had picked out for you. A surprising number of my courtiers expressed sincere regret to hear of your sudden illness. I'm sure they will mourn your passing as well."

His words gave her the courage to share a little truth with him. "Eventually, your people will rise up against you, Ifre. When they do, you will die. That will be a day to celebrate! My only regret is that I won't be here to dance in the streets."

Ifre snarled and slapped her, banging her head against the wall. Fisting her hair, he hauled Theda to her feet. "You speak treason, a crime that carries a death sentence."

She stumbled along behind him. "As if you've ever needed an excuse to kill. How many have died down here to feed your hunger for power?"

He yanked her hair hard as he sneered, "Not nearly enough, Theda, but rest assured you will be just one in another long line of sacrifices. And don't think it has escaped my notice that you've somehow managed to smuggle your ladies out of the city."

A small victory, but one she savored. "I wasn't about to let you harm them."

They'd reached the steps up to the dais. He tossed her to the ground while he studied his new altar. "I had warned you that if you did anything to thwart me, I would execute your stepson, but that would be an empty threat now."

Her stomach clenched as she guessed what he was about to say.

"Terrick has been dead for some time now. He was with the forces I sent to retake Lord Fagan's keep, and they failed."

Acid-hot tears burned down her cheeks. "You murdering bastard. I'm glad Armel didn't live to see what a monster you've become."

She expected Ifre to respond with another attack, but he laughed again. "And it's one of my few regrets that my noble brother didn't survive long enough to see what all I've accomplished. You'll be joining him soon, so perhaps you can tell him."

He returned to pull her up onto the dais. "Don't look at me like that, Theda. You chose to interfere with my plans for Captain Kane. If you hadn't, I would've stripped you of your fortune, but I might have let you live."

Then he paused as if to think about it. "No, you would've died regardless. You hate me too much for me to risk letting you live."

After shoving her into an elaborate chair, he pressed his fingertips against her temples and spoke some unintelligible words. A strange lethargy spread from her head down through her body.

"There. You'll do whatever I ask now."

It was if she were watching from a long distance as he untied the ropes on her hands and then used them to lash her arms to the chair. Her mind screamed that she should fight, that she should run. Something, anything other than to meekly sit there waiting for the pain to begin.

"You will remain right there until it is your turn to offer up your blood." He patted her cheek. "While you wait, you'll have a perfect view of those who will die before you."

As he looked over his new altar and checked the strength of the new chains, Ifre asked, "So, tell me, my dear, did Captain Kane charm his way into your bed, or was it the other way around?"

When she didn't answer, he returned to her side. "Answer me when spoken to."

His monster floated down to settle on her right arm. Its hideous eyes stared into hers as a hole opened up like a misshapen mouth. She screamed as soon as it bit down on her skin. The attack lasted but a few seconds before Ifre called off his monster.

"That's enough. We don't want to weaken her too soon."

The cloud released her arm and floated back up above Ifre's head, its color darker now. Her arm ached, but there was no mark on her skin. How was that possible?

"Are you going to answer my question, Theda, or shall my friend steal more of your life from you?"

What would the truth hurt? "Kane and I found each other."

"Interesting. Had I known you had a taste for dark-magic mages, I might have had you myself." His eyes glittered with a sickening heat. "Tell me, what did he promise you to get you to help him escape?"

"Nothing." She'd helped him because she'd wanted to, not because she expected anything in return.

"Who else helped you? That troubadour friend of his?"

All right, so he also knew about Averel. "It was just the two of us."

He stared at her for a few seconds before slowly nodding. "I think that much is true. You'll tell me far more eventually, but that's enough for now. I have business in the hall upstairs, but I will return soon. Then things will get most entertaining."

When he walked away, the cloud drifted to hover over the altar. Its hideous eyes yet stared at her, but it made no move to attack again. She slumped in relief, even knowing the respite would be short-lived. Rather than dwell on what was to come, she concentrated on the one person who had reminded her what it had felt like to be happy. In her mind's eye, she pictured Kane's face, all harsh lines and so fiercely intense. His body was lean and powerful, built for combat, yet he'd been so gentle with her. A complex man, one she would love unto the grave and beyond.

Thanks to him, she still held on to a small glimmer of hope. Kane had promised to return, and she believed he would. Even if he didn't get back in time to save Theda herself, he would save her people. Cold comfort, perhaps, but right now it was all she had.

Chapter 27

*G*ideon rode at the head of a column of foot soldiers marching four abreast, the last company to be moved into position. Merewen had called as many horses as she could muster to help transport their foot soldiers into position. Given the short distance left to ride, they'd put two men on each animal to speed up the movement of Murdoch's forces to the other side of the small valley. Once there, they would form up to march on the city.

The remaining horses ferried Gideon's men closer to the city, returning over and over again to carry his forces to the front. They'd made good progress, but he'd feel better when everyone was in position. With dawn nearly upon them, it was only a matter of time before Keirthan's forces realized the city was about to come under attack.

Two of the scouts broke free of the trees just ahead of where he rode. As soon as they spotted him, they rode hard straight for him. "They've sounded the alarm in the city, Captain!"

He'd hoped to get closer before encountering Keirthan's troops, but at least Murdoch's men were formed up and ready to fight. Gideon shouted to the closest sergeant at arms. "Blow the horns. Get everyone moving."

He'd no sooner spoken the words than a large band of horses came crashing through the woods with one man riding at the front of the herd. "Sir Murdoch thought you might need the horses."

Having delivered his message, the rider wheeled his

mount around to return to Murdoch. Without being told, the men who were afoot began clambering up on the horses in pairs. When they were mounted, Gideon led the charge to where the rest of his forces waited.

As he rode, he thought of his friends, praying for victory for them all. Damn, he wished they were all together rather than scattered this way. His gut told him their strategy was the right one, the only way for them to stand a chance of success. But he missed the comfort of having Kane and the others riding beside him.

When he reached the rise that overlooked the city, he paused long enough to offer up a prayer to the Lady of the River. "My lady, your warriors will do their best to see this battle won. Please watch over those who cannot defend themselves and the ladies who have so bravely joined us in this fight."

As he spoke the words, the duke's soldiers began pouring out of the city to join forces with the patrol that had sounded the alarm. Murdoch's men flanked them, blocking their retreat. If they made it back inside the city walls, this would turn into a siege, something the Damned could not afford. They didn't have enough time left before the solstice to starve a city the size of Agathia into surrendering.

Gideon drew his sword and bellowed the war cry of his people, gone now for all these centuries. From across the valley, he heard Murdoch echo his own challenge to the enemy. As one, the two forces surged down the hillside toward the enemy's gates, coming together with a clash of swords and a bath of blood.

Growing more tense by the minute, Kane restlessly patrolled the route to Keirthan's chambers while Sigil returned to fetch the others. He'd been about to turn back to meet them when he spotted a rider moving through the woods in the distance. All of the scouts had already returned, making it unlikely the intruder belonged to the rebel forces.

Kane recognized the rider as soon as he reached a small break in the trees. What was Sergeant Markus doing out here on this day of all days?

Only one way to find out.

Kane connected with Hob long enough to ask the gargoyle to startle Markus's mount. Hob dashed in and then out again, nipping at the horse's ankles. Within seconds it was rearing and plunging, finally unseating his rider. Markus hit the ground hard, but regained his feet as Kane rode into the clearing. He slid off Rogue's broad back with his sword drawn and stalked toward the guard.

"Ah, Markus, I had hoped we would meet again."

To give the man credit, he held his ground. Most men who faced Kane with Hob at his side broke and ran. This one drew his sword, although it didn't take Kane long to disarm him. He shoved Markus back against a nearby tree and held him there with the tip of his sword pressed against his captive's stomach.

"Care to tell me where you were headed?"

Markus was too busy staring down at Hob to answer. Kane tried again. "Was the duke sending you to seek aid from his nobles?"

Finally, the sergeant looked up. "What is that thing?"

Kane sighed with disgust. "A gargoyle. Since it is unlikely you've ever encountered one before, you should know that his venom is poisonous, and he hasn't yet fed today. Now, answer me. What is your business out here? Were you riding to request aid for the duke?"

Markus shook his head. "No. I've resigned my commission with the duke. I haven't spoken with him at all, not since last night when he ordered me to . . ."

He hesitated before continuing, his eyes shifting away to the side.

Kane brought the tip of his sword up to Markus's neck, the razor-sharp blade drawing blood. "When he ordered you to do what?"

The guard swallowed hard before answering. "He ordered me to take Lady Theda down to the chambers where he'd held you prisoner. Keirthan knows she helped you escape."

Fear for her knifed through Kane's heart, but he continued to talk, hoping to learn as much as he could before ending the man's life.

"We both know you provided him with any number of victims, even knowing what he had planned for them. Why quit now?"

Besides the fact that by betraying Theda, the bastard had signed his own death warrant.

Markus shrank in upon himself, as if he'd suddenly aged two decades. "Something you did weakened the duke's powers. He's desperate to rebuild it, and he's been using anyone he can snare with his magic. When I made rounds last night, the guards were missing. I found them down below, all dead. There had to be a dozen or more. I won't be the next one he catches."

Kane fought to keep from killing the bastard before he got the answer to one more question. "And Lady Theda, what of her?"

Markus shook hard enough to rattle his teeth. "He made her watch. I think she was in shock, but as of an hour ago, she still lived."

"And you left her there?"

Markus's head dropped. "To my shame, I did."

Kane stepped back, lowering his sword. "Pick up your weapon and say your prayers. Although I doubt the gods will listen to a man who broke faith with both those he was sworn to protect and those he was sworn to lead."

Markus didn't argue. As he faced off against Kane, he said, "Please tell Lady Theda I regret my actions."

He held up his sword in salute, and the fight began. It didn't last long.

Kane gritted his teeth and kept riding. He doubted Lady Lavinia could hear the battle being waged on the far side of the city, but the god-enhanced senses of the Damned painted a clear picture for him and the other three warriors. The fight for control of the city had begun. May the gods guide Gideon and Murdoch.

"We're here." Finally. "This is as far as we can ride."

Kane dismounted and stroked the stallion's nose. "Take the mares away from here, but not too far. If we fail, return to Lady Merewen."

The horse shook his head and stomped his foot. Rogue had the heart of a warrior and wanted to fight. Kane understood his frustration. "This tunnel is no place for you. Now, go, my friend."

As the horses moved away, Kane led his small force around to the far side of the hill to the hidden entrance. Kane knelt down to study the lock. As he worked on the mechanism, Duncan stood close by with Lavinia at his side. She hid her fear well, but Kane could taste it on the air. Sigil and Averel brought up the rear, both men scanning their surroundings for any sign of opposition.

It took him several tries before the lock clicked open because he kept picturing Theda chained and bleeding as Ifre Keirthan tormented her in retaliation for assisting Kane. He had to block out his fear for her, knowing he'd serve her far better with his emotions running cold.

It was time to call forth the other four-legged avatars. Within seconds, Averel's dogs and the huge wolf that belonged to Sigil joined Hob in prowling the area. Kane opened the door wide and motioned everyone inside. Before closing the door completely, he considered their options. The four men and their beasts could see to move in the darkness well enough, but that wasn't true for Duncan's lady.

"Lady Lavinia, a bright light will alert the enemy that we are coming. But if the darkness will bother you, I will light one."

Lavinia held out her palm, and he felt the stir of magic as a small ball of light flared to life. Kane smiled in approval. He should've guessed that she would know how to call mage light. Her control was good enough to ensure the circle of illumination barely extended an arm's length in front of her.

The light floated down to hover near their knees, reducing its visibility even more while lighting the way before her. When it was stable, she said, "Let me know when you wish me to douse it, Lord Kane."

He nodded as he closed the door behind them, making sure it locked. With battle fever raging within him, Kane started forward with his sword drawn and his friends following after him. If Keirthan wasn't in his chambers, they would have to fight their way through his great hall until they found him.

But find him they would.

The tunnel stretched on forever, gradually sloping downward to cross under the city walls. Kane cursed when he almost tripped over Hob for the third time. The gargoyle clearly remembered their last trip down the tunnel and had no interest in a repeat visit.

Kane stooped down to reassure his friend. "Steady, boy. We'll be leaving this tunnel behind soon."

He'd pitched his voice low, intending the words of reassurance for Hob's ears only, but both Sigil and Duncan responded anyway.

"Not soon enough."

They laughed softly, lightening their mood even if it had no effect on their situation. He needed to gauge how far they had left to go.

"Remain here. I want to make sure that we're not walking into a trap."

Duncan wrapped his free arm around Lavinia's waist and stepped back. Kane motioned Hob to follow him and started forward. He'd gone about forty steps when he heard voices speaking up ahead. Kane tightened the grip on his swords, straining to hear what was being said.

"Talk to Captain Markus, Commander. He should be dealing with the city defenses."

"I couldn't find him, Sire. No one has seen him since last night."

To Kane's relief, Theda spoke next. "Ifre, don't tell me Markus already regrets his promotion. Perhaps he had second thoughts, considering the short lives of those who were captain before him. Only Kane survived long enough to escape your clutches."

As glad as he was to know she was still alive and strong enough to speak, he worried about what would happen if she were to continue to taunt her brother-in-law. As tempting as it was to go charging in, Kane held his position. He needed to know more before he could figure out how best to attack Keirthan.

The other man spoke again. "Sire, the army awaits your orders."

Keirthan sighed in obvious frustration. "What would you suggest?"

"The capital is being attacked from two sides. Right now two of my three companies are defending the gates to the city and trying to hold off the enemy. They need reinforcements and fast. I can send the third company of army regulars to one gate, but I need your guards to join the fight at the south gate."

Keirthan snapped, "Send your men wherever you want to, but not my guard. Their job is to protect me, not the city."

"But, Sire—"

Keirthan cut off the protest before the man could speak another word. From the sound of choking, the bastard had used the same spell on his own commander that Damijan had used to immobilize Kane earlier.

"Don't argue. Do as I said and send all of your own forces to hold the gates against the enemy. Now, go and leave me to my work. I, too, shall play a role in keeping the city safe. The enemy will come to regret their decision to attack me."

The commander managed to whisper, "Yes, Sire."

As soon as his footsteps faded away, Keirthan began speaking again. "Theda, you would think even those fools should be able to hold the gate long enough for me to unleash my weapon. My enemies will die as my fury rains down from the sky. No one will oppose me once they know the true scope of my power."

Kane reached the end of the tunnel in time to see Keirthan chanting as he raised his knife over the chest of his latest victim. Kane bellowed in fury and charged forward, only to run into an invisible wall. He watched in horror as the duke brought the blade down in a sweeping curve, cutting deep into the man's chest.

The dark cloud immediately swooped down onto the struggling prisoner's chest, its color pulsing black as the night sky as it suckled greedily of the blood. When Damijan finished feasting, it turned its crimson gaze toward Ifre himself.

"More."

Keirthan glared up at his creation. "Not until you attack those outside the gate."

The cloud spun on its axis, picking up speed as three bright spots flickered to life in its interior. With a clap like thunder, bolts of light shot out from its center, disappearing straight through the stone walls. Almost immediately, Kane heard answering explosions in the distance. Memories of similar attacks on Gideon's avatar and Merewen's horses only fed his need to destroy the duke and his magic.

The cloud faded again as it gave voice to its demands. "More. Promised. Don't argue."

The duke's movements were jerky as he unchained the body on the altar and rolled it off onto the floor. With a flick of his wrist, another man stumbled forward from the back of the chamber, his eyes wild as he fought against the summons. For the first time, Kane noticed the ragged line of people clustered on the far side of the fire pit.

How had he missed seeing them? More important,

why hadn't the army commander said anything? As soon as the prisoner made it to the altar, the rest of the people disappeared behind a shimmer of power again. The same spell that prevented Kane from entering the chamber must also mask the presence of anyone behind it. Did that mean that the mage hadn't detected Kane's arrival?

He retreated to where the others waited for him. "Lady Theda has not yet been sacrificed, but he has others waiting to die. We've got to stop him, but there's a barrier between the tunnel and the chamber itself I couldn't break through."

Duncan frowned. "Lavinia, it sounds like the ward that you set in the abbey library. The one that made the books beyond disappear or made people forget that they'd even seen them."

She agreed. "It must be similar. If we can get close enough for me to test it, I should be able to counter it."

The four men formed up around her and moved out with swords drawn, their avatars providing rear guard. As they reached the end of the tunnel, Lavinia's mage light winked out, leaving only the dim glow from the chamber itself.

Kane stood next to Lavinia, speaking softly. "Will your earth magic counter his spell, or do you need me to try since my magic is closer in nature to his? It has been centuries since I wielded such magic. If I ever knew the right spell, I don't remember it now."

"Let me attempt it first. If that doesn't work, I will explain how you should try." She stepped in front of the four men and closed her eyes. "For now, when I nod, try the ward and see if you can push through it."

As she chanted, Kane listened carefully to the words. They came from one of the old tongues, one Kane had grown up speaking. If her attempt failed, he should be able to repeat the spell.

When she nodded, he stepped past her and slammed right into the same power that had stopped him before. She chanted faster, her voice growing in volume. The second time she nodded, Kane was able to push forward several more steps than before, but then the ward held again.

This time, Kane joined her, his deep voice playing counterpoint to hers. The power of their words increased until it stung his skin as they continued to call on the gods to break through the dark magic. Duncan and Sigil both pushed against the barrier, but it refused to give.

Sigil put his hand on Lavinia's shoulder and motioned for Duncan to do the same to Kane. As soon as they did, the wall of power flamed bright and shattered. The four men once again drew their weapons and stalked forward into the chamber.

So intent on her brother-in-law's atrocities, Theda didn't immediately notice they were no longer alone. It wasn't until the monster spun away from where it had been hovering over Ifre's shoulder that she spotted the newcomers.

"Kane!"

As soon as she said his name, she wished she'd controlled her tongue. Ifre threw up his hands, trying to cast the spell that would ensnare Kane and his friends in the same sticky mire that held all of the other prisoners in his thrall.

To her amazement, a striking woman stepped forward, her own hands glowing brightly. Then she tossed two balls of light, one at Ifre and one at the cloud. The effect was minimal at best. When Kane growled a series of words that sounded jagged and sharp to Theda's ear, the results were far more spectacular.

A burst of dark light burst over Ifre's head, sending sparks fluttering around him, temporarily freezing him in position. As soon as that happened, the prisoners broke free of the duke's control, including Theda herself. Ifre had been so confident in his magic, that he'd only loosely tied her wrists. Ignoring the pain, she jerked her hands free and bolted from the chair to help shepherd the prisoners from the room. She sent them pelting back down the passageway toward the door to the great hall, following just far enough to make sure they found their way.

This time Ifre hadn't limited his predations to the servants; several were nobles. She caught one by the arm. "Lord Kai, do what you can to get the army to stand down. I swear upon my late husband's honor that those at the gate are there to overthrow the duke, not to harm the people of Agathia. Tell them that I'm not asking them to surrender the city, only to delay any further attacks."

He glanced back toward Ifre. "I will do my best, my lady. They may not listen to me. Perhaps if you spoke to them yourself."

Torn between her love of Kane and her duty to her people, she made the only decision she could live with. "I must help them defeat Ifre. I will follow when I can."

When she returned to the chambers, it was a scene out of her darkest nightmares. Keirthan had broken free of Kane's attack. Right now the cloud was pulsing again, its color changing once more, growing blacker, with several spots of light flickering at its center. By the gods, Ifre was going to unleash his weapon here!

Once again, the woman mage moved up to stand beside Kane. She recognized Averel when he stepped into sight. The third man's eyes marked him as another of the Damned. It was the fourth man who had her crying out. "Terrick!"

Ifre recognized him at the same time. "Traitor! You bastard! You weren't defeated by my enemies! You joined them."

He barked a word at the cloud, which immediately shot another of its bolts straight at Terrick. Her stepson threw up his hands, easily deflecting the light, sending it arrowing straight back at its creator. Ifre staggered back a step, but continued to target his five opponents with bolt after bolt of sizzling power.

Between Kane, the woman, and Terrick, they blocked

the attacks, but they'd also retreated several steps as Ifre pushed more and more of his power into the bolts. That's when she noticed the cloud had circled around behind them, and he was driving them straight toward it. A few more steps, they would stumble right into the trap.

She shouted his name. "Terrick, behind you!"

When he didn't respond, she tried again. "Averel! Kane! Behind you!"

The warning came in time to save the two of them, but not Terrick. The darkness engulfed him, his screams ripping at her heart. Desperate to do something—anything— to save him, she charged up on the dais straight across to shove Ifre, hoping to break his concentration. As he tumbled over the edge of the dais, he caught her hand and dragged her down with him.

The impact knocked the breath out of her, but Ifre came up screaming like a madman. He pulled her up to stand in front of him, using her to block any more attacks as he resumed firing those bolts of light.

Averel and Kane faced off against him while the woman and the third warrior were focusing on Ifre's creation. Kane shouted at it in that harsh language. It shuddered and released Terrick. He fell to the floor and scrambled back toward his friends. Once again, the cloud had faded, its color now more white than gray. It was impossible to know whether the spells being cast by the woman and Kane were responsible or if Ifre himself had weakened it with all the power he'd been burning. She didn't care as long as it left Terrick alone.

While the woman watched the cloud, Kane turned his attention back in Ifre's direction. He stared past her at her brother-in-law. Did Ifre see his own death written in Kane's pale gaze?

"Release her."

Her brother-in-law laughed. "And what? You'll let me go?"

Kane sneered. "No. I'll kill you, but I'll make it quick. That's more than you deserve, and a better offer than what you'll get from your creation. Do you really think Damijan will continue to serve you? Already you are bending to its will."

Keirthan's answering laughter sounded shrill. "It remains mine to command, Kane. Surrender to my creation, and I will release Theda to your friends."

Then he splayed his fingers across her forehead. It felt as if he were jamming shards of broken glass into her skull. She refused to beg or give in to the pain, but she couldn't control the tears that streamed down her face.

"You or her, Kane. Your choice."

She could barely whisper, but she knew Kane would hear her. The question was whether he would listen. "Don't do this. He has sworn to kill me anyway. You know he can't let any of us live."

But Kane was already laying down his weapons and backing toward the cloud. When his friends tried to block his way, he shook them off. "I promised to make this world safe for Theda. I can't do that if he kills her. Trust me when I say that this is the only way."

Then he stared into Theda's worried eyes. "Have faith, Theda. I have lived all these centuries for this one moment."

The cloud was already floating nearer, its maw open and ready to attack Kane. For the moment, he held out his hand as if to hold it off with a small amount of his own power.

"Release her now, Keirthan, and I'll give you what you wanted from me in the first place: my magic for your pet."

It didn't take Ifre long to make up his mind. He shoved Theda aside. She stumbled slightly, but then quickly retreated to the relative safety of the far side of the room to circle around to reach Kane. She couldn't risk getting caught between Ifre and the others, not again.

Before she could reach him, Kane smiled at his companions before looking up into the cloud that settled over him. His body shivered and then went stiff. All she could hear was the sound of her own sobs.

Chapter 28

The battle at the gates had been going well until Keir-than unleashed a barrage of magical attacks on their forces. One of the bolts had missed them altogether, but two had hit right in the midst of the fighting. Gideon had lost a fair number of men, but just as many of the duke's own men had been among the fallen.

He and Murdoch had ordered their men to fall back and regroup. The Agathian forces had closed ranks and prepared to face the next charge. Before Gideon could give the order, a voice rang out from atop of the city gate.

"This is your commander speaking. Withdraw to the gate and stand your ground. Do not, I repeat, do not attack unless they attack you first."

What was going on? Gideon signaled for his own men to do the same. An uneasy stillness settled over the battlefield, the silence broken only by the moans of the wounded and the dying. There was one order he would give.

"Bring the wounded to Lady Merewen. Take any of their men who are willing to accept our help as well."

Then he slowly rode forward until he was within easy shouting distance of the gate.

"Know that I have offered your wounded the chance to be taken to our healer along with our own."

"Do I have your promise that they will come to no further harm?"

Gideon didn't hesitate. "My battle is with Ifre Keirthan for crimes against the people of Agathia. I have been sent here by the gods to end his evil."

He paused to draw another breath. "May I know your name?"

To his surprise, the gate to the city swung open far enough for a single man to ride through. He urged his mount into a fast trot, leaving his forces behind to approach Gideon alone. In a show of good faith, Gideon mirrored his action, stopping less than ten feet from his opponent.

"I am Bojan, commander of the army. I would know who you are to claim to speak for the gods."

Gideon urged Kestrel forward another few steps, close enough to enable Bojan to see the color of his eyes. "I am Gideon, captain of the Warriors of the Mist. We have served the Lord and Lady of the River, who have called us to end the evil that has taken root in your land."

Bojan stared hard at Gideon. "Your eyes are the same as Kane's, the mage-marked warrior who served as captain of the duke's personal guard."

"Lord Kane is one of us. He joined the guard to learn of the duke's strengths and weaknesses."

"And the troubadour with the dogs? I hear that he was similarly marked."

The man had obviously been gathering information. "Again, one of my men."

Commander Bojan moved on to another subject. "Lady Theda sent Lord Kai to ask us to stand down until she comes to speak to me herself. It would appear that Duke Keirthan had intended to kill not just Lady Theda herself, but several of the nobles in his court."

Gideon offered Bojan a grim smile. "He is guilty of killing many others. All of the nobles who have allied themselves with our cause have suffered such losses at Keirthan's hands."

Bojan didn't look surprised. "I will listen to what Lady Theda has to say. Know that I can and will defend my city, but I meant what I said to my men. We will not attack unless provoked. Agreed?"

For the first time all day, Gideon felt the stirrings of hope. His friends were still at risk, but perhaps the corner had been turned.

"Agreed, Commander. Other than to aid the wounded, my men will remain where they are. We will also allow your men to retrieve your own wounded as well as your dead. I regret their loss."

Without waiting for a reply, he rode back to where Murdoch waited on the hillside. Together they would hold vigil until they learned the fate of their four brothers-in-arms.

The cloud and Kane both remained motionless, neither one making a sound. It was as if both of them had been frozen in time. Theda prayed that meant that it wasn't too late to save Kane from grievous harm.

Meanwhile, Theda reached out to Terrick and helped him to his feet. An enormous wolf appeared at his other side. Any other time, she would have been afraid of such a large animal, but the only monsters in the room were Ifre and his creation. She and the wolf supported Terrick as they approached Averel and the others. The woman immediately threw up a ward to shield Kane from any more attacks from Keirthan, while the third warrior added a second line of protection around all of them.

"Sigil, come here."

Terrick broke free of Theda's grasp to approach the other woman, who persisted in calling him by that strange name. "Who are you?"

The woman shot Theda a hard look. "I am Lavinia, your late husband's half sister. Like Armel, I inherited a full measure of our father's ability as a mage but mixed with the magic from my mother's bloodline. I will do my best to ensure Lord Kane comes to no lasting harm."

"I thank you for that. Is there naught I can do to help?"

"Keep an eye on Ifre for us. I'm going to need Sigil's help to counter Ifre's magic."

Again that strange name. "His name isn't Sigil, Lady Lavinia. It's Terrick."

Now all of Kane's friends looked confused, especially her stepson. He stared at her in shock. "You truly know who I am?"

What was going on? "Yes, of course. You are Captain Terrick, my late husband's son by his first marriage. How could you not know that?"

Duncan interrupted the conversation. "Now is not the time for lengthy explanations. Lavinia, can you help Kane?"

"At best, I can only weaken the hold Ifre's monster has on him. If I were to destroy it, the spell could very well kill Kane, too."

Without waiting for anyone to react, she went to work. "Sigil, stand by me with your hand on my shoulder so I can draw on your power if I need it."

When the younger man did as she requested, she turned to Duncan. "You maintain the wards. Whatever you do, don't let them fail."

Finally, she glanced one last time at Theda. "If Ifre looks as if he's going to break through to us, let me know. Otherwise don't interrupt. The spell I'm going to attempt is delicate. Understand?"

"I do."

The woman immediately began chanting, blue light sparkling in the air around her. When at last she sent it streaming out to touch the cloud, it flinched, the first reaction it had shown since it had encompassed Kane.

As the blue light completed a circle around the cloud, it was as if that had been the signal Kane had been waiting for. From inside the cloud, he shouted words of power that rang throughout the chamber. The cloud immediately shot upward, leaving Kane behind, alive and unchanged.

Theda started for him, but then he held out a hand.

The gesture froze her where she stood. When he looked at her, she gasped. She'd been wrong about Kane being unaffected. His eyes glowed red and the mark on his cheek pulsed and writhed, now written in the same dark crimson.

"Stand back." His voice had deepened, his words grating to the ear.

As they all looked on in horror, he reached up to the cloud, caressing it as if it were a favored pet. Hob howled in misery, joined by two enormous dogs and the wolf, their cries echoing eerily around them.

Only Theda was willing to approach him. She ignored his warning and stepped closer. "Kane, what's happening to you?"

When he looked at her this time, she hardly recognized him. "At long last, you are seeing my true heritage. I had to do this to strip Ifre of his control over Damijan. To stop him from turning it on you. Listen when I say come closer at your own risk."

The cloud twirled happily over his head, its eyes now the same exact shade as Kane's. Across the room, Keirthan wailed in protest. "Give it back! I created it. It belongs to me."

Kane's laughter was dark and ugly. "Then you shall have it, Keirthan. I hope you enjoy the reunion."

The dark warrior pointed toward the duke. "Feed well, my pet."

When Ifre realized what Kane meant, he scrambled backward, but he ran into the altar before he'd gone more than a few steps. The cloud soared straight through the wards created by Lavinia and Duncan as if they weren't even there. Theda looked on in horror as the cloud flashed black just before it engulfed Ifre.

His screams soon turned to whimpers. Theda hated him and everything he stood for, but no one deserved to die like that. She ran to Kane, evading Duncan's and Averel's attempts to stop her.

Throwing her arms around his waist, she squeezed

hard. "Kane, stop it. Kill Ifre because he deserves it, but don't let him destroy you at the same time."

Kane heard Theda's words as if she were speaking from the depths of a well, but her touch was immediate and warm. He remembered how her hands felt upon his skin and the way their bodies had come together in joy. There was the taste of her kisses and the way her love soothed him. He fought against the darkness and the cold that had taken hold of his soul, pushing them back, pushing them out.

Hob bumped against the back of his legs, adding his own strength to Kane's. Then a pair of familiar hands came down on his shoulders as Duncan and Averel joined in. Lavinia was there, and Sigil, too.

If the others spoke, he didn't hear them. Only Theda's soft voice filled his head. "Come back to me, my love. I need you."

At that, the last of the darkness shattered, leaving nothing but the light of Theda's love and that of his friends in Kane's heart. He breathed deeply, bolstering his resolve with the support of those around him.

"I have to finish this."

One by one, they each stepped back, until at last it was just him and Theda.

He smiled down at her. "I came here to rescue you, yet once again it is you who has saved me."

Drawing his sword, he marched toward the dais. He barked a command in that same harsh language. The cloud lifted off Ifre with obvious reluctance.

Its eyes flashed brightly as it spoke. "Dark warrior, you have proven yourself to be weak. I will finish him and then I will feast upon you."

Kane smiled at it. "Damijan, it has been centuries since your kind last walked freely upon the earth. You have forgotten that it was my bloodline that bound you to the netherworld where you belong. We did it then, and I do so now."

He called out the words of binding, calling on the Lord and Lady to add the weight of their power to his spell. The cloud shrieked in defiance even as it began shrinking in on itself, fading to gray, then white, until all that was left were the two eyes. Even they paled, becoming smaller and smaller.

Kane called out the spell once again and then a third time. As the last word died away, there was a small pop and the last vestige of the cloud disappeared. Exhausted by his efforts, Kane staggered back. Theda and Averel caught him, supporting him when his own legs wouldn't.

Duncan looked down at Keirthan in disgust. "What should we do about him?"

Theda pointed at Sigil. "You should have inherited your father's title upon his death. It is your decision."

Sigil still looked doubtful. "Then as the rightful Duke of Agathia, this man's fate is my responsibility. He murdered my father and nearly killed me as well. He fed off my magic, stole my heritage, and even my name from me."

Kane stared hard at Sigil. "You've remembered?"

The warrior nodded. "Bits and pieces. Not everything, but I am Terrick, son of Armel, the late Duke of Agathia. In his name, as his sole son and heir, I claim the throne of this realm."

He moved past the three warriors to stare down at his uncle. "Ifre Keirthan, you are guilty of high crimes against our family and our people. For that, your life is forfeit."

Kane covered Theda's eyes, and Duncan did the same for Lavinia, as the man they'd known as Sigil personally carried out his first act as the new ruler of Agathia.

Chapter 29

Kane held Theda close, breathing in her warmth and savoring these last few moments of peace. It was late afternoon, yet he would not leave their bed until the very last minute. The summer solstice was upon them. Just past midnight, it would be time to stand at the river's edge and face the gods.

Theda had insisted on accompanying him and her stepson back to Lady Merewen's keep. It had come as no surprise that Sigil had ultimately refused to formally accept the title of Duke Keirthan until the Damned stood judgment at the river. He'd left Lord Kai and Commander Bojan in charge of the city and the realm.

Theda blinked up sleepily at him. "Is it time?"

"Not yet. You can go back to sleep."

She rose to stare down at him, her eyes narrowed in suspicion. "You were going to sneak away without saying good-bye."

He brushed her hair back from her face and knew he couldn't lie to her. "On the contrary, I said good-bye to you every way I could think of last night."

His body stirred at the memory. They'd retired early and made love until they'd both collapsed, too exhausted to continue. He'd taken her again during the night, and she'd awoken him in the early hours of the morning. Hunger had finally driven them down to the hall for the midday meal, but then they'd immediately returned to the privacy of this room.

He stared up at the ceiling, not wanting to see the pain that his next words would cause her. "I love you, Theda, but the journey to the mountain is one that the Warriors of the Mist make alone."

Theda pointed out the one flaw in that statement. "Lady Merewen is going."

"True, but that is because she is the one who called us."

And so Merewen would face the judgment of the gods as well, a truth that was killing Gideon. Returning to the river was never easy for the warriors, but this time was worse than any they'd ever faced. Four of the six would be leaving behind their hearts even as the gods claimed their souls.

Sigil was also torn between the vow he'd made to the gods and the duty he now knew he owed the people of Agathia. Most of his memories remained locked away, but he was a man of honor, one who took his family's obligations seriously.

Only Averel would return to the river, his heart intact, his duty clear.

"Well?"

May the gods forgive him, but Kane could deny her nothing. "You may come as far as the horses can go. After that, you and Lady Lavinia must return to the keep with Lady Alina."

Then, to forestall any further discussion, he showed her one last time how much he would miss her.

Theda and Alina followed Lady Lavinia up the mountain. Her mage light allowed them to make faster time up the steep trail, but they all despaired of reaching the river before it was too late. They'd only pretended to ride back to the keep, returning to follow their warriors and their hearts.

Lavinia's voice whispered on the cool night air. "I can hear the river. We're almost there."

Her words vanquished the last bit of Theda's weariness. All three women hurried their footsteps, determined to reach the top in time. It was not yet midnight and the beginning of the solstice, but time was passing.

She realized the trees had grown thin and there was a glint of silver in the distance. "There. I see it."

For the first time, the three of them hesitated. Kane and his two friends had given them stern orders to return to the keep. Kane had held her close and kissed her so sweetly. Then he'd tossed her back up in the saddle and slapped her mare on the flank to send it trotting away.

Her tears had choked her as she'd watched back over her shoulder as Hob and Kane had disappeared into the darkness. Watching him walk away when she knew she was going to follow him had been hard enough. Saying good-bye for good might just kill her.

Lavinia's mage lights faded away, and the three women clasped hands to give one another courage as they strode out of the woods to where the six warriors and Merewen stood watching the river.

Hob spotted her first, letting out his eerie howl. Shadow's answering scream echoed off the rocks, as did the wolf's mournful cry. The dogs and the two avian avatars added their own voices to the chorus.

As much as Theda appreciated their welcome, she wished Hob's master would say something. Kane stood off to one side, his arms crossed over his chest, his eyes pinned directly on her. She wouldn't back down, not when she could touch him one last time, hold him in her arms, and remind him how much he was loved.

She took a hesitant step forward and then another. As soon as she did, he held out his arms, offering her a safe harbor high on the mountain. As they came together, she was dimly aware of Duncan and Murdoch charging past her to claim their own ladies.

Kane buried his face in her hair, his breath tickling her skin as he murmured, "I'm glad you came."

She did her best to blink back the tears, but then it was too much. "I am, too. Don't ask me to leave until after . . ."

They both knew what she was trying to say even if she couldn't utter the words aloud.

Averel called out, "Look who is coming now!"

They all turned as one to face the path as Kestrel and then Rogue walked into sight. Behind them came the mares that had served Murdoch, Sigil, Duncan, and Averel.

Kane led Theda over to where Rogue had stopped, as usual, standing apart from the other horses. They moved to his far side, using his solid strength to carve out a small bit of privacy here among Kane's friends, both the ones who walked on two legs as well as four. Hob joined them, standing nose to nose with Rogue.

"Kiss me," Kane whispered next to her ear.

There was nothing she wanted more. Once again, he held her so gently, his kiss tasting of desperation.

Choking on her tears, she gave him her truth. "No matter what happens tonight, know that I will always love you, Kane."

"I want you to find someone who will make you happy, Theda. Don't live your life alone because of me."

Before she could respond, Gideon called out, "It's time."

She thought her heart would stop as the six men lined up along the river's edge. Their avatars stood beside them or sat perched upon their arms. Merewen stood beside Gideon, their hands clasped.

Theda wanted the same for herself. She pushed her way between Gideon and Kane, taking Kane's hand in her own. He gave it a soft squeeze without taking his gaze away from the river, which now roiled and foamed. Everyone shifted yet again as Lavinia and Alina joined the gathering in awaiting the arrival of the gods.

Finally, a woman and a man slowly rose out of the water, their power blazing in their eyes as they made their way down the long line of warriors and women.

Starting with Merewen and then Gideon, the holy couple silently stared at each person in turn. When they stood in front of Theda, she felt a short burst of pain, as if someone had pressed hard against the inside of her head. It ended as quickly as it had started when they moved on to stand in front of Kane.

He flinched, but held his ground. When they finally moved on, he slumped to the side. Theda wrapped her arm around him, offering him what support she could.

"What's wrong?" she whispered.

He didn't answer, his expression bleak. Had they judged him and found him lacking? How dare they? He'd sacrificed so much and asked for nothing in return. All of the warriors had. She would wait to see what the gods had to say for themselves, but she would not hold her tongue if they failed to understand the true worth of Kane and his friends.

Kane held Theda close at his side, hating that she trembled in fear. He would never suggest the gods needed to rush to judgment, but he wasn't sure how much more of this he could take.

Finally, the two gods conferred for what seemed like an eternity before once again facing the people on the shore.

It was the Lord of the River who spoke first. "You were called to save the people of Agathia. Many died, some at the hand of Ifre Keirthan and others at yours."

The Damned nodded as one, acknowledging the truth of that statement. The god continued on.

"Captain Gideon, you served us well, leading your men and your allies with wisdom."

"Sir Averel, as always, you proved yourself to be a man of honor."

"Sir Murdoch, you let your own prejudice and mistrust of magic color your opinion of Lady Lavinia but otherwise followed the right path."

"Sir Sigil, as promised, you will no longer be judged for the deeds you did in the name of Ifre Keirthan."

"Sir Duncan, you gave in to a moment of weakness

and almost let magic overrule your honor, but only almost."

"Lord Kane, you alone gave yourself completely over to the darkness of your bloodline."

Kane spoke for the first time. "I would ask that you not hold my weakness against my friends. It was not their doing, but mine alone."

"We have taken that into consideration, Lord Kane." The Lady of the River moved to stand next to her mate. "Know then, Warriors of the Mist, that we have weighed your efforts and will now render our judgment."

As their captain, Gideon spoke for them all. "We will accept your verdict without question."

Theda started to protest, but Kane shook his head. "It is our way."

"Lady Merewen, we trust you are satisfied with the service of our avatars."

"Yes, my Lord and Lady, most satisfied. The evil has been vanquished. My people are grateful to you."

"Then hear our verdict. Listen well and heed our words. Captain Gideon, Lady Merewen will need you at her side to help raise the son you have created with her during the night."

Gideon's face glowed with joy as he wrapped Merewen in his arms. "Thank you, my lady."

The goddess moved on. "Sir Duncan, Lady Lavinia and her abbey could use another scholar to watch over and guard its library. Young Sarra will need your protection, as well. We trust you will accept those responsibilities."

"It will be my greatest honor, my lady."

"Sir Averel, we thank you for your service to us and to our captain. Your life is now yours."

Without waiting for a response from the young knight, the goddess turned her attention to Murdoch. "You have ever stood at your captain's side. We see no reason for that to change. We are sure Lady Alina will be happy to share her home with you."

Then both of the gods drifted back to hover in front of Kane. Theda immediately moved to stand in front of him, once again doing her best to save him. He loved her for it, but he would not let her come to harm because of him.

"Forgive her, my lady. I am the one who let the darkness touch my soul."

Instead of getting angry, the goddess surprised him with a smile. "Lady Theda seems to think you are worth saving, but then so do we. May the two of you find much happiness together, Lord Kane. It is time for you to know peace in your life."

The Lord of the River now spoke. "Warriors of the Mist, on this night you are released from our service, but not from our hearts. Your honor has been restored. You will no longer bear our mark, and you will now live out your lives as mortal men with our blessing. You may keep your avatars, who can still rest in your shields, to be passed on to your eldest sons when the time comes. That is our final gift to you."

They looked at Gideon one last time. "Captain, as we have released you from our service, it is time to release your friends from yours."

Then the gods flowed back down into the darkness of the river, leaving everyone else in standing in stunned silence.

Finally, Gideon cleared his throat and met the gaze of each of his friends in turn. "No other man has been blessed with friends such as you. It has been my greatest honor to serve with each of you, but it is time to seek out lives that will bring each of you peace and joy at long last."

Averel looked around, his eyes wide in confusion. "But what do I do now, Captain?"

Gideon smiled at their young friend. "You live your life, Averel. I have released you from my service, but know you will always be welcome in our home."

Sigil spoke up. "Averel, I will need all the good men I

can find. That invitation goes for you, too, Lord Kane, and I would value Lady Theda's wise counsel as well."

Kane hadn't expected to walk down off the mountain and couldn't think beyond the moment. "Theda, what do you want?"

"That's simple, Kane." She smiled up at him. "I want you. All that matters is that we're together."

Kane held out his hand to Sigil. "I have some experience as the captain of the guard, Duke Keirthan, if you'll have me, provided you have no objections to me wedding your stepmother."

Sigil took Kane's hand in both of his. "I would be a fool to say no to either of those propositions."

Kane swept Theda up in his arms, tossed her onto Rogue's back, and then vaulted up behind her. "Take us home, horse. I have better things to do with the rest of the night than stand by the river."

Theda pressed back against his chest, her voice full of laughter. "I do like the way you think, Lord Kane."

Together they led the procession back down the mountain to the valley below, the warriors damned no more.

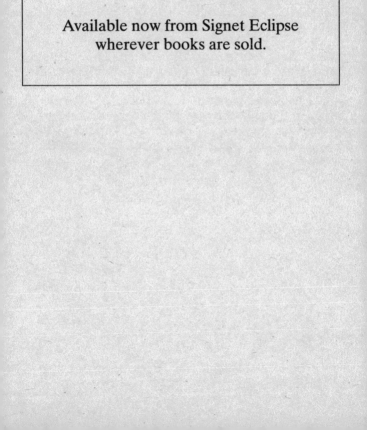

Don't miss the first book in Alexis Morgan's
Snowberry Creek series!

A Time for Home

Available now from Signet Eclipse
wherever books are sold.

"We're almost there, boy. Then you can stretch your legs."

Nick's canine companion was too busy sniffing the wind to care. Mooch had kept his nose stuck out the window since the minute they'd gotten in the truck. He reached over to pat the dog on the back, still carrying on the one-sided conversation.

"I bet it smells a whole lot different than the streets of Afghanistan. Doesn't it?"

Mooch thumped his tail in agreement. In truth, everything here was a whole lot different. Nick scanned the road ahead—there was so much green that it hurt his eyes. He had to tip his head back to see to the top of the firs and cedars that were crowded close to the two-lane highway. They made him claustrophobic. Too many hiding spots for snipers. Only one way through them, leaving him no avenue of escape.

Nick flexed his hands on the steering wheel and reminded himself that he'd left all that behind weeks ago.

No one here wanted him dead. Not yet, anyway.

"Think she'll forgive me?"

Nick hoped so, because he hadn't been able to forgive himself. Something in his voice finally had Mooch looking at him, the dog's dark eyes filled with sympathy. Of course, maybe Nick was only imagining that the mutt understood every word he said. There was no denying that the dog had known his own share of suffering back in his homeland.

Mooch's shaggy fur didn't quite hide the jagged scar where a bullet had caught him in the shoulder. He'd taken one for the team after he'd barked to warn them about an asshole lying in ambush. The bastard had shot the dog to shut him up, but too late to do himself any good. In retaliation, the squad had made damn sure it was the last time he ever pulled a trigger. Nick's buddy Spence had carried the wounded dog back to camp and conned one of the army vets into stitching him up. After a brief swearing-in ceremony, Mooch had become a full-fledged member of their unit.

In war, some heroes walked on four legs, not two.

Nick spotted a sign up ahead. He slowed to read it, hoping he was about to reach civilization. He'd left I-5 behind some time ago and hadn't expected it to take this long to reach Snowberry Creek. He had mixed feelings about what would happen once he reached the small town, but he and Mooch had been on the move long enough. Some downtime would feel pretty good.

But instead of announcing the city limits, the sign marked the entrance of a small cemetery. Nick started to drive on past, but a sick feeling in his gut had him slowing down and then backing up.

He put the truck in PARK and dropped his forehead down on the top of the steering wheel. In a town the size of Snowberry Creek, how many cemeteries could there be? He reached for the door handle and forced himself to get out of the truck. Sooner or later he was going to have to do this. Nick had never been a coward and wasn't about to become one now.

"Come on, Mooch. We've got a stop to make."

The dog crawled down out of the seat. Once on the ground, he gave himself a thorough shake from nose to tail before following Nick up the slope toward the rows of gravestones. Normally Mooch liked to explore new places on his own, but this time he walked alongside Nick, silently offering his support.

It didn't take long to find what they were looking for.

There were several granite markers with the last name Lang. Nick hung a right and followed the row, finally reaching a longer than normal stone that held the names of a husband and wife, most likely Spence's parents. Nick had to force himself to take those last few steps past it to stand in front of the last headstone.

He dropped to his knees on the green grass and wrapped his arms around his stomach. God, it hurt so fucking much to see Spence's name etched there in block letters. His eyes burned with the need to cry, but the tears refused to come. Instead the pain stayed locked tight inside his chest and in his head, a burden he'd been carrying since he'd held Spence's bloody dog tags in his hand.

As the memories began playing out in Nick's head, Mooch whined and snuggled closer. But even the familiar touch of the dog's soft fur couldn't keep Nick grounded in the present. His guilt and his fear sucked him right back to the last place he wanted to be. Just that quickly, he was in the streets of Afghanistan, riding next to Spence on yet another patrol. Instead of breathing the cool, damp air of Washington, Nick was sucking in hot, dry air and feeling the sun burning down from above as he got caught up in the past, living through it all over again.

The fiery depths of hell had nothing on the heat in Afghanistan in July. Maybe if he could've stripped down to a pair of cargo shorts and a sleeveless T-shirt, it would've been bearable. But only a fool would go on patrol without all of his protective gear, and Nick was no fool.

The back of his neck itched. It had nothing to do with the ever-present dust and grit that grated against his skin like sandpaper. No, there were eyes on them. Had been since they'd entered the city. A couple of well-placed shots had cut them off from the rest of the patrol. They were trying to circle around to catch up with the others.

Nick scanned the surrounding area, constantly sweeping the buildings ahead, looking for some sign of who was watching them. In that neighborhood, it could be anyone from a mother worried about her kids to someone with his finger on the trigger.

Leif stirred restlessly. "You feeling it, too?"

"Yeah. Spence, do you see anything?"

Before his friend could answer, a burst of gunfire rained down on them from the roof of a building half a block down on the right. A second shooter opened fire from a doorway on the opposite side of the street, catching them in the cross fire.

Nick returned short bursts of fire while Spence drove like the maniac he was, trying to get them the hell out of Dodge. Leif hopped on the radio, yelling to make himself heard over the racket. After calling in, he'd joined Nick in trying to pick off the shooters.

"Hold on! This ride's about to get interesting."

If more than two wheels were on the ground when Spence took the corner, Nick would happily eat MREs for the rest of his natural life. Not that he was complaining. His friend's extreme driving style had saved their asses too often. The M-ATV lurched hard as it straightened coming out of the turn.

"Fuck yeah, that was fun!" Spence's grin was a mile wide as he laughed and flung their ride around another corner.

The crazy bastard was actually enjoying this. Nick shook his head. He loved the guy like a brother, but damn. They made it another two blocks before the shooting began again, this time from behind them.

Leif yelled over the racket, "Ever get the feeling we're being herded?"

Nick nodded. The thought had occurred to him, but what choice did they have but to keep going? The street was too narrow to hang a U-turn and stopping sure as hell wasn't an option. He continued to scan the area for more shooters and left the driving to Spence, who knew the streets in this area better than anyone. It was like the man had a built-in GPS system. He'd find a way out for them if anyone could.

The gunfire was sporadic now with longer periods of silence between shots. The streets remained empty, as if the locals had been warned to crawl into the deepest hole they could find and stay there.

"Think we're in the clear?" Leif asked, still studying the rooftops and doorways for new threats.

Before Nick could answer, the whole world exploded in fire and smoke. A sharp pain ripped up the length of his upper arm as their vehicle started rockin'-and-rollin' on them. It went airborne and finally bounced to a stop, lying on its side up against a building.

With considerable effort, Nick managed to climb out. He retrieved his weapon and shook his head to clear it. The blast had left him deaf and, thanks to the cloud of dust and smoke, damn near blind. Nick found Spence more by feel than sight. He was lying facedown in the dirt with blood trickling from his ears and nose.

Nick checked for a pulse. Thready and weak. Son of a bitch, this was a major clusterfuck. He spotted Leif writhing in pain a few feet away. He crawled over to him.

"Are you hit?"

"My ankle. It's busted up pretty bad."

If the bastards who'd been shooting at them weren't already closing in, they would be soon. Nick needed to get Leif and Spence somewhere safe—and fast.

He got down in Leif's face. "Give it to me straight up. Can you walk?"

After one look at the twisted mess that had been Leif's ankle, Nick didn't wait for an answer. Neither of his friends could make it back to safety on their own, but which one should he help first? Spence was completely defenseless while Leif might be able to protect himself for a while.

On the other hand, Leif was bleeding; already his coloring was piss-poor. Nick crawled back to the rubble that had been their vehicle and pulled out the first-aid kit. He bandaged Leif's damaged ankle as best he could, but he'd seen enough wounds to know Leif was going to need surgery and damn quick. His decision made, Nick crawled back to his unconscious buddy.

"Spence, I'm going for help. I'll be back for you ASAP."

Then he muscled Leif up off the ground and half carried, half dragged the poor bastard as fast as he could. The rest of their unit would be pouring into the area, looking for them. A minute later, he spotted them two blocks down and waved his rifle over his head to get their attention.

Their medic hit the ground running. "What do we have?"

"His ankle looks bad, but we've got to go back for Spence. I was afraid to move him."

They carried Leif the rest of the way back to one of the vehicles. Nick patted his friend on the shoulder. "They'll get you to the medics. Save a couple of the prettier nurses for Spence."

Leif managed a small smile. "Like hell. Tell him he's on his own."

"Get yourself patched up. We'll be along soon." He stepped back and checked his rifle for ammunition. "Let's move out."

The medic stopped him. "You're bleeding, too. We'll get Spence. You go with the corporal."

No, not happening. He'd return for Spence even if he had to crawl. "I'm all right. Besides, I promised I'd come back for him. Wouldn't want to piss him off. The man's got a temper."

The medic didn't much like it, but he nodded. "Lead the way."

Nick's ears were finally starting to function again, and he could hear gunfire in the distance. Son of a bitch! He picked up the pace, doing his best to watch for hostiles as he led the charge back to where he'd left Spence.

When they were a block short of their destination, the deafening thunder of another explosion sent all of them diving for cover.

Before the echoes had died away, Nick was up and running, screaming Spence's name. He was dimly aware of the rest of his squad joining him in the mad race to save their friend. Nick's heart pounded loud enough to drown out the agonizing truth that he was too late, with too little. The building next to where he'd left Spence was nothing but a smoking pile of rubble.

He coasted to a stop at the corner. The horror of what had happened and what he'd done washed over him in waves. "Spence, where the hell are you? Come on, you dumb son of a bitch, this is no time for hide-and-seek."

Please, God, let him have regained consciousness and crawled to safety.

But he hadn't; Nick knew it in his gut just as he knew it was his fault. There was nothing left of their vehicle now except scrap metal. A huge hole had been ripped in the street right where Spence had been lying, and the building had caved in on itself, leaving the street strewn with rubble. While several of the men stood watch, Nick joined the rest digging in the dirt with their bare fingers, heaving aside rocks and jagged fragments of metal, looking and praying for some sign of Spence.

Finally the medic froze. He looked across at Nick and slowly lifted his hand. A set of bloody dog tags dangled from his fingers.

"Aw, damn, Spence."

Tears streamed down Nick's cheeks as he reached for the broken chain. He clamped his fingers around the small pieces of bloody metal and held on to the last piece of his friend with an iron grip.

The medic motioned to the rest of the men. When they had formed up, he took Nick by the arm and tugged him back down the street.

"Come on, Sarge, let's go get your arm looked at. We'll get you all fixed up."

Nick let himself be led away, but only because the longer they lingered in the area, the more likely it was that someone else would get hurt or worse. But they all knew there was no fixing this. Not today. Not ever.

Spence was—

A sharp pain dragged Nick back to the grassy slope of the graveyard. Mooch whined and licked the small mark where he'd just nipped Nick's arm. The poor dog looked worried. How long had Nick been gone this time? Long enough to be damp from the rain that had started falling since he'd knelt in the grass. The dog shoved his head under Nick's hand, demanding a good scratching that felt as good to Nick as it did to the dog.

"Sorry, Mooch. We'll get going here in a minute."

He pushed himself back up to his feet and dusted off his pants, focusing hard on the moment. It was too easy to get caught up in spinning his wheels in the past. He needed to keep moving forward, if for no other reason than he had to make sure Mooch reached his final destination.

Nick had something to say first. Standing at attention felt odd when he wasn't in uniform, but the moment called for a bit of formality. He cleared his throat and swallowed hard.

"Spence, I miss you so damn much. Wherever you are, I hope they have fast cars and faster women."

Then he sketched a half-assed salute and walked away.

LOVE
ROMANCE
NOVELS?

For news on all your favorite romance authors, sneak peeks into the newest releases, book giveaways, and much more—

"Like" Love Always on Facebook!
LoveAlwaysBooks